W H

Sarah Randall

BOOK ONE IN THE RANDALLS

GAIL HARIS

WHO IS Sarah Randall

Editor: Holly Ingraham, Holly Ingraham Editorial
www.hollyingraham.com

Formatting: Stacey Blake, Champagne Book Design
champagnebookdesign.com

Cover Design: Rocio Beauty Pixels
rociobeautypixels.myportfolio.com

Cover Model: Culley Williams

Blurb: Stacey Rourke, The Blurb Doctor
www.facebook.com/pg/blurbdoctor

My Boo. Because of you this was possible.

... Also because of you this book took longer because you kept distracting me with binge watching shows. But I don't regret a single moment ;)

I love you, Bobby. Thank you.

For everything.

Prologue

Dearest Olivia,

I love you. I love you more than words can describe. I need you to know that. I need you to remember that, especially after everything you have heard or will hear. I also want you to know I don't regret anything! You may not be my biological child, but I will always see you as my precious daughter. My Luv Bug. You must believe me when I say that raising you, loving you, and cherishing you have been by far the greatest joys I've ever known. My side of the story is kept in my journal. I won't ask you to understand why I did it. I honestly don't want you to understand; because, to understand my actions, you'd have to know that pain, and I would never wish that upon you. Please forgive me. Please remember me for how you knew me, not how you'll come to know me.

I love you forever and always,

Mom

I let the letter fall from my hands onto the floor. This doesn't make sense. I rush to the bathroom and dry heave.

Knock. Knock.

"Luv Bug? Are you okay?"

It's Aunt Andrea…or who I thought was my aunt.

One

"*M*OM! MOM!"

"In here, Luv Bug."

I rush into the kitchen and throw my bag on top of the kitchen table. "Angie said that Aaron Lancaster was asking about me! *Me!* Oh gosh. He might even ask me to Homecoming."

My mom chuckles as she closes the door on the dishwasher. "Aaron Lancaster, huh?"

"*Yes!* I've had a crush on him for the past two years."

"Has it been two years? Doesn't sound like a smart boy if he still hasn't asked you out. You're too beautiful and sweet to waste your time pining over an idiot."

I grab a bag of chips from the pantry and slam the door harder than necessary. "*Mom.*"

Of course she thinks I'm the prettiest, smartest, sweetest, and basically perfect-*est*. She has always gone on about how I look like an angel with my fair skin, blue-green eyes, long wavy blonde hair, button nose, and full lips. Her opinion is skewed so I don't think she realizes what a big deal this is. Mom must see my frustration because she walks over and wraps her arms around me. I try to nudge her off, but she kisses my temple and just holds me tighter.

"If you're excited, then so am I. You have the best judgement out of everyone I know, so this Aaron must be pretty special to have caught your eye. For two years, no less." I roll my eyes and she laughs. "He *is* pretty darn cute. Isn't he on the football team?"

I blush and look up at her through my eyelashes. "Yeah."

"And doesn't he work at the pizza place?"

I can't stop the grin that spreads across my face. "Yeah."

"I don't feel like cooking tonight. Wanna go out for pizza? Maybe call Angie and she can tag along."

I squeal as I do a little spin. I rush over and wrap my arms around mom giving her a big squeeze. "You're the *best*."

On the way to the pizzeria, we stop and pick up my best friend Angie. We're both cheerleaders and play on the community soccer team, since our school is too small for an actual school team. Don't be impressed by the cheerleader status. Our school is so small that if you can manage a cartwheel, you're on the team. We barely have enough students for a football team. Like me, Angie is an only child being raised by a single mother. She's wilder than me and to be honest, if we'd met in high school, we probably wouldn't be hanging out so much. But we met back in daycare and have been inseparable ever since.

"Hello, Cindy." Angie greets my mom when she climbs in the backseat. Her clothes hug her lean, tan body. Her brown hair hangs in loose curls. Her full pouty lips are already a little large for her face, but they are even more pronounced with her red lipstick. She swears it drives boys wild.

"Hey girl. Are you ready for pizza? I hear there's a handsome boy-"

"*Mom!*" My mom just laughs as I look back at Angie, who is also cracking up.

"I'm sorry, Luv Bug. I'll stop."

"You better behave. I shouldn't have told you." I groan.

"What? We're best friends. You can always tell me things. I was only teasing." She reaches over and squeezes my hand. She's right. She is my best friend, other than Angie, and my biggest supporter. I sometimes wonder if we're this close because it's just the two of us. But Angie isn't nearly as close with her mom. So, I guess we do have a special bond. I'm just lucky I guess.

"COME OVER!"

I hold the phone away from my ear as Angie groans and whines. "Ange, I can't. I *really* have to finish this history report."

"You can not be serious right now. Please tell me you're joking. It's *Friday*. You have all weekend! Come on, Liv!"

"I'm completely serious. You know how important getting a full ride scholarship is to me." Angie should be more concerned as well. Neither one of our mothers can afford college tuition.

"I also know how important Aaron Lancaster is to you. Can I persuade you by extending the invitation to him?"

"I'm so done with you. If I get half of my report finished, then I'll swing by. I haven't even asked my mom yet, so all your effort might be for nothing."

"She'll say yes. She loves me."

"She doesn't know your mom isn't home."

"And she won't, if you omit that information."

"I never lie to my mom."

"I didn't say lie. Now go ask your mom and get busy writing!"

I laugh. "Bye." I press end call and place my cell face down on the kitchen table. Mom isn't home yet, so I'll wait before I ask. Right now, I need to focus on Ancient Greek civilization.

Bbbzzzz. Bbbbzzz.

My phone keeps vibrating on the table. I have to get this paper written so I continue to ignore it. It's probably Angie again.

Bbbzzz. Bbbzzz.

My fingers tap away on the keyboard.

Knock. Knock.

Are you kidding me? Is everyone determined for my grade point average to drop? It's my senior year and if I'm determined to become Valedictorian, I don't even have the luxury of a B. I slam my laptop shut and stomp over to the front door.

Knock. Knock.

If Mom forgot her keys again…That thought is brought up short when I see the red and blue flashing lights cutting through the curtains. I peek through the blinds to see two police officers standing under the porch light. Taking a deep breath, I unlock the door and open it.

"Olivia Stevens?" The tall officer asks.

"Yes?"

"There's been an accident. Cindy Stevens is being taken to Memorial Hospital. Do you have someone we can call to be with you, or we can give you a ride?"

Mom? Mom's going to the hospital? What happened? What kind of accident?

"Olivia?" The voice brings my attention back to the present. "Honey, come with us and we'll get someone to help you through this."

Numbly, I close the door and follow the officers out. I don't even think I locked the door.

"Olivia? We've notified your Aunt Andrea. She's taking the first flight here. Sweetheart? Did you hear me?" They've sent Mrs. Barbara Jenkins, a social worker, to be with me. She hands me a cup of water and gently rubs my back.

I hear feet running down the hall and turn to see Angie. Her eyes are red-rimmed but she still manages to offer me a weak smile. Wrapping her arms around me, she squeezes me hard and then sits down on the other side of me.

"I didn't even get to tell her bye." My brain is struggling to accept what my heart refuses to believe. "She can't be gone."

"I'm so sorry," Angie croaks out.

Mrs. Jenkins leans closer toward me and whispers, "It's okay to feel whatever you're feeling." I turn my eyes to her and she nods. "You can cry. You can be angry. Allow yourself to feel. You don't have to be strong. I'm here to be strong for you. Don't lock yourself down."

My phone vibrates. Grateful for the distraction, I look over and read a text about prayers for me from one of my friends. I haven't responded to hardly any of them. Instead of responding, I open the last text Mom sent me:

Leaving the store now Luv Bug! I hope you're finished ☺ Just found Pretty in Pink and Sixteen Candles in the $5 bin!!!

Luv Bug. That's my nickname. It started out as Liv and somewhere along the way transformed from Liv Bug to Luv Bug.

Sounded like we were going to have another 80's movie marathon. I didn't get a chance to respond because I was busy. Scoffing to myself as I rub my eyes. *Busy.* My paper doesn't seem as important now. Angie takes my hand and squeezes it. "Want me to give you a ride back home? I'll spend the night with you."

"That sounds great, Angie." Mrs. Jenkins offers me a kind a smile and gently takes my hand. "I'll escort you ladies back home and I'm going to stay with you until your aunt arrives."

I nod because I don't have the strength to speak. Mom had been involved in a two-car head on collision. Her vehicle was hit head on by an older man passing another car. She was pronounced dead upon arrival at the hospital. He's still in critical condition. They believe he'll survive, and I hope he does. However, I don't know if I will.

∽

What feels like forever, but may have only been a couple of hours, I feel Aunt Andrea wrap me in her arms. I thought I was too numb to cry, but apparently not. Seeing her red puffy eyes and feeling the tightness of her arms around me brings me to my knees. My body physically aches. Andrea allows me to lean on her as she gently runs her fingers through my blond hair. I hold on to her and cry, grateful she doesn't tell me it's going to be 'okay' and she's 'sorry.' Because this isn't okay and it's not going to be. I'm seventeen and I've lost my mother.

"What happens now?" I voice my biggest fear between hiccups and muffled sobs.

"What do you want to happen? You're almost an adult. I don't want to disrupt your life any more by forcing you to relocate with me, but you're welcome to. We'd love for you to stay with us. Or we could see about you living here. I'm really not sure, but I'm sure Mrs. Jenkins will have the answers."

I pull back and frown. "Who?"

"Mrs. Jenkins. The social worker you've been talking to."

"There wasn't much talking on my part."

"And that's okay, sweetheart."

"I don't know what to do…"

"You don't have to decide now, Luv Bug. Let's get you some sleep and tomorrow, we'll take the day as it comes."

"Thank you, Aunt Andrea."

"Oh Luv Bug, come here." She brings me back to her in a warm embrace and I soak up all the comfort she has to give.

The next day, Aunt Andrea makes me some scrambled eggs before going to the funeral home. I told her I really didn't want to go, but agreed to pick out Mom's final outfit and gather a few photos. As soon as I walk into Mom's bedroom, my lip trembles. The further I step into the room, the more her vanilla scent invades my nose. My knees buckle and I collapse onto her bed. I fist the blanket and scream into the mattress.

Why? I only had one parent…

I force myself to calm down. Aunt Andrea will be back soon. She lost her sister and she's carrying the bulk of this. I can at least pick out an outfit and find some photographs. I walk over to the closet and grab the hanger with her favorite dress. With great care, I lay it on the bed. Using a small step ladder, I reach far back in the closest to grab the old albums on the top shelf.

I drop a few bulky albums. Stretching on my tiptoes, the ladder shakes a little, but I spot a box shoved in the far corner. I reach back using the tips of my fingers to slide the box closer. The ladder wiggles, and I have to stop to get my balance back. I stretch again and push harder, sliding the box within my reach. The dust is layered so thick it's almost cemented the box in place, but with a little more force, I hear a *pop* and the box drags dust with it as it slides toward me. I cough and close my eyes as a small dust cloud attacks my face as I pull the box off the shelf. I cringe when I sit the box down and look at my fingers caked from the thick layers of dust on the box.

The lid pops as it becomes unglued from the film. Now that the lid's off, I don't want to touch anything else with my filthy hands. I hurry into the connecting bathroom and wash up. Once clean and dry, I return to the box. My eager hands pick up a piece of small white fabric. I unfold it, and find it's a frilly baby romper.

Sarah

I smile at the sweet little romper that belonged to a little girl named Sarah. *Who's Sarah?* I've never heard Mom or anyone mention a Sarah. I lay the romper on the bed and continue to search for more clues in the little box of mystery. It's like a treasure hunt. There's printed photos of poor quality, like the ones you print off a computer. There's a dark-haired woman pushing a stroller through a park. There's another picture of the same woman, but this time she's with a baby and a young, dark-haired boy walking in the same park. There's several more, all of the same woman with two children in the same park.

Weird.

I stop and stare closer at one photo. There's a diaper bag with the name 'Sarah Randall' in cursive on its side hanging from the woman's shoulder.

Who's Sarah Randall?

This must be who the romper belongs to. Did Mom know these people? Are they from the town she lived in before she moved here? Aunt Andrea might know. Maybe they're related or a close friend from their hometown. Not recognizing anything from the photos, I place them aside to reach in the box and pull out a journal. When I open the journal, a folded, faded piece of paper falls to the floor. I close the book and bend down to retrieve it. I unfold the paper and my heart plummets.

No.

Three

"Luv Bug? Olivia? Can I please come in?"

No. No. No. It can't be. It's not true.

I lock myself in the bathroom and take my phone and swipe the screen. In the search engine, I quickly type 'Sarah Randall.' There's news article after article about a missing infant that was kidnapped in Lumberton, Missouri, Cindy's hometown. The little girl was last seen in a park. *In a park.* She was wearing a white romper with her name on the front. *The white romper. Sarah.*

I lean over and vomit into the toilet. The room is spinning so I grab the sink to help me stand. I turn on the faucet and splash water on my face.

"*Olivia! Please!* You're scaring me."

I throw the door open and stare into Aunt Andrea's concerned eyes. "Who am I?"

Andrea's brows furrow. "Honey, what are you talking about?"

Pointing to the bed, I wait for her to see the evidence of lies lying upon my kidnapper's bed. "Who's my mother?"

Andrea walks over and shakes her head. As she starts to read, I watch as a wash of horror crosses over her face and the denial in her wide eyes. "This isn't possible. Cindy was pregnant. She *was*. She left close to the time this happened but I-" Her face crumbles and her eyes seem to plead for me to what? Understand? Forgive? Agree and deny all the evidence?

Through clenched teeth, I stand firm and ask the question that's burning through me to know. "Did you know?"

"I knew about the missing child. Everyone knew. The Randalls are a big, wealthy family back in Lumberton. It was everywhere."

"Did. You. Know. About *Cindy?*"

"Olivia. We don't know-"

"We don't *know?* Did you read the letter? Why would she have this? *How* did she come to have this?"

Andrea picks the letter up off the floor. Her eyes widen as she reads the letter. She reads it again. I watch her hands shake as she places the letter on the bed. Her mouth opens and then closes. "I don't know what to say," she whispers. "Cindy wasn't… she wasn't in the best place there for a while. I thought moving away and having a baby had straightened her out. I thought she'd finally found happiness and stability. I never dreamed she'd stolen someone else's child."

"So, you're not really my aunt," my voice breaks.

Andrea rushes to me and wraps me in a tight embrace. "Never doubt that I love you. Cindy loved you. This changes none of that."

Pushing her away from me, I stumble back. "It changes everything!" I rush out of the room of deceit to the sanctuary of my room. I slam the door and lock it.

What do I do now? Who am I?

When I hear Andrea leave the room across the hall and walk away, I slip out. I retrieve the box, letter, photos, and journal. The only verification I have of my identity are here. I take them back to my room and spend all night examining the photos. This stranger was my mother, yet the woman I loved like a mother was really a stranger all along.

Four

Feb. 5

I read in a women's magazine that writing can help. So—here we go. I've nothing else to lose.

You know what phrase I hate more than anything? You can try again.

This wasn't a plant in my garden that didn't survive the winter.

*This was my **child**.*

*Apparently, only mine because Michael has moved on. He's moved on. And I can't. He says I need help. That **I** need help. What about him? Why isn't anyone wondering about how easily he can get over our loss. It's been only a couple of months since I miscarried during my third month of pregnancy. I'm not ready to try again. I'm not ready to move on. We suffered a great loss.*

Was it really a loss to him? Did he feel the baby? No. At this point I wonder if he feels anything…even for me. I hate him.

My sister Andrea is pregnant. I'm going to be an aunt. I, who went to great lengths to eat as healthy as possible, lost my baby. But Andrea, who smokes like a freight train, is experiencing a perfectly, healthy pregnancy. I don't even think she's eating right…

Can somebody please explain to me how this is fair?

I love my sister and I want to be an aunt. I'm just trying to understand. I loved Michael. I did. I loved Michael as much if not more than she loves Brad. Michael and I never even argued until my chance of motherhood was stolen from me. Brad and Andrea fight all the time!

It's not fair.

It's not fair.

It's not fair.

Five

April 18

Michael and I are divorcing.

He's divorcing me.

Michael is divorcing me. He accused me of being sick and depressed… Men don't know a thing. Not a damn thing. How can he understand my feelings when he doesn't even have any feelings? Having feelings and grieving now makes you a sick person? Well **HE** *makes* **ME** *sick. That asshole has left me stripped of everything. I don't know how I'll afford this house…*

I'm going to lose my home.

I now regret ever listening to him. I had a job, but HE suggested I quit while we try to have a baby to "help with stress." Maybe he was the cause of stress. He was the reason for all this. My job won't take me back. What will I do?

Our lives were going to be perfect…

Now, we hate each other. When did our love turn to hate? When we lost the baby, I guess we lost our love too. We lost our hearts. Too much has been said for us to go back.

I don't know what I'll do…

Time will tell.

Six

June 1

My sister Andrea is "worried" about me. So I drink. So I have a drink on occasion. Little Miss Perfect doesn't understand what I'm going through. Her with her sweet little house and sweet little husband. How would she know the first thing about what **I'm** *going through?*

There's nothing wrong with having a drink. I've had everything else taken from me, now she wants to take away the only thing that numbs the pain?

Am I bothering anyone?

Michael filed a restraining order. Over one little phone call. Prick. All I wanted was to know if he'd packed and taken my ultrasound photos. They were my photos. He doesn't deserve them. He sure as hell didn't give a shit when we lost the baby so what does he want the photos for?

I'm back to being unemployed. I had a few little jobs here and there…but here I am back to square one.

I bet **he** *likes that. He probably likes watching me suffer. Watching me struggle financially without him. He set me up this way. He left me this way. And the police have the nerve to act like I'm the villain?*

<u>Me?</u>

I bet him and Andrea talk about me. Laugh about me. I don't need either one of them. Tomorrow I'm getting a job.

And eventually I'll get out of this hell hole.

Seven

THE WOMAN WRITING THIS COULD NOT HAVE been my mother, but it's her handwriting. I wipe away the moisture from my face. This doesn't sound like her at all. *I knew her. I loved her.*

Cindy was torn between being happy and jealous for her sister. She felt as though she'd been dealt a huge injustice in life. Andrea still smoked during her pregnancy and argued with Brad constantly. Cindy went to great lengths to eat as healthy as possible and was madly in love with Michael. Reading her words, I felt her pain. It was hard not to. Without Michael to support her, she had to get a job. It's hard to imagine her never being employed before. The mother I knew was a career driven woman, working in management for a small company. This woman seemed to struggle with holding any job. She developed an alcohol problem. *I can't believe this! Mom never touched alcohol in all the years I knew her.*

This woman was a disaster. I have to stop reading. I don't want to remember Mom like this. I go back to my phone and read the words from the woman *I* knew. Her sweet, loving words in that final text message.

The sound of voices wakes me. Tomorrow is my mom's, no—Cindy's funeral. I don't even know how I feel. The more time I have to absorb this information, the more confused I feel. I was raised by…a stranger. She lived a whole other life I'd never known about. The woman that I've loved more than anyone for as long as I can remember, who was supposed to protect me, is the one I should've been protected from. She not only lied to me but isolated me so I'd never know the truth. Had she planned to eventually give me that letter? Was it back-up in case she ever got caught? I still have her journal, although I can't bring myself to read it any more right now. I'm not emotionally stable enough to receive any more information.

The voices continue. They're muffled, so I'm not sure who's on the other side of my door. I get dressed and slowly creak the door open. I tip-toe down the hallway to the bathroom. When I look in the mirror, I cringe. Makeup can only do so much. My eyes are swollen and red rimmed. When I've made myself at least presentable, I exit the bathroom.

I walk into the kitchen with my head held high, ready to face whatever new life altering discoveries await me. Aunt Andrea is seated at the table with Uncle Brad's hand holding hers. They look how I feel with their dark circles and red-rimmed eyes. On the other side of Andrea, holding her other hand, is their son, Noah.

I haven't seen him in years, but he doesn't look the way I was expecting. I know he plays football and it shows. He's filled out from the scrawny little boy that came to visit years ago. Gone is the baby fat from his face. He now has visible jawlines and cheekbones. Maybe I've been staring at photographs of Ancient Greek statutes too long, but Noah Wallace has the face sculptors dream about. His body is that of an athlete, with strong arms that I can see the muscles flex as he grips his mom's hand while watching me. His messy, blondish brown hair that used to be like a mop on top of his head is now trimmed and styled. The sides are cut shorter with the top longer and with a few strands hanging loosely over one of his thick dark eyebrows and hazel eyes that stare at me with caution. *Is he worried I'm going to snap?*

I probably appear like a wild animal with how I keep my distance from anyone and right now, I feel like one. *Who can I trust when everything has been a lie?* Across from them are the backs of a woman and of a male in a blue police uniform to me.

"Luv Bug." Andrea sighs when her eyes meet mine.

The officer turns around and stands. "Hello Ol-" He doesn't continue.

He doesn't know what to call me. *That makes two of us.* Who is Sarah Randall? Apparently, *I am.* I know myself as Olivia Stevens. In fact, she's all I've ever known.

"Olivia." I tell him with a blank face. "Please."

The officer and who I now can see is Mrs. Jenkins, exchange a look. She sighs and has trouble meeting my eyes. "Olivia, I'm sorry for your loss. Your mother's car accident was most unexpected and a shock to us all. None of us knew..." She clears her throat, "...what Cindy had done. The accident has brought all this out into the open." She turns to the officer and then back to me. "They need the box with all of its contents back. The letter, photographs, and...clothing. It's all evidence. See, sweetheart, there are some legal matters that need to be tended to."

The officer nods in agreement. "Miss Stevens, I know this is hard for you. It's a lot to take in for anyone, especially a young girl. You have parents that are still looking for you. They've been waiting a long time for this day. Would you like to meet your biological parents?"

Mrs. Jenkins whispers something to the officer. He gives me a single nod and steps outside. She gives me a hug. "I'm so sorry, Olivia." She pulls with her eyes full of sympathy. "If you will," she takes my hands in hers, "go get the letter and box. I'll give it to the officer."

I nod and go to my room. *They didn't mention the journal.* I take the box and letter but leave the journal and a photo of me as a baby with the dark haired woman. Listening to make sure no one is coming, I hide them under my mattress. Aunt Andrea may not have seen the journal; therefore, the police don't know about it.

When I give her the items, Mrs. Jenkins hugs me again as she turns to leave. "I'll come back tomorrow. In the meantime, please call me if you need anything."

Andrea wraps her arms around me and holds me close. She whispers against the top of my head. "I won't leave your side unless you want to be left alone."

I don't answer her. Instead, I turn my head to look around the house at all the photos on the wall of me and the only woman I've ever known as my mother. Her beautiful, smiling face scattered throughout the house. She was always smiling and laughing. My favorite is the one of us two years ago on the white, paint chipped porch swing in front of our house. Mom is holding my hands in hers, and we are looking at each other with our heads almost touching. We're laughing. I still remember the day so vividly. It was in the summer, but it had rained so there was a nice cool breeze. A few friends had come to visit. We had all sat on the front porch for hours drinking lemonade, talking and most of all, laughing.

I hang my head as Aunt Andrea rubs my back. How is all this happening? First, Mom, I mean, *Cindy* can't be dead. Second, Cindy wasn't my mother but my kidnapper. We were supposed to make lasagna and watch a movie that night. She went to the grocery store for supplies while I finished my homework. It was a normal night…until it wasn't. My only thought now is I wish I'd gone with her that day.

There's a knock on the door. I don't wait to see who it is or what they want. News has spread of Cindy's death. This isn't a big town, so everyone heard as soon as it happened. I push myself off of Andrea and go to my room, shutting the door behind me.

I refuse to leave my room, other than to use the bathroom. I keep flipping through photos in the photo albums. Memories flood my mind. Cindy trying to teach me how to roller skate but us both ending up with matching scars on our knees. Her teaching me how to swim. My birthday parties over the years, always in the backyard. The memories become too painful, so I walk over and fall on my pillow and smell her perfume. I begin to cry as I think about how she'd come in here to tell me good-night and we'd spend hours talking, sometimes into the wee morning hours. I roll over onto my side and press the button to unlock my phone. I swipe my finger through the more recent photos of us. Her trying on a ridiculous hat in a department store. A selfie of us with snow cones. A few more selfies of us making silly faces. I laugh out loud when I see the photo she had made me promise to delete. She's pointing her finger at the camera, wearing a bright pink, fuzzy bathrobe. Her face is completely green, except for around her eyes and lips. A pastel orange colored towel is wrapped around her head, and she's staring wide eyed and clearly screaming, having been caught in her current state. I'm so grateful now that I didn't delete it. I get a tight feeling in my chest, so I close out of my photos.

There's a knock at my door. I turn my head toward the door and try to call out, but my words get stuck in my throat. The person doesn't bother waiting long anyways. The door flies open and Angie comes rushing to my bed. She plops on top and curls up next to me. "You didn't answer my texts so I got worried."

I give her a small smile. "Thanks Ange. I'm sorry, it's just that-"

"Hey don't apologize. You've lost your mom. I'm just worried about you. What happens now? Think they'll let you move in with me and my mom?" When I don't answer her for fear I'll burst out crying again, she continues. "Or…do you want to move away? To live with your aunt?"

"Angie…" I clear my throat. "I found something out."

Angie sits up on the bed. "Shit. Did Cindy have millions stowed away?"

"If only it were something that simple."

"Olivia, what happened? It's not something crazy like Cindy had another family somewhere on the side."

"Actually…" I wet my lips. "I am the one that has another family."

Angie stares at me for a moment and then bursts out laughing. "That's not funny. Wow. Your face was so serious, you almost had—wait, are you *serious?*"

I nod my head with my lips pressed tightly together as I try to fight back the sobs threatening to break through. Angie wraps her arms tightly around me. After I take a moment to calm down, I pull away from my best friend that I may very well never see again for a long time if I move away.

"Cindy is not my biological mother."

"So you're adopted?"

"Not exactly. I—gosh, I don't even know how to explain. Google the name Sarah Randall from Lumberton, Missouri."

I patiently wait and then watch her eyes widen. She holds a screen up showing a beautiful, smiling young woman holding a baby. "This is *you?*"

I wring my hands together and nod. "I think so. I found some evidence in Cindy's closet as I was looking for stuff for the funeral. A social worker is handling most of the stuff with the police."

"Now what?"

I fall back on my pillow and throw my hand over my face.

"I don't know, Ange. This is so messed up. All of it. I just don't know." I look over at her. "Hey, but can we keep this between us?" She nods vehemently. I point a finger at her. "Not even your mom." She nods again.

"Of course. I won't tell a soul."

"Thanks. I appreciate it."

⟳

There's a knock on the door. I don't answer. Whoever it is, knocks again and then finally turns the knob. I didn't lock it, so I watch as the door opens a tiny bit.

Noah.

I give a sideways glance waiting for him to speak. He clears his throat and asks, "Are you hungry? Need any…anything?" I shake my head and he gives me a closed-lipped half smile as he slowly shuts the door back.

My cell vibrates with a text from Angie.

Angie: I'm sorry. I'm a horrible friend. I kind of told my mom…

Angie: It just slipped out I swear.

Angie: She promised she wouldn't tell anyone

I know that's a lie. Angie's mom is going to tell everyone. *Great. Just great.*

Angie: Please don't hate me.

I don't have enough strength in me to even be mad at Angie. Everyone was going to find out eventually.

I toss my phone and open Cindy's journal. I'm hoping by reading this, I'll gain some understanding. *Why did she kidnap me? How did she find me? Did the Randall family ever know Cindy? Did the Wallace family have any involvement?*

Eight

September 5

Andrea gave birth. She's a mother. I'm an aunt. *yay* That's possibly the closest I'll get to becoming a mother. His name is Noah. And he is perfect.

I want to be happy.

I am happy. I just… can't.

Nine

ER SHORT JOURNAL ENTRY CUTS ME. IT'S like she was too emotional and depressed to even write a full entry. It's weird that I'd just seen Noah at my door and then read about his birth in her journal. My mom did turn out to be a loving and great aunt. Her and Andrea both. Noah and I haven't seen each other much throughout or lives; in fact, we barely know each other. But I know Mom always remembered his birthday and kept up with his life. She mailed gifts and cards. Andrea was a little more involved in my life. She'd make it a point to come visit, but she had Brad to help with Noah when they couldn't all come.

All she wanted was to be a mom. And she was. She was a great mom. I cry until I'm so exhausted that sleep takes me.

⁂

It's Monday. I just had the weekend from hell. I sit alone in the dark in my room. This can't be real life. This can't be *my* life. I wait for the next shoe to drop. Instead, there's a soft knock at the door. I wait and Aunt Andrea calls from the other side of the door. "Olivia, it's me. I was wondering if you need help getting ready?"

With all that is happening and all that has been brought into the light, we've decided against a formal funeral for Cindy Stevens. We're going to the church and having a simple cremation. The preacher is going to speak and we'll say our goodbyes to a framed photo next to a box. *What can he say about a woman who'd stolen a child from her family?* I guess, we'll find out.

I open the door and turn on the light. Aunt Andrea wraps me in her arms. She kisses the side of my head and sniffles. She's been so strong all this time. Hearing her sniffle breaks me. It breaks the last shred of my heart. I squeeze her tighter and bury my face into her.

"I'm scared," I whisper.

"I'm here for you, Luv Bug. Brad and Noah are here too. Angie. Mrs. Jenkins."

I shake my head into her shoulder, feeling her shirt soaking up my tears. "This is only the beginning. I don't know what's to come. I've never left home. I feel—I feel sad, confused, embarrassed-"

"Ssshhh," She speaks into my hair as she pets the side of my head, while still holding me tight with her other arm. "You're allowed to feel all of those things. But know, none of this was your fault. You have no reason to feel embarrassed, Luv Bug. We're going to take this one day at a time."

I pull back and search her eyes. "Are we?"

She knows what I'm asking. Am I going to be able to continue my relationship with Aunt Andrea? She's been questioned about her involvement in my kidnapping and so far, there's nothing linking her to it other than being Cindy's sister.

She cups my face. "I'm here. And I'll always be here for you. If you still want to have any contact with me, that is."

I'm shocked that Aunt Andrea could possibly think I

didn't want a relationship with her. She bows her head and I see a single tear slide down her cheek. I reach up and cup her face. When her eyes meet mine I ask, "And give up the best peanut butter pie? You know yours is my favorite."

She sniffles. "I can make you some tonight, would you like that?"

"I'd love it, Aunt Andrea."

We take a moment to hug each other and shed a few more silent tears. Between being so confused and constantly nervous, I've had a painful headache since this all began. I need another minute alone.

"I'll be out shortly."

She nods and leaves. I shut my door and go stand in front of my mirror.

Who are you?

All the messages about a mother being the woman who defines you. Who am I then? I've always been so close with the woman who raised me. There were never any signs that she wasn't my mother, other than we didn't favor each other in looks. She loved me. She cared for me. She made sacrifices for me. Her life wasn't easy as a single mother, yet she never once complained. Yet who was she really? She kidnapped a child. She *stole* me from my family. Yet, I feel that she's been stolen from me. Maybe I was never meant to be hers to begin with. I wipe my eyes and blow my nose. I take one last look in the mirror at Olivia Stevens. Cindy's Luv Bug.

Taking a deep breath, I open my bedroom door. I focus on placing one foot in front of the other. I stop when I enter the living room. There's Aunt Andrea, her husband, her son and Mrs. Jenkins sitting in awkward silence. They turn their heads and stand when they see me.

Mrs. Jenkins smiles. "Your parents' flight has landed. If you're up for it, we can go visit them tonight or tomorrow. Whenever you're ready. They're *very* eager to see you."

Andrea dabs at the corner of her eyes, but gives me a smile.

What are my biological parents like? Will I feel an immediate connection to them? I have brothers and sisters now. What are they like? This is too much too soon.

"Tomorrow. Tonight, I want to focus on laying Cindy Stevens to rest." *And burying Olivia Stevens.*

⁓

We enter the small church. My heart breaks at the sight of an empty room. Not even Cindy's co-workers came to say their final goodbyes. The scandal of my kidnapping has overshadowed the death of a loving mother. I'm tired of everyone's pity. Once the news got wind of my kidnapping and Cindy's death, I received several messages. Most were "Sorry for your loss," but I'm sure now it's not the loss of Cindy, rather it's the loss of my life that might've been. Another popular one is, "Sorry for what happened." Again, I'm sure this isn't about the car wreck but rather the kidnapping.

I wonder if Pastor Rogers and his wife June are only here out of obligation. I hear footsteps behind me and turn to see Angie. She hugs me tight and whispers again how sorry she is.

"It's okay, Ange."

She gives me a sad smile and then moves on to give Aunt Andrea a hug. Uncle Brad clears his throat and mumbles about going to find a seat. *Shouldn't be too difficult.* I feel a large presence at my side and turn.

Noah.

This whole day we haven't spoken, and I think now he'll speak, but instead, he nods his head toward the front pews. He gently places a hand on my back and I follow him to the front and sit down. I'm a little surprised when instead of sitting next to his mom, he takes his seat next to me. Angie comes and sits on the other side of me and takes my hand in hers.

I watch as Pastor Rogers' wife, June, slowly makes her way to the piano. Her long, frail fingers tremble but never falter as she begins playing. The church looks as though it would on any given day. There's no flowers. Since Cindy is being cremated there's no coffin—simply a black box and a single frame with her photo smiling. Pastor Rogers makes his way to the front of the church. He stands and looks out. What must he think seeing only six people? I wonder if this is the smallest funeral he's ever officiated. He clears his throat and Mrs. June stops. I watch as she places her delicate fingers in her lap and awaits her husband to give his eulogy. I follow her gaze and wait to see what light he might shed on Cindy.

"We're gathered here today to honor the life of Cindy Stevens. She's preceded in death by her parents Mark and Debra Stevens. She leaves behind one sister, Andrea Wallace, who is married to Brad Wallace. And one nephew, Noah Wallace. Cindy was born…"

What about me? She left me behind?

I feel my chest rise and fall rapidly. I want to stand up and shout at him that he left out a daughter. She left behind one daughter, Olivia Stevens. I feel a heavy arm around my shoulders pull me close. I lean on Noah's warm, solid body for comfort as I stare at the man who speaks about Cindy as though she's a stranger. He *knew* her. She attended this church every Sunday.

And he knows me. He knows me as Olivia Stevens, daughter of Cindy Stevens. Yet he refuses to make eye contact with me. I stop listening and watch his mouth move. I don't hear what meaningless words he says, I just watch the motions. I feel Noah's arm tighten occasionally around me. I feel so broken as I sit here. I'm baffled. I keep thinking, this can't be real. None of this is real.

Finally, Pastor Rogers looks directly at me. I sit straighter, giving him my full attention. "There's a plan set in place for all of us. We don't know, and we may not understand, but we have to trust He has a plan. Let us bow our heads and pray."

I stand up. "I'd like to say something." Everyone stares wide-eyed at me as I walk up the altar steps. "Please." Pastor Rogers steps aside and I take his place at the microphone.

"Cindy Stevens was more. She was more than a dedicated, hard-working woman. She was more than a member of this church. She was more than a loving sister and aunt. She was…" I feel my throat tightening. I swallow and suck in a deep breath. My eyes find Noah's and he gives me a single nod. "She was a loving mother. She was my mother. She was so much more and deserved more," I choke. My resolve is crumbling. I just wanted—no needed—for them to know she did love me. And despite everything, I loved her. This church should've been full. In my peripheral vision, I see Aunt Andrea jump up and rush toward the stage. "She was a mother."

Andrea wraps her arms around me and allows me to fall into her. She leads me down the steps and holds me as the piano plays softly. Pastor Rogers leads us in prayer as I cry quietly into Aunt Andrea's shoulder.

Ten

January 3

    It's been a year. A long, painful year. I'm more alone than I've ever been in my life. Or that's how I feel anyway. I've thought about trying to get pregnant again. I don't have to be married. I don't even have to be in a relationship. All I need is a man for a few minutes.

    Who am I kidding? My body isn't fit for a child. I need to clean up my diet. My lifestyle. I'm no longer fit to be a mother or grow a baby.

    What have I become?

Eleven

January 5

Do you believe life has a way of winding around to finally landing you where you're meant to be? I do.

I didn't for the longest time, but in that moment...I did. Because through all the heartache and pain, I got a job at Tony's Pizza as a delivery driver and it brought me to steps that I'd otherwise never gone. The door opened...and there she was.

There she was!

I met those big blue-green eyes and my heart finally began beating again. This beautiful little pink baby with blonde curly hair. The most beautiful baby in the world was being presented to me. When the woman told me her name was <u>Sarah,</u> it took everything in me not to scoff.

Sarah? Really? For such a beautiful girl? The name is too common. This girl would not be <u>common</u>. A name instantly came to me. Olivia. That's her name. Olivia...

Then I hear the voice of a small child and look over the woman's shoulder. She notices me and looks over as well. She smiles and tells me that's her son Trent.

"Can you believe I'm already pregnant again? I just gave birth! I almost cried when the doctor told me."

Three. She has two here and one on the way. While I… well, it's just me, isn't it?

Once again, I'm reminded how unfair the world is. How cruel fate can be. Or maybe…maybe it's fate that brought me here to lighten her load… Maybe I'm not meant to birth my own daughter, but to be a mother to this little girl.

Twelve

*I*T'S ONE O'CLOCK IN THE MORNING WHEN I finally get to the part where I'm mentioned. I was about to fall asleep, but now I'm wide awake. Cindy had taken a job delivering pizzas. She was delivering a pizza to the Randall's home when Melissa opened the door holding me.

The way Cindy describes me makes my heart swell, as weird as that sounds. She thought I was the most beautiful baby. I laugh when I read that she didn't think the name "Sarah" suited me at all. I feel the same way, but maybe only because I was raised to feel that way. She was jealous that Melissa was pregnant and already had two healthy children. I can understand Cindy. I mean, she felt that this woman had it all, while she had nothing. It hurts my heart to think of how defeated Cindy must've felt. She was the best mother and did give me all her attention. Melissa's attention was divided amongst three children and a husband. Did this all work out for me? I'm suddenly drained, physically and emotionally.

Tap. Tap.

"Luv Bug?"

I roll over in my bed and see Aunt Andrea standing there with sad eyes. "Yeah?"

"Mrs. Jenkins will be here in an hour to take you out to lunch. You're meeting your parents."

"Are you coming?"

She bites her bottom lip and looks at the floor. "I don't—I think this is something…" She gives a humorless chuckle and shakes her head. She looks up at me and smiles, but it doesn't reach her eyes. "You'll like them. Don't worry. They're really good people and they have so much to offer you."

I raise up in bed. "I'd feel better if you were there. They might be my parents, but Aunt Andrea, they're still strangers to me."

"Strangers who already love you. They've loved you since before you were born and never once stopped. How can you be nervous when you've already swept them off their feet?" She attempts to joke. I roll my eyes at her. She walks the rest of the way into my room and sits next to me on my bed. "Mrs. Jenkins will be with you the whole time. If you really don't feel comfortable, I'm sure we can talk to her." She pats my leg. "You're almost eighteen, kiddo. Pretty soon you won't need any of us."

I scoff. "I doubt that. I'm a mess. I don't even know who I am anymore."

"Well, if it makes you feel any better, I'm forty-four and I still don't know who I am half the time."

We take a moment just to smile at each other. On the upside, if I move in with the Randall family, Aunt Andrea won't be so far away. On the downside, I'd rather move in with her. As if she can read my mind, she says. "Just give them a chance. They're who you should've been with all along." Her eyes glisten as she fights back tears. The strain in her voice and tremble of her lips shows that took a lot of effort for her to say. I nod. Aunt Andrea pushes herself off the bed and closes the door on her way out.

I walk into the living room and see two suitcases by the front door. Aunt Andrea and Brad aren't around, but Noah is standing there with his hands in his blue jean pockets.

"Ma and Dad are in the bedroom. Getting the last of our stuff."

"Oh," I nod. He nods. *This is awkward.* "I hope you have a safe flight back."

"Thanks." We hear footsteps outside the door. "That's probably your ride."

"Probably."

"Well, I hope you have a nice lunch with Richard and Melissa."

"Do you know them?"

"Not very well."

The doorbell rings. "More than I do," I say as I walk over to the door. I open the door and find Mrs. Jenkins, dressed impeccable as usual, in a grey suit. I look down at my jeans and grey long sleeve shirt.

"Ready?"

"Yeah—I mean, yes." I look over my shoulder at Noah and give him a closed lip smile. "Bye."

He gives me a slight nod and three-finger wave.

Mrs. Jenkins opens her car door for me and smiles. I thank her and ask, "Where are we going?"

"To the steakhouse down on Main Street. They're so excited." When I don't respond she reaches across the console and takes my hand. "Don't be nervous. I'm right here with you. And they're probably more nervous than you are. You're the one in charge. If you feel overwhelmed and need to leave any time, just say so. I'm sure your parents will understand."

My parents? Strangers.

No, I need to try to be positive. Maybe then they won't seem like strangers. In fact, I may have an instant connection with them since they are my biological parents.

The only family I ever knew of, other than Cindy, are my Aunt Andrea and her family. I barely recognized Uncle Brad and Noah. Aunt Andrea would send photos, of course, but it'd still been eight years since I'd seen those two in person. Over the years, they had come to visit us in Springfield, Colorado, but we never went to visit them. Since we lived in Colorado and they lived in southeast Missouri, visits could be expensive and time restricted. Thus, Aunt Andrea would make most trips alone since usually Uncle Brad and Noah couldn't make the trip due to conflicting schedules. I've only been around them a handful of times; however, I've maintained a close relationship with Andrea. She always tried to visit at least once or twice a year, but she called every day.

We pull into the parking lot and park next to a black sedan. As I'm exiting the car, I see the doors of the sedan open also. A very handsome, well-dressed older couple walks out. The man is tall and lean: he has blondish brown hair and slightly darker facial hair that's neatly close trimmed to his face. Everything about him is neat, right down to his pale blue, wrinkle free button down shirt and beige dress pants. The woman reminds me of a modern day Jacqueline Kennedy—everything about her. Her dark styled hair, clean classic beauty facial features, olive coloring, light makeup and fitted peach colored A-line dress.

She's the woman from the photograph. She's my mother.
This beautiful, sophisticated woman is my mother.

When she catches sight of me, she puts her hands to her mouth and nearly crumbles to the ground. She quickly regains her composure and comes rushing towards me in tears. She wraps her arms tightly around me and cries. I'm not really sure what to do, so I wrap my arms around her as well.

"You're here! You're really here! You're here," she continues to repeat between sobs.

The man joins us, teary eyed, and rubs his hand on his wife's back. "It's okay, Melissa. It's okay. Let's take her inside. I'm sure she's already overwhelmed," he whispers.

He turns to Mrs. Jenkins and shakes her hand, thanking her for all her support and help.

Melissa nods but keeps one arm around me to lead me toward the restaurant. "I-I'm sorry, Sarah. I am just *so* happy to have you in my arms again. Not a day has gone by that I wasn't praying for this day. Not a day." She squeezes me close to her side.

Sarah. That's the name that was originally given to me. I'm speechless and overwhelmed.

The man turns to me and smiles. "Sarah, I'm your father but, uh, you probably don't remember me, so I'd like to re-introduce myself. My name is Richard Randall." He hugs me and whispers, "I can't express enough how happy we are. We hope to bring you home."

Mrs. Jenkins smiles. In a gentle tone she says, "Let's go discuss this over lunch. Get to know each other again."

Melissa takes my hand in hers. She can't seem to stop touching me. As she's leading me toward the restaurant, my stomach drops. This is all too much. It's becoming too real. I make eye contact with Mrs. Jenkins. She's watching me closely and raises her brows silently asking me if I'm alright. *Am I?* I inhale slowly and exhale. *I can do this.* I give her a reassuring nod.

We're seated immediately and I'm grateful for the glass of water the waitress brings. Mrs. Jenkins carries most of the conversation, while Richard and Melissa smile at me misty-eyed. She's done her research on me as she fills them in on what a bright student I am and my extracurricular activities. When she's finished, she asks the Randalls to tell me about my siblings.

"You have two brothers and a sister. Trent is the oldest, he's twenty-one, Landon is barely a year younger than you, and Denise, the baby, is fourteen. Well, she's not a baby but the baby of y'all." Melissa grins at me.

I'm not sure how to respond. *Awesome? Okay? That's cool?* I nod and take another sip of water.

"You favor Landon so much. Doesn't she look like Landon, Richard?"

Richard nods and smiles. "You're definitely a Randall."

What does that mean?

Melissa reaches in her bag and pulls out an envelope. Her hands quiver slightly as she lifts the flap. She pulls out a photo and hands it to me.

Three strangers smile back at me. Stretching across the table, her manicured nail points to each head as she says, "Trent, Landon, and that's Denise."

I examine each face. Trent is definitely what I would picture as a big brother. Even from this photo I can tell he's strong and his hazel eyes look so tender and caring. I give Melissa a shy smile as I tell her, "He looks like you."

Pride beams in her eyes as she smiles. "He does. He looks identical to my father. Your grandfather. Dad passed away, but I can show you photos. I have one of him holding you."

I nod and stare into the brown eyes of what would look like me as a skinny boy. His smile is so wide that I can't help but smile back at the photo. We do favor each other. If I had brown eyes, short hair, and no curves. We favor so much in appearances, that I wonder if we have other similar traits. This must be Landon.

The final sibling in the photo is Denise. No doubt she's going to grow up to be a gorgeous woman. She's a tiny little thing here with braces. However, she has lots of Melissa's features.

"That's a year-old photo. Denise doesn't have braces anymore. And Trent's even bigger, if you can imagine that?

Landon still looks about the same." She gives a short chuckle. "He's such a mess."

Richard groans in agreement. The two smile at each other and then turn their eyes back on me. A sadness has crept into their eyes.

I hand the photo back to Melissa but she holds a hand up. "Keep it. I have some more for you to have. Some of you when you were a baby." She hands me the envelope. "And some of your brothers and sister."

"They'd love to meet you." Richard gives me a hopeful smile.

Mrs. Jenkins clears her throat. "Richard? You work in construction?"

"Yes. I own a construction company, Randall Construction. I also design homes as well as build them…I-" Richard gives a short laugh. "I'm sorry. I'm so nervous right now."

"It's alright. Take your time. This is a big moment for everyone." Mrs. Jenkins gives him a reassuring smile.

"Your father is very talented. He has designed some gorgeous buildings, not only in Lumberton, but in surrounding cities. He's a very talented artist."

I smile. "I enjoy art. I'd love to see some of your designs."

Richard's eyes turn glassy. "I'd love nothing more than to show you." A shy smile spreads across his face as Melissa pats his shoulder.

"Melissa? You bake from your home, is that correct?"

"Yes. I love to bake. It's more of a hobby, but I get quite a few orders for pies, cakes, and cookies for the school. You know, little things."

"Don't be modest. You've done some amazing birthday and wedding cakes."

"Oh, Richard. You're the artist here." She looks to me and smiles. "Your father is a smart man. He knows to compliment where his meals are coming from."

I giggle at the two of them.

So these are my parents. They seem nice enough, but they're trying to get me to live with them also.

Richard leans forward on his elbows. "Honey, we want you to come home. More importantly, we want *you* to *want* to come home."

I look to Mrs. Jenkins. She smiles reassuringly.

You're definitely a Randall. Maybe it's time to find out what that means.

When I return home, Uncle Brad and Noah have left. Noah has school and they couldn't miss their flight. Aunt Andrea must've already known I'd be leaving as well, if her somber mood is any indication. There's so much I want to say, but Mrs. Jenkins didn't leave as I had expected her to. Instead, she followed me in, offering to help any way she could. A part of me suspects she's there to ensure my safety in returning me to the Randalls. She's been pleasant, but her eyes watch Aunt Andrea carefully.

"Don't worry. I'm going to get everything situated here." Aunt Andrea tells me. She already has empty boxes in the kitchen.

"I can't fit all of my stuff in a suitcase."

"Do you want me to ship it to you? Any of your friends here that you want to give anything to?"

"I'll leave a box for Angie, if you don't mind?"

"Of course not. I don't mind at all."

We take a moment to just stare at each other. Mrs. Jenkins gently places a hand on my shoulder.

"We need to get your bags packed."

⌒

Once my suitcase and carry-on are full, Mrs. Jenkins tells me she'll see me bright and early in the morning. She assures me the Randalls will provide everything I will need and not to worry about whether I packed enough clothes or anything else.

I find Aunt Andrea still in the kitchen packing away plates and glasses. "What are you going to do with everything?"

"AH!" I giggle as Aunt Andrea grabs her chest. "You scared me to death! Whew. Let me catch my breath." She grabs another plate and wraps brown paper around it. "I think most of everything I'll try to sell. What doesn't sell, I'll donate. These plates were our mother's, so I'm keeping them. I have a woman that's supposed to do an estate sale or whatever. I don't even have to pack the stuff. People will come in, buy it, and take it."

"That's easy enough."

"Yeah, I thought so too."

There's an awkward pause between us. We never have these. I want to cry and tell her I've changed my mind; I'm going to live with her. But, a part of me is excited for this new family, new life.

"I guess you need to get some rest. Early flight tomorrow. Big day." I hear the slight crack in her armor. She's trying so hard to be strong right now.

"Wanna watch a movie? In my room? Before…before we go to bed?"

She smiles and narrows her eyes. "Depends…" Aunt Andrea grabs another plate and tilts her head at me as she wraps it. "What movie are you thinkin'?"

"Pretty in Pink?"

"You got yourself a date. I'll be in there in just a minute."

I rush to my room and get the movie ready. While I wait for her to finish with the plates, I take out the journal.

Thirteen

March 20

I saw Michael the other day. He was with her. His new blushing bride. I can't believe he got married so soon. After all we'd been through!

What's worse is they had a baby. A tiny little girl wrapped in a blanket that had "Karlie" sewn on it.

He must've ran right into her arms after me. She gave him a baby right away. That was supposed to be me. That was supposed to be us. But here I am smelling of greasy cheese and pepperoni. I couldn't help myself so I blurted out that I was expecting as well. I have a rounding belly but not from a baby. It's from weeks of alcohol, fast food, and lack of exercise. Lack of anything really, except alcohol.

After seeing their disgusting public display of affection and happiness, I drove by the Randall house again.

And there she was.

There she was.

Melissa was pushing her in a stroller as Trent rode his bike. Right on schedule. Melissa is such a creature of habit. She's also so self-absorbed. What's funny is I made it into a picture that she took and posted it on her MySpace page. Her selfie with the kids while walking shows me in my car parked on the corner of the Randall's street. I think I'll print it and save it.

It's my first photo with my new baby girl, after all.

Fourteen

THE NEXT DAY, I HUG ANGIE AND AUNT ANDREA goodbye.

"You better not forget about me. Call me soon and tell me all about your family. And tell me about your brothers. Are they hot?"

"Ew. Angie...don't make this awkward."

"Hate to break it to you, but it's already going to be awkward. Send me pics asap of them." *She's so boy crazy.* I roll my eyes. "And tell me all about your new school. I want to hear all the deets as soon as you get home."

"Alright you two," Aunt Andrea waves me and Angie apart. "Come on, Luv Bug, before you miss your flight."

I hug Aunt Andrea again. "I guess I'll see you in Missouri." Her only response is to hug me tighter.

I follow Mrs. Jenkins to her car. On the way to the airport she asks, "Do you want them to call you Olivia?"

I'm surprised by her question. *Do I?*

"Olivia was Cindy's daughter. I'm going to try and be Melissa and Richard's daughter. Sarah Randall is who I was meant to be."

"You are who you're meant to be. Be you."

Be me? I don't even know who I am.

"I'll be that person when I figure it out. For now, I'm going to try and move on as Sarah Randall."

Mrs. Jenkins parks the car. The Randalls are waiting for us at the door. She hugs me goodbye and tells me to keep in touch.

⁂

I'm seated on a plane in between Richard and Melissa Randall. This is my first plane ride, and I'm disappointed that my first experience is under such bizarre circumstances.

"Doing alright?"

I don't turn to look at Richard. I keep my head low and nod. I mean, I think I'm holding myself together pretty well considering I'm seated between two strangers that I'm going to live with.

"Do you like to read?"

I nod. Richard reaches into his satchel and pulls out a tablet and hands it to me. "There's a few mysteries on there." I take the tablet and can barely hear him mumble, "A few fantasy ones as well."

I smile and watch his cheeks grow a little pink. "I like fantasy."

My life seems more like a mystery right now than reality. I swipe the tablet screen but I don't really look at the titles. I mostly want to distract myself. I wonder if this wasn't my current situation, where would my first plane ride take me? I see a book cover with a castle. Maybe I'd be on my way to Scotland. Or a castle in Germany. Another cover shows a cityscape. New York City? Los Angeles? Wouldn't those be amazing places to visit. Never would I have dreamed it would be to Lumberton, Missouri that my first flight would take me. No matter how hard I try to daydream about different circumstances, I still slam back to my reality. Cindy had lived in the same town as my biological parents that she kidnapped me from.

Kidnapped.

Cindy Stevens is not my mother, but had been my captor. I still love her. I hurriedly glance over at Melissa, afraid she might have heard that last thought. I feel like I'm an accomplice to my own kidnapping, which is ridiculous since I wasn't even a year old. *Did I cry for my real parents or did I just immediately take to Cindy? Real parents…Cindy was like a real mom.*

Oh no. I'm about to start crying again. I wipe the tear away. I haven't had the courage to discuss my kidnapping with the Randalls, and they haven't brought it up. I might learn answers by reading the journal. Once I finish reading it, then I'll turn it in to the authorities. *Maybe.*

The captain announces we're getting ready to land. I hand Richard back his tablet. The plane begins its descent, and I feel my stomach plummet to my feet. I sit on my hands to try and stop them from shaking, but that only draws my attention to how much my legs are shaking. I swallow hard and try to calm my nerves before I vomit everywhere.

I need air. I need to get off this plane. I need air. It's too crowded. I can't breathe. I can't breathe!

A firm hand touches my shoulder. I look at the hand and my eyes follow up the arm to Richard. His eyes soften and he gives me a small smile.

"It's okay."

I can only nod as I try to take deep, calming breaths. He nods and gently squeezes my shoulder before dropping his hand. Melissa takes my hand in hers and soothes.

"That's it. Breathe in and out. It's going to be okay now. You're going home."

Home? Home is the other way. I'm going to a house with strangers. People begin to slowly make their way out of the plane. She nods and gestures for me to get out of my seat.

"When you're ready sweetheart. I know this is overwhelming."

I try to stand but fall back down. People are pushing and shuffling their way down the narrow aisle of the plane. Richard uses his body as a shield to give me an opening. This time I make my way into the aisle but immediately I regret it. I feel more claustrophobic than I did before. The pushing and shuffling seems to last forever. *I need air. I need to get off this plane. I need air. I need space.* I feel the hand on my shoulder and turn to receive a nod from Richard. He's behind me now and keeping some distance between us. I at least have a little bit of breathing room now. Slowly, ever so slowly, we approach the flight attendants thanking us for flying with them. As soon as I step off the plane and into the terminal, I exhale a sigh of relief, but I'm still nervous as to what I'm getting off the plane to. I have never felt more alone than I do right now.

Fifteen

UMBERTON, MISSOURI DOESN'T HAVE ITS own airport, so we have a thirty-minute drive after we land. I look out the window and absorb all my new surroundings. It's a drastic change from the mountains of Colorado. There's hills and trees until we enter the city limits of Lumberton. The land is flat with farm fields for as far as the eye can see.

I stare in awe at the beautiful neighborhood we've entered. Any one of these houses could hold three of the house I grew up in. We drive around a curve and pull into the driveway of a pink brick mansion with four huge white columns. The house is beyond gorgeous with two elegant iron front doors, several balconies, huge windows, and every fine detail shouts elegance. I can only imagine what the inside will hold. I don't want to exit the car.

I don't know these people. This is nothing like what I grew up knowing. I want to find Aunt Andrea and go live with her.

What if my brothers and sister won't like me? They're probably snooty. They won't accept me. They're probably ashamed or disappointed with me.

"We're here," Melissa sings.

I contemplate locking the door as Richard and Melissa exit the car with smiling faces. But I don't lock the doors. I gulp and open the door. I step out into the sunshine and birds chirping. Melissa takes me in her arms again, hugging the breath out of me. Richard gets my luggage and rolls it to us.

He gently nudges his wife and whispers, "She's home. We won't lose her again."

She's home.

The words feel heavy. This is it. This is my new home. Right now, it looks like a mansion that I'd never imagine as somewhere I'd live, but maybe it will come to feel like *home*.

That thought evaporates into a puff of smoke as I enter the foyer. The house alone makes me feel like an outsider, never mind the fact that I don't recognize the name Sarah as me and I know nothing of these people. I may be their child, but I've never felt so uncomfortable in a house before. *And this is to be my home?*

The entryway is all marble with a huge brass chandelier hanging from the ceiling. There are two marble staircases with the most beautiful, elegant iron railings I've ever seen. There are three large, open entryways that lead to other areas of the house: one straight ahead that looks to lead to a grand formal living room, one to my left that seems like a longer hallway, and one to my right that I can see is a formal dining room in the distance. They lead me toward the left side of the house. This hallway is covered with family photos. I pause when I see a professional photo of a young dark-haired boy holding a baby girl.

The baby girl has wispy blond hair and is wearing a white frilly dress. I've never seen a photo of myself so young, but I know that's me. Next to that photograph are a few more framed photographs of me. Some of me by myself, some are me with a very young Melissa and Richard, and one of them with me and the small dark-haired boy.

I jump when Melissa's voice is so close to my ear. "I wished we'd taken more photos of all of us together."

I'm left speechless. What can I say to that?

"I have your shadowbox in my bedroom. The outfit you were brought home from the hospital in and the newspaper clipping welcoming you into the world."

I still don't reply. I don't know what I can say to this woman who is my mother but is also a stranger.

She takes both of my hands in hers, looking me straight in the eyes as she speaks. "She may have taken you from this house, but you've always been part of this family. A lot of time was taken from us, but no amount of time nor distance could *ever* make you any less my daughter. You're family. And I plan on making up for that time." Her eyes become glassy. "I can't wait to fill up these walls with memories of my beautiful daughter with her siblings."

Richard clears his throat and gestures for us to continue down the hall. "We have time, honey. Let's not overwhelm her more."

Melissa gives my hands a little squeeze and shake before releasing them. We enter a very cozy den that's decorated in a very rustic theme. There's a large red brick fireplace with a deep brown-colored mantel. In front of the fireplace is a large, dark leather sectional, and the three individuals from the photographs sitting there, looking as awkward as I feel.

"We'll give you a recap of who everyone is again." Melissa whispers and winks.

Richard wraps an arm around me and squeezes me close to him. He releases me and holds me at arm's length. He shakes his head a little, and his eyes get teary again. "I just can't believe it. I didn't believe them at first, and I was skeptical until the moment you got out of the car. But," he releases sigh, "it's you. It. Is. You."

It's weird. These people have been searching for me for

the past seventeen years, but I've only just learned that they even exist.

I'm overcome with a flood of emotions. I'm happy, sad, confused, and intimidated all at once. I have a whole other family when I thought I was alone when Cindy died. But I've lost so much time. Not lost, it was taken from me. The three sitting in front of me have been raised in a life of wealth, which is something unbeknownst to me.

Richard wraps his arm around me again and leads me to stand in front of the fireplace. With his other hand, gestures toward the other siblings and he begins to introduce them.

"This is very strange to introduce you to your own brothers and sister. I can only imagine how you feel, dear. If it becomes too much for you at any time, just say so. Everyone will understand." We all stand there in an awkward pause. I gulp and nod.

"Well," he clears his throat and in a stronger voice announces, "this is your older brother, Trent. He's twenty-one, a junior at a university about an hour and a half away in Lexington, and he's working on a degree in physical therapy."

Trent favors Melissa with his thick, wavy, dark hair and blue eyes. He's extremely attractive. His athletic body is on display with him wearing a black Nike shirt and grey Nike basketball shorts. He stands to shake my hand. As he towers over me, he looks down and studies me. A wrinkle forms between his eyebrows and his eyes turn dark with a swirl of emotions. *What is he thinking?*

Before I can pull my hand away, he wraps me in a tight hug and rests his chin on top of my head. "I'm glad you're okay." His deep voice rumbles.

When he sits back down, Richard continues.

"This is your younger brother, Landon. He just turned seventeen and is a junior in high school." Richard sees the confused look on my face and hurries to explain that Melissa was already pregnant with Landon when I was taken, and he was born premature. "You two are barely a year apart."

Landon comes up to me with a warm smile and wraps me in a full hug with no hesitation. He's a spitting image of a young Richard. He has dark blond hair with a few lighter natural highlights, a button nose, and a bottom lip that's a little fuller than the top. It's almost creepy how many similar features we share, and our ages are so close together. My hair is slightly more blond. I'm seventeen now, but I'll turn eighteen in three months. The main difference that I can tell is that while I do bear a resemblance to Richard and Landon, I have Melissa and Trent's blue eyes. Richard and Landon both have brown eyes. My figure, I notice, has more curves than the lean stick figure of Richard.

"The long-lost sister has returned." Landon says with a wink and then goes back to sit next to Trent.

Richard waves over the petite girl. "This is your baby sister, Denise. She's fourteen and in the eighth grade."

Denise pushes herself out of her seat and quickly walks toward me. She has dark brown, thick, arched eyebrows, but her hair has been colored with an ombre effect so the top is dark brown and flowing into caramel tips. She resembles Melissa and Trent in all aspects except her frame. She's not very tall, even by fourteen year-old standards. She's lean yet athletic, and has a golden tan. The skinny tan lines on her shoulders indicates this is a natural tan.

Denise holds her hand out like she doesn't know if she wants to shake mine. I take her hand and shake it once. She gives me one more look up and down and looks at Richard. He nods, and she returns to her seat.

Melissa comes and wraps her arms around me again in a tight hug. She jumps back suddenly. "Where are my manners! Sarah, sweetheart, would you like something to drink? You must be starving. Come to the kitchen. Let's sit and have a snack. I'll get supper going and you can tell me about…well, about you!"

I shift nervously on my feet and nod. Richard looks to the kids "Why don't you all go to your rooms for now. Let your mom and Sarah have some time together. We'll visit at supper."

I'm relieved to hear that since I don't really want to talk about myself in front of everyone.

On the way to the kitchen, it occurs to me that I could quite easily get lost in this house. My home had two bedrooms, one bathroom, a living room, and a kitchen. We didn't really have a dining room. We ate at the kitchen table. I'm also not used to living with so many people. I have only ever lived with one other person. As far as I can remember, anyway.

Melissa sits me down on a bar stool in the kitchen. This kitchen is basically a restaurant-style kitchen, complete with a mini griddle built into the stove. She asks if a cold sandwich will do for now while she gets supper ready. I nod and in a matter of seconds, she quickly whips up a ham and cheese sandwich for me. After placing a glass of ice water down in front of me, she begins grabbing different ingredients out of the cabinets.

When I finish my sandwich, she sets a few vegetables in front of me on a cutting board.

"Here Sarah sweetie, you prepare the salad. I'll start seasoning the chicken and get it in the oven."

I'm grateful for having something to do, which I think is why she did it. I'm already more at ease with having something to keep my hands busy.

I'm cutting the bell peppers when she casually says, "I love to cook. What are some of your hobbies?"

I notice right away that nobody has mentioned or asked about my previous life with Cindy. The way they've acted with my return I know they care, but it is probably a painful topic for them. I desperately want to ask her to call me Olivia. This Sarah business is uncomfortable. I don't know who Sarah Randall is because I'm Olivia Stevens. I thought I could do it. Take on a new name and new life, but now I'm having doubts. I can't bring myself to say anything about my name, so I tell her about how I love to cook as well, and I enjoy art. We discuss other trivial facts about each other.

"I love pasta. I sometimes experiment by adding my own twist to recipes." I give a nervous chuckle. "Sometimes they work out…sometimes, not so much."

"I bet your dishes are delicious! I'd love for you to cook for us one night. We could make something together? You know, I'm not surprised. Your grandpa owned his own restaurant and was an amazing chef. He had a natural gift in the kitchen. He passed, but it sounds like his passion for cooking went to you. Ha, Lord knows Landon and Denise didn't inherit it. Those two burn toast. Trent enjoys cooking."

I analyze her movements, gestures, facial expressions, facial features, and every comment she makes. My eyes scan the luxurious kitchen again before focusing on Melissa. It's a dream. I can't imagine cooking in here. I can't possibly be a part of this family, this life. *What if there's some mistake?* I know there isn't. Mom—*Cindy*, already confessed everything in her letter. Melissa keeps the conversation light, and I find myself becoming more at ease. All too soon, though, supper is ready and it's time to move to the dining room.

I learn about each one's personalities through random chatter. Trent is very calm and laid back. Landon is comical but hot tempered, and Denise is very chatty and dramatic. I keep looking for similar traits between myself and them. I feel a little shot of excitement each time I hear something we have in common, so much that I want to raise my hand and say "Oh yeah! Me too! Me too!" Instead I remain reserved with a nod and a few mumbled, "me too." Going from a table of one other person to a table of five other people at supper is a little overwhelming. *Will I ever get used to this?* I can't help it, but a few times I think that maybe it was better I did grow up with Cindy. *Is that because she's the one who raised me? Nature vs. Nurture?*

Melissa shows me to my room, and it's massive compared to my old bedroom. I even have my own bathroom. My bedroom closet is about the size of my full bedroom back home. It's all too much and so overwhelming that I want to cry, but I won't in front of Melissa. She's watching me as I take in the room. It's truly beautiful with pale, powder blue walls, grey and white swirl marble floors, and all the furniture is a bright white. The bed is a large, four post queen with an iron canopy. There's a large armoire, vanity, and dresser. There are two white French doors that lead to a balcony with two long windows on either side that are decorated with white curtains. This room is more than I could have ever dreamed of having, yet I'm rather scared of it.

Melissa comes closer to me and rubs my arms "I'll let you get settled and get some rest. Please come to me for anything."

She wraps her arm around my shoulders and squeezes me tightly. I feel her about to break down again. I hug her back tightly because I'm about to break down as well. She releases me and rubs my arms again. She gives me a teary-eyed smile and walks to the door.

She has her hand on the handle about to pull it shut when she pauses. "You don't know me, but I know you. No amount of time or distance could ever change that. At any moment you need me, no matter the time, I'm here for you. I love you."

She shuts the door. I'm swallowed in the silence of the vast space. The big room feels so lonely. A little part of me is tempted to call for her to come back. Not to leave me alone. What would I say? Melissa Randall is my biological mother.

Am I supposed to call her 'mom?' It's much too soon to even consider. I'm so lost and confused that maybe I do need the space to sort through this giant mess. I throw my suitcase on the bed and open it. I didn't bring much from my old room as far as decorations and memorabilia, but I did pack a small painting I'd done last year in my art class. It's one of my favorites and I'm rather proud of it. It's an 8x10 canvas with a black and white checkered background. Alice from Alice in Wonderland is standing in the corner holding her hands behind her back. In the center of the canvas is a circle made of whimsical flowers, and in the center of that circle I painted:

I knew who I was this morning but I've changed a few times since then—Alice In Wonderland.

I can relate, Alice. I place the painting on the nightstand next to the bed, along with a couple of books. I grab all my toiletries and head for the bathroom. I'm surprised to find the bathroom is already fully stocked with everything from high end bath products to scented candles. There's even new razors and loofas. I hop in the shower and instantly feel better when the hot water hits my skin. I scrub the shampoo harder into my hair than necessary, and I do the same with the body wash, scrubbing hard as the hot water scorches my skin. I begin to let the tears fall until finally my body slides down the shower wall, and I cry uncontrollably. I don't know how long I sit on the stone tile and cry. My body is sore when I stand, and the water is lukewarm.

I get out of the shower and finish getting ready for bed. I crawl into my extremely beautiful and comfortable bed. I swipe my phone screen and read through all the unread messages from friends back home. I want to text back but decide not to. Even they seem like strangers now. What could I possibly say? I went from living in a tiny house to a mansion overnight. Most people would be ecstatic for the major upgrade, but I lost my best friend and mom in the process.

58 | **GAIL HARIS**

More than that, I feel like I've lost my identity. I don't have any trouble falling asleep because I'm just too exhausted, emotionally and physically, at this point.

$\sim$

The next morning, I wake up around nine and go downstairs to find breakfast ready for me.

"There's a little bit of everything. I, um," Melissa's cheeks turn pink, "I wasn't sure what you liked."

I nod and smile. As I sit down, she takes my plate and grabs the tong sitting on top of the plate of bacon. "Do you like bacon?" I nod and smile. She goes through every dish on the table the same way, turning my plate into the grand slam of breakfast platters. I hear a snicker next to me and turn to smile at Trent sitting at the end of the table.

"Jeez, Mom. You're going to overwhelm her with protein."

"There's still plenty for you, Trent, if that's what you're really worried about." Melissa winks at me. She places the plate in front of me and I'm almost scared to touch it. The food might topple everywhere.

"Sarah, I want you to make a list of all your favorite foods. And anything you don't like."

Trent raises his eyebrows. "Can I make a list? I'd like to put in requests for the weekends I'm home."

Melissa gives Trent a loving scowl. "Like I don't already fix whatever you want when you're home. You should hear what I have to go through with Denise and Landon. Saying I roll out the red carpet and prepare a feast when the 'golden child' has returned."

Trent must notice me looking around because he says, "Dad already left for work. Landon and Denise have left for school."

"They all wanted to visit with you again. But I told them you needed rest and we were going to let you sleep as long as you needed too."

Trent's phone beeps. He presses the side button and stands. "I hate to run, but I have to hurry if I'm going to make it back to campus for my afternoon class." We share a second of awkwardly staring at each other. Trent presses his lips together and comes over to me with slightly outstretched arms. I quickly stand, hitting my knee on the table, and stretch my arms. We hug and he pats my back. "Glad you're safe and home."

Melissa hugs and kisses Trent like he's a toddler and not a towering body of muscle.

With Trent gone, that leaves only Melissa and I at the table. I feel silly asking my mother who she is, but I don't want the conversation back on me.

"You said you're a stay-at-home mom but also run a baking business? How'd that come about?"

"It started out as a hobby, but I kept receiving so many orders for cakes and various desserts that Richard suggested I start a business."

I nod. I look around the house for inspiration for my next question. They'd told me that Richard owns a construction company. Judging by the house, he must be successful.

"Did he build this house?"

Melissa beams. "This one and all the others in this neighborhood. He also designed this one. He's quite the artist. However, it's not his dream house. This is more my dream. He was able to take my vision and bring it to life. I just blabbed about the kind of house I wanted and he sketched it in a matter of minutes. I'll never forget when he turned his sketch pad around to reveal his design, and then he turned that beautiful drawing into an actual house." Melissa pours herself another cup of coffee and comes to sit next to me at the table. "Your father is *very* talented."

I look around at all the fine details in the moldings, trims, arches, window placements and realize the house is a work of art. "I'd say so. This is a beautiful house."

"You being here makes it a beautiful *home* again." She reaches over and places her hand on top of mine "You're going to have to start school soon." She gives an audible sigh. "You have options on where you'd like to go. One, you can be homeschooled if you're extremely uncomfortable. Two, there's a private school in this district. Three, there is a public school where Landon and Denise go. You'd be in the same building as Landon, of course. He's a grade below you. I wanted to let you decide which school to attend since so much of your life has been out of your control." She gives my hand a little squeeze.

I sit my fork down and ask the first questions that pop into my head, "Why do they not attend the private school? Aren't those supposed to be better? Not to be rude, but y'all seem like y'all can afford it." *We only had one option back home so this is a little overwhelming.*

Melissa laughs and then holds her coffee cup with both hands to take a drink. She places the cup back on the table and says, "We're well off now, but that wasn't always the case. My parents were upper middle class and I went to private school. Richard is an alumnus of the public school, and he wanted our kids to still be down to earth. Not that I wasn't." She gives me a pointed look. "Trent loved public school because when he was there, they were doing better in sports. Landon and Denise followed in his path."

"What sports did Trent play?"

Melissa gives a humorless laugh "What didn't he play? He signed up for everything his schedule allowed. Trent is very athletic and probably could've gone pro in either football or basketball. Even though he loves sports, he wants to do something else with his life. He does a lot of volunteer work and loves physical therapy. Now, Landon on the other hand has no idea what he wants to do with his life yet. He does track. He's sharp, very smart. More than anything, he loves life and lives for the moment. Denise loves baton twirling, art, basketball, and soccer. She's already planning her future. She's unde-cided between pursuing a career in fashion design or reality television. I have no doubt she'll find some way to do both. Although I'd be more than fine with her dropping the dream of a reality show."

I laugh. "Well, she's only fourteen. I'm sure she'll change her mind by the time she graduates."

"What about you? Tell me more about your hobbies and dreams."

"I like to play sports for fun, but I wouldn't really call my-self athletic. I'm pretty good at soccer, though. I love art and reading. I don't know. My dreams… Not sure on my future just yet. At this point I'm taking the day as it comes."

Melissa smiles and nods. "Seems like the two girls took after their father. Both artists."

"I don't know if I'd call myself an artist."

"Humble as well." She takes a sip of her coffee.

"What about you? Are you the athletic one?"

She tilts her head in thought. "I was definitely competi-tive in school sports. Tennis, track, basketball…" She shrugs. "I was also a cheerleader. But Denise hates cheer. She chose twirling."

I think about what she asked me as far as school. I decide to go with the rest of them and attend public school, but I have one concern.

"Do you think it would be weird for them if I attend the same school? I don't want to embarrass them."

I know I'll draw a lot of attention at whichever school I attend. I would prefer that my new siblings not resent me if they receive any unwanted attention on my behalf.

Melissa looks as though I just struck her *"Embarrass them? Honey…why would you think they'd be embarrassed by you being there?"*

I look down at my lap and say, "Well, I've been featured

on the news as the abducted girl. I'm their sister that was kidnapped and now I'm back…People might look at me weird and gain them unwanted attention."

Melissa gets up out of her chair and takes me in her arms "Stop. Nobody is embarrassed, and you…." She takes my face in her hands and looks me square in the eye "Don't you ever be embarrassed or ashamed. Don't ever think less of your-self-*ever*! This whole situation is not your fault. I want you to know that every single person in this family loves you. We're so proud and happy to have you!"

Since I'm scared I'll cry or my voice will break, I settle for a nod. She smiles and kisses my forehead. She sits back across from me and I go back to focusing on my breakfast.

"Sarah?"

I look up from my plate. Melissa taps her nails against her coffee cup. "I don't want you to feel uncomfortable, but—" She sighs. "This is silly. I don't know why I'm getting tongue-tied and flushed. It's really not a big deal. Mrs. Jenkins suggested you attend a few therapy sessions. Just until you get adjusted. You've gone through a life changing experience. Your whole world has been flipped. I can't imagine."

I swallow and nod. I focus back on my breakfast because what more can I say? Of course I probably need therapy. My life is so screwed up how could I not? Add that to my other list of *let's make Sarah, Olivia, whoever the hell she is more not normal.*

"Please talk to me honey. I was worried you'd feel uncomfortable, but I really think it's for the best. So does your father and Mrs. Jenkins."

"Okay." I whisper.

Melissa bites her bottom lip and watches me for a moment longer. Finally, she sighs and offers me a tight smile. She whispers back. "Okay, then."

I finish my breakfast, and she finishes her coffee.

That afternoon, as I'm sitting on my bed sketching, there's a knock at my bedroom door. I look over to see Landon leaning against the door frame holding a thin hardback book.

"Come on in." I give him a closed lip smile as he pushes himself off the frame and strolls through the bedroom. He plops down on the bed and holds out his high school yearbook from last year.

"Thought you might want to get an idea of the school. Lay of the land so to speak."

I raise one eyebrow at his lopsided grin. "That's really sweet of you. Thank you. It's mid-September, so I'm going into the year late. Great way to start my senior year."

"Ah, don't look at it that way. You haven't missed much. This way you'll make a grand entrance."

"I don't want to. I want to ease in unnoticed and just get through the year."

"What? It's your senior year. It's the best year of high school. I'm already planning what pranks and shit I'm going to pull next year." I can't help but smile at his infectious smile. This is supposed to be the best year of school, but it's already the worst. Hopefully, Landon will get to have an amazing senior year.

I debate on asking him about Noah. If he knows him, but I've never mentioned the Wallace family to any of them; I'm too scared. I'm unsure how well they know them, or how they'll react. There are options for schools here, and it would be unlikely Noah and I'd be attending the same one. If we did attend the same school together, I could ask him questions and, hopefully, get some answers. Maybe Noah does attend public school. I don't ever recall them being well off, but that still doesn't mean he couldn't attend a private school. Sometimes money has nothing to do with it. Look at the Randall children.

Idly I flip the pages as Landon chatters on about how Trent was a legend at school with his athletic abilities while he scans social media on his phone. "I'm a legend in my own right, but sports aren't my thing. I do like track. Do you play any sports?"

"Soccer, but we didn't have a team."

"Why?" He puts his phone down clearly shocked.

I smile and actually laugh. It feels funny because it's been so long since I've genuinely smiled. "Our school was too small. We had a few community sponsored teams, but it was never the school. That lasted only six weeks out of the year."

"Huh…" He picks his phone back up and resumes swiping. "Well, we have a team. Two actually. Girls and boys. They're pretty good. Might look into it."

The yearbook is from last year so when I get to the junior class, I scan the W's. There he is. Noah Wallace was a junior last year at public, so that means he'll be in my graduating class. I was so lost in my own grief and confusion that I didn't pay much attention to Noah at the house or at the funeral. In fact, I can barely even remember much of it now. I mostly remember him comforting me at the funeral. He has grown up to be quite handsome.

I feel eyes on me, so I quickly turn the page. So much for taking time to study his face. Landon raises up and shows me his phone screen. "Do you have any accounts?"

Suddenly feeling embarrassed and weird for probably being the *only* teenager on the planet that's not connected on social media somehow, I look down and shake my head.

Cindy never allowed me to use social media growing up. The only means I had with communicating with friends and the Wallace family was through phone. *Now I know why she never allowed me to be on social media and why we never returned to her hometown.* That's partly why Noah and I probably never formed a cousin relationship or even friendship.

Aunt Andrea was the only one that really kept in contact. I remember us sending gifts to Noah for his birthday. Cindy would chat with him on the phone from time to time. I guess at the time, Noah and I were too busy with our own lives to worry about a cousin who lived across the country.

Landon shrugs casually, "That's fine. I was just curious." He pauses and studies me closer. "You know, I could help you set up an account if you wanted… It's up to you. No pressure. Just ask if you need anything, okay?"

Touched by the tenderness in his voice I smile. I turn the final page in the yearbook and then hand it to Landon. "Thanks."

"Any time." He takes the book and then strolls out.

If I see Noah at school, what should I do? What will *he* do? I'm so confused. Should I be sad or angry with the Wallace family? I really don't feel angry towards them. I'd like for Noah to be my friend. I want Aunt Andrea to still be my aunt and for all of us to still be family. I'm seventeen years old, and I just lost my mother, who I discovered through her death, is not really my mother but my kidnapper. This isn't what normal people go through. At least now I feel like I've got Landon by my side, except will Landon be okay with Noah there as well?

Sixteen

THE NEXT DAY, I GET UP EARLY ENOUGH TO join everyone for breakfast. While setting all the food on the table, Melissa announces that Trent was accepted into an early internship at the hospital by the University. Landon is elated for the news, while Denise seems like she couldn't care less. Richard beams with pride and says, "I knew he'd get it. That boy gets anything he puts his mind to," before he begins to shove food in his mouth. Melissa sits down and starts fixing her own plate. She turns to me.

"You have your first appointment today." I raise my eyebrows in confusion, so she continues. "Your first therapy session." My face falls and she hurries to continue. "Only for a little while. To help you get adjusted."

Denise grumbles without looking up from her plate. "Maybe you should go too."

Melissa gasps. "*Denise.*"

Denise continues. "Then maybe I could go to sleepovers like a *normal* teenager."

"Young lady, you're barely a teenager. You make your

bed, they make theirs. Everyone sleeps in their own." Richard gives Denise a pointed look, but she ignores him.

She hasn't got to attend a sleepover? Even Cindy let me spend the night with Angie.

"I'm four—*teen*. Hear the *teen* part? It's also part of the word *teenager*."

"Watch it or you'll be a grounded teenager." He scolds.

Denise pokes at her eggs with a fork and scoffs. "What's the difference than how it is now?"

"Try not having a phone? No wifi? Not going to the games?"

"Yes, sir."

Melissa gives a nervous chuckle and smiles brightly at me. "We should go shopping."

That gets Denise's attention. Her eyes are wide and bright, and not staring at her plate. "I want to go! Homecoming's in three weeks! I think Joey might ask me out. Even though I would rather go with Clint. I'm not about going solo, so I may go with Joey if he asks. Daniel was hinting about us going together, but ugh, no thank you."

Richard tells his daughter she's only allowed to go out to eat before the dance if Trent and Landon agrees to chaperone the dinner. This gets him an eye roll from both of his children. I doubt I'll be going to Homecoming, and I highly doubt I'll get asked to the dance. Before, I would never have missed a dance, whether it was solo, with a group, or on a date. But that was my old life.

Melissa smiles at Denise. "Sweetie, how about we all three go next weekend? We can make it a whole day of dress shopping. We can also go out to eat and have ice cream. But today, I'm going to take Sarah out for some new school clothes." She turns to me and smiles. "We never got to go school shopping." She shrugs and blushes. "Would that be...okay?"

As all eyes fall on me, I nod and go back to eating. An

awkward silence starts to settle. Landon immediately begins chatting about a new movie coming out that he thinks Richard and Melissa would enjoy. I look over at him and he gives me a wink. Landon seems to try the hardest to make me comfortable and something tells me, out of everyone in this house, he seems to understand me the best. Maybe it's because we're so close in age.

When I go back to my room, I check my phone. A few messages from Angie and a few other friends trying to reach out to me. My thumb hovers over the keypad on my phone. I feel like a coward for not at least sending them a thank you for checking on me, but I'm scared they'll ask more questions. I know I've been in this zombie-like state since the accident, but I'm not ready to enter the social world yet. I'm not ready to accept my reality. I'm not ready to fully accept the loss of my mother. The full loss of my mother as in she was my kidnapper and not my mother. I'm not ready to face my anger, fear, grief, any emotions yet. As long as I'm numb, I can't feel.

The least I can do is text Angie back.

Me: Sorry. Everything is good. They're super nice. I think my little sister doesn't like me.

Angie: You're just used to being an only child. Besides, aren't little sisters supposed to not get along with big sisters?

Me: I guess. It feels like she resents me. I think the parents were super strict.

Angie: I bet. I mean—their baby got kidnapped. Tell her to chill. Wait—so are they strict with you now?

Me: I haven't even tried to go anywhere. Ha. Where would I go?

Angie: Back to meeee ☺

A giggle escapes me.

Me: Maybe. Think they'd let me visit Spring Break? Or you come here!

Angie: If I could afford it, I'd be there.

I sigh. *I know you would Angie.*

There's a knock on my door followed by Melissa. "Sarah? May I come in?"

"Yeah."

Melissa opens the door and her eyes immediately fall on my phone. "I'm sorry. Am I interrupting?"

I shake my head and place my phone on my nightstand.

"It's time to leave for your appointment."

⁂

We all exit the house together, everyone going to their designated vehicle. I follow Melissa to her Lexus for therapy and a mother/daughter first day of school shopping.

The therapist's office is a small building and the waiting area reminds me of a comfortable chic living room...with a front desk. Melissa checks me in and then joins me on the grey couch.

"*Sarah Randall.*"

I admire an arrangement of white lilies. The white is a nice contrast to the light turquoise walls.

"*Sarah Randall?*"

Melissa gently pats my hand. "Sweetie. They're calling your name."

That is me. I'm Sarah Randall. I give an embarrassed smile and stand. "Sorry."

The lady standing by the door is younger than I was expecting. She's probably in her early forties. Her makeup is clean and simple matching the rest of her style. A plain sheer pink flowy blouse and khaki colored slacks. Her shoulder-length dark waves are loose but out of her face.

"Hi. I'm Rita Dawson. Have a seat."

I sit down on the yellow cushioned chair. "Hello. I'm... Sarah Randall."

"Would you rather I call you Olivia?"

I pause. "No."

"If it would make you more comfortable, we can?"

"No. Sarah is fine."

She sits across from me and smiles. We wait. I fidget wondering what I need to say or do now. Rita finally speaks. "Sarah." I nod. "How are you adjusting so far with your parents? Siblings?"

"Everyone is great."

"Details. I want to know how you feel."

"Confused."

"Understandable."

"Scared."

"What makes you scared?"

"Is this…is this over? Is another ball going to drop? Something else bad going to happen?"

"Are you afraid to get close to your new family? Since you've lost your mother?"

"I've lost everything."

"Do you keep in contact with any friends from back home?"

"One. My best friend Angie."

"Good. Don't isolate yourself with this. Why don't you find something that you loved from your old life that you can share in your new life."

~

Melissa tells me we're going to a mall that's thirty-minutes away because Lumberton doesn't have many options. We listen to the radio as she drives. Melissa, I pick up quickly, is a country music fan. Which is fine. I like country music, but Cindy and I always enjoyed our eighties stations. Or the old mixed CDs we'd made. Melissa uses Bluetooth. No CDs. I smile despite myself remembering how we'd still pull out that huge CD wallet. All the CDs had scribbles and whimsical writing made from Sharpies. I swallow the lump in my throat and try to focus on the present. Here with Melissa. Here with my real mom.

We go from store to store in the mall buying everything from expensive dresses to plain black ankle socks. These clothes are a long way from my under twenty-dollar outfits I typically purchase. After a few hours into our shopping endeavors, it becomes clear to me that Melissa doesn't want to simply buy me a few outfits for school. No, she wants to replace my entire wardrobe. I test my theory when I tell her I already own a winter coat, but her reply is she never got to buy me one. I try again by telling her that I have plenty of socks, and she shoots back, "Is it just me or does it seem socks get worn thin so easy? Let's go ahead and get some more. I don't know about you, but I'm *always* losing a mate to my socks. It's just socks honey, no biggie."

But it is a "biggie," because she insisted I needed new socks. I needed new everything, apparently.

When I have every possible garment that I could ever possibly need, she takes me out for a late lunch. I'm surprised that our lunch conversation goes so smoothly after all the tension from mission "Convert Olivia into Sarah." We discuss interests, movies, music, and even a little about sports. Both of us are careful not to let it go too deep and too personal. I relax and realize we can be fun and easy together.

After our lunch, Melissa takes us to an AT&T store. I don't ask any questions as we go in. "What kind of phone do you have?" she casually asks while examining the phones on display.

"Oh, I have an Android Galaxy." I take my phone out and show her. *Maybe she's thinking of getting a new phone. I know all the kids have one since they're always in their hands.*

She barely glances at it and turns her attention back to the ones on display "Are you happy with it? I have the iPhone and love the camera on it. Do you like the iPhone, or would you like to try another type of phone?"

Her question throws me off. When I don't immediately answer, she says, "Honey, we need to add you to our phone plan. I figured since we were here, might as well get you an upgrade. Which one do you like?"

An employee comes to check on us, and Melissa explains to him we're adding a line. Then, she asks him which is the latest iPhone model. She turns and asks me if I like the phone the man is holding. All I can do is slowly nod because it's an amazing phone, but it's way too expensive.

She whispers something to him and turns to me to take my phone. "Whoever is handling all the legal affairs will end the contract this phone is on. He needs to go ahead and deactivate it."

Before I can say anything else, she hands the store employee my phone. I'm hoping maybe he'll keep my SIM card by placing it in the new phone. Unfortunately, when they hand me my new phone, all my contacts are gone. I'm about to ask for my old phone back so I can at least get all my contacts and photos from it, but Melissa puts her arm around me to lead me out of the store.

"No." I stop her. "I need my phone back. I have photos and numbers on there. Please. I didn't get a chance to back anything up."

She pretends that the thought never crossed her mind, but I can tell it's an act. She uses overexaggerated hand gestures, and her voice is strained and drips with fake surprise. "Oh no! I'm so sorry, Sarah. I didn't even think of that. Let's go see if we can still get it. I told him we didn't need it, and they could recycle it or donate it."

She turns around, and the guy almost looks like he's expecting her.

I walk up to them, and he says, "Sorry, I *just* wiped it clean."

I'm barely able to contain the tremor in my voice. "You did it already? We only walked a few feet."

He holds the phone up. "I hooked it into the computer and pressed a button."

I cross my arms and narrow my eyes at him *"Pressed a button? Does that sound as lame to your ears as it does mine? Why the rush? Seriously, she just handed you the phone."*

He merely shrugs and Melissa feigns disappointment. We turn back to leave the store. I could be imagining it, but I could've sworn I saw out of the corner of my eye Melissa slide money to the guy when she shook his hand to thank him again for his "help."

I stop walking and turn to face Melissa. "I've kept quiet because I'm trying to adjust. But this is too far. I just lost everything. My phone had photos that were important to *me*. I have friends and I just lost all their numbers."

I don't even remember Angie's number! I never dialed a number. They were always instantly saved in my contacts.

"We can get their numbers, Sarah-"

"But not the photos! Those were memories! They meant something to *me*. You just wiped them away. I've lost my life! Do you not understand? I've lost-" My voice cracks and I turn away from her before she can say anything else.

She calls out to me. "Sarah! You haven't lost your life!" She rushes up to me and takes my arm. "You've been returned to the life you should've always had. I'm sorry you lost photos that were precious to you. I thought I was helping by getting you a new phone. I'm not tech savvy and didn't think anything about photos being on the phone. All I can do is apologize and help you reach out to your friends back in Colorado. You haven't lost your life, sweetheart. It's been given back to you. Make new memories. Starting now."

"I didn't want a new life. I was *happy*. I didn't want *any* of this to happen."

"You didn't want to come back...home?" The sight of Melissa's tears breaks through my hurt and anger.

"I'm sorry…I didn't mean it like that. I was happy when I was in a state of ignorant bliss, I guess you could say. I didn't know I wasn't *me*. Can you just go slower with me? Please. I'm trying to be who you were hoping for, but I can't become Sarah overnight."

Melissa pulls me into a tight hug. "I don't want you to be anyone else but you."

I don't even know who that is…Or how to be me anymore…

When we get out to the car, Melissa suggests we go see a matinee before heading home. My mood is bleak so all I can offer her is a shrug. She drives to the cinema, and there are only three shows about to begin in the next twenty to thirty minutes. We choose a romantic comedy and share a big bowl of popcorn and a bag of M&Ms. While we wait for the movie to begin, I reflect on all that has happened. I don't want to sound ungrateful for the new and stylish wardrobe or the expensive smart phone, but it feels like Melissa wants to remove any trace of my former life. Unfortunately for her, I'm not like my old phone where you can just erase all my memories and contacts with the push of a button. A life doesn't come with a reset button. I know she's wanting to erase what happened. I get that she's wanting us to forget it happened and pick up where we left off, me as her daughter and she as my mother.

But it did happen. Those memories still mean something to me. Cindy, Aunt Andrea, friends, everyone that I knew back home still mean something to me. It has all shaped me into the person I am now, yet she expects me to wipe it all clean overnight. *Well that was not supposed to be your life, so let's pick up where we left off and start what should have been happening all along. Cindy wasn't really your mother so you can't love her.* But I do. I still love her and the life I had. I never texted my friends back. Now, I for sure won't be able to. I should've quit wallowing and accepted their words. It's done now. Everything is done now. I try to quit reflecting on all this and enjoy the show. After another twenty-minute struggle, I force myself to get lost in the movie, and I begin to relax.

Since the movie let out at 5:15 PM, we get takeout from a restaurant for everyone's supper. When we get home, she tells me we can come back out to the car for the clothes later.

"Let's go in and eat first. I'm sure everyone is waiting at the door like starving puppies."

After we eat, I go back to the car to gather the bags of clothes. It takes two trips, but I take all my clothes up to my room and lay them on my bed. After a few minutes of hanging up all my new clothes, Melissa comes in with a black garbage bag.

She sits down on my bed next to my new clothes "I won't make you do anything you're uncomfortable with, but if you have any clothes that you don't wear anymore…or want to make room for your new clothes…you can put some in this bag. I can bring more bags if you need them."

Confused by her statement, I hesitantly ask, "Why would I throw away all my stuff?"

"Not throw away. Donate."

"Do you think my clothes are not good enough?"

Melissa looks panicked and rushes, "No, no! Oh gosh, no honey! I didn't mean for it to come out like that." She laughs and throws a hand up, "But now that you ask me that, I guess it did sound that way." She takes my hand, "Your clothes are lovely. Truly. But-" She squeezes my hand tighter. "Can I make a suggestion and you not get upset with me?"

I can already tell I'm going to get upset. But I nod.

"I feel like this is a new start for you. I know a new outfit sometimes makes me feel like a new person. I want you to embrace your new life, and I guess in a way, I figured new clothes were kind of a fresh start. Shedding your old skin, so to say."

I think about what she's saying. I don't see it that way. Honestly, I already had a lot of new clothes that I hadn't even worn yet. However, this means more to Melissa than she's letting on. It's written all over her face, no matter how she tries to hide it. She wants to rid me of any remembrance of Cindy. I knew this was coming, though. That's what I was worrying about in the theater. These are the clothes that *Cindy* had bought me, helped me pick out. Clothes I had worn while with *her*. I nod and tell her okay. I expect her to leave, but instead, she gets up and opens the bag. "This might be hard for you, so I'll help."

I almost have a panic attack because I thought she meant for me to do this in my own time. I kind of hoped I could keep some of my clothes and maybe not wear them in front of her. I don't want to start slinging them in the bag like garbage. I need a moment, but Melissa wastes no time going through my room and shoving items in the bag. I want to tell her to leave, but my voice doesn't come. How can I ask her to leave when she just spent a small fortune on me? This is her house. She's my biological mother and now legal guardian. Feeling defeated, I slowly stand and pick up the nearest item. It's a floral shirt that Mom—*Cindy*, had gotten for me. The shirt is made of a soft pink, sheer fabric with various bright colored flowers. She got it because she said it reminded her of a watercolor painting I'd done. I love it because it's so beautiful and flowy. I lay the shirt in the black bag. It seems to swallow the vibrant, beautiful shirt into darkness. I want to cry, but I hold it in for now. Melissa and I don't speak during the 'clean up.' When we are finished, she kisses me goodnight and leaves. I get in the shower and burst into tears, wishing the water could wash all of this away.

Seventeen

I WAKE UP BEFORE MY ALARM ON THE MONDAY of my first day of school. I lay staring at my ceiling, dreading what it'll be like at a new school. New school. New town. New clothes. New family. I even have a new name. I won't hear Olivia Stevens. People will call me Sarah Randall. Before I get out of bed, I say a silent prayer to Cindy.

Mom. I don't know why you did it. I can't say I regret it. I regret you leaving me more than anything. I don't know if I'd have forgiven you had you told me while you were alive. I guess I can't be mad at you while I miss you so much. I'm scared. I just wish you were here to talk me through this. Why? Why did all of this have to happen to me? Why you? Why couldn't I have just been born yours and you not have died? We were happy. I miss you. I forgive you. I love you.

I wipe my tears and climb out of bed. Rushing to the bathroom, I dry heave a little and then turn to the sink to splash water on my face. I look up and stare at myself in the mirror. I don't know the girl looking back at me. With shaky hands, I dry my face and hands. Then I get ready for school.

Instead of riding with Landon and Denise, Melissa insists on taking me for my first day. I pray she doesn't take it as far as walking me to my first class. We hop in her Lexus, and I buckle up while she starts the engine. As we drive the short distance to the school, she asks, "Are you nervous?"

I nod and explain, "It's more than simply starting a new school. I'm worried there will be a lot of attention on me. I mean, not only am I the new kid starting late in the year; I'm the new kid that was featured on Channel 6 for being kidnapped."

Melissa pulls the car over and turns to me "You don't have to do this if you're not ready."

I look out the window giving a one shoulder shrug. "I have to face it eventually." *All of it.* Sounding more confident than I really am, I turn to her. "People are going to whisper and ask questions anywhere I go. I'm just nervous."

She pats me on the shoulder "I'm proud of you. If anyone takes the conversation in that direction, just redirect it. You'll be fine. Landon will be there, too. He should be waiting at the door for you."

We smile at each other, and she pulls the car back on the road. The car stops in front of a very beautiful historic brick school building. It's much larger than my old school. It also seems cleaner and well maintained. Melissa leans over to give me a kiss on the cheek and wishes me luck. I take a deep breath and get out of the car only to wonder *where do I even go?*

I hold my backpack on one shoulder and see a group of students heading toward two big, double doors off to the far left. I decide to head in that direction. *Remember, your name is Sarah Randall. Sarah. Your parents are Melissa and Richard Randall.* I feel like I'm undercover or something, but nope, this is real. I walk up the steps and into the building. Although the building is old on the outside, the interior is very updated.

The students seem like the same as my previous school. One can easily pick out the groups: popular, nerd, jock, hipster, etc. The school I attended before was so small that the groups overlapped. You could be a little of all the groups. I was by no means a queen bee type, but I wasn't an outcast. Here I already feel like the outcast.

I jump when a strong arm comes around me. "Haha! Easy, Sarah! I came to see if you need help finding the office." I nod and smile at Landon. "Let's go, sis."

A group of guys wearing school jackets pass us and pat him on the back. "Yo, Randall!" We keep walking and all the way down the hall, people wave and smile at Landon, especially the girls show particular enthusiasm with him. As we keep walking through the halls, more girls keep throwing flirty smiles and waves at him. I begin to wonder if Landon is a player or if he's seeing anyone, "Do you have a girlfriend?"

He smiles and shakes his head, "Nah."

"Well it isn't because you can't get one. You seem very popular."

He squeezes me to him. "What can I say? I get along with everyone." He leans and whispers in my ear, "There was a special someone, but they moved. I haven't quite gotten over it."

I give him a wistful smile. "The one that got away, huh?"

He nods and with his arm still wrapped around my shoulder, gives me a little shake. "But now we have the one that came back!" He notices the stunned expression on my face and hurries to apologize. "Sorry, bad joke…"

I wave off the comment as he continues to guide me through the crowd of students.

"So, *Sis*, have you always been so quiet? Were you the shy girl?"

I chuckle. "No, actually I got along with just about everyone. I wasn't the most popular girl, but I was involved. I'm just taking it all in right now."

"Cool." He nods his head and stops by a glass door and holds it open for me to enter.

He leads me into the office and smiles at the lady at the desk. "Mrs. Jones, the lady with the answers. Good morning! This is my big sister, Sarah. She needs her schedule, please."

Mrs. Jones looks at me in awe. She's a tiny, elderly woman with glasses and puffy white hair that reminds me of the texture of cotton candy. She wears a pearl necklace, a floral button up shirt, and pale pink slacks. She slowly picks up a piece of paper and hands it to me. "Pleasure to meet you, Sarah. I am so glad you're here." She stresses that last part, and I pick up on her double meaning.

I take the paper and give her a smile, "Thank you."

Landon turns us back towards the door and waves. "See ya later, Mrs. Jones! Thanks again." He takes my paper and scans over my schedule as we walk. He gives me a nudge with his elbow. "Hey, look at this. We have sixth and seventh period together. You get to end your day with me."

I laugh at his excitement and follow him as he walks down the hall. I reach for my schedule in his hand but he holds it up and keeps walking. "Hey, um I need that! Where are you going?"

I catch up to him, and he stops at a locker. "This is yours." He slams his palm on the locker and announces, "Locker 286. I'm around the corner, down the hall, 355." He looks back down at my schedule. "Okay, looks like you have Mrs. Sanders for English. She's the second door on the right down there. Then, Mr. Barnes is all the way at the end of the hall. P.E is going to be in the next building so you might have a little trouble finding it. I'll meet you outside Mr. Barnes's door and walk you to P.E."

He hands me back my schedule. I'm so glad he's there to help me that I give him a hug. "Thank you so much, Landon. I really appreciate this."

He gives me a quizzing look. "What's wrong? I get you're nervous, but it'll be okay."

I sigh. "Everyone knows, right? I mean… about me?"

A look of understanding comes over him. He presses his lips together and nods. A bell rings, and he gives me another hug, with a voice laced in excitement. "You're going to be fine. Good luck, not that you'll need it," he winks, "and have fun."

He releases me and points toward my next class. I wave bye and head that way. I weave through students and walk into the classroom. A woman in her mid-thirties with brown hair in a messy bun looks up at me from her desk. She smiles and stands. "You must be Sarah Randall." She walks over to a bookshelf and pulls out a textbook. "The year has taken off to a slow start. We're running behind, so you haven't missed much."

She hands me the used textbook and then picks up a red folder off her desk to give me. "Your parents called, so most of your teachers should have everything ready for you to catch up on. I don't have assigned seats in here so have a seat anywhere."

I hesitate because even though there may not be assigned seats, I'm sure everyone has *their* seats. The second bell rings, sending students flooding into the room. I know I don't want to sit in the front with all eyes on me, so I decide to hurry and grab a seat in the back. A seat in the back is most likely someone else's spot, but I cannot handle the idea of easily being on display. I hurry and take a seat in the very back, right corner. Mrs. Sanders smiles at me and sits back behind her desk. The room is filling up quickly, but so far, nobody heads toward me. I notice everyone does have *their* seats since everyone goes straight to a desk without a second thought. A group of four pretty girls walk in giggling, but they stop when they see me. I get a sinking feeling in my stomach that I've taken one of *their* seats. I try to appear as casual as possible. It's obvious which one is the leader of the group. She raises her chin and straightens her shoulders as she comes charging toward me. She's petite with strawberry blonde hair that has a few pale blonde highlights pulled up on top of her head, full lips, and a small upturned nose. Her large blue eyes would be more beautiful if they weren't overshadowed with so much eyeshadow and mascara thick enough that I can see some of the clumps from my seat. She stops in front of my desk wearing a look of distaste.

She sits her books on my desk "I'm sorry sweetie, but this seat is taken."

"Oh, I'm sorry. Mrs. Sanders told me to sit anywhere. She said there aren't assigned seats."

She isn't used to taking no for an answer or people pushing back at her. It's clear by the complete bitch face she's giving me. She doesn't move, merely crosses her arms and stares me down. I begin to cower under her gaze and gather my belongings. I'm just about to stand when a deep voice announces. "She can sit there."

I stop moving immediately. I keep my eyes down and weakly say, "No. Really, it's fine. I'm sorry, I didn't know."

A large hand lands on my shoulder and keeps me from rising another inch out of the chair. "You're in my seat. And if I say it's fine, then I don't see why anyone else should have a problem." The statement is clearly geared toward the pretty girl in front of my desk.

"Sure, you can sit there. Welcome to your first day of school," the girl sneers, completely not okay with me sitting there. Her voice magically changes to sickly sweet. "If she's taking your seat, then where are you going to sit?"

This guy must be her boyfriend because she's a little too worried about his seating arrangement. He removes his hand, and I turn my eyes up. I feel the blood drain from my face.

Noah.

Noah takes the seat next to mine and puts his hands behind his head and stretches his legs "I'm taking Jeff's seat."

I assume the guy that takes the seat next to him is Jeff, and another guy follows taking the seat next to Jeff. The girl that was standing in front of my desk moves to sit in the desk in front of Noah. One sits in front of me, and the other two take seats in front of the guys.

Noah doesn't meet my eyes. Should I acknowledge that I know him? Are we pretending not to know each other? Does he not want to bring up how we know each other? My mind is running ninety to nothing and my heart is beating so hard it physically hurts. The girl in front of Noah cuts her eyes to me and sneers. I lean over and whisper to Noah, "I'm sorry. I really didn't know."

Noah chuckles. "How could you?" He leans closer to me, "Unless you did a little digging and purposefully signed up for the same classes as me and found out my seating arrangements." He raises an eyebrow at me and gestures toward my schedule on the desk. "Let me see. Should I expect you in any more of my seats today?"

I hand him my schedule, and he reads it. I notice that the girls in front of us are quiet and have their heads tilted. *Nosy bitches.* I grab my notebook and pen. I decide to not dance around the topic of whether we know each other or not.

Thank you for being so nice. How is Aunt Andrea?

I hand Noah my notebook. He looks surprised as he takes it, and I hear him sigh as he writes back.

You mean thank you for not being an ass? Seriously. Chill out. It's just a seat. She misses you. Your parents won't allow her any contact. I doubt they know we have any of the same classes. Well, they might know… Knowing them, they know.

I want to cry as I read, but I keep it together. I glance up at the girls and notice the one in front of Noah has her hands on her lap in fists.

You know them better than I do :)

Noah chuckles when he reads it.

I guess I do… that's weird.

This is so bizarre. A slight giggle escapes me. What else can I do in this situation? I might as well laugh rather than cry. The girl in front of me huffs so I give him a smirk when I hand him the book.

Is she your girlfriend?

She wants to be.

Pretty sure she thinks she already is. She's about to claw my eyes out.

He laughs harder. The girl in question turns around and taunts, "Aren't you a little old for writing love notes?"

Noah's good humor quickly dies and is replaced with annoyance. "Karlie, turn around and mind your own business."

Thank goodness Mrs. Sanders stands in front of the class and calls attention. I'm so relieved for class to begin. But then my stomach plummets when she says, "Class, we have a new student. I want everyone to welcome Sarah Randall."

Everyone turns and stares at me. Karlie has a look of shock, but then she gives me a smile that turns my stomach. She's going to try and be trouble for me, but I won't let her get to me. Surprisingly, I don't think anyone has made the connection with me to Noah. When Mrs. Sanders begins going over the English assignment, I write to ask him.

Does anyone know that we're cousins?

He doesn't look at me and keeps his eyes between Mrs. Sanders and the notebook as he writes. He slides the notebook to my desk.

Are we still cousins? I mean, technically speaking? As far as people knowing—Cindy left and never returned. None of my friends knew I even had an aunt. With us having a different last name as Cindy, not many people knew the connection when it hit the news. The Randalls know, but they said they'd keep it hush if we don't contact you. I'm glad you're even talking to me. Mom will be glad too.

A small smile pulls at me when I read that last part. I focus during the rest of the class on Mrs. Sanders. At the end of class, Noah stands and says he'll see me third period.

Karlie smiles at me. "Sarah Randall, my my. I guess I should welcome you back to Lumberton also."

She looks like she's about to say something, but Noah speaks over her, "Ignore Karlie and her minions. They lead boring lives so they may fixate on you. Try to take it as a compliment."

Karlie let's out an 'ugh' and leaves with her loyal minions following behind her.

Jeff and the other guy come to stand next to Noah. "This is Jeff McClish and Keaton Sloan." They nod and pat Noah on the shoulder, I guess letting him know they're heading out of the classroom. Noah nods to them and then pats my shoulder. "See you around."

As I watch them walk away, I wonder if the patting of the shoulder when saying goodbye is a Missouri thing or just a guy thing. I head on to Mr. Barnes's class for History.

Mr. Barnes is grouchy until he begins teaching. He's an older man with brown hair and beard mixed in with a few speckles of grey. His eyes are a bright blue that sparkle with animation when he discusses ancient civilizations. He wears a brown suede jacket over a hideous, green plaid shirt and jeans. He's tall with a slight belly. The man is almost comical with the way his mood changes so drastically. One thing I can say about him is, I love how passionate he is.

He passes out an outline for the chapter with questions we're to complete by the end of class. When the paper is placed on my desk, I immediately write my name at the top. They really drilled that into us in elementary school to write our name first thing on every assignment. I scan the questions first and then begin reading the chapter. When I'm finished with the assignment, I proofread my paper before turning it in. The first thing I notice is I got the very first question wrong. Where it says *Name*, I answered Olivia Stevens.

It still feels like *my* name. I bite my lip to keep it from trembling. My hand has a slight quiver as I erase what I'd written. It feels as though the more time passes, I keep erasing more and more of who I was and who I am. Very slowly, I write *Sarah Randall* as neatly as possible across the page.

When class is over, a girl from the far side of the room comes rushing over to me. She has long brown hair with high-lights, bright steel blue eyes, a cute nose, and full pouty lips.

"If I'd known who you were at the beginning of class, I would've sat with you! I'm friends with your brothers." She pauses and looks up as she is reconsidering her statement. "Well, I'm more like best friends with Landon and infatuated with Trent." She giggles and holds her hand out. "I'm Rachel Abernathy. What class do you have next?"

I shake her hand and tell her physical education. She doesn't have the same one, so she suggests we have lunch to-gether. I don't really have anyone else to sit with, so I agree.

Landon is waiting for me outside the door. He nods to my new hyper-active friend. "Hey Rae! See you at lunch." We walk down the hall and out the doors to the sidewalk. "I see you met Rachel. She's been my best friend since our elemen-tary days."

"She seems great. Lots of energy."

He chuckles at that. "That she does. But she's got the big-gest heart. She tries to hide that by acting over-confident. And she disguises how sensitive she is with all her bubbliness."

"Bubbliness? Is that a word?"

"I said it, so it is." We laugh as he opens a door that leads outside. "Come on. We gotta go out here and the gym is right there. So how was your first class?"

"It went well. Even though I met a girl name Karlie that instantly hated me."

Landon nods. "Oh, that was probably Karlie Snyder. Mega bitch. Avoid and ignore her."

We make it to the gym and the second bell rings. "Aren't you going to be late for your class?"

Landon shakes his head and waves my comment off. I debate if I should tell him about Noah. *Does he know that Noah is Cindy's nephew?* Instead I thank him again and head into the gym. As soon as I walk in and see everyone changing, I realize that I didn't bring a change of clothes. I go find the P.E. teacher and explain my situation. She introduces herself to me as Coach Brooks. Then, she leads me into the girl's locker room and asks if any of the girls have an extra set of clothes. A skinny petite girl with flawless mocha colored skin and a sassy bob haircut comes up and hands me a pair of shorts and a shirt. She smiles at me and tells me her name is Tara. She has a genuine warm smile and big brown eyes with long eyelashes. I read the words on the grey shirt she's wearing, *Sorry I'm late. I didn't want to come.* Combined with her hot pink running shorts and glitter nail polish, I like her immediately and decide I'm going to hang around her for the rest of this hour.

I go and put on the clothes she gave me. *Oh no. I'm going to get suspended if I wear this.* I go and tell the Coach that the only outfit available to me is inappropriate since Tara is smaller than me, so the top is tight around my breasts, and the shorts are a little too short and tight. She looks up and down at me and says it'll have to work for now.

We walk out into the gym and Coach Brooks does roll call. She tells us today for class, we're going out to the field for soccer. Inwardly, I jump up and down. We follow her in a line outside to the field. She has us spread out to do some stretches before we begin playing. As I'm leaning over to touch my toes, I feel eyes on me. When I raise up, I see the boys have come out to the field as well. *Great.* As if I wasn't already self-coconscious enough in this outfit. I scan the group and find the eyes that are burning my skin.

Noah.

He's standing tall with his hand holding the elbow of his other stretched across his chest. Through his loose hanging shirt with the wide openings on the side I can see his defined muscles stretch and bulge. The guy next to him is following his line of sight while speaking. Noah looks agitated. He doesn't respond. Just swaps arms staring with hard eyes and his mouth in a grim line. He doesn't acknowledge me staring back at him either. I finish my stretches feeling Noah's eyes on me the whole time.

Coach divides us into teams. *Thank goodness she didn't leave it for us to pick teams.* I recognize two or three girls from my previous classes, and I'm relieved to see Tara is on my team. I wander over toward her and casually stand next to her.

She turns to me. "Do you play soccer?"

"Yeah and no. We didn't have a school soccer team because we were so small, but I played community soccer and with friends. I play defense."

Tara nods and announces to the other girls on our team that I'll play center defender. As we get in our positions on the field, I see the guys head over to the track and start off on a slow jog. I ignore them once our game begins. I'm in the zone now.

It's clear that a few of the girls play on the soccer team because they're running circles around the other girls. Tara is one of them, and it turns out we work well together. She plays forward and is an aggressive player. She's also a great team player and good at communicating, and although you can tell she's skilled and likes to be the one to score the goal, she still passes the ball. I see a girl charging my way toward the goal, and I don't hesitate to cut her off. I run up and tackle the ball away. I dribble the ball up to the halfway line and pass it to Tara, who takes it all the way to the goal. She gives the ball a hard kick towards the upper right corner of the opposing team's goal, and it barely clears the goalkeeper's glove. Tara runs back, and we high five. The rest of the game goes about the same way. When the score is 5-2, Coach yells for us to head back to the locker room.

Tara walks up to me with her hands on her hips. Breathing heavy she says, "Good game! Have you considered joining the team?"

Before I can answer, we meet Coach at the door. "Randall! Good job out there. The season has already started, but if you want to play, we'd love to have you on the team."

I look back at Tara who is grinning and nodding enthusiastically.

"Yeah! I'd really like to join if I can."

Coach laughs. "Fantastic! Practice is tomorrow immediately after school. Our first game is next Saturday. See you girls tomorrow. Go get cleaned up; the bell rings in fifteen minutes."

*Oh my gosh. I just made the soccer team! I can't wait to tell…*My heart drops a little because I was thinking of her. I swallow the lump in my throat. I force a smile on my face and continue walking with Tara.

We enter the gym and hear the echo of deep laughter. The boys are also coming in from the other doorway on the opposite side. I get a little nervous because I know we're going to pass them to get to our locker room. I debate on how I should act. Do I wave at Noah? Do I give a nonchalant smile? Do I show my excitement and call out, "NOAH!? I just made the soccer team! Quick, call your mom now!" I don't know how to act. I'm kind of on a high right now from being asked to play on my first team sport. Since I got here, this is the first time I've felt a sense of belonging. The guys are noisy and rowdy with some pushing each other, smacking each other, all laughing and sweaty while entering the locker room. I'm trying to casually scan the crowd without it being obvious. Tara begins talking to me about the team, and now I'm having trouble dividing my attention.

"Our biggest rivals are next weekend. I wonder if Coach will have you play that game or not. It's a big game. Would you be able to handle that?"

We stop walking and I turn my full attention to her. "I'm always nervous before any game. But…" I shrug, "once it starts, I block everything out, and I get my head in the zone."

Tara has a look of understanding, but then, her eyebrows raise and her attention is focused on something behind me. I turn around to find Noah standing behind me with Jeff and Keaton. Up close I see more clearly the muscles through Noah's thin, white shirt that has the arms cut off, leaving the sides open all the way to the bottom hem and blue basketball shorts. My mind short circuits a little at how in shape he is. *How did that lanky eight-year-old turn into a fitness model?* And he's sweaty. But surprisingly I'm not grossed out. He wears it well.

Wait.

Did I just think he wears sweat well? And this is Noah! NO-AH! As in the guy I used to believe was my cousin.

He crosses his arms and cocks his head. "So, you're somewhat of a professional soccer player?"

Instead of answering, I keep staring. My brain can't form words. Tara smiles and speaks on my behalf. "Hey, Noah. Yeah, what a surprise, huh? She just came out and kicked butt, didn't warn any of us how good she is." She looks back and forth between us.

I stutter. "I—I mean. I told you I played."

Tara laughs. "Community team, yeah right? You didn't say anything about pro."

I roll my eyes with embarrassment. I don't like all this attention. "I'm not pro," I mumble lamely.

Noah doesn't take his eyes off me while he says, "I'll see you guys in the locker room."

Jeff and Keaton take the hint and scurry off. Tara hasn't moved yet, so Noah turns his gaze to her and stares. Her mouth forms an O and her eyes go wide. "Oh, um, yeah, I guess I'll catch you two later. If I don't see you before the period is over, how about you just bring my clothes back tomorrow? Or you can give them to me at soccer practice. Whatever. It's whatever." Noah clears his throat, and Tara smiles sheepishly and heads back to the locker room. She keeps sneaking peeks over her shoulder the whole way.

Once we're alone in the gym, I get a little nervous so I start shifting my weight from one foot to the other and swinging my arms back and forth, lightly clapping my hands and snapping my fingers. I probably look as awkward as I feel. "So…how was gym?" I ask.

"A little distracting." He makes a point of looking me up and down. "A lot of the guys definitely took notice of you, and I had to bite my tongue more than once. What're you wearing?"

I scoff, "Me? I didn't know I had gym today, so I had to borrow clothes. This ensemble is not my fault. What's your excuse? Is that even considered a shirt? Or did I miss the memo that togas are making a comeback?"

He chuckles at my lame joke and then says, "Okay, well we should both go put on some decent clothes then, huh? It's almost time for lunch, so you better hurry if you're going to shower. I'll meet you back here and walk you to lunch."

We go to our separate locker rooms. Most of the girls are finished in the shower and getting dressed. They all tell me great job and some are excited that I'll be on the team with them.

Tara corners me on my way to the shower. "Did you know Noah before coming here? How do you know him?"

I laugh at her head-on approach. She has so much excitement bouncing in her eyes that I wonder what Noah means to her. Since it isn't common knowledge that I knew Noah before coming here, I decide to be vague. "Um, I share first hour with him. I accidently took his seat."

Her eyes grow big. "Then what happened?"

I look around to make sure nobody is paying us any attention, "Well," I lean toward her and whisper, "he let me sit.. in..his..seat. Can you believe it? Then…He took the seat next to me." I'm being a total smartass, but I can't help myself.

Tara ignores the sarcasm and gasps. "He gave you his spot?"

I narrow my eyes at her and shake my head in disbelief at how ridiculous she's acting. "That's the polite thing to do, isn't it? What kind of guy is Noah around here? What's with all these questions?"

Tara grins. "Noah Wallace is…" she literally sighs, "Noah's hot. In case you haven't noticed, he's freaking hot. I've had a crush on him since middle school, like most girls, I'm sure." I roll my eyes and begin continuing toward the shower with her following me. "He's kind of a mystery, too. For him to be so popular, nobody knows much about him personally."

She narrows her eyes at me. "You've seemed to grab his attention, though."

I shrug. "I don't know about that. Um, I need to take my shower…Could we continue this conversation later?" *Or never.*

She keeps staring at me and then finally decides, "Maybe because you're new."

She wanders off, and I finally begin to undress. I know I'm short on time, so I take the fastest shower I've ever taken in my life. I'm drying off when I realize that I left my clothes in the locker room. I throw my hair up in a messy wet bun, wrap the towel around myself, and walk over to my locker.

I grab my clothes and almost drop my towel when I hear a low voice calling my name, my *other* name. "Olivia? *Shit.* Or…Sarah?"

The towel is sliding when Noah steps in looking around. He stops short and stares at me with wide eyes. The stupid towel keeps slipping while I try to keep a grip on it and on my clothes. Most of my thigh is visible and I'm showing a lot of cleavage and about to have one full boob pop out.

I struggle with my clothes and towel while hissing at him, "Noah! You're not allowed in here! Get out before Coach walks in!"

My shoes fall out of my hands followed by my jeans. The slit where I'm holding the towel together is starting to spread open as I bend over. I debate on bending over anymore for fear of giving him a serious peep show.

Luckily, Noah comes over and picks them up. "Coach has gone to lunch, along with everyone else. I got worried when you were taking so long."

He takes the clothes from my hands so I can readjust my towel. I feel like an idiot, but if he hadn't scared me, I wouldn't have been so clumsy. *That's my defense, and I'm sticking to it.* I go around back to the showers and get dressed.

I walk out and find the locker room empty. Noah must've gone back out to the gym. I find him sitting on the bleachers looking at his phone. My voice is a little too high when I announce my presence. "Ready?"

His eyes scan my body. He clears his throat and mutters, "Much better."

He stands up, and we start heading out of the gym.

"I guess you're going to take on the role of overprotective cousin?" I nudge him with my shoulder.

He looks down at me and smiles. Nudging me back, he asks, "Overprotective cousin?"

"You seemed to be bothered by me showing any skin and

the guys noticing me. And I already told you, my feelings haven't changed. I mean, I guess I can see why you might think I wouldn't see you as a cousin, still, since it turns out we aren't actually related. But I still view you guys as family. I miss Aunt Andrea and want to see her."

He looks straight ahead and is quiet for a moment. We're almost to the cafeteria building when he stops and whispers, "I, um, didn't know if you would acknowledge me today. None of us knew how you felt toward us—now that you're with your real family. They 'advised' us to stay away from you. And—and you have to know that we were clueless. Ma is worried sick that you don't believe her. Cindy told her that you were the result of a one-night stand."

"A one-night stand? I kind of wish she would've stuck with what she's always told me, that my father died in a construction accident." I don't even know why I'm offended considering she kidnapped me.

Construction accident. I just now connected the dots that Richard is in construction. Hmm. I guess now I know her inspiration for that story. Noah looks around and then leans toward me to whisper, "Maybe we can work something out for you to see Ma. I know she'd love that."

I clap my hands together. "Yes!"

He raises a finger to his lips and whispers for me to shush. He bites his lip like he's trying to keep it from smiling as we walk into the cafeteria. He gently holds my elbow and leads me in the direction of the food line. Noah explains the process of giving them my student number if I need to charge for food, or I can pay cash or card at the end of the line. He's explaining why I should avoid the meatloaf due to his bad experience when he abruptly stops, and his face goes hard.

I feel a hand on my shoulder as a deep voice whispers in my ear, "Sis, I don't think you should be associating with him."

It's strange to see Landon, who is so carefree, look angry.

It completely transforms his appearance. He isn't directing any anger toward me, but he's shooting daggers at Noah.

"We're not going to cause a scene, alright? You two continue through the line, but she needs to sit at *my* table."

Noah gives him a nod and looks away. I promise Landon I'll find his table after I get my plate. After Landon disappears, I lean toward Noah. "If they're so against us being around each other, why are we attending the same school?"

Noah whispers back, "The Randalls don't want more gossip and attention drawn to this situation. Cindy's death and your return is where they want it to end. If we were brought into it, more gossip would circulate. I already attended school here and so did their children. I didn't even know you'd be here today until first hour when I walked in and you were in my seat." He gives me a wink. "It's almost like you were waiting for me."

I give him a small smile and shake my head. It's our turn to get our food, so Noah grabs two trays and pushes them down the metal rail. I tell the lady which items I want, and Noah hands her my tray. I go for pizza, salad, and mac and cheese. Sans meatloaf, of course. Noah takes the roast beef, mashed potatoes, and vegetables. We both get water to drink. He gives my elbow a gentle squeeze as we start to go our separate ways. My smile starts out small and sad but he gives me another wink and I can't help as my smile begins to stretch across my face. I turn my face away from Noah and my eyes slam directly into Landon's. He's been watching us the whole time.

Rachel turns to see me and grins from ear to ear. "Sarah! Here sit by me!"

She pats the seat next to her and I take it. She's already finished eating so I have her undivided attention while I eat, which makes me self-conscious.

"How are your classes going? How do you like this school?

Have you made any friends? I mean, I saw you talking to Noah. Is he a friend? Talking about making an entrance. You walked in with Noah Wallace—Mr. Unavailable. Girls are either going to envy you or hate you. It's almost the same thing, isn't it? How's this school different from your other one? Have you heard from Trent? Is he coming home soon?"

She is firing questions at me before I can get a word out to answer the first one.

Landon watches us, amused, and finally intervenes, "Alright Rachel, that's enough."

Rachel gives him a confused look, so he explains, "You might be coming on a little strong."

"And nosy!" Another girl remarks.

"Sorry if I came off *strong* and *nosy*," Rachel tells me rather dramatically.

"And rude," the same girl remarks.

Rachel turns to the girl. "Anything else, Emily?"

The girl named Emily shakes her head 'no' and continues to eat her salad.

Landon gives me a wide grin. "We're all mad here." I roll my eyes but can't help but laugh. Is this going to be a new thing between Landon and I? Alice in Wonderland references. It's fitting that's for sure.

Rachel frowns and looks back and forth between us, making Landon and I laugh harder. "I'm so confused."

"It's an inside joke between us," Landon explains and then smiles at me. I feel warmth in my chest and can't help the ridiculous grin spreading on my face. Everyone around me begins to gossip about people and places around here that I don't know. I've no idea what anyone is talking about around me that they might as well be speaking in another language. I silently eat my food while everyone around me carries on speaking about their own world. Someone mentions a name I recognize from class so I look up from my plate. I want to participate in the conversation, but before I can voice a comment, they move on to a different topic. The bell rings, and we all take our trays to leave.

Landon asks to see my schedule again as we exit the cafeteria. I give it to him, even though I already know what class it is and its location. Next, I have Art II & III with Mrs. Taylor. I passed it earlier today on the way to gym. I'm excited because I've always had a passion for art. I'd mentioned this to Melissa in one of our conversations, so I wonder if she signed me up for it or if it's simply a happy coincidence. I'm also kind of excited to know that my father and sister have a passion for art as well. It's a connection to them, this family, this new life, but more than anything, it's a way to connect Olivia to Sarah. It's *me* remaining as *me* while everything else seems as an out of body experience.

Landon begins to explain about the class and where it is, but I interrupt him, "Landon, I appreciate all your help, but I've been to school before. Maybe not this one, but I'm not completely helpless. I already found the class earlier. Thank you."

Landon nods and smiles as he hands me back the schedule. "I guess I'll catch you sixth hour, then."

"I look forward to it. And that one I probably will need a lot of help with since I have so much catching up to do." I wave bye and head off to Mrs. Taylor's class.

The room is large with long tables instead of desks. It almost reminds me of a science classroom, except there is art everywhere. The room is whimsical with bright colors and various artistic decorations covering the walls. I go to Mrs. Taylor's desk that is colorfully cluttered. She's been my youngest teacher so far. She looks to be in her mid-thirties, attractive with wavy brown hair with caramel highlights, bright red glasses that make her long dark lashes pop over her hazel eyes, and her full lips are colored with maroon lipstick. She's wearing a flowy, burgundy maxi dress with big, black flowers and a black jean jacket. She looks very put together, except that her hands have all kinds of different color stains that make it look as though she just finished finger painting.

Mrs. Taylor gives me a bright smile as she turns her chair around to face me. "Well hello there! You must be Sarah. I'm Mrs. Taylor, but I let all my students call me Mrs. Carrie. Here, take a seat, take a seat."

She gestures out to the classroom. "We're about to start a new project today so this works out perfectly! You did miss two projects, though." She makes a face like 'bummer.' But immediately perks back up. "However, I think you can make them up," she snaps her fingers, "just like that. Lickity Split! So," she shrugs, "no worries."

She digs through all the papers on her desk, searching for something. Distracted, she waves me toward the table and chairs, "Go ahead and have a seat."

I take a seat in the back while she continues searching. Students begin to trickle in. Some acknowledge me and some don't.

Mrs. Carrie shouts, "Ah-ha!" She skips back to me and hands me two papers. "Complete these two just whenever you can. Then, you'll be all caught up." She claps her hands together and smiles at me.

I thank her and tell her I'll try to finish them as soon as possible. I read over my art assignments, a charcoal or black pencil still life drawing and a face study of drawing the other half of a face from a magazine. Both sound fun and I'm eager to get started. I'm placing the assignments in my backpack when I hear someone sit in the chair on my left.

I look up to see a guy that had been sitting with Landon at lunch; I think his name is Eric.

He smiles at me. "Hello there. I don't think we've actually met, even though I already know quite a bit about you. Name's Eric." He extends his hand.

I shake it and return the smile. "I would introduce myself, but it doesn't seem I need to…"

He laughs and stretches in his seat. Eric could be a poster boy for the 'boy next door' look. He has short blond hair with bangs styled off to the side, blue eyes, and a strong straight nose. When he smiles, I notice his perfect, straight white teeth. His cute dimples and strong jaw make him ultimately drool worthy. From the looks of his body, he must be a jock. Eric seems friendly, but he also strikes me as the type of guy that knows he's attractive.

"How do you know about me, again?" I playfully narrow my eyes and tilt my head.

I'm trying to come off casual but internally, I'm cringing. Praying he doesn't voice my fear that I'm known as the *kidnapped girl*. Worse, he may say he saw my face on the news. Best case scenario and most obvious is Landon. He was sitting with us at lunch. I want to be just Sarah, the new student. I mentally prepare myself for what my response should be if he does mention how I came here.

He gives me a mischievous smile and leans his elbows on the table toward me. "I make it a point to know about all the pretty girls at this school, Sarah."

I don't know if I should gag or laugh in relief. I give him a blank stare and flatly say, "Excuse me? Really, Eric?" I raise an eyebrow.

He chuckles. "I'm good friends with your brothers. Well, Landon is one of my best friends. I played football with Trent before he graduated and I run track with Landon."

He scoots a little closer. "The only reason you haven't seen me around the house is because your family wanted you all to themselves; however, now maybe it's time you share your time with others?"

I feel my chair being pulled away from him. I turn to my right and come face to face with Noah.

He laughs at my stunned expression and gives a mock, "Surprise."

I smile. "You didn't mention we have another class together."

He leans forward and whispers, "That's because, originally, we *didn't* have another class together."

Not sure if he is coming off as sweet or creepy. "I guess I don't have your seat then?"

Noah laughs. "Nope."

Eric slides my chair slightly closer but not as close as it was. "Wallace. How's it going, man? Suddenly feeling artistic?"

Noah merely nods and shrugs.

I lean over and whisper "How'd you get to change your class this late in the school year?"

One side of Noah's mouth curves up into a crooked smile. "Mrs. Jones loves me."

Mrs. Carrie tells us we're going to make collages. She gives us a list of requirements such as size, how many different items, and it must have a clear theme. We must write a short paragraph to turn in before the end of class about our collage's theme.

Eric nudges my elbow with his. "What's your theme going to be?"

"I'm between soccer, art, or books since those are what first popped into my head. What's yours?"

"Going with football. I think I will make the collage in the shape of a giant football."

"Oh, I like that. Very creative. Hhmm, I could steal your idea and do mine in a soccer ball. I could have the pictures divided into black and white and color photos to add contrast to the ball."

"I guess it would only be fair to let you steal my idea since I plan to steal your heart."

I stop for a moment to try and process what he just said.

Noah, however, bursts out into full belly laughter with tears in his eyes.

Eric gives me an unapologetic shrug but then narrows his eyes at Noah when he won't stop laughing. "Anyone talking to you, Wallace? Mind your own business."

Noah tries to gain his composure, but as soon as he looks at Eric, he loses it again. I can't help but giggle with him.

He holds his hand up and tries to speak again. "I'm—mmmm—I'm sorry. Ha, but does that *actually* work? Wait—first, I want to know how did you seriously, I mean *seriously*, just say that with a straight face?"

Eric's lips turn up at one side and he taps his pencil on the table. "Don't know. But Sarah can tell you if it worked or not."

Uh-oh. I begin to feel uncomfortable. I feel my face heat up as I rub my sweaty palms on my pants under the table. It didn't work but I don't want to hurt his feelings.

Noah shifts the conversation back to our project. "Well, I found my inspiration for this project. Lame pick-up lines. I'm going to have it in the shape of a heart. Do you care if I use a photo of you, Eric?"

Eric's answer is a sour look.

I smile at Noah and mouth "thank you."

He returns the smile and suggests, "I think you should do yours on books. I bet you could do something cool with your favorite quotes over pictures."

I nod in agreement and then ask him, "What are you really doing for your theme?"

"I'm going to keep it easy. Dogs. I can do the shape of a bone, and dog pictures are everywhere. Plus, if we need to draw anything, I'll draw Snoopy."

I giggle "Well it is *art* so there might be some drawing involved."

I turn back to start writing my paper. I decide to go with Noah's idea of books and reading. I can make a big outline of a book on poster board. I'll use my favorite quotes to outline the book and maybe add layers of quotes to add dimension as though they are pages of an open book. Then, I can have all my favorite books doodled, actual pictures, and maybe even draw some of the scenes. I definitely have enough ideas for the collage itself. For the reason of my theme, I describe my passion for reading and how it takes you to another world. The art of being able to see another world by using only words to paint the picture in your mind. Funny how I used to love to read because I got to become someone else. However, now that I am someone else, it's not as exciting. I've made the mistake several times today of signing 'Olivia Stevens' so I double check my name before turning in my paper.

When the bell rings to dismiss class, Eric leans over but loudly says, "Maybe I'll be over today."

He winks at me and then gives Noah a smug look before he leaves. I didn't think the comment would bother Noah, but I notice his hand is clenched in a fist.

I decide to distract him by bringing up his sudden interest in art.

"So, what class were you *originally* in this hour?"

"Study hall. I never did anything in there, anyways, except goof off. I was able to sway them to let me enroll in here so late because I thought it would look better on my college resume." He shrugs and gives me a lopsided smile. "Luckily, I've had Art I before, or otherwise, it wouldn't have worked out."

"Have you thought of a way I might be able to see Aunt Andrea?" I ask as we're standing up. Still feeling unsure about him changing his schedule, I rub my arm and look around.

He shakes his head. "Nah, but I wouldn't push it with your parents just yet. They'll already be upset that we're talking. I'm sure douchebag is going to inform them we're sitting next to each other in class. He probably went to find Landon now."

We're about to head in opposite directions when I grab his arm. "Tell them I said hello. Please?"

He gives me a single nod. Feeling awkward, I drop my hand from his arm and hurry off to my next class.

This is the first class I share with Landon. He's a junior, whereas I'm a senior, but we are both going to be taking Spanish I. I enter the class and notice all the seats are taken, except for the one next to him. It looks like the same group from lunch, including Eric, who's sitting behind the empty seat next to Landon. Rachel is sitting in the seat in front of Landon. Sitting next to her in front of what is my seat, I assume, is Emily. I can't remember the rest of the group's names.

I walk over, and Landon pats the seat next to him. "Saved you a seat, sis!"

Sis. Wow, that's still weird. I inhale and slowly exhale. *I am Sarah Randall and that is my brother Landon Randall.* Landon doesn't seem to be uncomfortable around me in the slightest. He's welcomed me with wide open arms and completely taken on the role as my brother. *Should I call him 'bro?'* I roll my eyes at myself for that ridiculous thought. I wouldn't call him 'bro' even if I'd grown up with him all my life. I don't think I would have anyways…

"I hope I'm not taking someone else's spot." I sit down, anyway.

"Actually, you are." Eric leans his desk forward. "But, since I'm such a nice guy, I gladly gave up my seat."

I smile at him, but when I turn around, I roll my eyes. *I'm sure you're a real gentleman.* Landon snickers but doesn't comment. Instead, he turns his attention to the guy sitting next to him. The teacher comes in, goes through roll call, welcomes me, and jumps right in on giving us a few vocabulary words to look up the meaning of and memorize by Friday.

Landon and I walk to our next and final class together,

Chemistry. We enter the class, and he walks with me up to the teacher's desk.

"Hey Mr. G. This is my sister, Sarah. She needs to get her book."

Mr. Gargus is an elderly gentleman with kind blue eyes and hair that's white as snow. He gives me a curt nod and turns around to grab a book from the shelf behind him. "Welcome, Sarah, welcome. I hope you are having a lovely first day. Let's end it on a high note, yeah?"

He hands me the textbook, and Landon leads us to the desks at the front of the room. I'm a little surprised we are sitting in the front row.

He notices my confusion, and says, "Yeah I know, front row, but this is one of my favorite subjects. Also, Mr. G is awesome."

A few people pat his shoulder or high five as they pass our table. Landon seems to be friends with literally everyone. *Almost. Everyone except Noah.*

Turns out Mr. Gargus is a fun and enthusiastic teacher. He makes jokes throughout the class and seems to have a friendship with all the students. Landon is outspoken in this class and chimes in throughout the hour. Those two make the class so entertaining that it takes me by surprise when the bell rings.

Landon tells me to go on to my locker and then meet him in the parking lot. I'm relieved to find out Melissa isn't picking me up. I open my locker and find a cell phone. It's not anything fancy. A small, simple, black phone. There is a folded piece of paper next to it. I open it and read; it's a note from Noah informing me that this is a phone that works on a pre-paid card so I can text without the Randalls having any knowledge. I open the contacts app on the phone, and it has four names and numbers listed: Noah, Andrea, Brad, and Angie. My vision gets blurry and I wipe my eyes. I immediately click on

Angie's name and send a text asking if it's really her. Then, I send a text to Noah thanking him. I get a response immediately from him:

Noah: *No problem. Be careful. Keep this hidden & try not to waste ur mins.*

Me: *But how did you get this phone? And when?!*

Noah: *I got the idea during Art & texted Ma. It's not that difficult to go to the store & purchase a Trac phone. She brght it to me & I slipped it in ur locker.*

Me: *How did you know which locker was mine?*

Noah: *Rmber what I said about wasting mins? UR doing it.*

I decide not to respond since it would be a waste of minutes just to text "Ok." I place my books in my bag and hide the phone in an interior pocket of my bag wrapped in Tara's gym clothes.

I find Landon standing by his Jeep talking to some of his friends. Once I get in the passenger side, he tells everyone bye and hops in. We pull out of the parking lot, and he informs me the junior high is a ten-minute drive from here.

Landon sighs. "I know you probably see Noah as a friend..." *Whoa! We're jumping right into it, I guess.* "...but you need to understand, his aunt ruined your life and ours. She kidnapped you from our *neighborhood.* Literally down the street. Do you know what that's like, to grow up knowing that someone in your family had been kidnapped? I always wondered if the kidnapper would come back for me, too. I mean, they probably didn't know about me since I hadn't been born, but it's still scary. Mom never stopped searching for you. She never gave up hope that you'd be safely returned. Sarah, we had no idea who took you and..." he takes a deep breath, and his face holds so much pain, "we are all so grateful that you weren't hurt. You hear what happens in similar cases and, thank the good Lord you at least had a decent life."

I haven't really thought about what worry and grief this family has gone through. It's still hard for me to see Cindy as a villain. An adoptive mother would be an easier pill to swallow. I think it's time to finally read her journal tonight. A final good-bye. This might show me who she really was, no matter how badly I don't want to accept any of this. I didn't want to accept her death, but I finally am. I didn't want to accept her as not my biological mother, but I'm trying. Am I? I haven't been. Just like I haven't accepted that she was my kidnapper. If I read the journal, in her own words, that she kidnapped me I'll be forced to accept it. Right now, the Randalls are like long lost relatives taking me in due to the loss of my mother.

Landon interrupts my thoughts. "Don't be upset if we want to keep you separated from them. Before all this, I thought Noah was a cool guy. I don't trust him now. We're still unsure what hand they had in all this. Maybe they really didn't know. The police didn't find anything, so most likely they really had no idea. If you were me, would you trust them?"

We pull the car up behind a black SUV to get in line to pick up Denise.

"If I were you? Probably not. As the person that actually *did* get kidnapped, I do trust him. I understand your side, Landon. But try to be patient with me. Will you explain to Melissa and Richard that I'm trying, but I need to adjust in my own time? I grew up with Cindy; she's all I've ever known. I can't remember anything as a one-year old. Noah is…a connection between both worlds. Funny thing is, I don't even know him that well. It wasn't like he was ever around while I was growing up. I saw him maybe two or three times as kids until…until the funeral. He was really there for me. And so far, I've been the most comfortable with him." Landon grimaces. "I'm sorry. He did make my day a little easier." I shrug. "And you did too, of course." That brightens his face.

He remains quiet, even after Denise hops in the car. She

doesn't seem to notice his lack of conversation since she stays glued to her phone.

When we arrive at the house and are getting out of the car, Landon mumbles, "I'll talk to them about giving you some time to adjust and about Noah. I can't make any promises to sway them, but I do see where you're coming from."

I smile at him and joke, "Is that why you were so quiet? In deep thought over how messed up all this is?"

He chuckles, and all the humor is back in his eyes as he says, "I try not to get into too deep of thought. This is a messed-up situation, but at least we can say we don't lead boring lives."

He turns and walks on into the house. Before I make it to the door, Melissa comes skipping out and wraps me in a hug. "How was it? Come on! Come on! Let's go sit in the kitchen."

She keeps one arm around me and leads me into the kitchen. I sit at the table while she brings two glasses of water and sits down.

Denise grabs a snack out of the fridge and kisses Melissa on the cheek. "Catch up with you later, Mom!" She bounces off out of the room.

Landon is leaning against the counter chewing on an apple. He gives me a nod and mouths, "Tell the truth."

Melissa turns around to look at Landon. "Come sit with us honey! I want to hear all about both of your days."

He comes and gives her a kiss on the cheek. "Nah, I'm going to get started on homework. You two have a moment."

The other two have left, so she gives me her full attention. "Well?"

I take a sip of water and begin. "Well, um, it was good. I think I might've made some friends. One girl is on the soccer team and her name is Tara. Speaking of soccer, Coach asked me to join the school's soccer team. I told her yeah."

Melissa is so happy and excited for me. "Yay! Oh, that's wonderful! We can go this afternoon and get your gear."

I stare at her wide-eyed for a moment and inhale a deep breath. She is really excited, so much that she's ready to jump and do anything. I almost feel bad that I hadn't thought of her when I first heard the news. I smile and nod. I continue telling her about today's events.

"Yeah, I need gym clothes. I didn't know I'd be in P.E and had to borrow clothes from Tara."

She laughs, "Oh no, but it worked out, huh? You not having clothes gave you two a reason to cross paths."

She's so happy, genuinely happy for me. Landon said to tell her about Noah, but I'm scared. I decide to go with an approach to paint Noah in the best light possible.

"I did meet one girl who was mean. She became very confrontational when I accidently sat in the wrong seat. It was Noah Wallace that made her leave me alone."

I can't read her face, so I have no idea how she's taking this. I continue, "He probably wouldn't have approached me otherwise. Please don't be mad at him or call his parents. I was surprised to see him. Why didn't you give me a heads up that he went to that school? Surely you had to know."

She takes a deep breath and exhales. We sit there in a moment of silence. Finally, she speaks, "Yes, Sarah, I knew. Of course, I did. Part of me wanted to see how you would react to him. I wondered if you would be angry with them or if you would allow him to still be a part of your life. I shouldn't be surprised that you're not angry. After all, she raised you from an infant as her own. It's not easy for me to accept that, and I still get angry thinking about it."

I take her hand. "I'm trying to adjust. It's a lot for me. Please be patient because I still haven't fully grasped all of this. I don't believe that the Wallaces were involved. Noah did make the day easier."

She makes a disgusted face, so I hurry to finish. "Landon helped as well, but all of this is so new. I don't even know

Noah that well but he's kind of middle ground between all this. I know you can't understand but-"

"I get it. Or more like I'm *trying* to get it." She puts her hands together. "If this will make it easier for you, then you can associate with Noah at school. Only, *only*, if you keep your contact with him to a minimum. I want you to make other friends. Don't attach to Noah simply because you find him familiar or comfortable. Just like you're trying, I'm trying. That's all we can do, right? Be patient with me as well."

She gives me another hug and then tells me it's time for my appointment with Rita.

∽

"Sarah. How was your first day at school? Tell me all the details." Rita smiles.

"I'm on the soccer team."

"And that's something you did *before*, correct?"

"Yes."

"Wonderful." I nod and she tilts her head. "How does that make you feel?"

"I felt a part of something. I wasn't Sarah or Olivia, new girl, kidnap victim, or any of that. I was just me. Part of a team."

"I think this is going to be good for you. What else happened?"

"I saw Noah."

"Noah, Cindy's nephew Noah?" Rita raises her eyebrows.

"Yes."

"And?"

"It was…confusing."

"Tell me."

"For one thing we've never had any kind of relationship, but through all this—he has been the one person I find comfort in."

"Maybe because he is a bridge between your two worlds."

"Maybe."

"How do your parents feel?"

"Yeah, speaking of them. Melissa got me a new phone."

"Really?"

"But she wiped my old one out before I had a chance to save my photos or contacts."

"She did? And how does this make you feel?"

"Hurt. Angry."

"Did you tell her how you felt?"

"Somewhat. I was upset and let her know."

"Sarah. You're building a foundation with your parents. You need to communicate your feelings."

"It's hard. I don't know them. The two people I should know, I don't."

∽

When we get home, Melissa asks for my help with supper. At supper, Landon talks everyone's ear off. Melissa tells Richard that I'm going to be on the soccer team. He's delighted for me. Denise brings up homecoming again, so we have plans to go shopping this weekend.

After supper, I help clean up with Denise.

"So…how was school?"

"Fine." She sounds pained. I wait to see if she's going to ask me anything but nothing. Funny enough, I had been hoping to avoid conversations about myself but right now, I'd like to try and bond with Denise. I wrap saranwrap around a bowl of steamed veggies and place them in the refrigerator. Denise huffs and puffs as she scrapes food in the trash. We both meet at the sink to rinse off dishes.

"Look. We're in each other's way. I'll rinse, and you place them in the dishwasher."

I nod and begin rinsing the dishes. I hand her a plate and ask, "So, what do you like to do on the weekends?"

"Nothing." She places the plate in the dishwasher and looks at me expectantly. I hurry and rinse off another plate. She takes it and continues, "Because that's all I'm allowed to do—is nothing. Don't you know I could get kidnapped?"

"I see." I feel my cheeks heat. I bite my bottom lip and focus on rinsing off dishes.

Denise sighs. "I'm sorry." My only reply is to hand her another plate. "I like to go to the movies, when I'm allowed. I guess my favorite thing to do is binge watch shows and gossip with my friends."

"I could go to the movies and I had one friend I could sleepover at her house. But, I wasn't allowed social media accounts."

"Gah. I guess neither one of us got a *normal* home life." She shakes her head and goes about shoving drinking glasses into the dishwasher. "So…" Her eyes brighten and a grin stretches across her face. "Spotted anyone you might have the hots for?"

I laugh. "What? I was more worried about figuring out my class schedule and where my classes are." For some reason, Noah's face pops into my mind. I quickly shake my head because no, that's weird.

"Oh puh-lease. There had to have been *someone* you gave a second look to."

I see his smiling face again and his dreamy blue eyes. *Wait. When did his eyes become dreamy?*

Denise ignores my silence and discusses how she finds almost every single one of our brother's friends 'hot.'

Once we are finished, she asks if I want to watch an episode of a show she is obsessed with. I agree and tell her I'll meet her in the den. I hurry up to my room and lock the door behind me. I pull the prepaid phone out to see if I have any text messages. My heart skips a beat when I see two unread messages. I open the first one. It's from Angie, and she tells me it really is her and that she misses me terribly and hopes to hear from me again soon. She also gives me her name on social media apps to download. The next message is from Aunt Andrea. This one makes me get teary eyed. She tells me she loves me and hopes to get to visit with me soon. She's so glad that Noah and I have classes together. She goes on to tell me that he spoke very fondly of me today. I want to reply but since I don't have any idea of how I'll get more minutes, I heed Noah's advice to save my minutes. After I hide the phone, I go back downstairs and find Denise in the den. She's wrapped in a blanket on the couch with a bowl of popcorn in her lap. I sit next to her and accept some popcorn.

She pops a piece in her mouth and sighs. "I always have to nibble on something when I watch anything. Even if I'm not hungry. Just like I always have to be covered, even when it isn't cold."

I smile and tell her I always like to eat while watching a show. Richard smiles at us as he passes through the room. It almost feels normal sitting here with Denise. However, for some reason that thought makes me anxious. I begin to wonder if this is how my life would've always been. Not that my life before this was by any means unhappy. My anxiety is beginning to make me feel nauseous. I decline her invitation to watch another episode pleading exhaustion. Once in my room, I lock the door and take out Cindy's journal.

Eighteen

March 27

If I'm going to do this, I have to do it right. Andrea can't know. She'd turn me in for sure. So, I have to lie. I told my sister that I'm pregnant. One-night stand. With the way I've been, she easily believes it. She's excited because I told her that I'll have to remain sober and clean. To help with the time frame, I told her I'm already at 8 weeks. It's stretching it, but Olivia is a couple of months old at least. I need to look up her birth announcement. I'm sure was in the newspaper somewhere.

Now I just have to find a place for us to live. We can't stay here. We can't even stay in this state. I hate to leave Andrea and baby Noah... I wish those two could grow up together. But they'll visit. I doubt we'll ever be able to come back here. Maybe years down the road we can come back. I can show Olivia where I grew up. It'll be nice.

Nineteen

A KNOCK COMES FROM MY DOOR. I HURRY AND stash the journal under my bed. I notice that I'm not even ready for bed, so I throw my pants off and wrap myself in my robe. I open the door to find Melissa and Richard smiling. I open the door wider and allow them to come in.

"We just came to tell you goodnight, sweetie." She gives me a warm hug.

Richard clears his throat. "Your mom told me about the Noah situation. I don't like it, but Landon shared his opinion with me this evening also."

My heart stops. *What were Landon's opinions? I thought he was going to be on my side.*

Richard speaks with a firm voice. "We set rules for a reason and expect you to follow them. Now, Landon fears if we come down too hard on you about anyone from… your past that you'll rebel. He pointed out that everything has been going smoothly, and I agree. We won't change your schedule to where you and Noah are in separate classes. I'm aware you'll cross paths with him at school, but only at school. Do not *ever* refer to him as your cousin. Do not discuss anything that has happened before today. Be civil but that's it. He's not related, so don't act like he is. You're not going to be pretend cousins."

I feel myself bristling at his tone and harsh words. Melissa hisses at him through gritted teeth. "*Richard.* Calm down. We talked about this."

"Landon assured us that this was the best way. To allow Noah to be a part of your life at school. But only at school, that is all I'm agreeing to."

I look up into his eyes. I see fear and pain. He's afraid of them and he's afraid for me. I watch as a look of sadness washes over him. Richard wraps me in his arms and kisses my forehead. "We're going to move past all this."

I'm not sure if he's telling me or himself. He releases me and offers a small smile. I'm about to pull away but he wraps his arms around me again and speaks above my head. "I just want to move past this. I'm sorry. I can't stand the idea of losing you again." I hear the break in his voice. "Sweet dreams, Sarah." Then he hurries out of the room.

Melissa gives me one last tight hug. "I'm so proud of you. Today was a big day and you were so brave! I love you."

After she closes the door, I'm left standing there stunned. I know their reasoning, but I still feel so confused by everything.

I hurry to the bathroom to get ready for bed. Then I crawl under the sheets. As much as I want to keep reading the journal, I simply can't. Everything that has happened today is finally catching up to me: school, Noah, the journal, the text messages, everything. With great effort, I get out of bed to go place the journal back in the inside pocket of the suitcase. I crawl back under the covers and as soon as my head hits the pillow, I fall asleep.

Twenty

I CAN'T BELIEVE IT'S ALREADY MONDAY AGAIN. I have caught up on most of the assignments I missed. Technically, it was only a month's worth of school. It was an excellent excuse to stay holed up in my room. My mind had simple tasks to focus on which for once made me grateful for homework. Noah and I didn't text any over the weekend. I assume he didn't want to use up the minutes. At school we keep conversations light. He still walks me to the cafeteria, but I always go and sit with Landon's group. This has drawn a little attention to us with me being the new girl and Noah is typically a mute—or so I'm told. Tara and Amber, another girl from the soccer team whom I've become friends with, sit with us now. I've found a nice outlet in soccer. When I'm on the field I'm not the new girl, I'm not Olivia or Sarah, I'm part of a *team*. I'm in the zone and all my personal problems cease to exist.

Today I've dressed up a little more. I added a little more makeup, nothing drastic, just more mascara and darker lip color. I leave my hair down and curl the ends. I pick out one of the nicest outfits Melissa purchased for me, and it compliments my coloring and figure. Reading the journal every night has made me understand more that this would've been my life already. Cindy had clearly been going through depression when she kidnapped me. She took me from my family. Reading it from her own words doesn't make it any easier, but I can't be in denial about what happened. A part of me still loves her, probably always will, but I need to embrace the family and life I'd had taken from me. At most, I owe it to myself and the people downstairs to *try*.

I go downstairs for breakfast and everyone is already there. Denise and Melissa both raise their eyebrows and smile at me.

"Oh my gosh. You look *hot!*" Denise reaches for a bowl out of the cabinet and places it on the counter. "Like why haven't you been doing that with your hair to start with? I'm being completely serious right now," she says while pouring a bowl of cereal. She walks by me carrying her bowl and raises her eyebrows. "Seriously."

Melissa touches my hair. "I agree, sweetie. Your hair is beautiful down. You look extra pretty today...any particular reason?"

Denise sits down at the table smiling like the Cheshire cat. "You mean any particular person? You *obviously* have the hots for someone!"

I frown and go to the counter to make some oatmeal, "Um no, just got up a little earlier than usual and had more time to get ready." *Besides, all girls feel better when they dress up a little.*

Richard and Landon are quietly watching our exchange from the table while eating their breakfast. After I sit down, Melissa reminds everyone about my game tomorrow. Then, after the game, we're going dress shopping for homecoming.

Denise looks over at Landon, and in a teasing tone, she asks, "So who are you asking this year? Is it *Rachel?*"

Landon rolls his eyes and shrugs.

Her eyes then fall on me. "Who are you *hoping* will ask you? Or..." she gets really animated, "are *you* going to ask them?" She wiggles her eyebrows.

They all stop what they're doing and look at me.

"Um...I haven't really thought about it. I don't even know if I'm going." I focus on my oatmeal. *Am I going to homecoming? Who would I go with? I wonder if any of the girls are going solo? I literally just started attending this school. I barely even know anyone! Except Noah. Would he be willing to be my date? Not sure the Randalls...I mean—my parents would approve. It'd be awkward because he reminds them of his aunt and of what happened.* I'm on the verge of a panic attack, and I already have a headache. It's not even eight in the morning.

Melissa gives a small chuckle, "Of course you're going. You can't miss your senior year homecoming. Is there anyone you hope to go with?"

I shake my head back and forth. *This is only my second week at this school people. Calm yourself.*

"You know, a group of girls might all go solo together. If you're worried about not having a date, we could have one of our friends' sons escort you," Melissa continues. She looks to Landon. "Honey, maybe you have a nice friend that might want to escort Sarah? You two could double date!"

Richard nods. "I would feel much better if you were there, son. She's been through a lot. We don't want someone to try anything."

All good feelings from this morning are gone. *Poof.* Just like that.

Luckily, it's time to go to school, so we don't dwell anymore on me needing a chaperone. As I'm picking up my backpack by the door, Richard walks over.

"Here." I look down and he's holding a small white piece of paper out to me. My eyebrows pinch together as I take the folded piece of paper. "It's your friend Angie's number. I called Mrs. Jenkins to see if she could get it for me."

I smile as I open the piece of paper to see in messy handwriting a series of numbers written. "Thank you."

"I explained to her that we lost her number when you got a new phone. I think Rita is right and… that you need your friend. I'm sorry if we're not getting this right, Sarah. Just know…" He sighs. "Just know that, we're trying. We want what's best and sometimes we don't know. It will never be our intention to hurt you."

"Thank you…" *Do I call him 'dad' or just Richard?* "Thank you for this. It means a lot."

There's good music playing on the radio on the way to school. Denise is totally feeling it in the back seat. She dances as much as her seatbelt will allow while not missing a single word from the lyrics. That added entertainment helps to bring my mood up another level. After we drop Denise off, Landon tells me he's excited for my game tomorrow. We discuss soccer all the way up to the moment when we walk into the school building. There, we part ways as I go to my locker and he goes to join a group of his friends. I pass him again on the way to class and wave. Unfortunately, I think Eric thought I was also waving at him. I guess it was a wave to everyone in general, but it was mostly just meant for Landon. My brother.

I smile to myself. I'm so used to being alone most of the time, it's nice having a sibling at school. A part of me knows without a doubt, Landon is there for me. It makes going to school easier. I have Landon. Speaking of Landon, I giggle as I pass Rachel skipping down the hall toward him. I turn around to watch him wrap her in a hug and spin her around. I see what Denise was talking about. She's been over to the house quite a bit and they clearly care about each other. Even if she does openly drool over Trent sometimes. I turn back around and walk into the classroom.

I'm surprised to find Noah already in the room. The first bell hasn't even rung, so it's still early. He's usually the last one to walk in. He gives me a crooked smile as I head toward my seat next to him.

"Hey, you," I greet him as I sit down, "You're here early."

He leans back in his seat and puts his hands behind his head. "I was hoping to get a few minutes with you. *Alone.*"

I smile. "Yeah, we don't really get to talk." I tilt my head in thought and voice out, "You know, we never talked before. Why?"

He shrugs, "We lived so far apart. We only met in person twice that I can remember, anyways…before, ya know, all this. Also, how were we going to keep in touch? You didn't have social media. I wasn't crazy about the idea of just talking on the phone to practically a stranger."

I scoff. "Aunt Andrea called all the time, and we talked. She came to visit us every time there was a deal on flights." I smile to myself. "She *always* wanted to talk to me on the phone."

Noah sits up in his chair and makes an exasperated sound. "Guys don't work that way. If you had had any social media accounts, we might've kept in touch. I guess now we know why your mo —why *Cindy* was so paranoid and strict about you and the internet."

Mom. That's what he had almost said. He was about to refer to Cindy as *my mom.* I still refer to her as my mom in my head, too. I've been making some progress on seeing Melissa as my mother.

Instead, I slip farther back by giving him a sad smile and saying, "You can still call her my mom. She did raise me. I know you struggle with calling me Sarah, and if it's just us, I don't mind hearing Olivia. Olivia is still what I call myself. Sarah seems…like a stranger. Honestly," I take a deep breath, and in a helpless voice I continue, "I don't know who I am, Noah."

He nods, and I think he may honestly understand what I'm trying to say. He seems to be the only person who seems to get me. Maybe it's because he knows both sides of the story.

Noah Wallace is probably the only person who can even begin to understand my struggle. I know I should be angry with Cindy but at the same time, I'm unable to hate her. I mean, I *am* angry with her, but I still think of her as my mother. It's not easy to toss aside seventeen years of loving someone. Aside from kidnapping me, she was a great mom.

I'm so lost in my head that I'm startled when Noah wraps his arms around me. I didn't even notice him get out of his seat. I'm stiff at first from the sudden envelopment, but then I relax and sink into him. I feel the strong chords of his muscles as they flex around me, tighten, holding me closer. I notice he's the perfect size. Big enough to encircle me into his body but not to where I feel I'm overpowered and going to suffocate. I feel warmth through the cotton of his shirt and smell the clean laundry detergent. I turn my head to rest on his shoulder and nuzzle into his neck, welcoming the comfort that I didn't realize I needed so desperately. I smell Irish Spring soap and a minor hint of a woodsy and spice scent. *Maybe cologne?* It's a comforting smell, or maybe it's just him. Everything about him from the feel of his strong arms, to the soft cotton of this shirt, to his steady breathing and all the clean warm senses enveloping me are comforting. *I could easily stay like this for the rest of the day.* He pulls back and looks intently into my eyes. His thumb wipes a stray tear from under my eye, and he gives me a sad smile.

"I'm sorry you're going through this," he whispers in a gravelly voice.

"You don't have to feel sorry for me. Don't feel any obligation, either. It's a really messed up situation. The sad part is, I don't know if I would change anything. I still love her. I'm glad I know the truth. I mean, I wonder if she would've ever told me the truth? I think the Randall family's great, too. It's just hard to leave Olivia behind and become Sarah overnight. That's what this feels like. I don't know who I am or who I want to be."

The first bell rings. I gently push him back toward his seat and wipe my eyes. "I'm sorry. I just dumped all this on you first thing. What did you want to talk about?" I feel so foolish for having that little meltdown.

He leans toward my ear and I get goosebumps as I feel his warm breath. "Be you." He leans back and looks into my eyes. "Just be you." He goes to his seat and flops down like he didn't just intently stare into my eyes and leave my whole body covered in goosebumps.

He casts me a crooked smile. "I just wanted to talk. I wanted to talk to you… Olivia? Sarah? Whoever the hell *you* are. I wanted to have a chance to talk to you about everything and nothing." He stretches and I can't help but notice his tan toned skin as his shirt lifts "Maybe we can get here early again tomorrow to discuss more of your identity crisis." He gives another crooked smile and winks. I roll my eyes at him.

I fight a smile as I say, "Or… we can both get here early again tomorrow and just talk."

He shrugs. "That's what happened today. We got here early and talked. *You* picked the subject. If I'd picked the subject, we would've discussed why you're so fixed up this morning." He makes a point of looking me up and down rather dramatically.

I hold my hands out as I ask, "Do I really look that dressed up today? I must really have been letting myself go because almost everyone has commented on the fact that I curled my hair. I know I gave a little extra effort, but…did I really look that bad all week?"

Noah throws his head back and laughs.

I huff. "Okay, that laugh is making me nervous. Is it a joke that I didn't notice how bad I looked?"

He stops laughing but his eyes sparkle and he's smiling. "Nah, Liv. You haven't looked bad all week."

Liv. Did he just give me a new nickname? Why do I like it so much?

I go back to focusing on the topic at hand. I give him a doubtful look so he quickly continues. "The hair style does suit you and it's a change from seeing it pulled back all week. Anyways, you never answered my question."

The class has filled up now, so I whisper, "Are you in protective big cousin mode? Denise thinks I've met someone, so she was giving me the third degree as well. Is that where this is going?"

He raises an eyebrow. "Protective big cousin mode?"

"Ya know, like a big brother that might be concerned about me dating." I chuckle to myself how ridiculous everyone is being.

Noah gives a small nod. "Okay." He lets the front legs of the chair drop to the floor and leans on his elbows on his desk. "So, have you met someone that you're interested in? If you haven't gotten his attention yet, I'm sure you will today."

I shrug and I'm about to tell him not really, but class begins.

⟡

In second hour, Rachel sits next to me. She tells me how cute I look and brings up homecoming. Of course, she asks if Trent's coming home for homecoming weekend. Everyone is in a buzz for homecoming. I guess two weeks isn't long enough yet to get in the school spirit. Rachel tells me how she's probably going to say yes to any of the guys from our group if they ask her. I probably enjoyed that she actually said *our* group too much. *I'm so lame. First today I was excited that Noah called me 'Liv,' and now I'm thrilled that I'm considered part of a group.* From what I gather, they've all just about dated each other or used each other for dates for social events like this. However, mostly Rachel and Landon always go as a couple.

The verdict is still out on what exactly their relationship is. She's alone a lot with him in his room, but he doesn't seem jealous when other guys flirt with her. He also isn't phased over her infatuation with Trent. However, he is overly protective of her feelings and always showering her with attention. It breaks my heart to think maybe he's pining for her, but she sees him as a casual or open relationship. I want to ask, but not sure if I'm to that point with our relationships. The curiosity is killing me!

After class, we find Landon outside the door, per routine now. Rachel asks Landon about Trent, but he merely rolls his eyes at her. My chest tightens as I watch intently for pain in his eyes. There's a hint, but then he smiles lovingly at Rachel and wraps an arm around her.

"I'm sure he's coming, but if you need a date…"

"I know," she grins as she wraps her arms around his neck and jumps on his back, circling his waist with her legs, "I've got you Lanny!"

He laughs and reaches back to slap her behind. She kisses his cheek and nuzzles her face against his. "My forever date. Even if I marry your brother."

"Oh my gosh! Get down!" He shakes her off, both of them laughing the entire time.

⸻

Tara is also caught up in the homecoming hype. She wants me to ask Noah if Jeff has a date. She's asked me a few times about how I managed to hit it off with Noah so well. Apparently, he has a very selective group of friends. He especially doesn't hang out with as many girls one on one as he has with me. The entire school has noticed and apparently, everyone is gossiping. *Great.* What nobody knows is this is only because we are...or were...cousins. I can't help but wonder if we would've been friends if none of this had happened. If I had simply gone to school here all my life, would I have been friends with Noah or remained with Landon's group? Noah seems popular as well but not like Landon. I've learned that Noah gained his popularity through sports rather than family status and being social. He plays football and runs track and is the star basketball player. Almost every girl has a crush on him, but surprisingly, he isn't a player —in fact, he has only had two girlfriends. He's smart and quiet and even with sports fame, he's kind of a loner. Landon, on the other hand, is the loudest person in a room, only does track, is extremely intelligent, and hasn't had a girlfriend because he doesn't want the commitment. Or he's in love with Rachel, who is in love with Trent. However, that doesn't mean he hasn't dated. He's typically always seen with Rachel but there've been other girls in between. As far as I can tell, Landon Randall is at the top of the social ladder.

During P.E., Tara asks me again if I'll ask Noah about Jeff at the end of class. I promised her I would, but she reminds me again at the end of class. She's borderline nagging at this point. I get dressed and ready faster than usual because I'm being rushed.

This is the first time I'm ready before Noah, so I go stand by the boy's locker room.

"She's hot dude. I'd like to kidnap her, ya know what I'm saying?" I hear a low voice say. My stomach sinks and I feel bile rise in my throat. I feel my cheeks flame and my hands shake. Suddenly there's the sound of sneakers squeaking and low grunting.

"Man, what's with you! C'mon! It was a joke. You got a hard on for this chick, cool, but take a joke."

I hear a low growl. "You don't joke about someone getting kidnapped, prick." *Noah.*

"Aight, aight. I'm sorry, okay?" It's the first voice again.

"Man, she's under your skin bad." Another voice.

I roll my eyes and lean my head back against the wall. Poor Noah. If only people knew he saw me as family, they might be more sensitive to what they say around him.

I hear a different voice speak. "What's the deal with you two? I see y'all talking a lot, sitting together and shit."

I don't hear a reply, so I assume he shrugged off whatever he said. *Guys are just as bad as girls with gossip.*

Another male voice, much lower than the others, begins to talk. "You know, I heard from Alex that Eric is planning to ask her to homecoming."

The first guy speaks up again. "Nah, Landon told Eric not to touch her, or he'd beat his ass. Eric told him, '*Like you'd be able to, pretty boy.*' But then Landon said, '*Aight, say I can't, but you know who can? Trent.*'"

Another guy, possibly Jeff shouts, "Yeah! You know Trent can whoop him. You might wanna watch out, Wallace. You're tough and all, but I wouldn't want to go up against Trent Randall."

There are some grunts in agreement.

The first guy speaks again. "Eric's been friends with them both since elementary school. Does he really think they'd let him go on a date with their sister? I mean, they *know* him."

Note to self, do not date Eric. Not that I was interested in him to start with. He's extremely attractive, but he gives off a creepy vibe. Something about him screams slimy and egotistical.

"Think they'd let Wallace here get anywhere near their sister? Whattya say, Noah? Is she worth getting your ass handed to you by Trent fucking Randall?" That sounds like Keaton.

Noah speaks too low for me to hear his response. If he even gave one. The guys are too busy laughing and making a hooping noise. I hear footsteps, so I decide to get away from the door. A few guys come out before I spot Noah, Jeff, and

Keaton walking together with their heads down, seeming to have a private conversation.

I'm afraid he isn't going to notice me, so I call out, "Noah! Hey!"

They look up and smile, Jeff's smile a little too big and mischievous. They walk up to me and stop. "Hello, Jeff. How are you?"

He's still cheesing when he takes a moment to look between Keaton and Noah before replying, "Doing good."

I decide it's silly to bother Noah about Jeff when he's standing right in front of me.

"Jeff, I was wanting to ask you about homecoming," I ask casually.

Jeff's face drains of all color, and he looks panicked at Noah. Confused, I turn to Noah, who also looks confused and pissed off at the same time. Keaton bites his bottom lip trying to keep from smiling.

"Did I miss something?" I give a nervous laugh.

Noah nods and puts his hands in his pockets. "No, all's cool." He lightly nudges Jeff.

Realization dawns on me that they think I'm asking Jeff to go with me. I start laughing, "Whoa! No! I mean, no offense, Jeff. Sorry, that came out wrong. Oops."

They visibly relax but Jeff plays hurt. "Well, gee thanks. What were you going to ask?"

"I want to know if you have date, just not for me." I smile.

Jeff gives his mischievous smile again. He makes air quotes. "For a friend, huh?"

I roll my eyes. "*Yes*. For a *friend*."

"Well if it really is for a friend… Let's see. That would mean you're asking for Emily? No, she likes to recycle her dates. Rachel? No, she sticks to Landon. Amber? Nope, unless she broke up with her boyfriend. Ah, yes. Tara. Must be Tara. You're asking for Tara…hhmmm. Interesting."

I tilt my head and narrow my eyes. "You've paid a lot of attention to who I've become friends with."

He shrugs as though it's not uncommon to stalk someone. "You're the new girl in a small school. Everybody knows who you've befriended."

I didn't really think this school was small. It's bigger than my old one. "Anyways. Tara? Homecoming? Don't be mean. She actually wanted me to ask Noah about you, but I figured this way would be faster and easier. Why not go straight to the source, right?"

Jeff gives me a thoughtful nod but then looks at Noah. "Alright man, I'll catch you later." He pats Keaton's chest and nods for them to go. Keaton throws his hand up in a single salute to me and they start walking off.

I call out, "Hey! You didn't say if you have a date!"

He doesn't even look back, just gives a single wave like Keaton just did. *Rude.* I turn back to Noah who's wearing a smirk. We begin walking out of the gym toward the cafeteria.

I nudge his shoulder with mine. "Speaking of homecoming," I say in a sing song voice.

He laughs and nudges me back. "What about it?"

I give him a sideway glance and smile. "Who are you going with? Apparently, everyone is going."

"What about you? Are you going with someone? Is that why you dolled yourself up today?" He looks at me out of the corner of his eye.

"I asked you first. And besides, I told you, you don't have to worry about me. I think the new fam has gladly taken on the role of protective guardians."

Before we enter the cafeteria, I look up at Noah expectantly. "Well? Homecoming?"

"Of course, I'm going to the game since I'll be in it. The dance I'll most likely attend with a couple of buddies."

"Oh yeah, you're playing in the game!" I can't believe I'd

forgotten that little detail. Especially since he's one of the big athletes here. "Well, I'm not sure on the dance yet, but I'm for sure going to watch you play."

He gives me a shy smile. There's a hint of pink to his cheeks. I smile to myself at how adorable he looks trying not to blush.

An idea occurs to me. "Maybe Uncle Brad and Aunt Andrea will be at the game? I might get a chance to visit with them."

"Yeah, they'll be there. They don't attend the away games but do come to all my home games. They'll be there, *especially* if you'll be there."

The way he emphasizes 'especially' makes me giggle and my heart swell.

Once in the cafeteria, Noah whispers for me to go to art early, and then we separate. I want to inform him that he didn't specify how early, but he's already heading toward his group of friends. I get in line and grab a tray for my food. After I fix my tray, I head towards Landon's table and grab a seat.

When I notice Noah taking his tray to the trash bin fifteen minutes early, I tell Landon I forgot some homework in my locker that's due today. He doesn't question me, thank goodness, but just nods, continuing his conversation with Rachel. Tara asks if I want her to go with me back to my locker, but I decline her offer. I hurry and dump my tray.

Noah is alone and waiting for me when I walk in the room. I go ahead and take out my sketch pad so I can at least finish my assignment that's due for this class. *I didn't completely lie to Landon. It's just not due until next week.* Noah watches me and compliments me on how talented I am. I don't agree with him, but I still like hearing him praise my art. This isn't the first time he's watched me draw and noted how impressed he was.

"So, you have a big game tomorrow. Nervous?"

"I will be for about five seconds before the game starts. It passes quickly once the game starts." I say.

"Yeah, I get that. I don't remember Mom ever mentioning you play before. Did you play at your old school?" he asks while watching me intently.

"The school didn't have a soccer team, but I did play with friends on a community club team." I smudge the charcoal pencil line I just drew to give more of a shadowy effect on my drawing.

"You know, I was thinking," he shifts slightly forward in his chair, "would your parents ever let you go to a friend's house?"

I look up at him surprised. I hadn't really thought about it since I had only just met everyone. I shake my head, "I doubt it. I don't exactly have friends right now since I've only known them for two weeks. Why do you ask?"

He sighs. "I was trying to think of ways that you could come see us."

I gasp. "You want me to *lie* to them about where I'm going? That's the oldest trick in the book." I give him a pointed look. "You're an only child, but the Randalls have three other kids that I'd bet money have already tried a stunt like that. I bet they are prepared for anything I might try."

He laughs, "I guess you're right. Okay. What about driving? You go shopping and we all bump into each other."

I grin and throw my hands up. "What a surprise!"

He waves his hand at me. "Mocking me? This display of immaturity is not becoming."

I giggle and go back to my work.

"Well, at least I'm trying, Liv. I'm actually surprised we're still in the same classes."

I blush that he used the name 'Liv' again. "Well I think Landon is our best ally right now. He already put in a good word for you. They said we are good to be around each other at school."

"Yeah, Landon and I used to be cool. I was closer to Trent since we played sports together. I'd been to your house a few times."

I pause my hand. This is all news to me. "They quit being your friend after…after Cindy passed away and all this came out about me?"

Noah rubs his jaw. "Trent popped up out of nowhere on the football field. At first, we all thought he was stopping by to say 'hi' since he'd played with most of us before he graduated. Instead, he comes charging at me. I had *no* idea what had gotten into him. Out of nowhere, he started beating the shit out of me."

He balls his hands into fists and acts out punching. "He kept screaming, 'Did you know? Did you know, asshole?' repeatedly with each punch." He lets his hands rest at his side, "I didn't know. None of us knew. I don't think they completely believe it. Well, I take that back. Trent and I had a long talk after he calmed down. We were close before, but it's not been the same…"

Noah looks sad. "He believes me, but he still can't let it go. I'm guilty by association."

I feel sad for them, so I try to comfort him. "He probably isn't allowed to be friends with you. Same with Landon. I doubt he really blames you for what your aunt did." I smile and shake my head. "Denise, now, Denise *is* the type to accuse someone of being guilty by association." I begin to tell him about my relationship with Denise. Our conversation takes a lighter note. It drifts to the topic of homecoming again.

"Well, I hope you go. It's senior year. You need to," he says. The first bell rings, and students trickle in.

Eric sits down and casually slides his chair close to mine. Noah pulls me closer to him. The difference is, Noah will scoot down as well to give me space. This has almost become a game for Eric. I think he flirts worse with me when we're in Noah's presence.

I think Eric feels Noah is competition, so he likes throwing it in his face that he has the advantage of being one of Landon's best friends. I just wish I could tell Eric that Noah doesn't see me that way so he can calm it down. He tells me he plans to come over tonight, loudly so Noah can hear as well. Apparently, Landon has a new video game they're going to try out.

He gives me a lopsided grin. "I'll be honest with you, Sarah. I want to come over and play, just not with Landon."

I keep looking straight ahead to the front of the room. *Maybe if I ignore him, he'll take the hint. At least he might stop talking.*

"I could tell Lanny that I'm going to the bathroom but get lost and find your room instead." He tilts his head and raises an eyebrow. "Do you have any games in mind that we could play together?"

Girls actually like this? I've heard the way the girls talk about him. I'm having a hard time understating why they like him, though. I mean, he's handsome…but then he talks.

"I have a game we can play now," I whisper to him.

He raises both eyebrows at that, and his mouth spreads into a full grin. "And what's that?"

"How about quiet mouse still mouse? You don't speak. You don't move. No more talking to me. No more moving closer to me or touching me."

He starts to speak, but I hold a hand up. "Nope, game's started."

Noah has his head down in his arms. I don't hear him, but I know he's laughing because his shoulders are bouncing. He finally stops and turns the page on his sketch pad. A minute later, he slides it to me:

I'm glad you stopped him. I was about to, but it wouldn't

have been that way. I can't get suspended or I won't get to play in the game. But at least I would've shut him up.

I turn to Noah and roll my eyes at him. He holds his hands out like what was he supposed to do.

Eric's an idiot. You would've been a bigger idiot if you got suspended over that idiot.

Noah takes the pad and writes:

Maybe so. Do me a favor and lock your doors when you are home. Like you said, he's an idiot.

The rest of the day flies by. When Landon, Denise, and I get home, we're surprised that Trent's truck is in the driveway. We go in the house and when Denise sees him in the kitchen, she runs over to hug him.

Landon pats him on the back, "Checking in? Don't worry we're all accounted for."

"You're such an ass." Trent lightly punches Landon in the shoulder.

I'm not sure what to do, so I stand back awkwardly. Trent smiles at me and asks me how I am. I give a short, "good." He comes up and hugs me. He's everything you'd imagine in a big brother. Strong and caring. He breaks away with a pat on my shoulder.

I'm surprised when he tells me he's excited for my game tomorrow, and he can't wait to watch it. Trent barely remembers me from when I was a baby. It feels nice knowing he came home this weekend to watch my soccer game.

Melissa begins prepping for supper as everyone starts to leave the kitchen. I stay behind to help. Landon calls out that Eric is coming over, and he'll probably stay for supper. I inwardly groan. *I guess I'll need to lock my door.* I debate about telling Melissa that I find Eric creepy. *What if she overreacts? Worse, what if she tells me I'm being silly?* I could also go to Landon. Eric is his best friend. He's known him longer and he is probably more like a brother than I am like a sister.

After supper, I go up to my room and take out Cindy's journal. I kind of want to text Noah about creepy Eric, but even if I said it as a joke, I think it'd cause him to worry. So, I decide against it. I'm about to start reading when I hear a light knock on my door. I walk over and put my ear against the door.

"I hear you Sarah. Let me in. I just want to talk," comes a low voice.

"Are you serious? You seriously came to my room! Go away," I tell Eric in a firm voice.

"Don't be like that. I'm best friends with your brothers. My parents are best friends with your parents. Honestly, they'd be glad for us to hang out. Open the door," Eric insists.

I hear another low, unhappy voice, "I'd hardly call us friends, much less best friends. Get the hell out of this house. I'll tell Landon you're *sick* and had to run on home."

I hear Eric take on a pleading tone. "Hey man, calm down. She invited me up here."

"Then why isn't she *inviting* you in? Don't bullshit with me."

"Trent, man, I was coming to just talk to her. We have classes together, ya know. I wanted to ask about an assignment."

There is no mistaking the threat in Trent's voice. "Get. Out. Or do you need help finding your way out?"

I hear footsteps quickly descending the stairs.

"Open," Trent clips.

I don't hesitate.

"Thanks," I whisper.

"Has he been bothering you? Don't lie." Trent points his finger at me.

I nod. "He's made comments. He's more annoying than anything."

He puts his hands on his hips. "Have you told Landon

what a douche his little friend's been? Did you tell him that he's going to use him as an excuse to get to your room?"

I sigh. "Trent," I feel defeated, "I just got here. I just started school here. I don't want to be trouble…any more than I already have been."

He seems to understand where I'm coming from and places a hand on my shoulder, "Really, Sarah? I get where you're coming from. And I don't like it. You're not causing trouble. You never have. Stop blaming yourself for the situation other assholes cause. It doesn't matter who they are or what the situation is. There's never a time when you let some creep harass you."

I push his hand off. "I didn't *let* him do anything. I don't know if you noticed, but I kept my door locked. How'd you know he came up here and was using Landon as an excuse?"

Trent looks around and then whispers, "Noah got in touch with me. He saw my truck in town and texted. Wanted to make sure you were okay."

I wasn't so sure about the last part of his sentence. I'm not so sure if he means Trent, himself, wanted to make sure I was okay or if Noah wanted him to make sure I was okay for Noah's sake. I give him a tight, closed mouth smile. I didn't have enough courage to talk to them, but Noah did. He did it knowing they hated him, and it might cause trouble for himself. Feeling completely awkward now, I decide to change the subject. The only thing I can think of to change the subject is Rachel.

"Um, Rachel keeps asking about you. She asks almost every day if I've heard from you or if you're coming home or if you're going to the homecoming game." He closes his eyes, shakes his head and walks out. *Alrighty then.*

With Trent gone, I close my door and lock it. Not because I'm worried about Eric anymore, but because I'll have Cindy's journal out. Before I begin reading, I go get my secret phone out of my bag. It took a lot of guts for Noah to message Trent. He did it on my behalf. The least I can do is tell him I appreciate it.

Me: Thank you. I'm fine. Eric got kicked out of the house by Trent.

I put it back in hiding. I snuggle under the covers and begin reading.

Twenty-One

April 5

I told my sister that I'm moving to Colorado. She didn't take the news well. But she finally accepted when I told her after the miscarriage, divorce, gossip, and my downward spiral of a life—that I needed this move. Which is true! I need a fresh start for me and my baby. Olivia is not going to be subjected to all my past sins. I leave tomorrow. I'm nervous but also excited. Here's to a new chapter in my life.

Twenty-Two

April 6

Luck is finally on my side! As soon as I left the airport I stopped at a diner for breakfast. They were hiring! They hired me immediately on the spot. I begin tomorrow. And get this, the woman working there knew of a place for rent in a nice neighborhood. The house is small but it's just going to be two of us living there. I need to work for at least two weeks and then I think I'll be able to ask for a few days off to go back for Olivia.

Hopefully I'll make enough in tips right off to go get supplies for Olivia. Andrea wants to throw me a baby shower, but I'm hoping to have the baby before then.

I don't know how I'll lie to Andrea about Olivia's age since she's already born and I'm claiming to be pregnant now. I'll just have to play it by ear. Besides I don't care what she thinks. All that matters is that I get Olivia.

Twenty-Three

WHEN I GO DOWNSTAIRS FOR BREAKFAST IN the morning, I'm greeted with a plate full of eggs. There's a little sticky note next to the plate that reads, "Eat Me."

I look over to a grinning Landon. Melissa sets a plate full of ham next to the eggs on the table. "You need your protein for the big game."

Richard is already fixing himself a plate, but he stops to wink at me. I give Melissa a tight hug and then join Richard at the table. Trent, Landon and Denise all come into the kitchen shortly after.

"So, I hear I'm not the only one that's athletically gifted," Trent says through a big smile as he sits next to me.

"Yeah, I hear that Landon is quite fast and Denise is awesome at basketball," I tell him before shoving a forkful of eggs in my mouth.

He laughs, "But what I heard is that you're a beast on the soccer field."

I blush. "Well, rumors spread like wildfire. Also, the more dramatic the better."

He pats me on the shoulder with a chuckle and we all focus on our breakfast.

Landon and Trent get in the Jeep, while the rest of us get in the Lexus. Once we arrive at the soccer field, everyone wishes me luck as I race off to join my team on the field. Some of my teammates are already doing stretches, so I drop my gear by the bench and go join them. As I'm sitting on the ground while holding my toes with my legs straight out, I spot the Wallace family in the bleachers. My heart leaps to my throat. I look around to find the Randall family. They're at the concession stand chatting with other people. I look back to the Wallaces, and we make eye contact. Aunt Andrea looks as though she's about to cry. I wave, and they return the wave. Noah gives me a thumbs up, along with a goofy grin. I see the Randalls making their way to the bleachers. Thankfully, they go to the opposite end. I don't have any more time to worry about those two families crossing paths because the referee comes on to the field. I'm surprised to find out Coach is going to let me start the game.

The first half of the game is intense. It's a more competitive game than what I'm used to. The team we're playing against is from a town that is just a few miles from our town, and even if I hadn't already been warned, I would've immediately picked up on the bitter rivalries they have between each other. By halftime, I'm dripping in sweat but I feel great. I'm proud of myself because I know I had some good tackles. I'm still nervous about whether or not Coach will let me play the second half, though. I'm the newest member on this team with only two weeks' worth of practice. I really want to play, but I know it isn't fair to let me keep playing. I drink my Gatorade and pace around the bench. I'm too worked up to sit. Coach comes to stand in front of us and goes over everything we did right and wrong. She points out the other players' weaknesses and which ones we need to guard better. She calls out everyone's name that needs to get back out on the field, and I'm shocked when I hear her call mine out. I don't hesitate. I'm back in the zone.

The second half is more grueling than the first with more fouls and more determination from each side. A defender on the opposing team comes after me as I'm about to cross the ball in the goalie box. As the ball leaves my foot and rises into the air, she gives me a powerful kick in the shin, causing me to go down. Before the referee even finishes blowing his whistle, I'm back up. I want to go after her because I know that was deliberate since the ball had already left me. She gets a yellow card and we get a penalty kick. I tell Coach I'm still good to play; no way am I letting them take me out. The penalty kick scores us another goal, which ties the game. The other team is pushing hard for another goal, but I keep blocking and kicking the ball back to their half of the field. I kick hard enough to pass the ball across the field to Tara, who is standing in front of the other team's goal. Then, she only has to turn around and kick it in the goal. This is how we scored the majority of our goals in practice, and it works here, breaking the tie and putting us up by one. There are only minutes left in the game. The other team pushes hard but never gets past our defense, until the final seconds of the game. One girl manages to break through and charges. I'm chasing after her and so is one of my other teammates. She kicks. Thank God Jennifer, our goalie, leaps into the air and catches the ball, taking a hard dive to the ground. When I hear the referee blow the final whistle, I almost want to cry. We all run at each other, hugging and jumping up and down.

As I'm jumping up and down, I feel a firm pat on my back. I turn around and find Uncle Brad smiling at me. I throw my arms around him. He pulls away quickly and looks around. Aunt Andrea comes up and hugs me so tightly that I can hardly breathe.

I return the hug with as much enthusiasm. "I've missed you so much!"

She pulls away and looks around also. "We have to go. They can't see us over here behind the crowd. But the team is about to scatter. I love you sweetheart." She gives me another hug and a kiss on the cheek.

She holds my chin between her thumb and index finger. "I'm so proud of you! You played one helluva game. Love you, Luv Bug!"

"I guess I should've been more worried about Eric. You're pretty damn scary and aggressive," Noah says.

I wipe some sweat from my forehead before it gets into my eyes. "I can be," I breathe out.

"Noah, c'mon. We don't want any trouble for Olivia. Especially after her big win. You were the main reason you all won, sweetie. You celebrate today."

Noah chuckles at his mom. "She's your biggest fan. You want to get an autograph real quick?"

"*Noah Wallace.* I said let's go." Aunt Andrea is visibly panicked. She's right, though. No good can come from the Randalls seeing them with me.

Noah gives my arm a gentle squeeze as he turns to walk away. "Good game. See ya Monday."

They hurry off, lost amongst the crowd of other people. I look and see that the Randalls are on the other side of the team searching for me —except Trent. He sees me and probably saw the Wallaces as well. We make eye contact, and he grabs Melissa's arm. She gives him her attention, and he points to me. He could've told them earlier where I was, but I'm so grateful that he didn't. They come rushing toward me cheering.

"Way to go! Atta girl! I'm so proud of you!" they all cheer.

Richard wraps an arm around me, "I'm taking you out for lunch. Let's go to a Taste of Tuscany. It's a nice Italian place."

As soon as we get back home, I go upstairs to get ready for my shopping adventure. It's a bit of a struggle to get up the stairs since I'm so full from the restaurant. Definitely my favorite place to eat. I take a quick shower, and instead of blow drying my hair, I put it in a braid. I choose a light grey sweater dress and boots to wear for the trip. Melissa told me the mall is in the next town a few hours away but it'll be worth the drive.

The mall is two stories tall and filled with high fashion stores. I check the prices of every item before I even consider taking it off the rack. Denise, on the other hand, grabs anything that catches her eye. Melissa assures me to try on anything I like, but I can't in good conscience take anything over two-hundred dollars to the fitting room. That makes this a very difficult task. If this was prom, the prices wouldn't bother me as much. Denise grows impatient with me so she begins picking out dresses for me. Our styles are different in the sense that she likes to show skin, and I'm much more conservative.

The dresses she picks out for me are lovely and stylish. Melissa sits on a couch and admires each dress we try on. Denise decides on an off-the-shoulder, black and white mini knit dress. It's very fitted with contrast, pleated trim and long sleeves with flowy bell cuffs. The dress reminds me of a retro, 60s style that I would look ridiculous in. However, her petite frame and confidence pulls it off. I almost choke when I glance at the price tag. The dress is almost *four-hundred dollars. Why?* It's not even a full dress. Not to mention, the dress is cute but rather plain —no bells or whistles. There's no bling. I can't figure out why this dress costs so much. She seems to love it, though.

When I'm in the dressing room, I decide to not even look at the tags. Melissa and Denise picked out the dresses, anyway. All the dresses are gorgeous. One catches my eye, in particular, because I see the tag has a red sticker so that means its marked down. I didn't think a store like this offered sales. There it is, though. Original price was three-hundred forty-seven dollars and now down to a measly two-hundred seven dollars. This is the one I'm getting. I say a silent prayer that it fits before trying it on.

The dress is a black mini-dress with a smocked, off-the-shoulder neckline; however, it's a little too mini for my taste. I do love the golden embroidery and threading against the black fabric. The top embroidery wraps around the entire dress. It has a vintage, elegant style and almost gives the appearance of a nude look behind the black lace. Thankfully, the dress fits like a glove. I walk out of the dressing room, and they both give praise. Denise suggests I wear pumps with the dress, but I find a pair of black heels that I adore. However, after checking the price, I all but throw the shoes down. Melissa already spotted me eyeing them, so she purchases them anyway.

Denise asks me, "Why are you so weird about prices?"

"Weird?"

"Yeah, it's not that big of a deal. You have to have a new dress and shoes for Homecoming. So *why* are you being weird about Mom buying them?"

"I don't have to have shoes that expensive. There's shoes just as pretty, only cheaper."

Denise rolls her eyes. "Cheaper price means cheaper quality. They may look pretty but your feet won't after hours of dancing." Then she speaks in a softer tone and leans closer to me. "Just let Mom spoil you a little. Enjoy it. She does." A huge smile spreads across her face. "I know I do!" She takes the bags of merchandise and does a little dance.

Am I being weird? If I'd grown up the same way as Denise, would I be more like her? Or would I still be more price savvy and a conservative shopper?

Melissa thanks the sales clerk again and then turns to smile at us, "My beautiful girls. You'll make these dresses look good. Whew. All that made me work up an appetite. Shall we?"

Denise loops her arm through mine and leads me out of the store. "Let's go eat!"

Twenty-Four

WHEN WE ARRIVE BACK TO THE HOUSE THAT evening, Denise and I join Landon and Trent in the den.

"Why don't you guys ever sit in the living room?" I look around and notice this room is not nearly as grand as their living room.

Trent is leaning back with his feet on the coffee table flipping through the channels. He doesn't take his eyes off the television as he says, "It's too stuffy and so much open space. We can relax in here."

I can't argue with that. I prefer this room myself. He stops flipping through the channels when he finds an action movie. We all sit together in a comfortable silence watching the movie. After a while, Denise yawns and heads upstairs.

Landon's phone dings. He spends a few minutes texting someone.

Finally, he leans over and lightly slaps Trent on the chest. "Hey, can you cover for me, man?"

Trent crosses his arms and narrows his eyes. "Depends."

His brother spreads his arms wide open and grins. "C'mon brother, just cover for me. I won't be out too late."

Trent doesn't respond right away. He rubs his chin, mulling it over. Landon's knee starts bouncing up and down as he stares at him. Growing impatient, Landon leans back and lets out a grunt. "Man, I've covered for you. You did crazy shit while you were a senior —worse than anything I'm wanting to get into. I guarantee it." He leans forward and emphasizes each word, "Guaran-freaking-tee it."

Trent rolls his head over toward him. "Who are you running around with tonight? And where?"

Landon runs his hand down his face. "You've gotten *so* uptight this year." He sees the seriousness on Trent's face and holds his hands up. "Alright, fair enough. I'm going out with Eric and the guys. I think Rachel's parents are going to be out of town, so some of us are going over there to chill."

For the first time, they seem to remember I'm still in the room.

Landon looks over to me. "Wanna come with? Travel further into the rabbit hole little Alice?"

Eric's going to be there? That's a hard no for me. I shake my head and feign being tired.

"Sure? You can hang out with Rachel." A thought occurs to him, and he turns back to look at Trent with a mischievous grin. "Or maybe *you* want to hang out with Rachel."

Okay, clearly there is something between Rachel and Trent.

"I feel out of the loop. It's probably none of my business, but...what's the deal with Rachel?"

Trent gives nothing away and casually replies, "What do you mean?"

I laugh and look at him like it's obvious. "Um, she asks about you all the time. You avoid any topic that has to do with her. And just now, Landon clearly implied you might want to spend time with her. Something is going on."

Landon looks amused at Trent, who is uncomfortable. We sit in silence until Trent realizes nobody is willing to budge. He clasps his hands. "Alright," he nods his head up and down, "you want to know what happened?" He looks back and forth between us. "Here's why I'm more uptight and concerned for you, Landon." He points a finger at me. "Take note as well, Sarah."

"Last year, while home visiting, I went to one of the house parties. I was careless and drank too much. It's not like it was the first time or anything. But, this time was different because I did sleep with Rachel." He bows his head and rubs his forehead. He groans and then continues, "It's not like it was my first time sleeping with someone. It certainly wasn't my first time sleeping with someone while drunk. It was, though, hers. I…" he takes a deep breath and looks at us, "I didn't know she was a virgin. She seemed so…she didn't give any signs…shit I don't know. I didn't realize it until we'd finished."

Landon, clearly disgusted, shakes his head. "Shit man, I didn't know that part of the story. Well, I only heard rumors that y'all hooked up. Neither one of you ever confirmed nor denied it. And afterwards?"

Trent's eyes are full of regret. "I was drunk! I was a complete and total dick. I got mad at her for not telling me because I wouldn't have slept with her. Even if I was drunk, I would've had enough damn sense to not go there. Then she told me that she *loved me*." Trent looks as though he's about to throw up. "It got crazy. She started spewing all kinds of feelings, loving me for years, and finally we were together. Then I realized that she was *sober*. I-I didn't know she had a crush on me. I thought we were both on the same page that it was going to be a casual hook up."

Landon looks pissed at this point. "We've known her forever. How did you not know she was obsessed with you? Is that what you think I'm doing? Unlike *you*, I'm not a total ass."

Trent rolls his eyes at Landon. "Like none of us screw around with friends?"

I'm mortified. My friends didn't sleep with each other. This seems weird and gross to me. Maybe I am too uptight, but I can't imagine a life of casual sex. However, it seems that incident changed Trent. Landon seems so upset with his brother for how he treated Rachel. I wonder if he has a thing for her. *Interesting.*

"Anyways, thanks for the advice. Don't be a dick, got it. Are you going to cover for me or what?" He gives his brother a hard look.

Trent nods. "Yeah."

Landon doesn't sit there a second longer. He pushes himself off the couch as he asks me if I'm going with him. I shake my head.

His eyes are hard as he glares at Trent. Then he offers me a tight smile. "Well, I'm late for a very important date." He gives me a small wave as he heads out the door.

Trent sighs and puts his head in his hands. I feel sorry for him because this seems to be eating away at him.

"Have you apologized to Rachel?" I tentatively ask.

He doesn't look at me. "I've tried, but it's so awkward whenever we do cross paths. Whenever I bring it up, she abruptly changes the subject. I feel like I can't fully apologize because she doesn't see how wrong the whole situation was. I'm so ashamed. She was sixteen at the time."

I stare blankly at him.

"The worst part is she still has a thing for me. I wasn't thinking when I…" he raises his head up to look at me, "I was selfish and a jerk. I'll never be that person again because I do care for Rachel *as a friend.* I've known her since we were kids."

He goes on to explain how that's why he barely drinks now and doesn't sleep around anymore. I can't help but feel at least some good came out of the incident.

Trent raises up and sighs. "It seems I'm determined to hurt this family."

"*What?*"

"I hate when Landon's mad at me. And I knew—I fucking *knew*—sleeping with Rachel would hurt him worse than anything. But I did anyways. Rachel is a part of this family too. She's grown up with us. I can't believe I did that."

"You didn't do it to deliberately hurt them though, right?"

"No. But I knew it would, so what does it matter the why of it?"

"It matters."

"Well, I didn't mean to be a distraction and run off so you could get kidnapped, but does that matter? You still got taken. Because of *me*."

"You were a child. A toddler, for crying out loud. Stop with the self-guilt. I'm sure Landon will forgive you and I forgive you. I know Rachel has already forgiven you because she's in love with you."

"She needs to stop. It's never going to happen."

"Why?"

"I made a mistake the first time with her, Sarah. I can't do that again. She's too young. She always has and always will be Landon's girl. I know they're back and forth a lot but that doesn't mean I should just swoop in. I think she has a crush. Once she got me, she wouldn't want me."

"Why do you say that?"

"Why would she? I'm bound to hurt her, and I couldn't live with myself if I hurt Rachel. I already have once out of a moment of weakness. I'm tired of letting the people I love down."

He flips through the channels until he finds a *Friends* marathon. Unsure where to go from that conversation, we fall into silence while watching television. After a couple of moments, we're lost in the show and laughing. Finally, we transition into idle chit chat, but for the most part, we sit in a comfortable silence.

When it starts to become difficult to keep my eyes open, I yawn. As I'm standing, Trent stops me, "Before you go to bed…"

I sit back down and give him my full attention. The way he says it makes me become wide awake and alert.

"…I was wondering if you have a date for homecoming?" He is completely serious when he says this. *Is he offering to escort me?*

I can't help it, but a laugh escapes me. "No…are you offering to be my escort?"

He gives me a half-hearted smile. "No, but I don't like the way Eric was behaving last night. I know guys like him, and I know him. I have a buddy that goes to the private school. Monday, sign him up as your date in the office."

I'm so confused. And slightly annoyed. "I don't understand…Let's back up for a second." I point at him. "You seem to think I need a date for homecoming because Eric was creeping around my room?"

He nods.

"I can handle myself."

"What's wrong with me finding you a date?"

"Because I don't need you to find me a date. Am I going on your resume as another charity work?"

"No, my plan-"

"Your plan is to have one of your friends be my date? Let's also note that you weren't the best type of guy, so I'm gonna guess you hang out with similar guys. So, we're going to substitute one creep for another? No offense." I give him a sideways look and raise my eyebrows. "Do you see how I'm struggling to understand where you're coming from? Also, what do you mean by 'sign him up in the office'?"

He actually gives a half-hearted chuckle. "Good points there. First off, anybody that comes from another school needs to be signed in at the office before the dance. The school likes to have time to call the other school and check them out beforehand. Next, Eric isn't the type to back off. He's going to be creeping around you throughout the whole dance. I don't want you to have a bad time. I also don't want Eric to lay on the charm and you fall for it." He notices the look on my face and chuckles again. "Something tells me his charm won't work on you, though. Anyways, he would definitely back off if he thought Luke was talking to you. And, I need this. It would make me feel a lot better since I can't be there."

I assume Luke is the potential date. A date would be nice I guess, especially one with no expectations attached to it. It seems everyone that I hang out with has a date, so this would prevent me from being the third wheel. What bothers me is that he thinks I can't handle Eric on my own. I know I can handle Eric, but I'm going to agree to Luke being my date since I'd like a date with no strings attached. It's a win for both of us. I let him know as much. I almost wonder if this is why Trent has been coming home so often. Is he trying to make up for my kidnapping? I'll ask Landon tomorrow if this is normally how often he comes home.

I almost bend down to hug him, but I stop myself. Instead I give a little wave and say goodnight. I don't know why I waved, that was probably more awkward than the hug.

With that awkward note, I scurry out of the room. I'm so exhausted that I don't even bother brushing my teeth or reading any journal entries.

Twenty-Five

THE SCHOOL IS FILLED WITH ENERGY ON Monday. It's homecoming week. It's homecoming week back in Colorado as well. Angie messaged me telling me that Aaron Lancaster is taking *her* to homecoming. I'm so excited for her—not jealous at all. I'm happy. Yes, I'm happy that my best friend is getting to go to homecoming with my crush. Not like he could take me, right? So, she should definitely go. I'm so lost in my thoughts when I get to my first hour class that I didn't even notice that Noah had been walking next to me.

I'm startled when he greets me, causing him to laugh. "You were in such a hurry to see me that you didn't even notice me? I'm flattered, Liv."

Liv. He calls me "Liv" when it's just us. I love it. I don't exactly know why I love that he calls me by that name, but I get a rush of excitement every time. I look into his gorgeous blue eyes...*Wait.* When did his eyes get so gorgeous? There's little specks of different shades of blue and even a little green. His lashes are so long and his dark eyebrows emphasize the light color of his eyes. I feel warmth spread to my cheeks and feel little butterfly flutters in my stomach. I shake my head. No. *No. This is Noah.* I'm being so weird right now.

"Um," I quickly avert my eyes from his face and slide into my desk. I pick at the corner of my notebook. "How was your weekend?"

"I went to a party and just hung out with friends."

I perk up and look over at him. "At Rachel's?"

His eyebrows raise in surprise. "Yeah."

I nod and smile. "Landon went too."

"Yeah, um, I saw him. We didn't hang out any though." He looks down and taps his pencil against the desk. "You should've come."

A little part of me kind of wishes I had gone now. *Maybe next time I will.*

"I have a date for Homecoming."

"*Really?*"

I release a chuckle. "Don't sound so surprised."

"I am. I mean, not because—it's just you just got here. I guess I shouldn't be since…" He shakes his head and gives me a shy smile. "Who's the lucky guy?"

"One of Trent's friends. Luke Jamerson." I notice his demeanor immediately changes. His jaw hardens, and his body becomes stiff. "I assume you know Luke."

"He's an alright guy, I guess. Extremely cocky and stuck up, but since he's doing Trent's bidding, he'll be on his best behavior with you. Hopefully."

I smile, but he still doesn't seem at ease. "Then why are you still upset?"

He tries to tell me it's nothing, but I push.

Finally, he sighs, "I guess I'm nervous he'll be taken with you and forget he's only there to be a guard dog."

I think about it for a moment. It's interesting that he doesn't want anything more to happen from this date. *Is it because it's Luke or would he feel this way about anybody? If it were any other guy, I'd think he was jealous and wanted to date me. If Noah could take me to the dance, would he?* I pause my rambling thoughts a moment and stare at Noah's handsome face. *Where did that come from? Noah taking me out on a date?* I feel myself blush at the thought and decide to focus back on Luke. *What if Luke is cute, sweet and nice? Maybe I'll want him to like me.*

"So, what if he does? I haven't met him yet, but I don't know. I might want this Luke character to be 'taken with me,' as you put it." I tease him but he isn't finding any humor in this.

His only response is to shake his head. I decide to let it go and change the subject to his mom. "I wish I could visit Aunt Andrea."

"It'd be so much easier if you had a car. We plan a trip to the store. Tell them you're used to going shopping by yourself. Surely, they'll understand and respect that," he offers.

The bell rings dismissing class and I tell him I'll try to figure out a way to gain private access to a vehicle.

I open my locker door but it immediately slams back shut. Stunned, I stare at the perfectly manicured slender hand holding my door shut. Karlie Snyder leans her shoulder against my locker door and tilts her pretty blond head. "Listen, I don't know who you think you are, but I've been patient with you since you're new and all. That ends today, though. So, to avoid any confusion, I'm gonna lay it out for you—Noah Wallace is off limits."

"I'm sorry but—"

"I don't think you are sorry, but you will be. Your deer in the headlight, sweet homegirl from Colorado routine isn't going to work with me." I open my mouth but she holds a hand up. "We're done. I don't want to hear another word out of you, especially to Noah."

And with that, she spins around slinging her blond ponytail in my face and walks off.

What. A. Bitch.

As I sit across from Rita, I can't help but be more annoyed. *Why me?* Why does every aspect of my life have to be so confusing and complicated? Why am I seventeen and in therapy already?

"Care to share your thoughts? You look like you're concentrating hard over something."

I turn my head to meet her eyes. "How long do I have to come here?"

"As long as you want."

"Really?"

She smiles. "Yes. I'm here to try and help you, Sarah."

"Help me what? How are you going to help me? There's a girl now at my school who hates me simply because Noah is being nice to me. Every time one good thing happens something bad follows."

"I can't stop the girl from bullying you, but I can help you work through your feelings. Help you with how you respond. I can also just be someone you talk and vent to. Does Noah know how this girl is treating you?"

"Somewhat. I'm not sure he knows how psycho she is. My best friend is going to Homecoming with my crush. I'd hoped that would've been me. I feel betrayed even though that's stupid because it's not like I could've gone."

"Your feelings are not stupid. You liked this person and the person you trusted is now going with them. It's okay to be upset. Don't downplay your feelings. Don't treat your feelings as though they're not important."

"Aaron would've gone with Olivia. She's gone. I'm Sarah."

"You're you. He would've gone with *you*. Have you still been drawing?"

"Not much."

"Draw me something. Next week."

"What do you want?"

"Anything."

⌇

While sitting at supper, everyone shares tidbits of their news. I've been content to listen and enjoy my meal.

"Sarah, how's school?" Melissa takes a bite of salad.

"Good. It's really going well." I take a sip of my water to hopefully gives someone a chance to jump in on the conversation.

"Rachel got the position for yearbook editor." Landon never fails to step in.

Melissa beams. "I'm so proud of her. She's such a dedicated and hardworking young lady."

Denise rolls her eyes. "Is she only doing this to make sure y'all are on every single page?"

Landon chuckles. "That, and to ensure an embarrassing photo of Karlie is published." I can't help but grin. Landon catches me and nudges me with his shoulder. Melissa doesn't miss the exchange.

"Karlie? Is she still being rude to you, sweetheart?"

"Oh no. Everything is cool between us." *If you don't count her slamming my locker door and threatening me to not speak to Noah.*

Denise scoffs. "Yeah, right. I'm in junior high and even I've heard that she has a mark on your head." Landon shoots her a scowl but she ignores him. "Everyone knows that even though they're not a couple, she's claimed Noah as hers."

The clanking of Melissa's fork dropping to her plate is the only sound. She exchanges a look with Richard. Landon shoots daggers at his baby sister. Denise shrugs and goes back to eating.

Melissa clears her throat. "I'm afraid I'm struggling to keep up. What does Karlie liking Noah have to do with Sarah?"

Landon starts to speak but Denise beats him to it. "She's convinced Sarah is after Noah. Apparently, he's like extra sweet to her something. Completely ignores Karlie if Sarah is in the room." Denise turns to me and gives me a smile like I deserve a high five. I want to crawl under the table.

I turn to Denise. "How—how do you, um, who told you this?" I look to everyone at the table. "Noah is just a friend. Ha. He doesn't like me like that." I don't know if I can say the same for me. I hope nobody can read through me, I'd be mortified. *What would Aunt Andrea think if she thought I liked her son? Can Karlie read through me?*

Denise rolls her eyes. "Karlie's cousin is in my grade, April Snyder. She said Karlie has been complaining about you."

"Sarah?"

I turn to look at Richard's questioning face. "Noah's being extra nice because… I think it's a misunderstanding since people don't know our history."

Melissa frantically shakes her head. "There's no history between you two. Not really. I was afraid he'd cause trouble."

"Mom," Landon's tone is pleading. "It's Karlie. She's obsessed with the guy. If he even acknowledges a cat over her, she'd lose it."

I frown at him and he gives me a sheepish smile. "Bad example? Sorry."

Denise, Landon, and I start laughing. Soon Richard and Melissa join us. Denise begins discussing a jacket she saw online.

It's Landon and Denise's turn to wash dishes so I go on up to my room. I finish some homework and then decide to go ahead and go to bed.

After tossing and turning for about an hour, I finally throw off the covers. I slide out of bed and go downstairs for a glass water. I creep downstairs, not wanting to disturb anyone. I tip toe into the kitchen and open the cabinet. I pause when I hear a voice.

"You were determined to have her part of your family, weren't you?" she slurs.

My stomach drops. *Oh no.* I ease further toward the other end of the room toward the voice. It's dark in the house but not pitch black. I see a lamp on in the living room. I peak my head around the doorframe to find Melissa on the phone. I have no idea who she's talking to, but my heart rate picks up.

"She. Is. My. Daughter. And no matter what you do or how much you try, she'll never be yours. She's mine!" Melissa is slurring, but her words carry a punch with the venom she spews in them. "*Olivia?* That'll never be her name. It's a nickname. You sent your sneaky, no good son after her. She is vulnerable and confused! He swoops in and charms her."

I turn back into the kitchen and slide down the wall, falling onto the floor. I lay my head into my hands to try and stifle my cries. My shoulders shake uncontrollably. I'm so emotional with my loss of Cindy, my loss of everything I thought I knew, and now I may lose what I have with Andrea and Noah. I thought we were moving forward. I don't want to keep being reminded that the Wallaces are supposed to be my enemies when I don't feel that way. I don't want to keep being in the middle of this battle between Melissa and Cindy. Cindy's gone. The battle should be over. I don't hear what else she says. I can't hear over my own cries and screams inside my head.

I feel strong arms wrap around me and envelope me in warmth. It's Landon. I sink in and momentarily calm down. He whispers words of comfort in my ear. I cry harder. My body is beginning to hurt, and I'm sure there are no tears left. Eventually, I black out.

When I wake up, I'm in my bed. My head hurts, probably from all the crying. Melissa is never going to move past her grudge. I don't blame her, honestly. However, this isn't the life I want to live.

I check the clock and it's four in the morning. At this point, I don't know if I have the strength or motivation to care. I decide to read until it's time to get ready for school.

I finally get to the journal entry of the day of my kidnapping. I get chills as I read.

Twenty-Six

April 18

It's been a year since Michael and I decided to separate. A lot can happen. I was at my lowest—but today, I feel at my highest. Here's what happened:

I wore a straight, blonde wig that I had used for a 70s costume, big sunglasses, and for added detail, I drew on a mole. I had never been so nervous in all my life. I almost turned and walked back to the car. When you want something, though, you must go for it. My Olivia was within reach. They always like to go for a walk in the park. I watch them leave the house. I circled around to make sure they were alone. I park the car behind some trees a little distance from the park.

I jog back to the park, terrified I'd miss them. When I see them in the distance, I begin walking and looking around frantically. Melissa looks perfect of course. My resolve becomes even stronger in the moment I take in her perfectly styled hair, nice designer clothes—that are ironed, and she's wearing makeup that makes her face appear flawless. How does she have the time and energy to look so amazing with young kids?

I'd never call myself an actress, but I have to brag and say I nailed my prepared speech. I gave real tears when I told her my puppy had gotten loose and was lost.

Of course Trent went crazy excited when he heard the word puppy. They said they hadn't seen him but would help me keep an eye out. I pretended to see something by the bushes near the road and as predicted, sweet Trent took off toward the road… right when a car was turning onto it. Melissa screamed his name and chased after him.

Leaving me alone with the perfect opportunity.

I picked Olivia up as gently as possible and wrapped the blanket in the stroller around her. I heard the car honk and could hear Melissa scolding Trent, her voice full of worry and fear. He kept shouting back at her worried about the lost puppy. So worried about saving the missing puppy.

Once I had Olivia securely wrapped and in my arms—I ran. I ran as fast as I could. Of course, the jarring motions startled her. But I continued in a hard run. I'd almost made it through the tree line when I heard Melissa's screams. I knew I didn't have much time before she gathered her wits enough to call the police. I didn't even strap the baby in the car seat. I held her in one arm and drove the car with the other. It was extremely unsafe, but I panicked and did not want to get caught.

Once I got outside city limits, I pulled over and strapped her in her seat. I had grabbed her favorite toy when I grabbed her so I handed it to her and it seemed to soothe her. After 20 mins of driving she dozed back off.

For the first hour of driving, my heart beat so fast in my chest that I wasn't sure I'd survive it. I kept thinking that any minute, I'd see sirens in my rearview mirror. Any minute, we'd get pulled over. I needed to use the restroom, but I wouldn't stop until I cleared the state line. At one point I had to pee so bad that I just pulled over, went around the side of the car, popped a squat and got back on the road. It was a miracle the baby slept so well. We were able to drive three hours before she woke up. I'd already packed baby food so I fed her and changed her diaper in the car. I drove another three hours before we stopped at a hotel. That's where we are now.

I can't believe it. I'm so excited, scared, anxious, overjoyed, and a bundle of emotions. I'm a mother! I finally have my baby girl! My Olivia. I'm Olivia's <u>mother</u>!

Twenty-Seven

I SIT THERE AND TRY TO IMAGINE ALL THIS. The part about Melissa's screams gives me chills. I can't imagine how she must've felt when she saw a stranger running off with her baby. The helplessness. She was trying to help her! And she had to save her son! The woman I knew that raised me would not have been so cruel. She stole her baby right out from under her nose. My mother would've never purposefully endangered the life of another child. Would she? Reading this from Cindy's own account does make me more compassionate toward Melissa. I should've been more understanding toward her before. After all, it was her baby that was kidnapped. Melissa had her baby kidnapped under her nose while trying to prevent her son from being hit by a car. She lived her life never knowing what happened to me. She probably lived with fear of losing her other children since it happened so easily with me. Melissa has been a victim through all this. Regrettably, I could never see it that way.

My eyes begin to feel heavy. I set my alarm to wake me just in case I sleep hard. My last thought before falling to sleep is, *I'm going to make sure to give Melissa an extra long hug at breakfast.*

The next morning, I go downstairs for breakfast. No one acknowledges what happened last night. I wonder if Landon talked to Melissa, but everyone seems normal. He watches me with a concerned look in his eyes. However, he merely asks me how I am, leaving it at that. Before I leave for school, I do wrap Melissa in a strong hug. I don't say anything, I just hug her.

I text Noah good morning and ask how his night went. He never mentions anything about Melissa calling Andrea in any of his texts. He doesn't say anything about it at school, either. However, I know he knows she did and probably knows what she said. I can see the worry in his eyes when I pass him in the hall. Then in class he looks at me with caution and concern. I decide since he isn't bringing it up, then neither will I. No good can come from discussing it. What's done is done, and it's not like Melissa's feelings toward Andrea are a secret. It's not going to change anytime soon, either.

Twenty-Eight

I DON'T SEE NOAH AS I'M WALKING OUT OF THE school. Landon and Rachel are standing by the steps, so I stop next to Landon. It's the big Homecoming game tonight. This is an event not only for the school, but the entire town it seems. Rachel and Landon fill me in that everyone, literally everyone, goes to the game so everyone dresses their best when they know they're going to be seen.

"Most women use the bleachers as their big runway moment."

"Runway?" My eyebrows pinch together.

Landon stares at me wide-eyed. "Fashion runway. You'll see." He chuckles. "You'll see."

Rachel slides a little closer to me and Landon. "Is y'alls brother coming?"

Landon rolls his eyes. "I'm done. It's time to go home."

Rachel grabs his arm. "C'mon. Tell me. Will he be at the game?"

"You'll be cheering so what does it matter? Not like you can sit with him." Rachel pouts her lips. "Yes, Rach. You know he *always* comes back for Homecoming." Landon turns to me. "It's a reminder of how great he once was."

"And still is," Rachel hurries to say. "Nobody has yet to beat his score."

"Oh yes, Madame President from the Trent Randall fan club Chapter One. You should write his biography. Tales from a lovesick fool."

Rachel flips Landon off and we all laugh.

Trent did come back for Homecoming, and he brought a girl from college with him. Her name is Maggie Tyson, and she's extremely beautiful. She looks like she was Photoshopped, and my heart hurts for Rachel. I know she'll see them at the game. I desperately wished Maggie was hideous, or at least of average beauty so it wouldn't be such a hard blow for Rachel.

Denise suggests wearing something cute but warm for the game. She waggles her eyebrows at me. "Tomorrow night you'll wear that super hot dress. Luke will probably devour you before you even make it to the dance."

Denise's date, Clint, and Luke arrive at about the same time. Luke is beautiful. I normally wouldn't describe a guy as beautiful, but he is. He has short, sandy blonde hair, bright blue eyes with a hint of green, a tan, bright white, beautiful smile, and strong, masculine facial features, and he's clearly a football player. He's wearing jeans that are not fitted but hug his legs in all the right places. The black button up dress shirt he has on stretches over his broad chest and arms.

He greets me with a warm hug, and his voice is strong and deep. "Sarah! Pleasure to finally meet you."

He smells divine. I'm completely smitten with him. He does that half hug thing that guys do with Trent. Everyone else gets a nod or handshake for a greeting. Landon comes downstairs to join us.

"Landon, is Rachel not going to stop by before going to the game?" Melissa looks around.

Landon gives Trent the side eye, but then he smiles at Melissa. "She's there. She had to be there early since she's cheering."

"Well I wanted some photos of all you kids together."

Landon groans. "Mom, we still have the dance tomorrow. We can take photos then."

A sad looks passes over Melissa's face. "You can never take too many photos, son. Every moment is precious."

Landon nods and stands next to me. Melissa takes a few photos of all of us before we leave. Landon gives Luke a snarl and then tells us he'll meet us at the game. I wonder what Landon's *obvious* issue is with Luke as we walk out to the car. I make a mental note to ask him about it tonight after the game.

When Luke and I are settled in the backseat of Trent's SUV, he whispers in my ear, "You look amazing."

I'm only wearing jeans and a cute sweater, but I give him a shy smile. "So do you." He winks at me and takes my hand in his.

When we arrive at the football field, we find the bleachers are packed. Luckily, Trent knows someone who waves for us to join them at the top. I'm really excited for the game since Noah is playing. I read the program they gave us at the gate entrance with everyone's numbers so I scan the field for #24. I can't help but notice Eric is #31 since he's listed close to Noah's name. I find him on the field as well. I won't deny that I thoroughly enjoy seeing Eric get tackled.

I scan the cheerleaders to look for Rachel. I spot her and wave. She shakes her poms poms in the air. Emily does an amazing backflip and I cheer loudly for her. I spot Karlie front and center. I squint harder at her and notice, along with her excessive makeup and glitter, she has #24 painted on her cheek. I frown and narrow my eyes at her. Then I scan the field for our mutual favorite player.

My eyes follow Noah as he plays hard. I get lost in the game and begin cheering openly for him.

"Quite the football fan. You'll have to come to some of my games. I'd love to have someone so enthusiastic cheering me on."

I blush at Luke. "I'd love to come to a game. What's your number?" My eyes go wide. "I mean-" I let out an embarrassed laugh. "Your jersey number. So, I'll know who to cheer the loudest for." *Not much better.*

He gives my knee a little bump with his. "My jersey number is eight."

The game only has a few minutes left when Trent surprises me by telling the group he wants to introduce me to someone. He tells them if we're not back by the end of the game, we'll meet them back at the car.

"Who is it we're meeting?" I'm practically running to keep up with his long strides as he leads me toward the locker rooms.

He smiles. "One of the players."

I gasp. "What?" *Could it be Noah? Even if not him, I might still get a chance to see him.* I can't stop the smile that stretches my face. "Why?"

He stops and turns to me. "Sarah, I know this is hard for you. I love my—*our*—parents, but they go about some things the wrong way. Like this. Noah didn't have anything to do with what happened. If y'all get along, why not let him help make this transition a little easier?" He shrugs again. "I saw how excited you were with our team winning. It wasn't because of your school spirit. I figured that you'd want to get a chance to congratulate him."

I throw my arms around him and force the tears to stay at bay. "Thank you so much," I whisper into his neck.

He holds me and pats my back. "That's what brothers are for, right?"

We hear the buzzer, and the crowd goes wild. He pulls me over to the gym entrance, where we see the mob of red jerseys heading our way. I'm bouncing up and down as I spot Noah, dirty and sweaty carrying his helmet. He looks momentarily stunned to find me there with Trent. I wave, and he continues toward us.

"Good game."

He gives a light laugh but still looks uneasily at Trent. But Trent surprises us when he holds his hand out. "Good game, man."

Noah shifts his helmet to his other hand and shakes his hand.

"You were great!" I blush at my outburst. I smile and in a more controlled voice tell Noah, "I'm so proud of you."

He looks a little embarrassed and waves my compliment off. "Nah, but thank you." We have a moment of smiling at each other, when suddenly Noah frowns. "Where's Luke?"

Trent answers, "They're back at the bleachers, or maybe the car by now. You'll see him at the dance. He's escorting Sarah." As Trent finishes the sentence like no big deal, I think he's oblivious to how everyone seems to snarl about Luke.

He nods his head and clenches his jaw. "So I heard. I gotta go shower, but thanks again guys."

As he passes me, he whispers, "You look very pretty, Liv."

We walk back to the car to find the rest of our group with some new additions standing around laughing. Luke turns toward me and casually throws his arm across my shoulders. He easily guides me farther into the group. Trent wraps both of his arms around Maggie's waist. I glance over to Rachel to see her slap Landon on the chest and nod toward the other end of the parking lot.

Landon announces to the group, "See you guys later. We're heading out."

"Wanna hang out at the house?" Trent calls out to Landon.

Landon looks back at Rachel and then to Trent. "Nah, I think we might catch a late movie. See ya." He takes Rachel's hand and they walk away, turning into dark shadows in the scarcely lit parking lot.

Luke whispers into my ear, "What about you? What are your plans tonight?"

I shrug and smile, honestly not sure.

"Well, you could invite me over, and we hang out with your brother. I mean, Trent already invited me over, but I'd feel more welcomed if you did. It would be more like you wanted to hang out with me, rather than Trent." He gives me a shy smile.

I look up at him and bite my bottom lip. "What's wrong with being invited by Trent?"

He removes his arm from my shoulder and shoves his hands into his pockets. It's not well lit in the parking lot, but I think he's blushing. "It's always better to have a pretty girl invite you over rather than a big, hairy guy."

I laugh. "Trent's not hairy."

He gives a low chuckle and then smiles sweetly at me. "I guess he isn't that hairy. But he is big. And you are pretty. So most of it was true."

I hope he can't see me blushing as I squeak out, "Luke, would you like to come hang out at the house with me and my big, not-so-hairy brother Trent?"

"Wow, thanks for the invitation. I'd love to but I have plans."

I scoff and smack his arm. He grabs my hand. "I'm kidding! Please forgive me. I couldn't resist. Hey, let me make it up to you. I'll buy us a pizza."

"Pizza? Where'd that come from?"

"I'm hungry. Figured you might be too, so it's a win win. And everybody likes pizza."

Trent walks over to us with his arms still around Maggie. "I'm hungry too. I didn't catch all that conversation but I did hear Luke's buying pizza. Let's go."

Once we've all climbed into the SUV, Luke calls and places an order for five pizzas for pick up. By the time we get across town to pick up the pizzas, they're ready. The hairs on my arm stand up when I see the name. *Tony's*. This is where Cindy had worked. Luke waves his hand in front of my face. "Hey. Where'd you go?"

I smile and shake my head. "Lost in thought."

"Don't tell me you're already planning out to ditch me?"

I smile. "Not yet."

He grins and my heart skips a beat. "Alright then. Let's take these pizzas and see if I can keep you interested in me."

"The pizzas will definitely help."

Laughing, he grabs the pizza and I follow him out.

When we finally pull into the driveway back home, I realize why he ordered five. Two other cars are already there. We go inside to find a few more of their friends sitting in the den. We eat pizza and watch movies until one in the morning. Landon still hadn't come home. I'm too tired to sit up for him. I send him a text to make sure he's okay before going to sleep. He replied instantly that he's been doing the same thing we're doing…except at Rachel's house.

꿏

After lunch the next day, Denise and I go to the salon for hair and make-up. In the past, I'd always done my own hair and make-up for events. It's nice to get pampered for a change.

Denise is sitting in the salon chair next to me and we're both being laid back to get our eyebrows waxed. She's very particular how she wants them waxed.

"I want to keep them slightly thick. Just the strays on the bottom and maybe a little off on the ends. But keep my arch. I need an arch." Then in a hushed tone I hear her say, "And don't forget the middle." She points between her eyebrows. I smile to myself. She's so self-conscious. I don't think I was that insecure in junior high. Yet, she has nothing to be insecure over. She's Denise Randall. Beautiful, stylish, intelligent, and has everything she could want in life.

I relax as I feel the paper being pressed firmly to the wax. *Riiiiiip. Ow!* I flinch but hold back a yelp.

"Isabelle told me that her brother *really* likes you."

"Who's Isabelle?"

She huffs and groans. "Luke's little sister! Duh!"

I feel the rip and screech. "*Luke!*"

She giggles. "Yes! Luke Jamerson is into you!"

I raise up and stare at her. "He barely knows me. Are you sure?"

If Isabelle is anything like Denise, she's probably overreacting. Denise raises up as well. We face each other and try to stifle giggles at our red blotches around our eyebrows.

We are led to chairs in front of large mirrors. We take our seats and they begin brushing our hair. I look at Denise's reflection in the mirror as she answers me.

"Isabelle and I were chatting on the phone and she said Luke has *never* acted this way. He's so pumped for your date tonight."

"I don't think it's really a *date* per say. He's acting on Trent's behalf."

Denise casually shrugs as her hair is styled. "Maybe that's how it started, but I doubt that's how it is *now*."

"You think Luke thinks this is a date?"

She gives me a mischievous smile. "One can only hope, right?"

"How does everyone know Luke so well if he goes to a different school?"

"He *used* to go to the same school as us. His younger sister still goes to public. Luke transferred in high school for sports and better opportunities for colleges. Trent should've done that but there's no telling Trent anything. He liked where he was."

Denise turns her attention from me to offer plenty of suggestions to the hair stylist. I smile at her because even as she's somewhat bossy she still comes off adorable. It's part of her charm.

⁂

We go back to the house so we can put on our dresses. I'm still nervous about wearing mine because it's more revealing than what I'm used to.

We hear the doorbell and my heart flutters. I had a really nice time with Luke yesterday. I'm also a little nervous that this will be the first time I'll be alone with him, even if it's only for the short car rides. I'm riding with Luke in his car since after dinner, we're all going to separate places. Trent and Maggie are joining us for dinner, but can't join us at the dance. Denise and Clint will be going to the middle school building. Denise isn't thrilled that Trent is acting as a chaperone on our dinner date, but I'm relieved. I'm pretty sure Denise doesn't want me at her dinner date, either. But once again, I'm relieved because the more the merrier.

⁂

When we arrive at the dance, all eyes are on us. Luke, apparently, is quite the heartthrob around here. Even though he attends a different school, he's still well known. He excuses himself to run to the restroom, leaving me standing alone. Noah saunters over to me, and he looks quite handsome. He's similarly dressed as Luke. However, his outfit is not the high fashion designer brands. He looks like he should be on the cover of a magazine, nonetheless.

He gulps and clears his throat, "Um, wow."

I give a nervous laugh. "I know right? Everyone is staring." I lightly slap his chest. "Thanks for warning me that Luke draws attention whenever he enters a room."

Noah purses his lips together and shakes his head. "I'm afraid you're mistaken as to why everyone's staring. Have you looked in the mirror this evening?"

I raise my hand to my face and look down at my dress. *Did I spill something? Do I have toilet paper on my shoe?*

"Did I spill something? Is my dress tucked into my underwear? Quick, tell me. This is embarrassing." I panic as I keep examining myself.

Noah touches my arm to get my attention. I stop and meet his eyes.

He gives me a boyish grin. "You look incredible. I mean, I don't think anyone can keep from staring." He loses his grin and becomes somber. "Luke's a lucky guy." He turns his eyes away from me to stare out into the dance floor. "He's here with the most beautiful girl in the room."

My heart skips a beat, and I throw my arms around him. "Thank you, Noah. You always come to the rescue to put me at ease." He hesitantly wraps his arms around me. I sigh and relax further in his embrace. His hold becomes more firm. Something shifts between us. I hold him tighter, and his hand travels to the small of my back.

"May I cut in," a deep voice cuts through our trance.

I look up and smile at Luke. Noah reluctantly releases me and tells me he'll catch up with me later tonight. Luke rests his hands firmly on my hips, and even though I don't feel like dancing, I decide it's better to let him think that's what Noah and I were doing. I don't know how I'd explain hugging another guy from school. Nobody except the family knows about Noah being Cindy's nephew.

Luke gives me a playful smile. "I'm going to have to keep a closer on eye you, Miss Randall. I walk away for five minutes, and someone is already trying to steal you away."

Nice choice of words there. I wonder if the term "steal me away" was intentional.

I try to give him a playful smile. "What would my big brother, Trent, say?"

"Trent?"

"You slacking on the job?"

"Oh, I'm not worried about him. I'm more worried about losing *my* date."

He winks at me and holds me closer. He definitely knows how to turn on the charm. I'm not used to flirting. I couldn't date before, so there was never really any point. I turn my head and blush. I feel someone's eyes on me and look over to find Noah watching us. His jaw and fists are clenched. Then, I see Karlie come up to him and drag him out onto the dance floor. I don't know why, but I hate the idea of him dancing with her. *I want to dance with Noah.* I shake my head to clear the thought away. I'm here with Luke.

The music changes to an upbeat tempo. Luke slides behind me and begins to perform some dance moves that I'm not completely comfortable with. They seem very suggestive. I'm not sure what I'm supposed to do in return. I bend my knees and bounce awkwardly. Landon comes to my rescue by pulling me away and into a group of people. It's basically everyone we sit with at lunch. Instantly, I feel relief, and I'm comfortable enough with this group to dance. I throw my hands up and begin swaying my hips. Tara cheers me on, and Rachel joins in front of me. Landon is performing outrageous dance moves with Emily. We dance this way through three songs. I'm breathless from dancing and laughing so hard.

I leave the group to get a cup of punch. Luke is by the punch table talking with a few of the football players.

"There she is." He raises his cup to me. He turns around and gets me my own cup of punch. I gladly accept it. He leans his shoulder against mine. "That's the second time I've had you taken away. Nice dance moves by the way. Maybe I can have the next one?"

I nod and take another sip of punch. It's really good. I finish the cup and gladly accept a second. I'm so thirsty from dancing and this punch is cold and sweet. Luke asks if I'm ready for another dance, and I agree to dance with him. It's a fast tempo song, but before I can be nervous, he dances our way back to the rest of Landon's group. I'm touched that he probably did this so I'd feel more comfortable. This time, I'm much more relaxed dancing with Luke. I sway my hips freely and let my head roll from side to side. When the song is over, his smile and excitement is so contagious that I find myself smiling with as much enthusiasm. He asks if I would like another drink, but I'm slightly distracted noticing Karlie still hanging around Noah. I take the cup absent-mindedly and allow Luke to hold my hand leading me across the floor.

I take a long drink. I notice he keeps getting closer to me, but I don't mind. In fact, if I'm being honest, I like the feel of his warm, strong body. He's really buff. He might be the buffest guy I know. *Is "buffest" a word? I don't know. I don't care.* After the third cup is gone, I feel so light and carefree. In the back of my mind, I get a nagging feeling that something is wrong. A song comes on that I recognize from the radio, and everyone gets excited. Luke wastes no time dragging me back onto the dance floor. This time, he's even more comfortable with me. His hands begin to stray from my hips to other neighboring areas. His mouth is against my ear breathing heavily. My mind is fuzzy because I'm unsure if I'm wanting him to stop or not.

Landon calls out my name. I look over and he takes my hand. "You feeling alright?"

I giggle and nod. "Have you tried the punch? It's delicious. Here." There's not much left in my cup, but at least he can sample it. "Drink me!" I shout and begin laughing hysterically at my own joke. When Landon doesn't laugh, my eyebrows furrow. "Get it? I'm referring to our joke."

He tugs my hand. "You look a little flushed. Wanna take a break?"

"She's fine, man. Let us dance." Luke nuzzles my neck tickling me. He eases us further into the crowd. His strong hands knead my waist. I close my eyes and focus on the beat of the music. His body is in sync with mine, and it's starting to overpower my senses. I feel the movements starting to become obscene, so I try to allow some space between us. However, he pulls me back and keeps a firm hold on me. I try shrugging him off, and the effort is making me tired.

My eyes feel heavy. "Luke, I need to go sit down."

"Nah, you just need to relax right here with me. I've got you." His hands snake around my body.

I shake my head and try again to shrug him off. *What's wrong with me?*

Suddenly, Luke is gone, and I sway with the loss of support. Landon and Noah are standing there looking pissed.

I go to Noah and whisper, "I don't know what'th wrong with me, but I don't feel tho well."

He looks me over and sniffs at my mouth. I back away, confused as to why he's sniffing me.

He stares at me intently as he asks, "Did you know the punch is spiked?"

I'm dumbfounded. I shake my head and stare at him. I can't believe I was so stupid. I didn't taste any alcohol, but I should've realized it was the drink making my head fuzzy. If Noah thinks I'm a complete idiot, he doesn't show it.

Instead, his tone is full of understanding. "One of the guys offered me some punch earlier. When I saw how you were acting, I figured you must've had some." But then his tone is clipped and cold as he glares daggers at Luke. "However, when I was offered punch, they told me it was spiked."

Landon gets in Luke's face. "Did you seriously give her a

spiked drink? Trent asked you here to keep that kind of stuff from happening. I told him it was a bad idea to trust you."

Luke laughs. "Oh, c'mon man. I offered her a drink, I didn't *force* her to drink it. She didn't seem to mind."

Landon shakes his head in disbelief. "She didn't know! Did you tell her it was spiked? No, you didn't!"

Luke throws his arms out. "Like she couldn't taste it? There was a lot of alcohol. You can taste it!"

Noah steps up to him and seethes, "You were a prick for not telling her."

Luke shakes his head in disgust and mumbles, "Whatever."

We're drawing attention, and a faculty member breaks through our group, "Is there a problem here?"

Landon gives a carefree smile. "Oh no. There isn't a problem."

Tara and Rachel get on either side of me and lead me over to the bleachers.

"Hey are you alright?" "How are you feeling?" "Are you going to be sick?" "Do you need to go home?"

Their questions seem to be coming at me rapidly but in drawn out, slow motion at the same time.

I look between the two of them and grumble, "Did you two drink any?" They both give me a "duh" look. *Did everyone drink? I must be the only one causing a problem. If they get caught, it'll be my fault.* I feel guilty and foolish. The thought never crossed my mind that the punch could be spiked. That would've never happened at my old school. We didn't even serve punch at dances. *Maybe that's why.* It's nice of the girls to sit here with me, but I know they'd rather be dancing. I try to assure them I'm fine, but they don't leave until Noah and Landon arrive.

"Do you need me to take you home?" Landon asks, kneeling in front of me and handing me a cup of water.

"I'm fine!" I cringe when I realize how forceful I said that.

It's not their fault. I shake my head but then get dizzy. I take a few deep, calming breaths. I take a long gulp of water. "I'm sorry. For snapping at you. I already feel better. I think I might have just drunk the punch too fast," I confess sheepishly.

He gives me a chuckle but then in a more serious tone says, "Luke should've told you it was spiked. *Dick*. He's such a dick."

I sigh. "It could be possible he assumed I knew. Everyone seemed to know *but* me."

There will be no swaying Landon otherwise. He argues, "Still, Sarah. It's common courtesy to mention that little tidbit of information. He was here because Trent trusted him. He knew better than to offer you a spiked drink."

I roll my eyes. Another reminder that he was here on Trent's behalf. He was probably trying to have fun while babysitting, and I proved what a baby I really am.

Luke stalks toward me, but Noah and Landon stand, blocking his path. I'm frustrated that this is still happening. "Guys, stop."

Noah looks uneasy about allowing Luke to come sit next to me.

Luke looks between the two guys. "Care to give us a minute? I need to apologize to my date."

They give him a hard look as they walk only a few feet away.

He opens his mouth, but I cut him off, "I'm sorry, Luke."

He looks baffled and laughs. "What? Why?"

I take a deep breath and begin, "I noticed I was feeling funny after the first cup, yet I drank a second cup. And then a third cup."

He holds his hand up. "In no way is this your fault. I should've told you, and…if I'm being honest, I wanted you to let loose a little."

He should've told me, but I assure him, "Either way, I'll

let Trent know it wasn't all your fault." I think about it and maybe it was his fault. "Only most of it."

He waves the comment off. "I'm not worried about him. How many times do I have to tell you?"

"You're doing this as a favor to him. I assumed you didn't want him mad at you." I pick at my fingernails.

He places his hand over mine, and I look up at him.

He gives me a crooked smile. "I think you might be missing something. Trent asked me to go to this with you, but I'm here because I want to be." He eases closer to me and inclines his head toward me. "In fact, I want to be on a few more dates with you. Anywhere else you need an escort?"

Unsure whether or not I want to go on another date with Luke, I remain quiet.

"For now, why don't we have another go on the dance floor?" He holds a hand out and helps me stand from the bleachers.

Noah and Landon are still watching us. They both shoot disapproving looks at us. *Looks like those two found a common foe.*

I watch Karlie saunter up to Noah again. *Ugh, speaking of "foe." Or more like common hoe.* I smile to myself at my own little joke. I watch them through narrowed eyes. *She needs to get over him. He's way out of her league.* As a ballad begins, Luke wraps his arms around me. Noah allows Karlie to lead him onto the dance floor next to us. Landon is dancing with Rachel a few feet away. I can see Noah has a firm grip on Karlie, trying to hold her back to maintain some distance between them. She is pawing all over him. *She had the nerve to refer to me as pathetic.*

Luke nuzzles his nose in my hair and then whispers in my ear, "Have I told you how amazing you look tonight?"

I'm not really paying attention to him because I can't get over how ridiculous Karlie is acting. Noah must feel my stare because he looks over at me. His eyes narrow and his jaw hardens. He pulls Karlie closer to him. She gives me a smug smile while rubbing her hand up Noah's neck and through his hair. She looks back at him as she brings her hand back down and lets it lay against his jaw, whispering to him. I feel myself getting hot with anger. I try to be subtle and ease myself and Luke towards them. I feel Luke's body against mine, but my eyes are on Noah. The gentle sway of his hips and his strong hands on Karlie's hips. We make eye contact again. Both of us staring through the narrow slits of our eyes. The song ends, and immediately, Noah drops his arms and stomps away. Luke, however, is still holding me.

"Whenever you're ready to leave, just let me know," he whispers.

I smile and nod. "Thank you. Can we leave in, say, ten minutes? I need to tell Tara something before I leave. But I think I'm ready to go home."

He gives me that guy nod for "cool," "alright," or whatever they mean with that.

It's not really Tara I'm wanting to go see. I find Noah by the punch table filling a cup.

"Is that for Karlie? I thought you said you were coming stag?" I sneer.

He scoffs at me. "Uh no. It's actually for me. And I am here alone."

I cross my arms and debate if I should ask him if he's interested in her. Instead, I ask, "Have you met her parents? What's her dad's name?" I have a hunch. I just want to know if this is the same guy. It shouldn't matter. But this is the man that's baby hurt Cindy and pushed her to her breaking point. Maybe it was because of them she kidnapped me. And now, that same child is trying to hurt me.

Noah narrows his eyes. "Still a little tipsy there, I see. Um, random but yes. Her parents come to school functions so, yeah. Her dad's Michael. I don't know him well. Mom can't stand the guy…oh."

I feel hot angry tears at the back of my eyes. I probably shouldn't hold it against her for her father's past sins, but considering I already don't like her—now, I despise her. *Speak of the devil.* She puts herself between us.

Her eyes stay on me as she sweetly tells Noah, "A gentleman would offer a lady a cup."

I keep my eyes on her as I imitate her. "Why yes Noah, I would *love* to have a cup. Thank you."

She narrows her eyes at me. "Excuse you."

I let out a cold laugh. "Oh, you've got to be kidding… You were referring to yourself as a *lady?*" I point out to the dance floor. "Was that lady-like when you were out there dry humping his leg?"

She barks out a laugh. "Says the little hussie that practically gave Luke Jamerson a lap dance twenty minutes ago. And don't try that innocent bullshit with me, honey. He 'spiked' your drink. *Right.* Afraid to lose your girl-next-door angel persona? You went to a different school. Not a different planet. I'm not buying your little act."

Noah hands me a cup and places a hand on the small of my back. He mumbles into my ear, "Ignore her, Liv. Let's go."

Him whispering the nickname he has for me immediately calms me down. Karlie says a few choice words about Luke being here out of pity, but I don't pay any attention to her. I allow him to lead me over to a quiet, dark corner.

He takes a drink, and after he swallows, he asks me, "What was that all about?"

I raise my chin and puff out my chest. "I think it's ridiculous how she was behaving with you."

"Okay," he draws out, "but why do you care?"

I'm starting to get aggravated with him. "What do you mean 'why do I care?' Why wouldn't I care?"

It's his turn to sound aggravated. "What I mean is, why do you care when you've got golden boy all over you?"

I roll my eyes. "Golden boy wasn't pawing all over me and acting like a dog in heat!"

He takes a step closer to me and is right in my face when he growls, "What about what happened ten minutes ago? What would you call that? Or even better, what about twenty minutes ago when Landon and I had to practically pull him off of you? Looked pretty heated to me."

He takes another drink. He has a point, and I know it. Since I can't think of an immediate comeback, I drink as well, and I notice this cup isn't spiked. "Is yours spiked? I notice this one tastes different, more like the punch I'm used to." I try to sound light.

He grunts at me, but answers, "Mine is. Yours isn't. I think you've had enough for tonight."

My mouth falls open and closes. We've had tension all night tonight. I reach over and take his cup from him. "Your attitude is starting to get old. You're not responsible for me, ya know. I don't know if this is some protective family thing you've going on."

I take a big drink and make it a point to stare at him as I swallow. His jaw clenches.

"What? What is it? Did Aunt Andrea tell you to look out for me at school? Are you supposed to be on babysitting duty as well?" I sway again but regain my balance.

He takes his cup back. "No, Liv, I'm not on any babysitting duty. Funny how you're getting uptight about me sticking my nose in your business. You stare daggers at Karlie every time she touches me." He gives me a playful smile. "You even told her that she was *not* a lady."

I raise my eyebrows and shrug. "Well, is she?"

He shakes his head back and forth. "Far from it."

I start to smile but then frown. I lean forward and point

my finger at him. "How do you know she's *far from it?*" Leaning forward causes me to sway. I reach out and grab his arm to prevent myself from falling. He steadies me with his other hand, placing it on my waist.

"Whoa. I hear guys talk. She's made offers."

We're holding each other so close that we can feel each other's body heat. For a moment, I think we might kiss. I want him to kiss me. But that would be weird. I've thought of Noah as a cousin for years, but I never really knew him. Truthfully, we're in no way related. *Does he still think of me as a cousin?* The drinking has given me a little courage, I guess, because I reach up to him and caress his strong jaw. His eyes grow wide, and I think he stopped breathing. He seems surprised by the gesture. I lick my lips, and his stare becomes heated, focusing on them.

"Do you like Karlie? Ever take her up on any of those offers?" I whisper.

His voice is hoarse but sure. "No. On both accounts."

My thumb begins to trace his bottom lip. "Good."

Our trance is broken when Tara walks up. She hisses, "Sarah. Sarah!"

Noah reluctantly releases me and steps back and puts his hands in his pockets.

"Sarah, Luke is searching for you! What the hell?" She looks back and forth between us. She takes me by my elbow and leads me away from Noah.

"Hey, I need to tell Noah bye." I start to pull away from her, but she jerks me forward.

"No, what you need to do is go back to *your date.* You came with Luke! What was going on between you and Noah? I know y'all flirt all the time," she scolds me.

I laugh at her. "Noah and I don't flirt! He's…" Oops, I almost called him my *fake* cousin. I spot Luke talking with a group.

Tara stops us a few feet away, clearly wanting to know what's going on. "Look, Noah's hot. I mean, he's really hot. But you're here with Luke Jamerson. I know you're new and all, but Luke is a big deal. A really big effing deal. He's so popular that he doesn't even go to this school and is still the most popular guy here. Not to mention he's gorgeous! I don't even know how you can think about Noah or any other guy right now with Luke in the same room."

I stare at her and blink a couple of times. I think about what she said. "Then why don't you go dance with Luke?" *Why am I suggesting this? I should be running to Luke…but I want to go back to Noah.*

She looks at me like I'm crazy. "Like he would give me the time of day. Honey, I would *love* to dance with Luke Jamerson. Especially the way you did earlier tonight. Unfortunately, I'm not even on his radar."

"Well, he's only here with me because of Trent," I remind her. Even though Luke told me he wants to be here with me, but I don't tell her that part.

Tara shakes her head at me like I'm the most pitiful sight. "You really don't pick up on things, do you? Maybe Trent asked him, but he's only had eyes for you all night. If he was here on your brother's bidding alone, he would've ditched you at the door and hung out with other people. He would have danced with other girls. He sure as heck wouldn't waste his time getting into it with Landon or hunting you down. Luke's the kind of guy that does only what he *wants* to do. Even if it is Trent Randall asking. Luke effing Jamerson likes you…for some reason, no offense." She looks me up and down.

Luke must've spotted us because I watch him heading our way. "I don't know how I feel about Luke. Even if he is into me."

"Girl you're crazy."

"I'm starting to believe I might actually be."

Tara giggles and then I feel strong arms wrap around me.

"I can't seem to hold on to you. Next time we go out, it's going to be somewhere you can't wander off."

Ignoring his comment, I tell him, "I still need to find Landon."

Luke takes my hand and we search for my brother. When we find Landon and tell him bye, he offers another twenty-times to drive me home himself. However, I allow Luke to drive me home.

We're sitting in front of the house, and neither one of us has moved. *Should I invite him in? I'm not sure if Trent is home. He might have wanted to see him. Do I want him to come in? He should've told me about the drink, so I don't think I'm going to encourage this date any further. I wonder what Noah is doing? Did he leave with Karlie?*

Luke clears his throat and brings me out of my rambling thoughts. "Here. So your parents don't smell any alcohol on you." He hands me some breath mints and travel size can of Febreeze.

Clearly, he is prepared. Nice. I don't know what to make of this since I've never drank with my friends before. I don't want to risk any confrontation with my new parents, so I pop a few mints in my mouth and give a light spray on my clothes.

"Thanks. I had a wonderful time. Thank you." I reach for the door handle.

Luke gets out of the car and walks around. We walk up to the front door together, and I am unsure if he's planning to follow me in.

He stops and holds my hand. "I had fun tonight, so much that I think we should go out next weekend. How about Friday night we go to a movie?"

"I play soccer, and we have games every Saturday morning. Depending on what time the movie let out, it could be a late night." I stand up straighter and narrow my eyes at him.

"Besides, what you did was shitty. The more I think about it, the madder I get. I'm starting to sober up."

"Stop thinking about it then."

I reach for the doorknob with a growl. He quickly reaches for my hand. "I'm sorry! I was trying to make a joke. A bad joke, clearly. I'm sorry. Let me make this up to you. Huh?"

I pause and look at him. He takes that as a victory.

"Saturday night it is! You can even take a nap after your game." He leans forward and gives me a peck on the cheek. He calls out as he is walking to his car, "I'm leaving while I'm ahead. I don't want to make a bigger ass of myself. I'll text you until then."

I wonder for a minute if he knows my number, but I'm sure he's gotten it from Trent.

All the lights are off in the house, but as soon as the door shuts, I hear Melissa call out, "Honey?"

I guess that could be for anyone, but I go ahead and answer, "Um, it's me… Sarah?"

I don't know why I say it like a question. I guess I'm still not used to the name. It still is a question for me. *Should it be by now?* I don't understand why I still hold on to the memories and love of a woman who lied to me my whole life, while the woman that gave birth to me and searched to have me back is right here. I want to embrace this family and *be* Sarah.

I hear her heels clacking against the marble floor as she quickly approaches. It was sweet she waited up for me. Cindy would sometimes, but she usually had to work early in the morning. Most parents do, I guess, but it's still difficult for me to wrap my head around them treating me as their actual daughter. I'm practically an adult who's moved in with them. How can they still look at me with so much love and automatically assume the role of parent? Why can't I automatically assume the role of daughter? She's grinning, anxiously waiting to hear how it went.

"It was great. Luke was nice, and he asked me to go out again. I mean, if it's alright. If I'm allowed to date," I hesitate.

She nods her head vigorously. "Oh yes! Luke's such a nice boy!" She gives me a knowing smile. "Handsome too, huh?"

I see this as my opportunity to bring up the issue of having a car. That would give me so much extra freedom, opening the opportunity to visit the Wallace family.

"The thing is…I like Luke, but I'd like to have my own car for any dates. Just in case I wanted to leave early or maybe it gets awkward…like this conversation. I would feel better if I had a car." I scramble with my words. I see a flicker of confusion cross her face, so I hurry, "I'd get a job and work towards buying my own car."

She takes a deep breath and nods. "I see. Well, Trent has a car, and so does Landon. Obviously, we won't think twice when Denise turns sixteen about getting her a car. Of course, any teenager wants their own car."

She wraps her arm through mine and leads me into the kitchen. I have a seat on a bar stool by the buffet counter. She promises to discuss it first thing in the morning with Richard. We move on to discuss the game, the dance, and my next soccer game over a bowl of chips. I omit the part about the punch and Noah. Denise is already in bed, but Landon strolls in around midnight. He only stops for a second to kiss Melissa on the cheek and appraise me. He finally asks if I'm okay and then goes to bed. It's nearly two in the morning by the time I make my way up the stairs to my room. I hear the door slam and Trent and Melissa's voices fade as I make it to the top of the stairs.

Twenty-Nine

HE TONE OF CINDY'S ENTRIES CHANGE drastically after she made it to Colorado with me. She was positive she'd get caught, yet she didn't. Cindy wasted no time in announcing to Andrea that she was farther along than what she thought in her pregnancy; therefore, it'd be a while before she could travel. She knew if Andrea saw me right away, she'd realize I was not Cindy's since the timing didn't add up. To make up for it, she was already a couple months pregnant when she left for Colorado, and I was born early. It worked out since Andrea was too nervous to travel with Noah so young. Cindy found photos online of babies to send to her sister, claiming they were me. She was hoping to someday return with me, since she hated being away from her sister. Her parents were getting old, and their health was getting worse. That was another concern she had. The hype over my kidnapping was too great, though. Unfortunately, as I continue reading, her parents passed away before she could visit them again. This was after I'd been missing for an entire year. By this time, she'd become good friends with a woman from work so she left me with her for a weekend while she went back for the funeral. Andrea was shocked that she hadn't brought me, but Cindy told everyone I was ill with strep throat.

I skip a few pages about mundane, everyday life. Her passages are less frequent and further apart in dates. I've been with her two years now.

Thirty

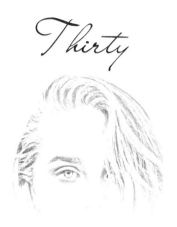

Feb 17

    …the older my Olivia gets, the more clear it is that she doesn't physically resemble me. That's fine because I tell everyone she looks like her deceased father. Which is true. Not the deceased part but her father. I still check up on the Randalls. Their social media accounts, articles from newspapers from back home, every now and then Andrea tells me tidbits about them. Unknowingly, Andrea fills me in on all kinds of things I'm curious about. I'm pleased that Melissa had a healthy pregnancy and safe birth. My gosh. The one she was pregnant with while Olivia was a baby—now we know as Landon—favors Liv Bug so much that its uncanny. They both took after Richard. Which is a compliment. He's a very attractive man. Not that Melissa isn't a looker herself. She has two babies, beauty, wealth and a handsome loving husband. Which is why I've let go of any guilt I had. I'm so blissfully happy and so is little Olivia. Obviously. I'll always be grateful to the Randalls. They've given me an extraordinary little girl. And maybe they'll have another daughter. I'll let them keep that one ;)

    They have wealth. They have a happy marriage. My gosh, I deserved to at least get something. I'll settle for my beautiful daughter any day over marriage, wealth, and all that. I'm happy with just Olivia. My Liv Bug. Or Luv Bug! Yes, that's her new nickname. My little Luv Bug.

And she's happy. She's such a happy and loving little girl. Today she tried to play soccer with the bigger neighborhood kids. I didn't want her to play because I was afraid she'd get hurt. But the other mother said 'Let her play, Cindy!' She ran out there like she was as big as them. She was pretty good for as little as she is. After their little game, she ran across the yard and threw her arms around me screaming, "I did it Mom! I thored!" I didn't care that she scored—oh, I was proud of her. But she said—"I did it MOM." Mom. She ran to ME. She was so happy and she wanted to share it with ME. I've never felt such pure happiness in my life as sharing her joy.

Melissa has children she gets to do that with. TWO. She can even have more. I always wondered if I should tell Olivia she was adopted—but I'm too scared. I can't lose what I have. I won't lose this again. I lost a baby once. I never got to know or hold that child, but I did love. I loved that baby with all my heart. I've held Olivia. I've been raising her. I know her better than the Randalls do. I love her more than my own life. I wouldn't have a life without her. So I can never tell her she was adopted. What if she wanted to search for her real parents? Started asking questions? Looked at me differently? Worse, what if she learned the truth?! She'd hate me. I hope I never see that day…

Thirty-One

ND SHE NEVER DID SEE THE DAY. IT'S DIFFICULT for me to read this and separate the two versions of her. On one hand, I see how shattered the Randalls were with losing me, and Cindy is the villain, a deranged woman who took me from my *home* and lied to me my entire life. On the other hand, I read how much she *loved* me, how she was a broken woman desperate for a child to love and seeking a new life. I recall some of the moments I had shared with her, and I want to cry because right now I *miss* her. I really do. I want to talk to her about this. I also want to talk to her about boys and ask for advice about my feelings with Luke and Noah. But if it hadn't been for her, maybe I would love Melissa. Maybe I would be comfortable enough to talk to her about boys. Maybe Noah and I would date like a normal couple because we're not cousins and it wouldn't be weird. *This is so messed up. I don't know how I should be feeling right now.* I close the journal and throw it across the room. I lay my head in my hands and cry. I cry until I'm exhausted and sleep takes hold.

I hear a light tapping on my door that stirs me awake. I look at my phone to check the time, and its past noon. I open my door to find Trent.

"Can I talk to you for a minute? Sorry if I woke you, but I have to get back to school." I let him in, and he sits on my bed.

Turns out Landon had filled him in on *everything* that happened last night. He wants to hear my side of the story, and he plans to have a long chat with Luke. I give him my version that paints a less ugly and dramatic picture than Landon's. Trent doesn't give anything away as to how he feels about what happened.

He gives my knee a quick pat while standing up. "It's time for me to get going. All that matters to me is that you had a good time. I'm glad."

I pick at my thumb nail, avoiding eye contact, and ask, "Are you mad at Luke?"

He shrugs and leaves.

Later that evening, Melissa calls me to come downstairs. I see Richard and Melissa first as I walk in, sitting on the cream-colored sectional. Across from them is Luke, sitting on the other half of the sectional. He's holding a dozen pink roses, but that isn't what has me gaping at him. His eye is swollen and a horrid shade of purple, along with a busted upper lip.

"*Luke!* What happened?" I raise my hand to cover my mouth to keep me from saying more.

He gives a light chuckle. "Looks that bad, huh? This is nothing." He speaks in a loud voice, more toward Richard and Melissa than me. "I was just telling your parents about how I had a rough football practice."

Melissa shakes her head. "Luke, did you not wear your helmet?"

Richard stands and comes by to pat him on the shoulder.

"Boys sometime roughhouse a little on the field. I remember those days. Trent had plenty of them too."

"Ugh, I could barely handle Trent's games. Glad that's behind us. Well, we'll let you two visit." Melissa stands and her and Richard exit the room.

"How hard did you get tackled?" I stare at his face.

He smirks. "Actually, I didn't get tackled on the field. I was just telling them that. Trent was giving me fair warning to treat you like a lady next weekend. I would anyways, of course, but let's just say, the message was well received. Worse is to come if I get out of line."

"Wow. Worse? So, what brings you here now?" I ask him.

He smiles at me and nods toward where Richard and Melissa had exited. "I wanted to ask their permission. Before, I was escorting you to homecoming through Trent." He raises up and hands me the roses. His voice turns husky as he whispers, "These are for you."

I've never had a guy give me flowers before. I blush and sniff the roses. They're beautiful, and the gesture is sweet.

He clears his throat. "I'll see myself out. If you're still up for it, I can pick you up at five on Saturday?"

I simply nod, and watch as he exits out of the room. I catch sight of him at the door as he waves bye to everyone.

At supper, Melissa tells Denise and Landon about Luke being the perfect gentleman by asking for permission to take me on a date. Landon grunts and scoffs through the entire conversation. I don't miss the fact that no one has told them about the punch incident.

Seeming to finally have had enough of Melissa and Denise describing Luke as a dream, Landon sneers, "Isn't he laying it on a little thick? First, the weekend isn't even over, and he's already showing up with roses to make plans for next weekend? Eager much?"

I take offense to his tone. "Hey! Can't a guy be overly excited to date me?"

Landon narrows his eyes at me. "Yeah, but he's too eager. I don't trust him."

Denise sighs. "I think he's so romantic. Wow, you have the most popular guy in school bringing you roses."

Landon snaps, "He doesn't even go to our school, so how is he the most popular guy in school?"

Denise raises her eyebrows and speaks in a tone that clearly implies he's slow in understanding things. "That's how popular he is. Luke Jamerson is the most popular guy in *every* school. He's basically a celebrity in this town. Maybe even the surrounding areas."

He rolls his eyes in disgust. "Why? Because he's good at sports and works out? His family has money? You know who he is really? He's a fake, selfish, snob, and a total ass. Not sure I see the appeal."

Richard gets onto Landon about his language and changes the subject. The rest of our conversation is more pleasant. I speak when necessary, but my mind is still wondering what history there is between Landon and Luke. This is about more than how Luke acted at Homecoming.

When I get to my room, I check both of my cell phones. The private one has messages from Andrea and Noah. Andrea asks about homecoming and life in general. Noah reminds me to get to school early tomorrow so we can talk. On my regular cell phone, I have several messages from Tara wanting to know what was happening with Luke. Rachel is curious about Trent. *Pretty sure that's the only reason she wants to be friends with me.* I respond to everyone and then hide my private phone.

I get ready for bed but I'm not tired yet. I grab my sketch pad and charcoal pencils. I wander downstairs to the den. I sit sideways on the couch and tap my pencil against the pad. I'm enjoying my new school. I love my soccer team. I've made new friends. I have an extremely popular and attractive guy interested in me. I'm developing a relationship with my new family while getting to keep contact with Aunt Andrea and Noah. Maybe this is who I was always meant to be. Maybe this is Sarah Randall.

I draw a curved line down the side of the page. Then another. I hear footsteps and look up. Richard enters the room.

"Not tired yet either?" I shake my head. He holds up a sketch pad and points to mine. "Great minds think alike. Or artistic minds I guess." He smiles and releases a light, awkward chuckle. "Mind if I sit in here with you? I promise to keep quiet."

I nod and watch him as he sits on the couch next to mine. He flips the pages and then picks up his pencil. He holds it up and waits. I hold mine up and he smiles. And we begin sketching. We don't talk. We don't even look at each other's drawings. We sketch in silence until it's time to go to bed.

"That was nice. Maybe next time you're not ready for sleep and want to sketch, come get me?"

"Yeah."

"Good night, sweetheart."

"Good night…"

Thirty-Two

*H*URRY AND GET READY FOR SCHOOL. *IF I HAD my own car, I could already be on my way.* I'm thinking this as I eat my breakfast. As if he reads my mind, Richard lays his newspaper down to address me.

"Sarah. Your mother and I discussed you having a car last night."

Uh-oh. His tone doesn't sound favorable.

"When is the next day that you don't have soccer practice?"

I swallow the cereal in my mouth and answer, "We don't practice on Wednesdays."

He nods, looking at Melissa. She is bursting with excitement. "How about Wednesday then?"

I look back and forth between them. Confused, I draw out, "Wednesday what?"

Richard gives me a wide grin. "To take you to get a new license. You need a Missouri license and then after that, we go look for a car."

I drop my spoon in my bowl and stare at him. I sit there a moment trying to wrap my head around what he said.

He seems unsure about my response. "We can look at any cars you like. Melissa said you wanted to get a job to buy a car. We can help you buy a car, Sarah. Or is that something you wanted to do on your own? I'm sorry, I'm having trouble gauging your reaction to this."

He seems nervous and flustered. I release a shocked laugh. I asked for a car, so they're going to go buy one just like that. Cindy wanted me to have a car, but we couldn't afford it. If I ever needed to drive, I drove hers. For school, I would carpool with friends. Sometimes, Cindy would even carpool so I could have the car. I forget how wealthy this family is, even though this monstrous house I live in is a constant reminder.

I blink a couple of times and hold my hands out, "I-I... Wow. Um, ha, I can't...believe it. That's so generous of both of you."

Melissa begins clapping. "Oh sweetheart! I wanted to surprise you with a car for your birthday, but Richard thinks we should allow you to pick it out."

Richard gives me a sad look. "I don't think you need any more surprises in your life right now. Even if it's a good surprise. It could still be overwhelming. You choose your own car, sweetheart."

I realize what he's trying to do. I haven't had many choices and he's wanting to let the next big moment in my life be on my terms. I get to choose. Tears pool into my eyes. I run around and give each one of them a hug.

⌖

I arrive to Mrs. Sanders class early to find it empty. I sit down and start sketching while I wait for Noah. After a few minutes, I look up to find Noah watching me.

I shriek, "Ah! You could've said something. Wow, you're quiet." He merely shrugs and continues to stare. *Okay.* I go back to sketching and ask him if he had a nice time at the dance. He doesn't answer, so I look back up. I notice a red spot on his cheek bone, maybe a slight bruise that's already fading. I zero in on it and reach out to touch it. He flinches but doesn't move.

"What happened here?" I lightly touch next to the spot. I notice his eyes have different speckles of blue and green, maybe a little grey even.

"I, um, got into a bit of a disagreement." He looks away and moves out of reach.

I urge him to continue, "That's a bit vague. Do all your disagreements end this way?" He doesn't answer so I push more. "Tell me what happened."

He huffs and grumbles as he wipes his hand over his face. "Yesterday, I had a disagreement with Luke."

I almost shoot out of my seat. "That was *you*! He came by the house, and he looked far worse than you. He said Trent did it!"

He gives a chuckle. "Trent might have had a disagreement with him as well."

Does nobody think I can handle myself? Did me being a kidnap victim turn into me becoming a victim of everything? Do both of these guys now have a huge guilt trip and feel like they have to make up for it by beating up Luke? "Did you both gang up on him? Over what? Do not say it had anything to do with that freaking punch from the dance."

Now he looks annoyed and pins me with his stare. "That 'freaking punch' was spiked. You could've gotten drunk, and he could've taken advantage of you. Are you seriously that naïve? Trent trusted him, so he had every right to be upset —no exceptions. And for your information, I wouldn't gang up on anyone. I fight my own battles, especially against some douche like Luke Jamerson. Trent had already delivered the message. I just made sure it was received."

I snarl at him while considering if I should deliver my own

message to *him*. He lets out another huff and holds his hands out. "Look, it's not like it was at the same time. Apparently, Trent stopped by his house as he was leaving town. I ran into Luke at the gym. He was bragging about how he *let* Trent play the protective big brother to his new sister. Then he said he had every intention of still trying to date you and continue where y'all left off at the dance. I approached him because clearly, the message hadn't been received."

I roll my eyes. "Believe it or not, I can handle myself. You're both blowing this out of proportion. What? You wanted to be the one to play the big brother role?"

I watch as his jaw ticks, and his right leg jumps up and down. He's agitated, but he doesn't speak. I go back to working on my sketch. A few minutes pass, and the first bell rings.

He doesn't move when he asks, "Are you really going out with him this Saturday?"

I don't waste my time by looking up at him; I just give a casual "mm-hhmm." He gives a low grumble of inaudible words, but I don't bother trying to make out what they are.

Throughout the day, everyone keeps asking me about Luke. Are we dating? Is it serious? Did he really take on Trent to date me? A few girls even ask, "What makes you so damn special?" *Ouch! That one stings.* Honestly, I don't even know why Luke is interested in me. I think gossip and rumors have spread like wildfire all over the school —and possibly surrounding schools. It's extremely uncomfortable and I'm not really sure what to do with myself or how to handle it. I give vague answers throughout the day. Tara and Rachel are the only ones I tell the whole story to. While Landon shoots everyone down with a "*Sarah has more class than to date the likes of Luke Jamerson.*"

At lunch, I ask Landon, "Why do you think everyone cares so much?"

He lays his sandwich down on his plate with a sigh.

"First, you're Sarah Randall. You went missing for *years*." He stops and holds a hand up when he sees my eyes grow wide. "Ssshhh, I know, I know you don't like to acknowledge that people know you for that. I understand that it makes you uncomfortable having people still gossip about it. Sorry, but they do, and they *will* continue to. That's the way it is."

He gives a matter-of-fact shrug and then continues, "Second, Luke Jamerson is," he gives a grand wave with his hand, "an athletic god. Prince Charming to some foolish girls. The American golden boy. Truthfully, he's a glorified ass, but whatever."

He goes back to eating his sandwich while I sit there dumbfounded. We sit there a few more minutes before he places the sandwich back down with an audible huff. "Really, you still don't get it? You two dating is the juiciest gossip this pathetic town has had in a long time. You're both hot topics around here. So, of course, you're going to make headlines by dating," he holds his hand out as if he's reading a marquee, "*Playboy Star Athlete Luke Jamerson Dates Returned Darling Sarah Randall.* Oh! Or better, *Randall Family Finally Has Sarah Returned to Them Only to have Quick Luke Steal Her Heart. Could her heart be lost for good this time?*"

I slap his hand down and laugh. "Stop it! That's ridiculous!"

He gives a half-hearted laugh. "This town is ridiculous."

I get an unsettling feeling and voice my fears to Landon, "Do you think that's why Luke is interested in me? Only for the attention it might bring?"

He shakes his head and acts like I'm ridiculous now. "No. I highly doubt that. He'd have to think you're more popular than him, and his ego is too big for that nonsense. He has an interest in you personally if he's bothering with a date."

I examine him and finally ask, "Why do you hate him? Straight answer."

He stares at me, and I can't read the emotions going through his eyes. Finally, he leans down and whispers, "Later. I'll tell you tonight at home."

I don't push him anymore, and our conversations go back to lighthearted topics.

The rest of my day flies by, and before I know it, I'm home getting ready for bed. I hear a knock at my door, but before I can answer it, Landon comes strolling in. He flops down on my bed and throws his hands behind his head.

"Get comfortable." I joke.

He answers with a smirk. I finish getting ready in the bathroom and come out to lay next to him. Landon jumps right into it.

"I'm gay, Sarah." I watch his Adam's apple bob. "Nobody knows except Rachel. I think Trent's suspicious. Everyone else is clueless. Except...for maybe Luke Jamerson."

I'm honestly shocked. I'm speechless. I feel like I should say something. Should I show how surprised I am? Should I pretend like I'm not surprised? I don't think anything is *wrong* with him being gay, but he obviously feels it's wrong. Would Richard and Melissa be upset?

I stutter, "O-okay...but why are you telling me? I am only asking because you said you haven't told anyone else. Why me then?"

He turns to look at me and gives me a sad smile. "You know what it's like to feel different. I think you have a pretty good idea of what it feels like to be a member of this family but not *feel* like part of the family. I can't tell them —not yet anyways."

I take his hand and give it a reassuring squeeze. He's right in that I know exactly how that feels. He squeezes my hand in return and then focuses on the ceiling.

"There was this guy." He gives a half-hearted chuckle. "Isn't that how most stories begin? Anyways, there was this guy named Marcus Duncan. He went to the same private school as Luke. As you know, Luke is friends with Trent. He used to be buddies with Marcus as well. That's how I met Marcus. He would bring him around, along with a couple of other jocks. Long story short, Marcus and I…well, we became *close*."

I give a little "oh" and nod to show I'm following.

He takes another large swallow and continues, "I don't know how, but somehow, it leaked that Marcus was gay. Luke not only quit being his friend, but he gave him so much pointless shit for it."

When his voice begins to tremble, I cut my eyes to see unshed tears in his eyes, and the hand I'm holding visibly quivers.

He takes a deep breath and continues, "I still don't know how no one has found out about me. I don't advertise that I'm gay, but I was quite close to Marcus. Anyone could see it. If I had to guess, I'm sure—no —I know, Trent is protecting me. Luke would've gone after me, I know it, but he wouldn't dare go against Trent. But Marcus didn't have a big, cool brother to protect him. He was fair game to God only knows what. He was at the same school with Luke, did I mention that? Anyways, he was. He was at that fancy private school where all the kids are even more cruel because they believe they are untouchable. Somehow, their money makes them better than everyone. What happens when you get a group of spoiled, self-righteous people in one place that all think like that? They attack the first person that comes along that's different."

He goes quiet, and I don't know if I should ask what became of Marcus.

After a few tears trickle down his face, he continues, "Marcus wouldn't speak to me after the rumors first started. I tried calling, texting, going to his house, but he refused to acknowledge me. I heard about everything that happened to him because people around here love to talk, especially people like Luke. It seemed he couldn't wait to come over and talk about everything that happened at school. Trent would always tell him to 'shut up,' or 'it was wrong.' Luke would only laugh." He turns to me and stares so intently into my eyes, I almost want to flinch. "He *laughed*, Sarah. Laughed."

He focuses back on the ceiling, and I watch his nostrils flare for a few minutes.

Then, he whispers the next part, "Marcus couldn't stand it anymore. Who could have? He might not have had a brother to protect him, but thankfully, he did have understanding parents. They moved. I never saw or heard from him again. I still want to know why he turned me away. I guess I never will."

We sit there for a moment reflecting on everything he had just revealed.

Finally, I offer, "He didn't want you to go through it. He must've loved you, Landon. Maybe he knew his parents were going to move. Maybe he was afraid it would be worse for you. I think he was trying to protect you."

"Maybe."

Luke bullied Landon's first love and cast him into social exile. If I had to guess, I'd also bet he knows the truth about Landon's sexual preference as well. I can't date Luke now. I'd feel as though I was betraying my brother. *My brother*. I smile to myself, realizing that I do see Landon as my brother. I want to protect him. I wish I'd been here for him sooner. Maybe we could've stopped Luke before he tortured poor Marcus. Maybe it wouldn't have changed anything. At this moment, one thing has for sure changed—I hate Luke Jamerson. What kind of person treats another person that way? I'm overcome with a sudden urge to shield and protect Landon. But something tells me, he doesn't need me to protect him. He just needs me to be there for him. To love him for him. Isn't that all anybody wants? To be loved for simply being themselves. Not their name, sexual preferences, religious beliefs, social status or skin color—but to be loved for who you are, not what you are. Who Landon loves doesn't change who he is any more than whether he calls me Sarah or Olivia. He's still my brother and I still love him. My chest hurts and I fight back tears. Being grateful in this moment feels wrong because I was brought back to him through Cindy's death.

I continue to lay there holding his hand for comfort. A thought comes to mind. "Why is Rachel the only one that knows?"

He shrugs, "We've always been close. We both were in love with people we couldn't be with. She's always been in love with Trent. She'd use me to try and get closer to him. The funny thing is, I'm hurting her chances more than helping. Trent's not going to date her if he thinks there's the slightest chance harm could come to me as a result. She'll never abandon our charade either. It helps to keep rumors flowing about me being a lady's man and other stupid shit. We don't claim to be an exclusive couple or anything."

"She's a great friend."

"The best. I hate to see her hurting over Trent. Sometimes I think about coming out so she'll be free of me."

"Landon, I think Rachel's love for you is genuine. Sounds to me she loves you. There're different types of love, and you have the greatest one of all. A true love that doesn't require anything in return. She loves you, probably more than Trent. Give the girl some credit. If she's meant to be with Trent, it'll happen."

"Like you were always meant to be here? It happened."

I smile at him and squeeze his hand tighter. "Yeah. What's meant to be, will be. And I was always meant to be here by your side. That's where I'll always be."

Landon's right. I was always meant to be a part of this family. It took a while, but it happened.

Thirty-Three

I'T'S WEDNESDAY MORNING. I'M BEYOND
ecstatic that after school, we're going car
shopping. I try not to let it bother me so much
that these people are buying me a car. They're my family, and
slowly it's starting to feel more that way. I'm going to accept
this car with the hope I'll pay them back. This car will allow
me some freedom, at least.

When I get to class early, I bounce over to Noah. He
laughs at my excitement as I sit down.

"Aren't you just a ray of sunshine?" he says as he draws.

"I might get a car today! And it's not the idea of getting a
car, but the idea of freedom. I might even be able to come visit
y'all." I stress while trying to maintain control of my voice.

"That'd be great! Oh man, Mom's going to be thrilled. I'm
not going to tell her yet. Let's wait until you actually get a car
first."

I bite my lips trying to contain my huge, goofy grin. We
smile at each other and then burst out laughing.

The day drags since I stare at the clock through most of
my classes. When it's finally over, Richard and Melissa are in

the parking lot waiting to pick me up. They giggle at me when they see me bouncing toward them. The first place we go to is the DMV to work on getting a Missouri State license.

I'm surprised when our next stop is a BMW dealership. I vigorously shake my head in refusal, explaining that they're too expensive. I still have hopes of repaying them, but with a BMW, it would take forever. I don't know much about cars, but I do know that BMW is a luxury car. They take me to another dealership that I'm unfamiliar with, and before I can see any prices, they have me in a baby blue sports coupe. I love it immediately. That's the one I drive home without ever knowing the price.

After we get home, Landon comes running out the front door. "Whoa, an Audi A5. Nice!"

"Super cute, Sarah," Denise beams, as she pushes past Landon.

I give everyone a ride around the block. Plus, I let Landon drive it once around the block. I don't let Denise drive, but I do let her take charge of the radio. It's fun and it seems normal. I text everyone when I go to my room. Aunt Andrea is delighted, especially with the idea of me getting to visit. Noah can't wait to see the car and hopefully drive it. I laugh at the wink face emoji he adds to the end of the text. With my regular phone, I text Tara and Rachel. I get a text from Luke asking how the car shopping went. I'd forgotten that I'd mentioned it to him before Landon told me everything. I still haven't cancelled my date Saturday. I'm about to text him to cancel when my phone begins ringing with his name on the screen.

I answer and give a tentative, "Um, hello?"

I hear the smile in his voice as he says, "I'd rather you tell me than reading a text. I want to hear how excited you are."

Nervously, I laugh and begin to tell him. He laughs a few times at either my excitement or my lack of knowledge about cars. His low voice in my ear makes my stomach flip. He really is easy to talk to and seems genuinely interested in what I have to say. *Ugh, that sounds so cliché.* But my mind drifts back to Landon and what a horrible person Luke *really* is.

"Listen—about Saturday. I'm going to have to cancel."

"What? No. Please don't."

"Look I just don't think—"

"It's Landon isn't it? He hates me, I know. What if I talk to him?"

"No. Leave Landon out of this."

"Can we keep talking? I don't want to hang up. You've never talked this much to me. Let's keep it going, please?"

"I have to go. Bye, Luke."

⁂

Rita opens the door to the lobby and smiles. "Hello, Sarah. Ready?"

I nod and follow her back. She sits in her chair and I sit across from her.

"Did you bring me a drawing?"

"I'm still working on something."

"That's fine. Does drawing help?"

"Yes. I've started doing it with Richard."

"Your father?"

She knows who I mean. But I've caught on that she likes to do this, refer to them as mother or father. "Yes. My father. It's been really nice. I enjoy him sitting there with me and both of us sketching."

"That's wonderful. How are things with your mother?"

"She can't let go of her resentment. I want a relationship with the Wallace family. Plus, I'm worried things are getting more complicated between Noah and I."

"How so?"

"It feels wrong, but I think I have feelings for him…"

"And why do you feel it's wrong?"

"Because at one time I thought he was my cousin."

"But he's not and you two didn't grow up together, did you?"

"No."

"I would like to ask you this—are you attracted to Noah because he's the bridge between both your worlds or because of *him*?"

"I'm not sure. There's just something about him."

"How does your family feel about this?"

"I haven't said a word. Not even hinted. They can't even stand the idea of me being around him. I'm constantly terrified Melissa is going to call or say something."

"Why?"

"Because she has before."

"Have you tried speaking with her or Richard about this?"

"No. Not really."

"You need to. We can do it here if you would feel more comfortable."

"I'll think about it. They bought me a car."

"Wow." She raises her eyebrows and gestures for me to continue.

"Yeah, but sometimes I worry they're buying—not buying my affection. I don't know. Not that they're trying to make up for what happened, but I don't know."

"Because of the new phone and clothes?" I nod. "Do they purchase these kind of things for the other children?"

"Yes."

"Maybe this is just their way. They're not giving you more or less. They're giving you the exact same treatment they would any of their kids. Speaking of, how's your relationship going with your siblings?"

"Actually, really good." I smile.

"Oh, I like seeing this." She smiles. "This is the first time you've given me a real smile."

Is it? Well, when your entire world has been turned upside down, sometimes it's hard to smile, Rita. "Landon and I have gotten really close. I feel like he understands me the most. Trent has some guilt issues he's working through, but he's an amazing big brother. Denise is…Denise." I release a light chuckle.

"Denise is a fourteen-year old. Yes." She chuckles and nods. Rita tilts her head in thought. "I'm sure Trent does seem to have some guilt he's been carrying over the years. It must've been hard for him to feel responsible for the distraction needed for your kidnapping. He probably feels very protective of not only you, but all his siblings now."

"It's not horrible to have so many people that care and want to protect me, but I don't like feeling like a victim. Maybe victim isn't the right word. I want some independence. I don't like feeling helpless. I'm just trying to figure out who I am, but I need some space to do that. To learn what I'm capable of. Who I am and what I like. I'm just confused and sometimes it can be stifling."

"Don't forget to bring a drawing. Keep drawing and expressing yourself."

Our time is up. We move my appointments to monthly now.

⁓

The next two days, I only drive to school or run errands with a family member. I'm not going to push for solo rides yet since I don't want to seem too eager and raise suspicion. Friday night, Luke texts me to ask for one more chance at a date. I leave my room to go find Landon before he goes to a party. He's styling his hair in front of his bathroom mirror.

"Luke texted again about a date. No way am I going."

He meets my eyes in the mirror and says, "You can't do that. You used this date as your main base for getting a car. I highly doubt that was your main reason, but they bought it. Keep the date, but do not accept a second. Not for me, but for your sake. The guy is a royal prick." I nod and leave him to finish getting ready. Surely I can tolerate him for one dinner.

⁂

It's the morning of my soccer game. I'm so hyped with this being game day and my first official date tonight. I have so many mixed emotions. On one hand, what Landon has told me about Luke has me disgusted. Plus, the whole punch incident. On the other hand, what our phone conversations, roses, and the feelings I get with him has me captivated. Once again, I'm so confused with how I feel. *This year will be known as the year of confusion. I'm confused with who I am, who my family is, and who my love interest is. Heck, I'm even confused with my own name!* As I'm getting ready for my game, I text Luke that I'm going to meet him at the restaurant instead of him picking me up. After I send the text, I put my phone away and head out for the field.

I spot the Wallace family on one end of the bleachers and the Randalls on the other end… along with Luke. We end the game with a win, placing us currently second in the league. Coach feels if I'd been there from the beginning, no doubt we'd have been first already. The Wallace family doesn't come to congratulate me. In fact, Noah is staring daggers in my direction. It's most likely due to the two big arms holding me now in a bear hug.

Luke.

I wiggle free and put my hands up. "Easy there."

I'm surprised he even came to the game. I can't figure out why he is so into me. Maybe because I don't act like the other girls. I see the way they look at him. He is handsome, but I think Noah is… *wait*—not going there.

"Great game. Congratulations on the win."

"Thank you. Well, thanks for coming. I think I need to get going. My ride is waiting for me."

"Yeah, of course. Don't let me keep you. Besides, I get to have you all to myself this afternoon." He winks as he walks away.

I decide that even though I'm not planning to continue a relationship with Luke, I can still enjoy tonight. I can still have a good time with him tonight as *frenemies*.

∽

Denise helps me get ready because I think she's more excited for the date than I am. She goes on about how she's had a crush on Luke *forever* and he's the *greatest*. She stresses how lucky I am and she wishes she was old enough to date him.

"You know in a couple of years, our age difference wouldn't even matter. Sorry," she blushes. "I should stop drooling over him. He is your date. I can be really rude sometimes," she shrugs. None of what she says bothers me since I have no intention of continuing a relationship with the infamous Luke Jamerson.

The doorbell rings ten minutes before I'd planned to leave. I can hear Melissa and Richard making a fuss over someone downstairs. I go down and there's Luke looking handsome as ever. They adore him, so of course they're ecstatic that we're going on a date.

I make eye contact with Luke as I slowly descend the staircase. He gives a dramatic sigh and grabs his chest, "Beautiful!" He holds a hand out to help me down the last few steps.

"I told you I'd meet you at the restaurant," I whisper to him.

He doesn't release his hold on my hand as he whispers back, "This is a date. A decent guy would pick you up, not expect you to drive yourself. Although, I'm sure you're excited to drive yourself now."

"A decent guy would respect what his date tells him."

He sighs when he sees the stern look on my face, "I'm sorry. You said you would meet me there but here I am. I like the extra time we get riding together. You learn a lot about a person during car rides." I narrow my eyes, so he continues, "I can follow you to the restaurant, I guess."

I shake my head and mumble, "I'll ride with you."

He gives a full smile showing off his perfect teeth. He should consider becoming a model or movie star. He continues to hold my hand until we get to the car. He opens the door for me and waves bye to everyone as we drive off.

"You really look beautiful, Sarah." He takes my hand and holds it as he drives.

I ease my hand from his and decide to start up a conversation. "So, care to explain that line about 'getting to know people with car rides?' Did you mean through general conversation or are there certain telltale signs people give away while in a car?"

He gives me a crooked smile as he chuckles. "Oh, there are a lot of things people reveal while in a car. For example, the kind of music they like. They don't have to come out and say they like the song, although most do. They might know every word as they belt it out or mumble along. They might tap their hands or bust out crazy dance moves in their seat. Music tells a lot about a person. A song can also bring on a funny story. How many times have you heard a song and it brought up a memory that you then go into a whole story about? I could go on, but you get the idea. I mean, that was only a few examples, but there's lots to learn while in the car."

I think about what he said while we go down the road. He doesn't ask me where I'd like to go, but surprises me by stopping the car in front of A Taste of Tuscany. I know the little place. In fact, I love it.

"This is your favorite place, isn't it?"

I'm baffled that he knows that. "Um, yeah. How'd you know?"

He gives me a pleased smile but doesn't answer. He gets out of the car and is at my door before I have a chance to open it. He helps me out and grabs a hold of my hand again. Once again, I ease my hand from his and place them in my back pocket as I walk.

After we are seated, Luke begins to ask me questions about myself, and I, in return, ask him about himself. He's really starting to grow on me. He's ridiculously attractive, charming, and witty at times. However, I can't get over the conversation I had with Landon and our whole spiked punch experience. I want to ask Luke about Marcus. The date is going so well, though. Besides, I have a feeling he would try to charm his way around the conversation. I push the urge away and continue enjoying his company. Our conversation flows from one topic to the next with ease. We love a lot of the same movies and music. I'm surprised that he has a soft spot for *Titanic* and The Beatles. He wants to travel the world before he's forty and encourages me to branch away after graduation.

"Life is meant to be lived! Where have you always wanted to go?"

I think it over and finally answer, "I think the Grand Canyon would be amazing to see. I'd want to watch the sunrise. Maybe even take some colored pencils and sketch it."

He smiles at me with genuine excitement. He throws his hands up. "Let's do it then! Spring break, me and you! We're going to the Grand Canyon. We camp out and that morning, you can sketch your heart's desire of the sun rising over the magnificent Grand Canyon."

"That's crazy. What high schoolers just plan a trip to the Grand Canyon? With a stranger no less?"

"I think stranger things have happened…" *I can't argue with him there.* "Besides, I have some money saved up. You don't have to wait until you're a certain age to live life." He raises one eyebrow and tilts his head. "If you want to do any, um, nude portraits at the Grand Canyon, I could strike a pose for ya?"

I laugh and break off a piece of my breadstick to throw at him.

"What? I'm a big supporter of the arts!"

We laugh and discuss other destinations and what all adventures await. Before I know it, we only have fifteen minutes before my curfew, and we're walking out of the restaurant.

When we get to the car, he opens my door; however, he stops me before I can get in by kissing me. He takes me completely by surprise that I stumble. He catches me with his strong arms and holds me firmly in place. I could get lost in his soft lips and firm hold. He smells amazing. I place my hands on his shoulders for support and then use them to gently push him away. I can't do this. My loyalty lies with Landon.

He smiles at me. "I've been wanting to do that since you first walked down the stairs."

He's so endearing with that husky voice. His eyes seem so kind and sincere that it makes my heart melt. I almost want to lean in for another kiss. It's unnerving how charming he can be. The allure of him. How can this be the same guy that Landon described? Being so unsure with myself right now, I get in the car with no comment.

We listen to the radio in comfortable silence. I catch my hand tapping to the beat of a song. I peek over and see him watching me out of the corner of his eye and with an amused expression on his face.

"You're an eighties fan. Nice. This song does have a good beat."

I have to bite my lip to keep from laughing. "Maybe I like just this one song. You can't analyze me from one song and one car ride."

"Nope. But you didn't respond to any of the other stations. I changed the station three times during our drives. You also tapped to another eighties song on the way to the restaurant."

I nod and we fall into back into silence. He breaks the silence when we pull into the driveway.

"This was nice." He takes my hand and kisses my knuckle.

I smile and nod as I try to as politely as possible ease my hand from his grasp. He puts the car in park, and we sit there. I try to figure out a way to get out of the car without making this awkward. I look at the house and say, "Well, I'm sure they're waiting for me."

I begin to slide out of his grasp, but he stops me with a firm hold. "Wait."

I turn to look at him and he smiles. "Do you have any plans for next Saturday?"

I have an internal panic attack. I gain some control and lie, "Oh, yeah I actually do."

He still hasn't released his hold, so I assume he's waiting for more details.

"I promised to help with an art project for school. It's a group project. Saturday is the only day that we can…because some of them work…yeah…" I look back at the house and then to him. I take a deep breath and breathe out, "So, thank you. This was really great of you to pick me up and buy my food."

I don't even know if I made any sense just now. I don't even know what I'm trying to say. I'm so awkward, and I just want this to be over.

He laughs. "I'll be more than happy to pick you up and buy you food anytime."

I open the door as he opens his. I hurry to the front door as I hear him coming behind me.

"You two have a nice time?" Richard opens the door scaring me half to death.

I'm relieved, though, because this saves me from worries about a goodnight kiss.

"Yes, sir. We sure did." Luke sticks his hand out to shake Richard's.

"Wonderful. It was good seeing you, son. Tell your parents we said hello. Probably see your dad tomorrow on the golf course. Drive safe on your way home." Richard gives Luke a hug and then puts his arm around me.

I assume Luke will leave after Richard gave his farewell. Once again, he surprises me by leaning in for a kiss. I catch him this time at the last minute and turn my head. He catches my cheek, barely missing my lips. Richard frowns at Luke, growling, "Goodnight Luke. Off you go. Drive safe."

Luke whispers in my ear before pulling away, "Sweet dreams."

⬌

While laying down in my room, I go through my text messages. I reply to Rachel and Tara, telling them we'll talk at school. Landon knocks on the door and comes in. He lays down next to me, and we discuss the night.

"Don't fall for his shit, Sarah." I give a small chuckle, but it only offends him, "I'm being serious. That guy is toxic." He holds a hand up to emphasize his point, "*Poison.* He's *poison.*"

I give a sad smile, for him and myself. Luke hurt him by bullying Marcus. Now, I'm hurt for falling for his charm. He hasn't actually done anything to hurt me. But Landon feels so passionately about his loathing for Luke that there's no way I could maintain a positive relationship with him if I pursue a relationship with his nemesis. At the end of the day, I'm going to choose Landon. He's the brother that I just discovered. He's family. He's all I have now.

He continues, clearly unfazed by me, "He is the most untrustworthy person I have ever met in my life." He visibly shakes, "I can't believe he kissed you. Did you brush your teeth? Please tell me you used some strong mouthwash. Kills 99.9% of bacteria. Might want to go get checked out in the nurse's office Monday. We can go to the hospital now."

I hit his shoulder. "He didn't use tongue if that'll ease your mind."

Landon nods. "It does. I'm glad to hear it. Are you going to go out again if he asks?"

"Of course not. He's been super sweet, a little pushy, but I still hate to hurt anyone feelings."

Landon waves off my last comment. "No worries there. He doesn't have feelings. The only thing you could possibly hurt is his ego."

I laugh and turn on my side. "Do you think I'll ever feel like Sarah Randall?"

He turns on his side to face me. "Do you think I'll ever feel like Landon Randall?"

I raise my eyebrows. "You are Landon Randall. You've always been. You know who you are."

"Think so? I'm still chasing the white rabbit as much as you are, Alice."

⊗

I go downstairs and find Richard in the kitchen eating some grapes at the island. I hold up my sketchpad and give a little wave. He nods and leaves the room. I go on to the den and get comfortable. Richard walks in and takes a seat next to me. We both begin sketching. I can see his work, but I'm still working on my original sketch. I make tiny curves in the center and then focus on big and little lines in a circular motion. When it starts to get late, Richard stands.

"Thanks for coming to get me. It helps me unwind before bed."

"Me too."

"Good night, sweetheart."

"Good night…"

Thirty-Four

NOAH DOESN'T GET TO SCHOOL AS EARLY AS HE normally does on Monday. I'm a little aggravated but try to not let it show. He finally walks in, with barely a glance my way.

"How was your weekend?" I ask him as he sits down.

"Alright."

That's it? "Nothing more to share?"

He just nods while looking straight ahead. I feel a little hurt that he isn't talking to me. I honestly would like to know what he did. He doesn't ask about mine, I guess because he already knows I went on a date with Luke. A little part of me wonders if he cares that I went out with Luke because he's concerned or…could he be jealous?

Karlie struts in with a smug smile. She winks at Noah as she sits down. I turn to watch him merely nod at her. *Please no.* Noah is handsome, no denying that. He's going to have girls crushing on him. The thought of him with Karlie makes me want to vomit. Yes, she's beautiful and the head cheerleader so she's popular. However, he deserves better. She's probably better than me since at least it wouldn't be so complicated. *I don't know why I just compared myself to her.* Deciding that Noah may not feel up to talking, I try a different approach. Maybe he'd be more responsive to writing. I pull out my notebook but before I can write anything, she speaks.

"If you want to know about our weekend together, go ahead and ask. I'll be happy to tell you."

I narrow my eyes at her and purse my lips together. *Deep breaths. Don't let her get under your skin.*

She smiles at Noah, and then sneers at me, "No point in wasting trees. Be eco-friendly."

I smile at her. "I already asked how his weekend went. He said it was just 'alright.' Didn't sound like it was that exciting."

This seems to infuriate her. *Mission accomplished.* Before she can begin a rant, Noah speaks, "Did anyone finish the assignment? I think I'm missing something in my notes."

I raise my eyebrows at his feeble attempt to change the subject, but it works. Karlie is beside herself going through her backpack in search of her notes. She's glowing when she hands him her notes. After class, I don't bother saying anything else to Noah. Even though I went on a date with Luke, I hate that he went on a date with Karlie. I'm so confused with how I feel, but I know I can't look at him knowing he was with her. I manage to avoid him during third period and lunch as well.

I walk into art class to find Eric and Noah already in their seats. Eric is wearing a smirk while Noah looks indifferent. That indifference is driving me insane. *What's his problem?* I can't figure out why he is treating me with such distaste. *Have I in some way made him angry?* I'm really annoyed with the fact he went out with Karlie this weekend. Is it because I don't like her personally and I think he deserves better, or is it because I don't like the idea of anyone *with* Noah? *Am I jealous?*

Not long after taking my seat, Eric begins talking. "Sweet Sarah Randall. I hear that you're *extra* sweet. It's a shame I didn't get to find out for myself. I should have been smarter and gone to your house when Trent wasn't around."

I look at him confused and disgusted. "It wouldn't have mattered if he was there or not."

I scoot my chair closer to Noah as Eric watches me. "I guess that's because I'm not good enough for you? I'm no Luke Jamerson, but we could've had a good time, nonetheless." He leans toward me with a smug smile. "We still can."

I shake my head, cringing. Eric suddenly stops talking and looks away from me.

Noah leans over glaring at Eric but speaks to me, "Ignore him. He's an idiot."

He seems tense so I ask, "What's going on?" Then I lean closer and whisper, "Why have you been so standoffish with me?"

He shrugs. "Not sure what you're talking about."

I give a humorless laugh. "Right. Okay, fine. If that's how you want to behave, go ahead, but I'd rather you tell me so I can make it right."

He raises his eyebrows and leans closer. "I don't think you were too worried about what I thought when you went out with that douche."

"Seriously? I told you I was going and guess what? Nothing happened. We went out to eat, and he took me home. It's none of your business, but I don't plan on going on anymore dates with him."

I huff and cross my arms. His facial features soften as he scoots his chair to the point we are completely against each other. He whispers, "Why are you not going out with him again? Did he…he didn't…did he do something he shouldn't have?"

I love that he cares, but I'm a little unnerved that I'm secretly hoping he cares more in a jealous way. Before I allow myself to focus on that feeling, I shove it aside to examine what he might be implying about Luke. I shake my head and ask, "Nothing happened. Why are you so upset?"

He huffs, and I can tell he's exasperated that I'm having trouble figuring this out. "I'm upset that I knocked that guy out for you, after he gave you a spiked drink, and then you were willing to go on a date *alone* with him. Also..."

He fidgets and looks around the room. He's making me nervous with this dramatic pause, so I urge, "Also?"

He sighs. "Also, Luke is telling everyone that *something* did happen."

I practically shout, "What? Okay, he did kiss me once on the lips, but it was by surprise. I didn't encourage him and avoided all other kissing opportunities." I feel myself beginning to panic, "What exactly is he saying?"

Noah shushes me and whispers, "I would rather not say. I don't believe anything happened...now."

I'm taken aback by his last comment. "What do you mean 'now'? Is that why you've been acting this way? You think I did something with Luke over the weekend?"

He rushes in an agitated tone. "What was I supposed to think? Like I said, the guy gets you tipsy and feels on you all night in front of everyone. You turn around and go out on a date with him. He went around telling everyone you liked it so much that you wanted more, and this time, y'all weren't interrupted."

My heart sinks, and my face feels flushed. I'm mortified. This is why everyone has probably been obsessed with asking me for details. Noah has probably been protecting me the best he can. No wonder he's so angry every time it gets brought up.

"Nothing happened. One kiss. No tongue. I haven't accepted a second date." I decide to change the subject and put the focus on Noah. "What about your weekend? Karlie indicated you had a nice time with her?"

He scoffs. "Please. A group of us all went to the movies. She happened to sit next to me."

I'm pleased with how he doesn't seem to reciprocate the same feelings toward her as she does him.

He gives a smirk. "Well…one little thing might've happened." He pulls some hair away from my ear and whispers, "She stuck her hand down…" He pauses. My heart stops. I can't believe he's telling me this. I want to stop him, but I also want to know what exactly went on between them."…my popcorn bowl."

I chuckle and give him a sideways look. Noah mocks surprise."What did you think I was going to say? Um, I don't know what kind of dirty mind you have. Also, it was a PG movie, I'll have you know."

Trying to disguise how much I really care, I ask as casually as possible,"You two only shared popcorn?"

He mimics my response from earlier."Nothing happened. It's none of your business, but I don't plan to share anymore popcorn with her."

We both burst out laughing. The rest of the day goes back to normal between us.

I get a text from Luke after school asking me how my day went. Funny he should ask. I decide to confront him about everything over the phone so I can gauge his reactions. He answers on the second ring.

"Hey you."

"Hey yourself. Have you been telling people that something more happened Saturday? Like—we did more than go out to eat?"

"What? That's crazy. I wish. Ha."

"This isn't funny. People have been whispering about me all day."

"That's because you went out with me. Ignore them. I haven't said anything. I don't kiss and tell. People like a juicy story. If they don't hear one, they'll make it up."

"Then maybe we should hold off on anymore dates. That

way they won't have anything to tell."

"You're going to not date just because some people are bored and exaggerate a little?"

A little? Wow. And, I'm still going to date. Just not you. I bite my tongue and wait for him to finish. "I understand though. There's a lot of attention that goes with dating me. It's fine."

"Yeah. Well, bye."

"Bye, Sarah."

If he's upset, he hides it well. I feel like that phone conversation went well. I find Landon to tell him about it.

He shakes his head and says, "You're so cute. Luke isn't going to take it well that he was turned down. Just wait."

…Well, crap.

Thirty-Five

Dec 12

I haven't written in here in years. I guess I felt like I needed to talk to someone about what's been going on, but who can I talk to? Nobody would understand. Olivia is fourteen and wanting more independence. Around here it's fine. I let her hang out with her friends, go where she wants. But I try to keep her away from anything that could leak back to the Randalls. She's been wanting to have access to social media. All her friends have accounts. Why can't she? Why can't she be like everyone else? She's so lame that she doesn't have her own account when literally everyone at school has an account. I'm surprised with what a strain this has been between us. Even Andrea is team Luv Bug having social media. She wants to be involved in her life and goes on about how easy it would be. My sister is so annoyed with me that I won't let Luv spend the weekend with them this summer. I can't. I can't take that risk. She can't go visit. And she most certainly cannot have her face plastered all over social media.

She'd really throw a fit if she knew I had accounts. I keep mine private and under a fake name. Gotta keep an eye on those Randalls.

Even if I was strict with who she could be friends with and kept the account private—her photo could still get leaked back to them. Especially if Andrea added her! I know my sister means well, and honestly, I'm surprised she hasn't noticed how much Olivia looks like the Randalls. Then again, she's not close to them. They don't run in the same circles. Probably the only reason Noah associates with them is through sports. What fate is that? Noah, friends with Olivia's brothers! And Noah, what if he added Olivia to his friends list? Not that those two ever talk—but what if this caused them to start communicating more. That'd push all of them to want her to go visit. I can't take her back!

It's asking for trouble. No, begging for it. We have a good life. We're happy. Her social media phase will pass. She just doesn't want to be an outsider. I tried telling her that not everyone has an account. Even my own ears thought it sounded lame. But what's a mother to do? I have to protect my daughter. The older she gets… the more I fear I'm going to lose her.

Thirty-Six

ONCE I LEARNED THE TRUTH ABOUT CINDY, I'D suspected that's why I was kept away from social media. Reading it from her and having confirmation doesn't make it any easier. I remember those conversations. They were the few arguments we had. Funny, now I can have a social media account, but I don't want it. I close the journal. *It's hard to admit, but I was raised by a crazy person. Does that make me crazy for a part of me still loving her?*

And funny enough, whereas Cindy let me go everywhere alone but no social media, Melissa lets me have all the online freedom in the world just no traveling alone. I finally get my chance to go somewhere alone. I need supplies for my art project. To my surprise and delight, everyone is busy. I grab the keys and my secret phone. I text Noah that I have at least a thirty-minute window. While waiting for him to reply, I go ahead and rush through the store. I walk out within ten minutes. With perfect timing, he texts me to meet him at a general store nearby. I'm a little perplexed because I'd wanted to go to their house.

I hop out of the car, but before I enter the store, I hear Noah calling my name from a few feet down the street. I speed walk toward him, looking around the whole time.

When I reach him, he answers my thoughts. "I can't let you go to our house. Your parents are most likely tracking your phone, so leave it in your car. Let's go to the restaurant down the street. It's less crowded, and none of your parents' circle of friends go there."

We enter a casual place that only serves sub sandwiches, Balto's. I spot Aunt Andrea right away. She gets up out of her seat when she sees us, and I rush into her arms. We both hug and cry until the guys clear their throats. We can't help that we're so emotional since this is the first time since Cindy's death that we have been alone together. I sit down next to her while Noah and his dad sit across from us. We all fall into easy conversation about anything and everything. I tell them all about the Randalls, especially how I'm developing a close relationship with Landon, and also slowly with Denise and Trent as well.

"Noah, didn't you and Landon used to get along really well? Nah, you were closer to Trent. Since y'all were both so competitive in sports. Landon ain't much into sports I don't figure." Brad asks his son.

Brad doesn't speak much but when he does, it's always with a deep drawl and very country.

Noah's only response is to shrug and nod.

"Landon participates in track and cross country." I inform him.

He nods and focuses his attention back on his sandwich. Andrea encourages me to continue speaking. I go on to tell her I still keep in touch with Angie.

She gives me a sad smile. "Sweetie, I hope so. Maybe when you get older and on your own it'll be easier. Won't be that much longer, now will it?"

I smile at her, and she begins talking about how she can't believe we're about to graduate.

Something has been nagging at the back of my mind. "Aunt Andrea?"

"Yes, Luv Bug?"

"Cindy was married before?"

I watch Aunt Andrea swallow and her eyes have trouble meeting mine. "Yes."

"His name was Michael?"

"How did you know?"

"I…" I don't want to mention the journal. "I heard someone talking. Briefly. I didn't catch his last name though. Would you tell me, please?"

"Snyder. Michael Snyder."

"*A tiny little girl wrapped in a blanket that had 'Karlie' sewn on it.*" Cindy's journal entry. Karlie Snyder *is* Cindy's ex-husband's daughter? I just needed the confirmation. Now that I have it, it doesn't really change anything does it?

Noah reminds me that I should be getting back. "They'll be worried, and we don't want them to have any reason to take away your driving privileges."

I give a teary goodbye hug to everyone. Noah walks me back to my car. Before he turns to walk away, he gives me a peck on the forehead. All the way home, I ponder that kiss. Was it meant to be intimate? Was it out of sympathy? Was it meant to be comforting? Or was it simply a kiss like Andrea or Brad would give me?

❧

The days have been going smoothly, so I'm a little surprised when out of nowhere, Noah apologizes again for how he acted over Luke.

"I'm sorry. I was kind of a jerk about the whole thing."

"It's okay. I've been acting a little immature and petty. So let's just let the whole thing go." I accept his apology and decide to take this opportunity to ask him if he knows anything about the bullying at Luke's school. "Since we're discussing Luke, do you know anything about him bullying kids? Maybe any guy named Marcus?"

"Ha. You're so subtle." I roll my eyes. "He was good buddies with Landon so I'm guessing you've already heard some of it?"

"I want to hear what you know."

"It was two years ago when Trent was a senior, Landon was a freshman, and Luke and Marcus were sophomores. It happened at the private school. But it was so bad, that we all knew about it. I heard a few of the pranks were covering the inside of Marcus's locker with gay porn and leaving suckers in the shape of a penis on his desk. The school didn't get involved very much since all the kids had important parents."

I don't even know Marcus, but I want to cry. That could've easily been Landon. Nobody should have to go through that.

As soon as class is dismissed, I find Landon in the hallway and rush to hug him. Fighting back tears, I whisper, "I'm so sorry what Marcus went through. If you ever come out, know that I'm here for you."

He shifts uncomfortably while returning the hug. He pulls away and looks me in the eyes. "Who've you been talking to?"

My eyes grow big as I realize he must think I've been talking about him. "Oh! I just asked Noah if he knew of Luke being a bully. What he said about Luke was horrible and cruel."

He nods in agreement. The bell rings so I hurry and give him one last bear hug before heading off to my next class.

In Art, I'm doodling a landscape while I wait for class to begin. It's missing something, but I can't figure out what it needs. I smile to myself as I imagine what Bob Ross might suggest. *Maybe a happy little tree over here.*

Noah plops down in the seat next to me and leans over my shoulder. He's intrigued with my love for art, especially my sketches. He tells me he has a surprise for me and to meet him in the supermarket parking lot after school. I keep pestering him to give me a hint, but all he'll tell me is I'm going to have to ditch my car and phone. *That doesn't sound suspicious at all.*

After school, I let Landon know I need to go to the store. He offers to go with me, but I tell him I enjoy my few little private trips of freedom. Thankfully, he lets it go.

As I'm about to pull out of the parking lot, he leans on my car and says, "You know, I'm not stupid. Nobody gets excited about going to the store for *supplies*. Also, didn't you just go to the store the other day? Might I suggest, you're going to Rachel's for a study session? Hhmm? Don't worry, I'll cover for you." He holds his hand out. "Your phone. I'll leave it at Rachel's house in case they track it." I give him my phone and he puts it in his back pocket. He winks and walks over to his Jeep.

I drive to the supermarket parking lot where I leave my car and hop into Noah's truck. Before I shut the door, he tells me to go ahead and grab my bag. I give him a quizzing look but go with it. He drives about twenty minutes outside of town before I ask, "Where are we going again? How far away is it?"

"A little bit further."

"Not going to give anything away, huh?"

He doesn't take his eyes off the road as he speaks through a smile. "Nope. It'll ruin the surprise."

We drive another couple of minutes and the scenery before us begins to change. Gone are the flat lands as far as the eye can see. The road begins to curve more and have hills. It almost feels like a roller coaster. I look out my window and marvel at all the trees with their red, gold and brown leaves. There's rolling hills with a few cows scattered lazily about. Noah takes an exit, but I miss the name since I was so distracted by the beautiful scenery. The first sign of civilization since we left Lumberton is a Subway connected to a gas station. We pass it and find a couple of farmhouses on down the road. Noah makes another turn, and the road becomes rougher.

The road is one you would've had to have been looking for and known was there. It's easily hidden by all the trees, and it's more of a dirt path than a road. As we drive down the narrow path, I smile with excitement. It's almost like something from a fairytale. The plain dirt road seems like a secret passageway that must be leading to someplace enchanting with how there are so many trees stretched over the road. It's a sunny day but with all the thick trees, the road is mostly shaded with the exception of few rays of sunshine poking through. The gold leaves gently drift down from the trees and a few sprinkle over the truck. I stretch up in my seat and it seems the road is this way for as far as the eye can see.

Just as before, Noah suddenly turns onto another path that could easily have been missed. It's an even more narrow and bumpy road, but not as long. No sooner had he turned the truck, we're up a small hill and then parking the truck in a clearing. Noah grins as he shuts the truck off.

"C'mon." With a smile and nod to exit, he opens the truck door. I hop out and take in my surroundings. The ground is covered in leaves and large, gray, moss covered rocks are scattered about. Noah takes my hand and begins leading me on what I think used to be a path, but it's hidden by all the leaves. I look up to the tall beautiful trees as the sun shines through the different fall colored leaves. A few red and gold leaves fall as we walk.

We've only walked a short distance when I faintly hear flowing water. He pulls my hand and leads me off the path between some trees until we come to an opening on a hill that has a stream running through it. On down, I can see that there's a small water fall on large, misshaped rocks. The water cascades down into a small bank that would be a great spot for sunbathing. The stream continues down for as far as the eye can see. This may actually be a small river. I'm not very good with geography, so I'm not exactly sure. The water does seem deep, and I bet this spot is popular in the summer for swimming. As opposed to right now, I'm sure the water is freezing. The location is beautiful and peaceful. There are colorful trees everywhere except for where the water is. It's almost like they're protecting and hiding a secret hidden fountain. My imagination runs wild creating my own little fairytale. I can't wrap my mind around how beautiful and magical everything seems, and it's barely an hour away.

Noah tugs at my hand again and begins to lead me down a small slope. The leaves are everywhere and hiding some of the rocks. I try to watch exactly where Noah places his feet. I step but my foot slides on the leaves and I also feel a rock come loose. I try to grab a tree branch nearby to catch myself, but I'm not fast enough. My eyes squeezed shut waiting for impact, I feel two strong hands on my waist and as a reflex, I reach out and grab two biceps. I hear Noah chuckle.

"You okay there? I should've warned you to wear outdoor shoes, but I didn't want to give anything away."

I slowly open my eyes prepared to answer him that I'm fine, but my words get caught in my throat. He's so close to me. His warm hands are practically burning through my sweater. We stare at each other and I think we've both stopped breathing. Noah really is handsome. His eyes are so warm and kind. His lips look so soft yet firm. He is both tender and strong. My stomach suddenly feels like it's in knots, and

I swallow and part my lips. He seems like he is inching closer and his eyebrows pinch. He searches my face.

Is he silently asking to kiss me? I nod, and my hands squeeze his arms. *Yes, kiss me.*

He clears his throat and in a husky voice says, "Good." He sits me upright. He clears his throat again and in his normal good humored voice says, "I was almost afraid I hadn't caught you in time. We'll go a little slower. It's not much further."

Oh right. He was asking if I was 'alright.' Suddenly, I feel foolish for thinking Noah was about to kiss me. He probably doesn't see me that way and might never. Despite us not actually being related and never having a family bond, he probably still thinks it would be weird to be attracted to me. I'm grateful for his friendship, either way, and it was really nice for him to bring me out here. This place feels special. I wonder if it's special for him. I've been here five minutes, and I love it. Slowly, he leads me down a few more feet, and I find a tree that's fallen. It must've been down for a long time with all the moss and vines that's wrapped around it. He opens his backpack and pulls out a blanket and snacks. He lays the blanket in front of the tree and we sit, using the tree to rest our backs against.

"Surprise." He nudges my shoulder with his. He gestures out to the scenery before us. From this spot, we have the perfect view of the waterfall and stream, with all the vivid gold and red from the trees that form a beautiful backdrop. "You seemed to really be struggling with that landscape. Maybe you'll get some inspiration from here."

"It's beautiful," I gasp. I nudge him back. "Do you ever swim here?"

His eyes brighten. "You bet. Wanna go for a dip?"

I laugh and indicate my clothing. "You should've told me the surprise, and I would've dressed appropriately."

He waggles his eyebrows at me. "Swimsuits are optional

out here. And I wouldn't recommend getting your clothes wet, might make for a cold ride home."

He grabs a bag of chips and casually pops one in his mouth. I struggle to get my blush under control. Was that Noah flirting? Maybe that was a matter of fact; we are out in the country. Deciding to quit dwelling on it, I open my satchel to take out my sketch pad and colored pencils. I flip open the pad and stare at the scenery before me. I grab my pencils and lightly outline the stream. Then, I focus on the scattered trees.

As I'm making outlines of the landscape, I feel Noah's eyes burning on my face. I don't take my eyes off my paper, but I let out a nervous laugh. "What?"

He's still staring. "Nothing. I'm enjoying watching you draw. I think I enjoy watching you as much as you enjoy doing it."

"And why's that?"

He leans back on his elbows. "You make goofy facial expressions."

I immediately drop my pencil and look over to him. "Excuse me?"

He laughs. "Nah, I'm just messin' with you. You do make a lot of different facial expressions. They aren't goofy, though. They're cute. Sometimes, you raise your eyebrows like you're surprised by what you see, even though it seems you've been looking at the same thing for twenty minutes. Sometimes, you look angry, like you can't get it the way you want it. Sometimes, you seem happy and content, relaxed and at peace." He leans forward and places his thumb in between my eyebrows and pushes the skin down. "My favorite is when you do this. When you look like this, you look like a pissed off bulldog pup."

I slap his hand away and then push hard on his shoulder. He falls to the side with a laugh.

I shoo him away with my hand. "I appreciate you bringing me here, but you can leave now."

"I would, but how'd you get home?"

"I can call you to come back or call someone else for a ride." I pick up my pencil, but before I begin sketching again, he sits back up but closer this time.

"One, you couldn't call someone else. No service. Two, you said Landon has your phone. Three, I wouldn't want you to call someone else. It wouldn't be a good idea, anyhow. Melissa would ask how you got here."

Noah puts a strand of hair behind my ear and gives me a sad smile. "I think your family is afraid I'm going to kidnap you."

Before he can pull his hand away, I lean my cheek against it. "It wouldn't be kidnapping if I went willingly, would it?"

He stares at me for a moment, looking like he's fighting an internal battle. Suddenly, he leans forward but pauses momentarily with his lips barely touching mine. I'm not sure if I should move or not. On instinct, I close my eyes and wet my lips. With my eyes closed, all my senses are heightened. I feel the warmth of his breath, the smell of the grass, the sounds of the trickling water, and a bird chirping in the distance. I also hear Noah's breathing. I can tell he's as nervous as I am, with his hand slightly shaking. His hand suddenly becomes firm against my cheek, and he pulls me slightly closer. His lips are soft and gentle. I want more, but I'm too scared to do anything. He pulls back, and I open my eyes.

"We kissed." *I'm so lame.* Obviously, we kissed.

He stares at me a moment and slowly responds, "Yes... we did..."

We both stare at each other, waiting for the other one to take the lead. There's a light cool breeze. I stare deeply into his eyes. I look down to his semi full lips. They're parted. I notice the contrast between the cool breeze and his warm breath. We're so close. If I was to lean an inch closer, we'd kiss again. Or if he was to lean in an inch. I want him to. I like Noah. I *like* him. Not as a family member. Not as a cousin. As a girl liking a boy. We're not related. Our relationship wouldn't be weird. Him being my cousin was a lie, but my attraction to him is real. I know it is. He must feel the same since he kissed me? But he isn't moving. Finally, he gets up and gathers our things.

The kiss was perfect. It couldn't have been more perfect, but suddenly we become silent and awkward with each other. I hurry behind him. He helps me through the path back to the truck. I do the only thing I can think of. I go back to familiar ground. When he starts the truck, I mention, "I'd like to see Aunt Andrea again."

He slams his hand on the steering wheel and turns the truck back off. I don't understand his sudden outburst. I'm still holding the seatbelt barely above the buckle because I'm too nervous to buckle it in case I need to hop out of the truck quickly.

He unbuckles his seat belt and turns to face me. "Dammit! You need to quit referring to my mom as your aunt. I agree with your parents on that one."

I'm on the verge of crying because I don't know where this is coming from. I'm dumbfounded and hurt. He's sending so many mixed signals. The seatbelt slides out of my hand and pops when it hits the interior of the truck.

He continues in a firm voice like he's scolding a child for the hundredth time. "Cindy wasn't your mom. Your parents are Richard and Melissa Randall. Ben and Andrea Wallace are in no way blood related to you. Hell, they aren't even related to you by marriage. Therefore, in no way are *we* related, do you understand?"

I'm blinking fast and trying to hold it together as I nod.

He's breathing heavily. "Good. Good because I need you to understand that it's been driving me crazy, this cousin bullshit. It makes what's about to happen seem wrong and weird."

Before I can even comprehend what he just said, he has his hand behind my head and crashing his lips to mine. I wrap my arms around him and crawl up the seat to get closer to him. We're both breathing heavily and touching each other everywhere. His tongue pushes its way into my mouth. My body is already pushed up against his, but I want to be closer. I *need* to be closer. I'm so relieved and excited that he does feel the same way. I wasn't crazy. We have a real attraction to each other. I keep pushing against him and running my hands all over his body. He starts to get impatient and pulls my shirt over my head. He begins kissing my neck but then suddenly stops.

"Shit," he sighs.

Once again, I'm dumbfounded. *Who sighs, 'shit' while making out? I'm not following his train of thoughts today.* Mixed signals!

"I'm sorry. I'm rushin' this. You deserve more than a hot and heated session in an old pickup." He hands me my shirt.

Frustrated with him, I ask, "What do you mean, Noah? Are you saying you do or you don't want to be with me?"

I'm getting really irritated, but he looks at me like I'm missing something that should be plain as day. "Of course, I want to be with you. Did you miss the part where I was about to take you in my truck? If I didn't stop myself when I did, I would've tried to go all the way with you. Right now." He pushes his body against mine.

It's so warm and firm. I desperately crave his touch, so much that I know without a doubt I would've let him take my virginity.

He holds my face in his hands, and what he says next surprises me. "We're both inexperienced in this area, but I do know I want our first time to be special. It'll be special no matter what, but I don't want it to be rushed in my cramped truck with the fear of your parents hunting for you. In fact, before we do anything I want us to first go on a proper date. Okay?"

I smile and whisper. "Okay."

He gives me a few more lingering kisses. Leaning his forehead to mine, he whispers, "We need to get you back to your car, but before we do, I want to make sure one thing is clear." He leans back and tells me to open my eyes. I hadn't even realized that I'd closed them. He has an intense look on his face and his voice is strong when he says, "You're my girlfriend now. You're not my cousin, so never refer to my mom as *Aunt* Andrea again. Never. Again." Then he whispers in a pleading voice. "Please." I laugh, but he's still so serious. "No laughing. No more auntie or protective cousin crap. I was never being the protective platonic figure. I was being the jealous guy wanting you to be his." He gives me one more kiss and then slides me back to my seat.

I buckle up and give him a sideway look. "It's not going to be easy to quit calling her Aunt Andrea. That's how I've known her all my life. It just flows."

He turns the key and gives me a pointed look. "Try."

Thirty-Seven

BY THE TIME I ARRIVE HOME, THE HOUSE IS DARK. I'm about to climb the stairs to go to my room when I hear a faint sound coming from my left side. It's so faint that I'm not sure I even heard anything, but then I hear another sound that resembles glass breaking. I debate on going to investigate or sneaking into my room. For some reason, I'm compelled to go see what it is. My feet are moving before I can talk myself out of it. I see a faint glow coming from the den. I creep down the hall and try to listen for any other sounds. I hear sniffling and muffled cries.

It's Melissa.

I peak my head around the corner and gasp. She's standing in front of the fireplace with a glass of wine in her hand. She turns her head to look at me, and I see her face is red and blotchy. Her eyes are blood shot and puffy. What has my heart in knots and sends me running toward the fireplace is what she has in her other hand. My mother's journal. Or rather, Cindy's journal. I reach for it, but she pulls it away.

"What? Just what do you think you're doing, *my daughter?*"

The way she says "my daughter" makes me stop and my blood run cold. Her voice is off. She's clearly drunk, which might be the reason there is meanness laced in her voice. She lifts the journal up and holds it open with one hand in front of her. She takes a long sip of wine and then chuckles while staring at the pages.

"That sorry bitch actually wrote down all the details of how she plotted, schemed and finally *stole* you. From *me!* She then goes on to write about the *joys* of motherhood. As if she was *ever* your mother. Fucking delusional." I flinch. I've never heard her swear. I've never heard her raise her voice. Then again, I've never seen her in this condition. She turns to face me again and holds the book to her side. "Delusional! You were taken and held captive by a pathetic psychopath who managed to raise you to *love* her. Did you love her?"

I don't want to answer that, so I look at the floor.

"Sarah. *Sarah!*" She yells at me. Then she pauses as if a thought has occurred to her. "Oh, I'm sorry." She speaks in a hushed ominous tone. "You're not Sarah, right? Your name is *Olivia.*"

Her voice grows so cold that I'm beginning to get a chill up my spine. "Well, *Olivia*, did you love her?"

She isn't going to let this go. I desperately wish Richard would wake up. Maybe Landon could calm her down. I gulp and whisper in a pleading tone, "She was all I knew. I thought…I thought she was my mother."

Melissa is visibly shaking, and I can't tell if she's about to cry from anger or grief. She paces. I'm about to panic and go for help. She seems like she's on the verge of a mental break down. She stops and turns to me. Her facial expression has me terrified. "But she wasn't! She was never your mother!" She shouts at me with so much resentment that I feel she's angry with me, but for what? *That I did not leave her willingly.*

I stare at her in disbelief. "You act like I ran away to be

with her. I was a child! I was an infant! Why are you yelling at me?"

Melissa narrows her eyes at me. "Why did you keep this journal? You know the *truth*. You know more of the truth than anyone. How long have you *known* that we were searching for you? Did you want to stay with her even after you discovered the truth? You never even wanted to be found!"

I throw my hands up. "I *never* knew until she died! She had the journal hidden and left me a note in her will. You honestly think I was okay finding out about all of this? This is horrible!"

She takes another big drink from her wine glass and gives me a sour look. "Then *why*, daughter dearest, didn't you turn the journal over to the police? It was hidden *here* in your room."

I cross my arms and hold myself. "I haven't even finished reading it. I was too scared to read it for a long time."

She pours more wine into her glass as she continues to question me in a clearly disgusted tone. "Why read it to start with? Once you learned who she really was, why read any more of her deceit?"

I rub my arms, unsure of how to continue, "Um, well she said she wanted to explain. I was curious. What does any of this matter? I'm here now, and she's... dead."

Melissa nods and narrows her eyes at me. She raises her glass to me. "You are absolutely right, my sweet girl. That bitch is dead. I'll drink to that!" She takes a drink from her glass before placing it on the fireplace mantel. Then, she lifts the journal up. "And *none* of this matters." She throws the journal into the fireplace.

I scream and rush around the sectional toward the fireplace. Melissa, however, stops me by pushing me onto the couch. My scream must've woken everyone up because I hear the pounding of feet coming down the stairs.

Landon comes rushing in and freezes when he sees both of us in tears. Richard and Denise do the same. Melissa looks back and forth between me and them before she finally crumbles to the floor. Her whole body shakes as she sobs uncontrollably. Richard touches my shoulder and asks if I'm all right. *Of course not!* But I merely nod. He then hurries to his wife's side and rubs her back, whispering what I assume are comforting words. I should feel pity for this broken woman, but I can't. *How could she? How could she throw away my mother's journal in the fire without a single thought? Okay, Cindy wasn't my biological mother and she did destroy Melissa. What about consideration for me that I still wanted to read it?*

I feel two arms wrap around me in comfort.

"I'm here for you," Landon whispers. I sink into him and allow my tears to flow freely.

Denise goes to her mother and asks her what happened. Melissa cries out, "She still loves her! She still loves her! She'll never see me as her mother!" Her voice begins to crack and we can barely understand her, "She'll never love me that way! Don't you see?"

I've had enough with feeling blamed for this. I've had enough with her constantly making me feel guilty that I had a relationship with a woman who raised me. I especially have had enough with not being able to move on with my life.

I stand and shout at her, "You won't let me! You won't give me a chance because you keep bringing her between us! *You* bring her between us! You focus more on her than you do me! Everything you do with me, you bring her into it! New clothes, because of her. New phone, because of her. You want to erase my life with her, but some of that is what made me the person that I am. If you could just allow us to spend time together freely, with no resentments, then maybe we could grow closer. It's like you resent the fact that she cared for me. Why can't you be happy that I did at least feel loved and got along with her? Be happy for me that I had a good life growing up when I could've easily been abducted and abused. This was terrible for you, I get it, but you're taking your anger toward Cindy out on me."

I catch my breath and cry, "Our relationship can't grow into love because you are filled with too much hate!"

I run out of the room. I continue to run out of the house, down the driveway, and out to the street. The cold night air burns my wet face, but I keep running. I run until I'm out of breath and my legs feel like jelly. My throat burns and my sides ache. I flop down on the cold ground and stick my head between my legs to try to catch my breath. I feel nauseated and exhausted. Once I've calmed down, I stand up and begin walking back toward the house.

Headlights approach me and as it gets closer, I can see it's Richard's truck. The truck stops, and since I'm exhausted, I hop in.

It's quiet in the truck, with only the hum of the engine. He doesn't say anything right away, but he doesn't go back to the house. He drives around the block twice before he begins, "She's jealous. She loves you *so* much but she's jealous, Sarah. Please, try to understand. I hope you never know the pain of losing a child. We all thought we'd lost you, except Melissa. She never gave up hope."

He pauses. I think he's fighting for control of his emotions. He shakes his head as if to clear it. "We lost you. The hardest part was that you were taken right in front of her, we're supposed to keep you safe. She was there when it happened. You have no idea what that did to her. She was *there* with you… and that woman slipped in and took you away. Melissa felt like she didn't even get a chance to fight for you. You slipped through her fingers."

I look out the window. It's dark but I can make out the shapes of playground equipment in the distance. He turns left, driving around another block. His tone changes from depressed to disbelief as he speaks, "Then, we get the call that you'd been found and were returning home." He shakes his head, and says, almost as an after-thought, "You know, we almost sold the house."

His eyes glisten and he clears his throat twice before speaking again. Then he says more firmly, "We'd discussed selling the house because it was a constant reminder, but Melissa had some crazy notion that you might find your way home. We couldn't live with it, but we couldn't quite move past it, either. She blamed herself. She blamed herself and tortured herself with your memory almost every single day." He clears his throat and then slowly exhales. "Anyways. When we found out you were coming home." He cuts his eyes to me and shakes his head. "It was unreal, and we didn't believe it."

He's quiet and in deep thought. I don't know if I should respond to what he's telling me. When I think we're finished with our talk and going to the house, he makes another left turn.

"Then, there you were at our front door. But you weren't our baby anymore. I guess a little part of me almost wished they would've showed up with you just how you were. Like we would pick up right where we'd left off. I got a call while at work that my baby girl had been kidnapped. Then, I get the call while at work that my teenage daughter had been discovered and was returning home."

"Seems things are always happening when you're at work?" I offer him a tight smile.

He nods in agreement. "You're a young lady now, practically an adult."

He makes another turn leading away from the house. He clears his throat again and quickly wipes at his eyes and nose. "She lost all that time with you. *We* lost all that time. We missed so many firsts with you and were not able to mold you and help you grow. That hurts. What hurts more is that *she* got to. She got to experience what was supposed to be ours—our moments. Your mother is jealous that another woman got to experience everything, and that same woman also got to experience your love."

He doesn't turn again but pulls into the driveway. He puts the truck in park but doesn't turn the key. He looks broken as his head hangs low. "We all love you. She loves you. I think she was expecting you two to immediately form a mother/daughter relationship. None of us know…we don't know what to do or how to make this right. I'm sorry for…everything."

He turns the truck off, opens his door, and climbs out. I sit there and try to make sense of everything.

The house is dark and quiet as I make my way to my room. I find Landon sitting outside my door.

"I wanted to make sure you were…well, I know you're not alright. Want to talk about it?" he asks.

I shake my head. He stands and follows me into my room. I flop onto my bed and hug my pillow. I feel the bed sink beside me as Landon wraps his arms around me. I don't know how long Landon stays, but I know he's still holding me when I fall asleep.

Thirty-Eight

THE NEXT MORNING, I GO DOWN FOR BREAKFAST, and everyone acts as if nothing happened. I decide to go with it. There's no point in arguing or bringing it up. It'll only make things more awkward.

I'm about to walk out the door for school when Melissa gently takes my arm. "I'm sorry."

Her eyes plead for my forgiveness. Even though I haven't forgiven her, I give her a half-hearted hug before walking out.

⌘

As soon as I find Noah, I rush to him and squeeze him as tight as possible. I'm about to start crying again. "Can we find somewhere private to talk?"

He nods his head and leads me to his truck. I'm surprised when he starts the engine. "Hey! We have class in fifteen minutes. Where are we going to go?"

He looks me up and down. "You said more private. Plus, you seem like you need the day off."

I hesitate before finally relaxing into my seat. He waits until we're at the edge of town before asking me what I wanted to tell him. I begin telling him everything. I watch his facial expressions as I recall the horrible incident with the journal.

We reach the next town, and he pulls into the parking lot of Aunt Becky's Kitchen. He doesn't turn the truck off until I finish speaking.

He lets out a heavy sigh. "I-," he lets out another sigh, "Shit, I don't know Liv. This would seem less awkward if I called you Sarah. Olivia was my cousin, so I'd much rather you be Sarah Randall. I don't agree with what she did, but I understand. She's hurt, bitter, jealous, and… I mean, in her mind, you love the woman that hurt her more than anyone. You don't see it that way because in your mind, a loving woman raised you. Cindy is two completely different people to you both."

He explains it better than anyone else has so far.

"Who was Cindy to you, Noah?"

"Honestly, nobody. I didn't know her that well. Yeah, she'd send gifts on birthdays and holidays. It's not like I miss her. That sounds terrible, but I just knew of her. Like you. I met you a handful of times, but you were someone that I knew existed and was out there. She kept her guard up around herself and you. Mom sent photos of me all the time, but Cindy only sent a couple photos of you. She didn't want us to be close. Now we know why."

He takes my hand in his. "You don't have to stop loving her to love Melissa. You're not betraying her by accepting Melissa. Honestly, from what it sounds like, I think she'd want you to have Melissa as your mom. She'd want you to be happy and loved."

"I just think Melissa could've went about last night-"

"Dude. She just read some sick stuff. I mean, put yourself in her shoes. She read about how a stranger *stalked* her and planned the abduction of her daughter. I kind of want a drink myself after hearing about that. Give the woman a break."

Despite myself, I laugh a little. He's right. That had to have been horrible to read from the mother's perspective. *My life is so messed up.*

"This is heavy stuff for an empty stomach. Well, I didn't eat anyways." He shrugs and gestures toward the restaurant.

I smile and nod that I'm ready to go in. "There's always room for blueberry pancakes."

We get out of the truck and enjoy a delicious breakfast with no more heavy talk. I look around the small diner and ask Noah if he knows which one is Aunt Becky. He laughs and looks around. He points to a middle-aged lady behind the register. "That's Aunt Becky's grand-daughter. Aunt Becky passed away about ten years ago. Mom talked a lot about her. Apparently, we went to the funeral, but I was a little kid, so." He shrugs then continues, "She left this place to her daughter and niece. Their families now manage it. Funny, Aunt Becky had only one daughter and so did her sister; now their daughters each only have one daughter. Seems like they only have girls in that family."

I take another bite of my pancake. "The food is amazing."

He nods in agreement before putting a fork full of fluffy scrambled eggs in his mouth. "That's why we're here."

After we eat breakfast, Noah suggests we go hang out at the mall. We rent the motorized animal scooters for kids. I get the panda, and Noah chooses the tiger. We crack up as we zig zag at a snail's pace through the mall. There aren't a lot of people since the stores are just now opening so we have the halls to ourselves, allowing plenty of space for us to spin around and play bumper cars with our "set of wheels." I keep laughing every time I look at Noah's long legs bunched up trying to fit on the tiger.

Between fits of giggles, I get out, "It's going to break! Any minute now one of those little wheels are going to go rolling down the aisle."

He tries to appear offended, but the twinkle in his eyes conveys otherwise.

I shake my head at him. "There's no way you're comfortable."

We finally tire of the mall and decide to catch a movie. When Noah orders a combo with two drinks and large popcorn, I lean in and whisper, "Are you going to let me stick my hand down…" I make it a point to look down and back up to his eyes, smiling mischievously.

He coughs a laugh as he takes the popcorn from the gentleman at the concession stand. He raises an eyebrow at me as we're walking toward the theater room. "Down?"

I wink. "Your popcorn bowl."

"Oh yeah, you reach right on in there. Get a handful. But be careful, it can get messy."

We burst into the theater laughing. We have the room to ourselves, thankfully. Through the whole movie, we make jokes and enjoy sharing the bowl of popcorn.

On the way home, I confide in Noah again about how I don't really like the name Sarah or Olivia now.

He nods and declares, "Then I won't call you either one. I can just go around saying Honey, Sugar Pie, Baby Doll."

I give him a mock look of horror and beg, "Please don't."

He pats my knee. "Nah, but how about Olah?"

I stare at him and he clarifies, "It's a combination of the names. Just like you're a combination of both the women that helped mold you…"

He stops and glances over at me. I hold up my hand, "Stop. I get that you're trying to go deep with this but no."

I'm worried I might have actually hurt his feelings, but once again, his eyes give him away. We start laughing at the same time. He continues to throw out the most ridiculous name combinations.

"You always call me 'Liv.' Maybe we should stick with that," I suggest.

He waves it off. "That's a nickname from your old name, though. I'm not going to lie, sometimes it's weird to think I'm dating Olivia. What if someone asks, 'Hey, seems I remember Andrea mentioning you have a cousin named Olivia,' and I'll be like, 'Yup! That's the one!' Referring to you as 'Liv' helped ease my mind, sorta. I do think Landon's nickname for you is fitting. The whole Alice in Wonderland bit."

I want to tell him I like the nickname and for him to keep calling me 'Liv.' However, I decide to drop the subject. I don't want to revisit last night and everything that has happened this year again. I lay my head back against the seat and enjoy the ride.

Noah begins scanning radio stations when I hear one of my all-time favorite songs come on. I quickly stop him and turn back until I hear "Hold Me Now" by the Thompson Twins. I can't help myself as I begin belting out, "*Hold me now, warm my heart, stay with me.*"

He laughs and gives me a knowing smile. "I take it Aunt Cindy was always jamming to the music of her youth? Mom's *always* blasting the 80s."

I nod and continue singing freely. He licks his lip and bites his bottom lip. I'm caught off guard when he sings at the top of his voice. I burst out laughing and then join him. "*Hold me now, whoa warm my heart, stay with me!*" It's like we're having a contest to see who can sing more theatrically. When the song ends, we laugh and poke fun at each other's singing.

I begin to sing a little of the next song but stop when he asks, "I take it you know a lot of 80s tunes?"

I nod my head and clarify. "And a lot of 80s movies. Cindy was always listening to music while she drove, cleaned, whatever she was doing. Then every time we'd have a movie night and it was her turn to pick she'd pick an 80s movie."

We pull into the school parking lot. He parks right next to my car but still gets out to stand next to me as I put my bag in the car. I'm unsure if I should just get in the car or stand there.

I choose to stand there grinning at him. "I really had fun. Thank you for today. I really, really needed that."

He responds with a sweet and gentle kiss on the lips. He pulls away. "I had fun, too. I'll get here early tomorrow. Hopefully, you'll have a better night than last night."

He rolls the window down in his truck blasting, "Don't You (Forget About Me)" by Simple Minds.

I start my car, but before I leave, I send a quick text to him.

Me: *Today was great. Thanks again. Also you have great taste in music. ;)*

Noah: *See you tomorrow. And "don't you forget about me"*

Me: *Smooth. You made fun of Eric for cheesy lines.*
Noah: *Did Eric's line work?*
Me: *No.*
Noah: *Did mine?*
Me: *Maybe*

⌀

Melissa is waiting for me at the kitchen table when I walk into the house. She raises her head when she hears me enter the room.

"We need to talk, Sarah."

Her eyes are puffy and filled with sadness. I sit down and wait for her to continue. I have no idea what to say, so I'll let her carry this conversation.

"Would you like something to drink? I think I need another cup of coffee." She gets up and goes to the coffee pot.

I have learned that when she's nervous, she always wants something to eat or drink. I think she does this mostly to have something to do, especially with her hands. I have the same habit, so I accept a cup of coffee as well. We both play with our cups for a moment.

Finally, Melissa speaks to me with a defeated and worn tone. "Sarah," she takes a deep breath, "I'm so sorry for last night. I know you skipped school because of last night. I know you went out of town. I don't know who you went with, but I have a pretty good idea."

I interrupt her, "What, you can't track everyone's phone?"

She narrows her eyes at me and retorts, "No. I can't. But I can call the school and find out if Noah Wallace was absent as well."

She holds a hand up as to stop herself and regains control of her temper. We both take a sip of our coffee.

"I'm sorry for last night. You've no idea how sorry I am. I lost my temper. I should have *never* behaved that way. I love you so much." Her voice cracks as though she's about to cry. She stops and takes another sip of coffee. "I know you're upset and confused, but you cannot skip school. You can't take off without us knowing. I was so worried. I didn't know…" She sniffles and takes another sip of coffee. "I didn't know…I didn't know if you were going to come home."

She breaks down now and sobs, so I walk around the table and hold her.

"I'm sorry I skipped school. And I'm sorry that I didn't tell you. I figured you'd track my phone anyways…but that's no excuse. I'm sorry too," I tell her as she cries on my shoulder.

She finally pulls away and grabs a napkin to wipe her eyes. I go back to my seat since I'm not sure what to do. I play with my coffee cup again, waiting for her to speak.

"I think we're both at fault here. You shouldn't have skipped school. However, I realize how I've been behaving has just made things harder for you. I really am trying, Sarah. I'm so sorry. I just want you to be *safe*. I want you to be safe and happy."

I shrug and lamely murmur, "I am safe and happy."

She shakes her head. "You're safe, but I don't believe you're truly happy. If having a relationship with the Wallace family would make things easier for you…"

She sucks in a deep breath. This is very difficult for her, I can tell.

"As long as you will communicate with me, you can have a relationship with them. I can't stand the idea of you sneaking around. I also realize they had no involvement in what happened. They love you too… and if this will help our relationship…" she lets the last sentence hang in the air.

I'm so excited that I'm about to cry. I go around the table again and hug her tightly.

"Thank you," I whisper.

∽

During my now monthly therapy session with Rita, I finally confess about the journal and that's its now burned.

"How did that make you feel, that she burned something of Cindy's that you'd kept?"

"I was hurt. Angry. But I told her. I let out a lot of those pent-up feelings. Then I ran away. Richard got me and we shared a moment. I think a lot of good actually came out of it."

"Good."

"I also found out that the girl that has been bullying me is Cindy's ex-husband's daughter."

"Really?"

"Yeah. Just when you didn't think this couldn't get more messed up, huh?"

"Well, this isn't a very big place." Rita smiles.

"Did you just make a joke?"

"I'm capable of it from time to time."

"I like this side of you, Rita."

"So, once again Noah was there for you. Offering you comfort."

"Yes, yes he was. Actually, Melissa gave her blessing for me to have a relationship with the Wallace family. We're kind of a thing now, I think. Noah and I."

"You think?" Rita raises a brow and smirks at me. I can't stop the corner of my lips from turning up as I give her a shrug.

"I don't know how serious this is going to be, but I'm excited to see where it goes. Still a little weird to call my boyfriend's mom my aunt."

"And—"

"It was a joke!" I burst out laughing. "I'm really starting to feel more a part of the Randall family. I'm happy being a part of their family. I feel like my life is coming together."

Thirty-Nine

VEN THOUGH MELISSA GAVE PERMISSION FOR ME to have a relationship with the Wallace family, I knew better than to push my luck. Noah and I keep our relationship mostly at school. I text Andrea every day from the private phone still.

I appreciate the effort Melissa is putting forth and felt it best to take baby steps. Which is why I'm so surprised that at the end of our Thanksgiving meal, Melissa announces for my eighteenth birthday, *everyone* is invited—including the Wallace family. The Randalls are throwing an extravagant party for me next week. Again, I appreciate the effort Melissa is making by allowing them to attend.

After I clean up in the kitchen, I grab my sketch pad and head to the den. Richard is watching television but when he sees me, he smiles and turns it off. He reaches over and grabs his sketch pad off the end table.

"I was wondering when you'd be back."

"You could've gotten me."

"Nah, I can wait." His eyes hold mine. "I can wait for whenever you're ready."

We watch each other as we flip the page. I take my pencil and hold it up. He grabs his and tips it toward mine. Then we begin. We sketch in complete and total silence until my neck is stiff and my eyes feel heavy. I yawn and he chuckles. "I think it's time to call it a night."

"Yeah."

We flip our sketch pads closed.

"Good night, sweetheart."

"Good night…Dad."

The house has been transformed into a winter wonderland theme with lights everywhere, and there's enough food to feed a small country. Outside, there's a huge tent and a stage has been set up. There's a live band playing a mix between Christmas tunes and contemporary hits.

I'm having a wonderful time. I visit openly with Andrea and Brad. I dance with Landon, Denise, and Trent. Tara and a few girls from the soccer team are here, and I dance and hang out with them. Most of my attention, however, goes to Noah.

Trent brought Maggie, and they look like a royal couple together as they dance. However, at one point, I spot him and Rachel off together chatting.

He leaves her side and comes to stand with Landon and me. "Having a nice time, birthday girl?"

"This is amazing, how could I not?" I make a show of looking around.

"Mom can get carried away with parties," he nods, "but she'll be thrilled to know you've enjoyed it."

I look over and find Rachel watching us with longing in her eyes.

Landon must see it as well. "Hey man, can you do me a favor?"

Trent nods and pats Landon's shoulder. "Anything for you, man."

He nods toward Rachel and asks, "Have one dance with her. Tell Maggie she's just your kid brother's best friend or Sarah's best friend."

Trent sighs and pinches the bridge of his nose. "Don't you think that's leading her on a bit?"

Frustration clear in his voice, Landon hisses, "I don't get it. What's the problem? You like her, but you reel her in only to throw her back out again, like you're freaking fishing. She's a great catch." Landon sticks his nose up with a huff, then points toward Maggie with his chin. "Is Rachel not sophisticated enough?"

Trent chuckles and shakes his head. "You know that's not it. And I'm trying not to keep 'reeling' her in, as you put it. She's young, and it's only a puppy crush. She's been fixated on me since we were all little kids. Wait until she goes to college and expands her horizon from this small town. Then, I bet she won't even give me a second glance."

Landon nods. "Good. I hope she doesn't, because you don't deserve her." He still presses, "It sounds like you should go get that dance while she's willing to give you the time of day. You better come to your senses before she does."

Trent turns on his heels and strolls over to Rachel, and we watch as her face lights up. She eagerly steps into his embrace. We watch as they dance, but alarm bells go off as we see Maggie heading toward them. Not wasting any time to see how it will play out, Landon rushes to her. He doesn't even give Maggie a chance to decline. He plasters a huge grin on his face as he swoops her off her feet and twirls her around the dance floor. Once the song ends, Trent unwinds from Rachel with a smile and goes back to find Maggie. He stays with her for the remainder of the night.

As the party is winding down, Noah tells me he has a gift

for me. He asks if it would be possible for me to leave. I go find Melissa and Richard to let them know I'm leaving for a little bit.

"I hope it's okay, but Noah wanted to take me out for a little bit. He said he has a birthday surprise."

Melissa brings her hands in front of her and entwines them together. "Are you two a couple now?"

"Yeah. We are. He's really nice and he gets me."

She starts to speak again, but Richard gently places a hand on her shoulder. "As long as you're being careful."

I nod but I can see the worry in Melissa's eyes. She smiles. "Okay. Promise you'll check in with me?"

I hug her. "Of course."

Richard squeezes my arm. "Have fun sweetheart. Be home before it gets too late."

"This has been the best birthday ever."

Melissa's eyes brighten. "Ever?"

I almost want to laugh at how hopeful she sounds. "Ever."

Noah takes me back to the stream at the reservation. I refer to it now as our spot. He starts a small fire. We unfold some blankets, and we cuddle under them. I giggle when he turns "Hold Me Now" on his iPod. I take it from his hands to find he created our own playlist.

"Best birthday present." I cuddle into him more.

"There's one more." He hands me a beautifully wrapped, flat square box.

I open it, and inside is some kind of form. I read it, and my eyes fill with unshed tears. I look at Noah and search his face, trying to understand what he's given me.

He fidgets for a moment but then clears his throat. "You said you didn't know who you are, but I think you do know who you are. The problem is that you identify a part of your-self with the name Olivia and what that name means. The same with the name Sarah. Maybe you'd feel more *you* if you chose a new name to identify yourself. Cindy chose Olivia and molded you into who she thought Olivia should be. Melissa has been trying to change and mold you into who she thinks Sarah should be. I figured that since you're eighteen now and graduating, it's time for you to decide who you are. Who do you want to be? Maybe a new name will help you with that identity crisis you seem to be suffering with."

I make an ugly choking sound as I try to swallow a cry. I read over the court form that is to legally change my name.

Noah quickly tells me, "But you don't have to change your name. You can remain Sarah Randall. I thought you should know that you have the option. I didn't know if this had even crossed your mind."

I throw my arms around Noah and cry into his neck. He pets my hair as he holds me and rocks back and forth. I pull back and kiss him, trying to convey my gratitude in that one simple kiss.

I sit back and grin. "I love this. Thank you so much."

He shrugs. "I didn't do anything. It's all up to you, really."

I kiss him and then sigh into his arms. We sit there, warm, cuddled under the blankets, and stare out at the stars while listening to the sound of water lapping from the stream and cheesy 80s music.

Forty

CHRISTMAS MORNING IS LIKE A DREAM IN THE Randall's mansion. I wake up to the smell of fresh baked cookies. At first, I thought I was dreaming but nope, Melissa is baking cookies. The house is beautifully decorated. Landon said she does it every year because Christmas is her favorite time of year. He informed me she goes a little overboard on everything Christmas related. I love her enthusiasm. I think when I have children, I'll want to bake cookies on Christmas morning, too.

Like my mom. I smile to myself and continue walking through the house. I notice there are new frames in the hallway.

Me.

There are several new photos blended in with the others. There are a few professional photos we've had done since my arrival. A few are moments I didn't realize anyone was capturing. I'm laughing and my eyes are sparkling while I'm eating frozen yogurt. I remember that day. Homecoming dress shopping. We'd stopped for a snack. There's one of me with all of them laughing on the soccer field. We look…like a family. There's one I remember taking right before Trent left back for school. Seeing all four of us standing side by side, the resemblance. There's no question that we're related. I gently run my finger down the smooth printed canvas. Our smiles are genuine. My smile now is genuine. A sense of peace washes over me. I love my family. I'm happy to be here. And seeing these photos on the walls, brings me more peace and joy than I could imagine they would. It's like an acceptance here. A feeling of belonging. They really do see me as part of the family. My face is worth printing and taking the time to hang up next to theirs. It may sound silly, but it means the world to me. I take another moment to let the emotions wash over me. Then I smile and follow the sound of laughter and Christmas music further into the house.

There are stockings with our names on them over the fireplace and beautifully wrapped gifts under the tree. It doesn't seem real.

I'm only used to me and one other person on Christmas. Occasionally, we might've joined with my best friend Angie and her mom for the holidays. We would get gifts from Aunt Andrea mailed to us. The most decorations we had was a medium size fake Christmas tree. We'd eat a bowl of cereal for breakfast. The most cooking Cindy did for Christmas lunch was a precooked ham that just needed to be heated in the oven. Then we'd lounge in pajamas watching whatever Christmas movies were on television. Nothing like this. This is a scene straight out of a Hallmark movie.

As I take it all in, I'm happy. I'm so blissfully happy. This is all a little overwhelming and surreal, but I'm excited. I'm excited to spend Christmas with *my* family.

I'm surprised when the doorbell rings. Melissa obviously isn't surprised because she rushes to the door. "Come in! Come in! Thank you so much for coming on Christmas!"

I peak around the corner to find the photographer whom

Melissa has used for the three family photos we've already taken since I arrived.

"Mom, I can't believe you hired a photographer! It's Christmas," Trent groans.

"It's our first Christmas as a whole family, young man. Watch your tone with me. I want every moment captured. I'm terrible with a camera. Your father is even worse. You kids aren't going to keep up with taking photos. What was I supposed to do?"

She turns to the photographer. "I really do appreciate this. Please make yourself comfortable. I might forget to offer, so help yourself to anything to drink or eat. Seriously, help yourself. I want both natural and staged photos."

The photographer, Hallmark setting, and room full of people is making me feel dizzy. They must sense my unease because everyone takes turns trying to comfort me. Melissa invites me to help cook. Richard, Trent, and Landon invite me to watch the Christmas movie marathons. Denise asks me if I want to join her while she scans media sites. I spread myself throughout the groups. Before I know it, everything begins to feel natural, and that I almost forgot about the photographer, *almost*.

It's not until the photographer leaves that Melissa announces it's time for gifts. I'm so nervous. Everyone just starts passing out their gifts at once. I gather the ones from me and hand them to each one of them. I didn't really have money for presents, even though I could've asked. I either painted them something or made a design on canvas with mod podge.

For Melissa, I painted a canvas the color of her kitchen and used mod podge to paste a photo she'd had made of a family photo. Denise, I made a fashion collage from magazines she likes with quotes mixed in. Landon, I did what I knew he'd love, a self-portrait of him in black and white. Trent, I did a simple design with a quote about never giving up. And for Richard, I gave him a mix of mod podge and sketches of the houses he'd done.

I open the gifts they got me. Denise got me several athletic outfits. "Because ya know, you play soccer."

Landon's gifts have me bursting out laughing. One is a T-Shirt with the Caterpillar puffing out smoke and it reads *Who Are You?* The other one is a framed family photo that has only the smile and eyes of the Cheshire Cat and reads *We're all mad here.* And then there's a small white stuffed bunny rabbit. I absolutely love it. All of it.

Trent got me a beautiful bracelet that has '*Randall*' engraved on it.

Melissa got me a ton of art supplies, along with a gift certificate for private lessons.

Richard walks over and hands me a simple red gift bag with white tissue paper. I open the bag and pull out his sketch book. I smile at the tattered and worn edges. I flip open the first page and my heart is in my throat. It's a sketch of a baby. "*My daughter*" is written in messy handwriting at the bottom. I flip the next page. There's a sketch of *me*. It's me focused and looking down. My hair hangs loose. *Has he been sketching me the whole time we've been drawing together?* I look at the bottom. "*My daughter.*" There's no name. Just my daughter. I look over at him. I want to speak, but I can't. I lick my lips and try to find the right words, but they just won't come.

"Does this mean you're finished sketching?"

He shakes his head. "No."

"Good."

His eyes are bright and shimmer with unshed tears. I place the sketch pad down next to me and walk over and wrap my arms around him.

Later that night, Noah comes by to bring me my gift. I can't wait, so I give Noah my gift to him first, which is a painting of our spot along with a gift card to his favorite store.

He hands me mine and I waste no time tearing into the paper. He bought me a special edition "Alice in Wonderland" hardback book, along with a dangly charm bracelet. There are a few sparkling stones between each charm. I examine each charm: a tea cup, a soccer ball, a paint pallet, a pendant that reads "Do you suppose she's a wildflower?" and a flower. *I love it.*

Noah claims he didn't know me before. But sometimes I feel like he knows me better than anyone. This gift couldn't be more perfect. He couldn't be more perfect.

                                                    ~

For New Year's Eve, we are attending the annual party that the local country club hosts. The theme is Gatsby, so we all dress in roaring 20's attire. Denise and I wear flapper girl dresses, but Melissa goes for a more conservative, long, 20's style dress that is very dazzling with stones and sequins. The guys get off easy with a tux and bowtie. Trent brings Maggie, Landon brings Rachel, which is a little awkward, and I get to bring Noah. He looks very handsome with his hair slicked back and a white tux.

Landon and Rachel kill the dance floor with their dancing. Landon has the ability to make anyone look great on the dance floor. He drags me out there a couple of times. I do notice Trent's eyes on Rachel on more than one occasion throughout the night, especially when she does dance with anyone other than Landon. Next, Landon grabs Denise. She's been pouting a little in a corner sipping her Shirley Temple. She is pushing against him and has her feet firmly planted to the floor. I rush over toward them.

"Denise? What's going on? You're normally the life of the party."

She rolls her eyes and her lips form a thin line. Landon answers my question.

"Clint's a no show. He apparently went to another party with Isabell Jamerson."

"I thought you and Isabell were friends?"

Landon waves his hand and shakes his head. "Don't go there. I told her there are *plenty* of other guys here that would kill to dance with her. She's too good for him anyways."

"I agree. And who needs friends like that? Get out there and forget them. You don't need a guy to have a great time. I'll dance with you!" She scowls at me. *Ouch.* "Hey! I'm trying here."

"Don't take it personally. That's just how our sweet little sister is." Landon grins wider when Denise continues to scowl.

Noah, Keaton, and Emily come over to join us. I smile at Keaton and Emily, "Hey guys. I didn't know you two were here."

Keaton nods toward Emily. "Well, I'm no member of the country club, but Emily's family is. I'm here as her date."

Noah nods. "Same here."

Keaton lightly punches Noah in the arm and they jokingly mumble jabs at each other while I turn my attention back to Denise. I notice she's standing up a little straighter and has a more pleasant expression on her face. *Did I miss something?*

Emily sighs as though she's bored. "Landon, where's Rachel?"

He points over to the other side of the room. "I think she's eating her emotions by the buffet."

Emily nods in understanding. "Trent's here, isn't he? I better go fulfill my duties as bestie by joining her." With that, she turns on her heels and heads toward the buffet.

Landon throws his arm around Denise's shoulder. "What about you? Wanna go eat your feelings away with them? Might make you feel better?"

Denise quickly slides out from under her brother's arm. "I'm *fine!* I don't have any emotions to eat. I mean, I don't need to do that. I mean, because I'm not upset over anyone. Because, I just came here to have a good time. I mean, I didn't, because-"

Landon tilts his head at her. "Are you okay? None of that made sense. I think you've really lost it, sis."

If looks could kill. Her eyes blazed at Landon.

Keaton chuckled. "What did I miss?"

Landon throws his hands up. "That's what I want to know, too! She was all pouty over her little boyfriend Clint bailing on her. Now she's just acting plain weird. Middle schoolers man."

"Awe, don't let that little dweeb bring you down. You're way too pretty and nice for that. If you need a dance partner, I'll be happy to assist."

Denise smiles and shrugs. "Okay."

Keaton extends his elbow, "Shall we?" She blushes and accepts. He leads her out to the dance floor. As soon as there is some distance between us, we all burst out laughing.

"Well, she got over Clint quick. Serves the little shit right." Noah says.

"Yeah, that was so nice of Keaton to step in." I smile at Noah.

He smiles back and nods toward his friend. "Sloan's a pretty good guy. He's a sucker for a damsel in distress."

Landon groans. "Which is why he's with Emily. She's *always* in distress. I love her, but she's so dramatic."

The night is filled with music, laughter, and a few drinks. However, the night is almost spoiled when Luke approaches me as I'm leaving the restroom.

"May I have a dance?" he asks smoothly.

I smile. "I don't think that's a good idea." I wave with a "Happy New Year."

I begin walking away, but he catches up to me. "I guess you prefer slumming it then."

I turn around furiously, but I'm hoping I misheard him.

"It makes sense. You were raised in the slums, right? He's familiar, more in your comfort zone. I get it. Have your fun with him. When you're ready for someone more in your league, someone who your family would be proud of, then come to me. I just might take you back."

He winks as he causally strolls off with his hands in his pockets. I charge after him. I grab him by the elbow, swinging him around to face me. I pull back and slap him as hard as I can. His head flies to the left.

"I'm with Noah because I deserve better than you. If I decide I want to 'slum it,' then I'll come find *you*, but don't count on it. I don't think I could ever get that low."

I turn my back on him and go find the rest of the group. I don't tell any of them what happened. *No sense in ruining their good time over a loser like Luke.*

We're all gathered together around the fireplace in the lounge. Noah has his arms around me as we shout out the countdown together. At midnight, we kiss and whisper, "I love you," to each other. It's our first time saying it. For a moment, it's just us. But a few bumps and cheers bring us back. We laugh and steal one more quick kiss. Then, we go around hugging everyone else, all of us shouting, "Happy New Year." We only hang around an hour longer. We all leave exhausted but smiling. My feet hurt, my throat is sore from laughing and yelling, and I can barely hold my eyes open, but what an amazing start to the new year.

Forty-One

SCHOOL RESUMES COMPLETELY DIFFERENTLY THAN when I first arrived. I'm grateful for the new year. Last year, I became two completely different people with two completely different worlds. Now, I walk into school confident and eager for the day to begin.

I have a meeting with my guidance counselor about college applications. I haven't discussed much with my family about where I'll apply. They want me to remain local since they just got me back, but I want the full university experience. I could go to the school that Trent attends to meet in the middle. It would be somewhat of a compromise since at least he'd be there. But I'm tired of having them hovering over me. I care about them, but it's time for me to get to be *me*. I apply to the same university as Trent, but I also apply to several others that are farther away.

Noah isn't applying to any schools. He's planning on going into the military and has been since his freshman year. I knew this before I even came to live here. Andrea had been so worried when she first told Cindy about it. He doesn't want to add the financial burden to his family, so he's going to join the military. This way, he'll be able to attend veterinary school.

We haven't discussed this in much depth, especially since we just now became serious. I don't want him to go, but I know I should not expect him to change his plans because we started dating. I'm a little upset that he doesn't seem that concerned with how him going into the military will affect our relationship. Maybe he doesn't think it'll affect us. Maybe it won't. Long distance relationships work for people all the time, but for some they don't work. Time will tell which relationship we'll have.

I decide to leave the issue on the back burner and focus on enjoying how wonderful everything else is at the moment. My school, home, and love life have all been spectacular. I have an extra skip in my step as I walk down the halls.

I pass Rachel in the hall as she slams her locker door. She hurries over to my side and we fall into step together. She adjusts her book bag as she asks, "Have you thought about what you're plans are after graduation?"

I shrug and explain how I'm still unsure about…well *everything*.

She tells me as we walk to class that she's wanting to become a nurse. She's hoping her and Landon can get an off-campus apartment for wherever they attend together. Obviously, they won't be able to room together if they live in the dorms. I ask her why she doesn't room with any of the other girls from our lunch table group, like Emily.

"Emily's great, but she doesn't always get me. Landon is my best friend for life. We've had this deal worked out for years. We're each other's go-to for everything."

We enter the classroom just as she's finished speaking. Tara must've heard her because she chimes in, "Why won't you two just admit you're in love with each other? We all know you and Landon are going to end up getting married."

Rachel and I exchange a knowing look. We sit down and before anything else can be said, class begins.

At lunch, everyone begins discussing prom. The girls and I make plans to go dress shopping. Landon is more worried about planning an after party. We all laugh at his crazy ideas.

"I feel like we need to do something wild that no class has done before. Let's go break into a zoo."

Keaton shakes his head. "Nah man, I think someone has already beat you to it. Didn't the senior class four years ago do that?"

Noah nods. "Yeah, the ones from the private school."

Keaton takes a bite of his sandwich. "Dude," he speaks between chews, "I don't have enough money for bail. My parents might let me rot. I'm up for wild, but let's keep it where there's no chance of getting caught."

"We could plan a toga party. Surely somebody's parents are leaving for the weekend." Emily suggests.

Landon considers it but still doesn't seem convinced. "We need to keep thinking. Everyone, you have your assignment. Epic after prom. I expect to hear your ideas next week."

Noah leans toward me and whispers. "I have some ideas for us, but I'm not sharing them."

"Oh yeah?"

"It won't be wild, but it'll be *in* the wild."

"Our spot?"

"Our spot."

"I like that."

"I guess if we wanted to make it wild you could bring your paint and I'll be your canvas."

I shake my head and turn around and he begins tickling me.

"I think we need to think more on it, too." I tell him.

"Skinny dipping?" He raises an eyebrow.

"Dude, what? Skinny dipping? I'm in. Hey Landon, Noah has some ideas. He just suggested skinny dipping to your sis."

Landon narrows his eyes at Noah.

Noah clears his throat. "Jeff, get your mind out of the gutter. I was asking if she liked this healthy dip called Skinny Dip. It's fat-free…"

"We have to go." I take my tray and stand up. "Art. Remember? Project."

"Yeah, art project. Bye y'all."

We hear their laughter as we leave. I turn to Noah, "Skinny Dip?"

I know I should wait, but I can't. I decide to address the concern that I have between me and Noah. I want to know where our relationship stands after graduation.

We sit down and I lean on my elbows on the desk. "Noah, what are your plans after graduation?"

He sighs and leans toward me. "You know already. I'm already enlisted. As soon as I graduate, I'm going into the army to pay for school. My options are limited. This is the only way for me to get a college education."

I try to argue, "What about your grades? You're really smart. Scholarships? You're really involved in activities. Test scores? You've scored really high. Sports? You're really athletic."

He cuts me off, "I'm really poor!"

I'm taken aback by his tone.

His voice softens as he repeats, "I'm really poor. Thank you for all the faith you have in me to get in school by other means, but there's a lot of competition for those scholarships. The military is a guarantee I'll have a good opportunity."

The hurt and disappoint must be on my face. He groans. "I'd already told you that I planned to enlist. I'm sure you knew even before you came here. I know Mom talked about it all the time with Cindy. She never said anything?"

It's plain he is reminding me I knew this well before we began a relationship. I want to tell him that was *before* we became a couple. Has nothing changed for him? Several questions keep running through my mind. What do we do after graduation? How long is he going to be away? Are we going to see other people?

I nod in defeat. I finally voice my biggest fear. "What about us?"

The bell rings, sending a crowd into the classroom. I would rather not discuss this with an audience, especially with Eric strutting in. Noah takes my hand and gives it a reassuring squeeze.

"After everything that's happened, how can you of all people lack faith that life will always put us where we're meant to be?"

It's because of everything that's happened, I'm a little unsettled.

⟡

I chat Rita's ear off about Noah and his decision to go into the military.

"What about you, Sarah? What are your plans? What do you see for your future? Sarah's future?"

"I'm considering going to the same college as Trent. I've applied there."

"Have you discussed it with Trent?"

"Not in great detail. But he wants me there. I still sometimes think about going back to Colorado."

"Do you ever keep in touch with Angie?"

"No. We've kind of drifted apart."

"Are you upset by this?"

"Yes and no."

"I see."

"I called Richard, Dad."

Rita's eyes go wide. "That's huge! Why didn't you already tell me this?"

"Well, I said it and then kind of ran off to bed."

"Wow. That's great. So your relationship is going well, then?"

"It is. Melissa and I are getting there. Landon's the best. Trent is a really good guy, but I sometimes think he really is the one that should be here right now. Denise is, well Denise."

"I'm so glad to hear all this. Did you finally bring me a drawing?"

"Yes."

I reach next to my chair and grab my satchel. I pull out my sketch pad and flip to the picture I'd been working on during my sessions with Richard. Standing up, I walk over and hand Rita the sketch. Her eyes scan the page and she shakes her head. "You are so talented. This is extraordinary. Are you not finished?"

"No. When I finally decide who I am, I'll finish it. Until then, this is all I can give you."

"Keep it then. Continue to work on it. You're doing beautiful work, on both ladies."

I take back the sketch of me. Half of my face is drawn while the other half is there but lightly faded.

⁂

The next day, I keep thinking about Noah's decision about the military. More importantly, what my decisions are going to be. I could go to school in Colorado, retreat to familiar grounds. Going to school with Trent wouldn't be so horrible. I try to think about who am I and who do I want to be. That night, I lay in bed and think about my life. I refuse to continue being Sarah Randall. I pull out the paper to legally change my name and stare at it. I fill out half of it. Then, I fill out my college applications. Tomorrow, I'll submit it, along with applications for colleges.

I go to Landon's room and knock on his door.

"Come in."

I open the door to find Landon sitting at his computer desk. "Hey."

He turns in his seat and leans back. "What's up?"

"Wanna hear something crazy?"

"Crazy, huh? It's gotta be pretty wild to be considered crazy around here. Stop lurking in the doorway. Get in here." I enter the room and sit on the edge of his bed. "So, tell me."

"I'm thinking about changing my name."

Landon raises his eyebrows. "Changing it to what?"

"I don't know. I just don't feel like Sarah is me."

"You want to be Olivia?"

"I don't know. But I'm going to change it." I lean back on his bed and smile at the ceiling. "I'm going to legally change my name. I just need to figure out what I want it to be."

Landon gets up. He plops down next to me on the bed. "I like it. I can't wait to hear what your name is going to be."

"Me neither." We both start laughing.

Forty-Two

It's April. Time has been flying by since New Year's. When I get home from school, I'm surprised that Trent has come to visit for the weekend. He hasn't been home in almost two months. A couple of his buddies that he graduated with are also in town, so they decide that this calls for a mini reunion, aka party. The get-together tonight is at this bridge that's not far from the conservation where Noah takes me.

I ride in Trent's SUV with him, Landon, and Rachel. She's beside herself that she's riding with Trent but trying to play it cool. She asks him about Maggie, but he tells her she was busy this weekend with charity work. Rachel snorts and rolls her eyes.

We turn onto a gravel road and pass an old cemetery that's in the middle of nowhere. The headstones and statues give off such an eerie feeling, yet they seem peaceful at the same time. I plan to come back this way again so I can sketch. The bridge is further up the road. We drive to the other side, and there's a wide opening where everyone has parked. There's even a levy. This is a known popular spot for everyone to drink. I'm sure there's an actual name for it, but nobody seems to use it. The stream that I'd been sketching flows into the river that the bridge is built over. It's not a large river, and the water is still. The bridge itself is concrete and not very long but plenty of feet wide.

I'm anxious about seeing Noah since last time we talked, it was a tense discussion over his plans to join the military after graduation. I knew this was always his plan, but secretly I'd hoped he would change his mind. It makes me sound so vain and selfish to hope he would change his plans over me, especially when his decision is to serve our country and relieve his parents of a financial burden.

I find Noah with Keaton, Jeff and Tara sitting on an open truck bed. Tara leaps off and grabs my hands. "I have to tell you something!"

I smile at her and pull out of her clutches. "All in good time, I just got here. I want to at least go tell Noah hello."

I skip over to him. I plaster a smile on my face hoping we don't spend the night together stiff and standoffish. He gives me a soft kiss and then offers me a drink. I'm not much of a drinker, but after a few sips, it doesn't taste so horrid. Noah and I chat a few minutes with Jeff and Tara as buffers before she finally grows impatient.

She drags me away from the guys, giggling. When we're at a safe distance from being heard, she stops walking but keeps giggling.

"Tara, how much have you had to drink?"

She laughs harder. "Not that much, really. I'm just so excited!"

I join in her laughter, even though I'm clueless as to what it's over.

Finally, she says, "Jeff and I are together!"

I'm puzzled as to why she's laughing over this. I tilt my head. "Congratulations? I thought you two were already together."

She laughs again. "Thank you! We are…but now we're *official*. Also, I have decided I'm going to have sex with him at prom."

My eyes almost pop out of my head, which causes her to laugh hysterically.

"It's not like I'm a virgin. Wait, are you?"

I nod and take a drink. She pauses for a moment and stares at me, "Really? Wow. Well, what about you and Noah?"

I take another drink before I answer, "We're officially together as well."

"Not what I meant…"

"I plan to wait. I love him, but…" I have almost emptied my cup by this point. I make a motion of shaking my cup. "I think I need a refill."

I begin to walk away when she stops me by gently grabbing my shoulder. "Hey, I'm sorry if I made you uncomfortable. I think it's great you're waiting to be with someone you're sure about. It's not that common anymore, but I think it's great."

I fidget awkwardly for a moment before stammering, "Well, um, I hope you and Jeff have a wonderful time…having sex…um…yeah, I hope it's good."

I bow my head as Tara bursts into fits of uncontrollable laughter.

When I make it back to Noah, his eyes are guarded. He's not sure what to do and honestly, neither am I. With courage from my slight buzz, I begin dancing around him. He doesn't dance. He wanders away from me to his truck. I stand there awkwardly watching him walk away since he didn't ask me to follow him. For a minute, I'm afraid I might have just made this awkward situation worse. However, when his truck begins blasting the Thompson Twins "Hold Me Now," I'm beside myself. He comes back to me and takes my hand and twirls me around.

Tara shakes her head and I hear her say, "Y'all are such nerds!"

The smile that stretches across my face actually hurts, but I don't care. The sunset is gorgeous and there's a perfect breeze. If we were alone, this would be considered romantic. Rachel, Landon, Keaton and Emily join in on the dancing while everyone else laughs and cheers us on.

Noah goes back to his truck when the song is over to turn it off. I follow him and thank him for the dance. He pops the the tailgate of his truck, and effortlessly lifts me to sit me on the bed. He climbs up and wraps his arm around me. We sit and watch the sunset together. He kisses my temple and whispers against my skin, "I love you."

I turn and look back into his eyes. "I love you."

"It's all going to work out, you know?"

I look back out into the sunset. I look over at all our friends laughing. My life has been like a puzzle that someone dumped all the pieces out, and it didn't make sense. I think about how all the pieces in my life are finally fitting together. Slowly, a picture is starting to form. There's a bigger picture yet, though. I just need to finish putting all the pieces together.

I nod. "Yeah. I do know. Just promise me that no matter what life throws at us, I'll still have you. No matter where we end up next. We'll still keep in touch."

"Promise. And hey, you've got social media now."

"That's right. No excuses. There's plenty of access to me."

He slides even closer and places his warm palm on my leg. "How much access is there to you?"

I stare at his hand and then back up into his heated eyes. We're mostly shadowed by the night. Only the moonlight. The group where everyone else is has their vehicles forming a circle with their lights on and a bon fire.

My breathing picks up. "Plenty."

I allow him to slide his hand further up my leg. We've

made out, but we've never gone very far. He's about to explore new territory for us. Forbidden territory.

Suddenly, we hear a commotion close to us. We walk over to find Landon and Luke yelling and pushing each other's chest. I scan back toward the crowd to find Trent chatting with some other college students. I rush over to him to let him know. Noah, Jeff and Keaton are already trying to talk the guys down. I can't make out what they're fighting over. They keep shouting and pushing at each other.

Trent jumps in the middle, "Hey! Cool it!"

Luke laughs. "Oh, here we go again." He's definitely drunk as he sways and laughs. He points to Trent. "Big brother swoops in to save the little bitch."

Everyone looks at me. *Were they fighting about me?* But Luke is smirking at Landon.

Landon narrows his eyes and growls, "Move Trent. Let me handle him."

Luke bellows louder. "Whooo! I bet you'd like to *handle* me. I bet you'd love to wrap your hands around my—"

Trent cuts him off with a punch to the face. Luke catches himself before he falls. He pulls his hand from his face and looks down at the blood. When he stands to his full height, I see that his lip is bleeding. He laughs, and there's blood coating his front teeth.

Trent points at him, "Shut it! I mean it, Luke. Don't be such an asshole. Let's just walk away."

Landon's eyes are red, and he's downing another beer. With him and Luke both drinking, things could've gotten out of hand. I'm so relieved that Trent is here to settle this. Luke nods and licks his lips. Trent shakes his head in disgust and turns to Landon. "Are you good, brother? Seriously, don't let that…don't let him get to you."

Landon nods in return and drinks another beer.

Trent doesn't quite believe him. "Hey, c'mon, let's go

party." He gently shakes his shoulder and gives a halfhearted laugh.

Landon sets the bottle down on the railing of the bridge. "You know, you didn't have to protect me against him. And I don't mean today. I know you said something to him when Marcus came out."

Everyone is quiet now and listening. I know exactly what he means, but I'm not sure anyone else has caught on. Except for Rachel probably.

Trent shakes his head. "Don't do this, man. Please, let's go have fun. Or do you want to leave?"

Landon nods. "Okay, will you go grab my phone? It's on one of the trucks over there."

As soon as Trent is by the truck, Landon charges Luke. He grabs him around the waist and tackles him to the ground. They roll around throwing punches. Trent runs back over. Both guys are back on their feet and pushing each other. They make their way to the side of the bridge by the railing. Luke holds Landon by the shirt collar against the concrete rail and lands punch after punch on him. Trent is almost to the guys when Luke punches Landon so hard it sends him over the bridge. Before anyone can react, Landon is going over the side, but somehow, he had a hold of Luke and took him over the side with him. Both guys fall into the black water with a loud splash.

I feel Noah take off beside me into the water. Trent is about to jump over the bridge when a couple of guys grab his arms. They tell him to go around to the bank. Everyone turns on their flashlights on their phones and rush toward the water.

"Call 911!" Trent runs and then dives under. I can't breathe. This isn't real. I keep shaking my head and thinking it isn't really happening. Trent and Noah finally return, pulling an unconscious Landon out of the water. Two other guys come back with Luke, who also appears to be unconscious.

We hear sirens off in the distance. Trent makes quick work on performing CPR on Landon.

I rush to his side but try not to be in the way. "Any way I can help? Trent tell me what to do!"

He doesn't seem to hear me as he keeps trying to revive our brother. The longer time passes with no response, the more my heart sinks. I keep praying that he'll open his eyes, spew out water and suck in a deep breath like they do in the movies.

For a second, I don't hear anything but the swooshing of my heartbeat. I'm staring in horror and disbelief as Landon lies there wet and motionless. He still has color in his skin. I focus on that. He isn't a sickly blue like when people are dead in the movies. His cheeks still hold a shade of pink to them. I stare at his long brown eyelashes. Water still drips from them and I keep thinking that I see them move. But it's not Landon moving them. It's Trent pushing so hard on his chest that his head is jolting a little.

Everyone is panicking. I hear screams and shouts *What do we do? Is he breathing? He's not breathing?* People are crying and calling their parents. I hear glass from a bottle shattering. One of the guys is shouting at another one that's trying to perform CPR on Luke.

"He's not dead. He can't be dead. We've jumped off that bridge a hundred times. You're not doing it right!"

"Then you do it!"

"I'll do it!"

"Did someone call the police?"

"Hell no, what if we get caught drinking?"

"That's not what's important right now!"

"I called! They're on their way!"

"Shit."

"Please God. Please."

But Luke's not moving and neither is Landon.

"We're too young to die. They can't be dead." *That's right. We're too young to die.*

I almost don't hear the sirens over the commotion. The ambulance arrives to take them away. *Thank God.* I just know that once Landon and Luke are in the care of trained medical professionals, all this will be fine.

I stare at the wet outline left from Landon's body in the dirt. I watch as they lift his still motionless body onto the stretcher. They quickly attach wires to him. Another set of sirens approach. Everyone hurries to their cars as the police approach, picking up the beer cans and bottles on their way.

We give a brief statement, and they inform us they'll be in touch. Noah offers to drive us to the hospital since Trent is in such a shaken state. "I've already called your parents. They're going to meet us at the hospital."

Rachel climbs in as well and holds Trent's hand. "He's going to be okay. He's going to be okay, right? He's going to be okay." She keeps mumbling through silent sobs to herself.

When we arrive at the hospital, we wait in the waiting room. Melissa and Richard arrive shortly after. A frantic, older couple along with Isabell comes rushing in, demanding to speak to someone. I assume they're Luke's parents.

It seems like forever before a grim looking nurse comes to the waiting room. She informs Noah and Rachel they'll have to stay behind, but the rest of us are to follow her. Another nurse approaches and takes the Jamersons. Instead of going to Landon's room, we enter what looks to be another waiting room. The doctor walks in with a grim face, and we know.

"I'm so sorry. Landon Randall did not make it. He suffered severe head trauma. There was nothing we could do."

We learn a few minutes later that Luke Jamerson suffered and died from a broken neck.

Landon's not dead. Landon did not die. Landon is still alive. This is a messed up dream. A nightmare. You'll wake up. You're going to wake up. Please wake up! Trent pulls my hands from my ears and shushes me. I hear screaming and uncontrollable sobbing. *It's me. I'm screaming and sobbing.* I look around me as if seeing the hospital for the first time. My face is wet, and my nose is running. Melissa is a wreck as Richard is trying to comfort her, but he seems like he needs comforting himself. Denise has her face buried in her hands.

I push Trent off and tell him to go to Denise. *I'm okay. I'm okay. I'm okay because I know this isn't happening.* Trent wraps his baby sister in his arms. He's trying to be strong for her, but I see the tears slowly dripping from the corner of his eyes.

The doctor leaves us, and Noah and Rachel enter the room. Rachel is hysterical. She rushes over to Melissa and they squeeze each other. Noah's eyes are red as they focus on me. His lips are moving, but I can't hear him. I don't hear anyone now. There's only a loud swooshing noise in my ears. *It's too much. This cannot be happening again. I lost the woman that I thought was my mother. I get a new family only to have the one person I bonded with taken away. No. He isn't. He can't be. I won't accept it. Wake up. Wake up. Wake up!* Noah is shushing me again, telling me he's here for me. I think I may have been voicing my thoughts. He's trying to hold me, but I keep shaking my head and swaying. *What if he dies, too, now?*

I wake up in my room. I don't remember falling asleep in here. I jump out of my bed and run to Landon's room. He'll be in bed asleep. I'll wake him up, and we'll laugh together over that ridiculous nightmare. I swing the door open. Denise and Melissa are asleep, curled in the fetal position on his bed. Denise has mascara streaks down her face. I crumble. The tears begin to silently flow as I make my way to the bed. I crawl behind Melissa and hold her. I must have woken her because I feel her body quivering in my arms. I hold her as we wordlessly cry together. The bed still smells like him. I can almost feel him in the room. *He isn't gone. He can't be.*

Forty-Three

WHEN I GO DOWNSTAIRS, I'M NOT surprised that there's no morning breakfast. Since I've lived here, there's been breakfast on the table. Every single day. Instead, Richard and Melissa are sitting at the table discussing funeral arrangements. Trent comes into the room carrying two of Landon's best suits.

Melissa looks up and her lip quivers. "He loved the blue. He felt it made him look like a GQ model. It did. He was so handsome," she reaches over and squeezes Richard's hand, "like his daddy. So, so young and handsome."

She sucks in a deep breath and releases it slowly. Trent gives a single nod and walks away with the clothes.

"Is there anything I can do?" I whisper.

I didn't even do much to help with Cindy's funeral. Planning a funeral makes it real. I don't want to deal with the reality of this. I want to crawl into a hole and pretend it never happened. Maybe I can pretend that Landon is on vacation, and I'll see him again soon. I've never been extremely religious, but I find comfort knowing that one day, I'll see him again. I just didn't want our time apart to be so sudden. I do believe that all things happen for a reason, but I still wonder what reason there could possibly be for Landon's death? *Why would the Lord take someone so young? Landon was the most tender hearted and good person I'd ever met.* Richard asks me to help Denise select photos and music for the funeral. Melissa would have the final say over everything, but we could go ahead and narrow it down for her.

I ease out of the kitchen and head back to Landon's room to find Denise. Trent is in the room as well going through Landon's items. He sets a pair of dress shoes next to the blue suit on the bed. He goes through the drawers and pulls out a pair of navy blue dress socks. "These match?"

Denise sniffles and nods. She's swiping her finger through her phone. When I get closer, I see that she's on his social media pages. "I'm trying to find his best photos. Mom will most likely make us use a professional photo, but I kind of like candid ones better."

"We can have the professional on big display but maybe make a board with all the favorite candid ones. A collage."

She nods. "I like that. I'm having trouble on song choices. None of the songs that he liked would be appropriate."

Trent calls out from the closet, "He'd love that even more."

I give a chuckle because that's true. We go through photos, song choices, and accessories. We don't speak to each other much. It's an eerie silence but a little calming. I have a headache, so there isn't the stress of having to hold up my end of the conversation, at least. I find several photos of Landon and Rachel. She was almost like my replacement while I was gone. Her, Landon and Trent were quite the trio for some time. *Interesting.* I set aside a photo of them as kids all dressed up for Halloween. They went as characters from Toy Story 2. Rachel is dressed as the cowgirl Jesse, Trent is Buzz Lightyear, and Landon is Woody. I missed out on all that. I missed out on all that could've been, as well, with Landon. I suck in a deep breath. I wanted more time with him. I want the time I missed with him. I'm owed time. Cindy robbed me of time with my family. God robbed me of time with him.

Why? Why couldn't I have been discovered sooner? Maybe Cindy didn't have to die for me to be discovered. Aunt Andrea could've realized that something was off, and that there was a girl missing that fit my description. Nobody thought it was strange that Cindy runs away and is supposedly pregnant around the time I conveniently go missing? I lost that time. I accepted it. But how am I supposed to accept it this time? He could've survived that fall. Luke could've too. But they didn't. Why? I wipe my eyes and excuse myself. I'm getting myself worked up, and it's not fair to Denise and Trent. I don't want to upset them more than they already are. I can't imagine having a lifetime of love and memories with Landon and then to lose him. At least they do have those memories and love. At least they had those shared times. He was the type of person that the amount of time didn't matter because you fell in love with him instantly. I'm kidding myself if I think that since I had less time with him, then this might make his loss less painful. I'm just grateful for the time I was blessed with. *What else can I do?*

After I compose myself, I go back into the bedroom. Denise has a stack of photos. I'm surprised there are so many of me. I smile at the collage she's putting together. Even though they had way more time with him, Denise has included me in the collage just as much. Trent tells me stories about the photos that I'm not in. I laugh despite myself, because all stories with Landon end in laughter. It's five in the afternoon before we see Richard and Melissa again. They stand outside the door to ask if pizza will work for supper.

We all eat our pizza in silence at the kitchen table. Then, we each take our plate to the sink quietly. Before we all go to our bedrooms, Melissa reminds us to have our clothes ready for in the morning, not to leave it last minute. She gives us all a weak kiss goodnight and then scurries off with her head bowed. I go to my room and cry.

First, I cry because I miss Landon. I miss the easy comfort he offered. The laughs he could easily bring. His charming personality. If he was here, knowing I was sad, he'd hold me until I fell asleep.

Second, I cry because Luke will never get to travel the world like he wanted. I remember the conversation we had on our date and how I had liked him. He'd been sincere when he encouraged me to go paint the Grand Canyon. Isabell also lost a brother. I cry for her and his parents.

Third, I cry because I know Noah is going to leave me. My phone has dozens of missed texts and calls from him. I can't right now. I can't speak with him. He's going to the military no matter how much he loves me. He's going to travel the world. He's going to find someone with less baggage. Someone he doesn't share so much weird and tainted history with. Or what if while overseas he's in combat and… no. No. My mind cannot go there even if that is the pattern my life's been thus far. Loss. So much loss in time and loved ones.

Fourth, I cry because no matter how exhausted I am, I can't sleep. My mind will not allow rest. The funeral is tomorrow, and all I can do is stare at my ceiling cursing fate for being so cruel. Landon and Luke were so young with bright futures, yet they're gone.

⁓

At the funeral, Noah is sitting on the church steps. He raises up and takes my hands. "I'm here for you. Whatever you need."

"I need strength."

"I can do that. Let me be strong for you."

"This next part I think I have to go alone."

"You can do this. And when it's over, I'll be here for you."

They give us a moment for the family to be alone with the casket. I don't want to see Landon like this, but there's something I must do. Each step toward the casket is painful. My chest is constricting and I feel as though I can't catch my breath. When I finally make it, I glance at Landon's peaceful handsome face. No matter how at peace he looks, I can't bear to look at him.

I hold my wrist up. I take the tiny silver rabbit charm off my bracelet, and gently place it in his jacket pocket. I ignore how stiff and cold his body feels and try to focus on the soft fabric pocket.

Your white rabbit, Landon Randall. No more chasing.

The charms on my bracelet jingle. I squeeze the matching rabbit charm that I'd added last night. I squeeze it until the metal hurts my tender fingers. The pain in my fingers actually bring me some relief. Two strong hands and two soft, delicate hands take each of my arms. The delicate, soft ones remove my fingers from the charm. When feeling returns to my fingers I glance over wide-eyed in their direction. *Denise.* I look to my other side where the strong hands are. *Trent.*

Both Trent and Denise are standing and looking the same on either side of me. Their teary eyes and pursed lips are staring down at Landon resting. They look back to me and nod toward the pews. None of us speak. I don't think we could even if we wanted to. I lean down and place a kiss to Landon's cold, stiff cheek. I squeeze my eyes tightly closed trying to keep the pain and tears in, but I feel them slip through. My body shakes with silent screams. I raise up and look down and notice a tear trailing down his face. If only this was Wonderland and our world was full of magic. Could my tears bring him back?

I can't bear to turn my back on him. So I walk backwards to the pew and take my seat between my brother and my sister.

The funeral was beautiful, but it seemed surreal. Now that I'm lying in bed, I'm forced to acknowledge that it happened. The whole day seemed as though I was somebody else watching everything play out. It wasn't me at the funeral, and it sure wasn't Landon in the casket. I vaguely remember Rachel singing a beautiful ballad, and Trent standing in front of everyone, speaking moving words mixed with scripture. I think he even used a verse I had suggested. I can't remember exactly what was said or sung. I remember watching people cry, but their cries were muffled. Everything seemed as though I was outside a glass looking in. Not clear glass, either. Everything was muffled and hazy. I vaguely recall an attractive young man introducing himself as Marcus to me. But maybe I'd only wished Marcus was there because I know Landon would've wanted him there. The whole day was as though I was trapped in a cloud of haze. My body was there, but my mind and heart seemed as though they were detached. I can't even make out what was or wasn't real today. *Did I even eat?*

I stare at the ceiling. I'm looking but see nothing. I'm listening but hear nothing. I don't even have a taste in my mouth or smell in the room. There's nothing. I'm numb. All I can think about is how he's gone. I know if I go down the hall, he won't be there. I know in the morning, he won't be in the kitchen. I know when I go back to school, he won't be there. He won't be in my classes. He won't be at lunch. He won't be at prom. He won't be at graduation. He's not going to college. He won't finally get to be with Marcus. Landon is gone. For the first time, I understand Melissa. Except, I have nobody to blame. I guess no one really took him from me. *Did Luke? If Luke hadn't been a bully, we'd have him or would something else had happened? Did God take him? Is there anyone to blame? Does it matter since he's not coming back? Was all this just meant to be?*

Once again, in the blink of an eye, my life has changed.

The following day is Luke Jamerson's funeral. I honestly didn't care if I attended or not. However, the Randall family had known him since he was a toddler. I couldn't exactly skip out on his funeral. It passed in a blur to me as well. The only time I seemed to snap out of it was when Denise went to Isabell to give her condolences, Isabell sneered. I didn't hear what was said, but Denise walked away looking ashamed. I couldn't muster up enough energy to check on her. The Jamersons are cruel, and Denise would be better off to avoid them anyways. My grief over Landon has me in a stupor. I noticed that Luke had a more elaborate funeral that I found to be tacky. Was this a competition as well? Who could outdo who with the funeral?

The town seemed to mourn the death of Luke more than the death of Landon. Of course, Landon was well liked. Both boys were charming and attractive. Both also came from wealthy families. Luke, however, was all that and more since he was a star athlete. He had such a bright future, "a tragic waste," people cried. Trent, disgusted with how everyone behaved, vowed not to return to this town after this weekend. He told all of us if we want to see him, we'll have to go to him.

Back to back funerals have left me exhausted and numb. I slowly climb the stairs to my bedroom. The house feels empty and cold. It was beginning to feel like a home, but with Landon's absence, it feels bleak. I'm at the door to my room when I see Rachel exiting Trent's bedroom. She looks startled to see me, but then she ducks her head and pulls a piece of her hair behind her ear as she scurries past me. Trent comes out a few seconds later, shirtless and in gym shorts. He wears a guilty expression but doesn't say anything and doesn't move. I rush into my room and shut the door.

Forty-Four

THE NEXT NIGHT, I FIND MELISSA IN THE DEN drinking again. At least she's not alone this time. Richard sits with her. I hear her sobbing as she pours herself another glass of wine. I walk into the room and clear my throat to let my presence be known. She doesn't even acknowledge me, but he looks over. His eyes are puffy and bloodshot. The smile he offers is so heartbreaking. It appears he has aged at least ten years in these past few days.

"I came to check on you," I whisper weakly. *Honestly, I don't know why I came in here.* Morbid curiosity, I guess.

Melissa gives a scoff that's so cold, the hair on the back of my neck rises. She puts the glass to her lips. "We should be checking on you, my dear. We are the parents." She takes a drink and slams the glass down. She wipes her mouth with the back of her hand and sighs. "It's a parent's job to tend to their children. To protect them. I," she places her hand over her heart, "I…I should receive the award for best mother any day now."

Richard shakes his head and whispers, "Melissa, please."

He squeezes his eyes shut and bows his head, but she

continues, "Why not, Richard? I've had one child go missing and buried the other? I've managed to have my daughter kidnapped in my own home. I have buried my son. My handsome, vivacious, outgoing Landon. He could light a room up as soon as he entered it."

She says more, but I can't understand her at this point. She's sobbing so heavily, and her words are jumbled and slurred. She sucks in a deep breath and regains enough control to pour another glass. "I get one child back, only to have another one taken from me, *permanently*. There'll be no surprise phone call. There'll be no day that we walk out the front door to find him." She lifts the glass to her lips and asks into it, "Will there, Richard?"

He shakes his bowed head and softly cries, "No."

She takes a drink and then looks disgusted at him and repeats, "No."

Melissa fixes her eyes on me. She smiles, but it doesn't reach her eyes. I feel extremely uneasy and decide I should go back to my room.

"Sarah." She stands and comes over to me.

She embraces me in a hug. The minutes pass, and she's still holding me firmly. Finally, she pulls away and pets my hair and the side of my face. I can tell she's about to break down crying again, which makes me want to cry.

"Go to sleep, honey. Get some rest. It's a school night," is all she says and turns her back on me.

I hurry back to my room and lock the door. I want Landon back. I want to lay next to him and talk about chasing white rabbits. I want Noah. If I ran to him right now, I know everything would be okay. Until it's not. Because eventually, I'll lose him as well. He's called every day to check on me. He's brought me food and tried to get me to leave the house other than to go to school. But, I can't. I want him to stop. To stop being so damn perfect because it's only going to hurt worse when I lose him. I dive into my bed and cry. I feel as though I'm going to cry until my body breaks. My chest hurts and I begin dry heaving. I feel sore and sick. I'm breaking. My mind and body are breaking with each tear.

⚓

When I pull into the school parking lot, Noah is leaning against the building in front of my parking spot. He pushes himself off the wall as I get out of the car.

"Sarah…"

"Don't, Noah."

"What have I done?" He steps in front of me blocking my path.

"*Nothing.*" I grit my teeth.

"What's going on?" He holds my elbow, preventing me from side stepping him.

"I can't lose another person. I can't go through something like this *again*. Don't you understand? I'm breaking. All of this is breaking me. I won't survive another loss."

He gently places his hands on my shoulders. "You're the only one that decides if you lose me or not. I made you a promise that I wouldn't leave you no matter what life threw at us. I keep my promises." I glare at him. I'm too hurt and angry. I'm bitter at what life's been throwing at me. He honestly expects me to believe he can keep that promise? His jaw ticks as he purses his lips and narrows his eyes. He drops his hands and takes a step back from me. "I guess I should've asked you to promise the same thing."

I don't answer. I duck my head and sidestep him. I march forward to the entrance of the school.

I go to my classes and want to cry when I spot the empty chairs that were Landon's. Nobody will sit in them. They also won't sit in his spot in the cafeteria. His track jersey is hung up in the gym. This Friday everyone has agreed to wear black button ups and sunglasses or black cocktail dresses in honor of Landon's stylish fashion. A bench and tree are being placed by the track field.

But as the weeks go by, school, along with everyone there, seems to slowly move forward, leaving me rooted in a depressed hole. The only other person at school that seems as affected by Landon's absence is Rachel. She has lost her best friend, and after seeing all the photos from their history, a brother. She attaches herself more to me with the loss of Landon. We both agree that our usual table at lunch is too difficult to keep using, so we find a new one. A few of our friends join us at the new table, but most remain at the old one. Noah, Keaton, Emily, Tara and Jeff join us at our new table.

As we're walking to our lockers after lunch one day, I can't stop myself from asking her about Trent. It's been bugging me since I saw her leaving his bedroom.

"Rachel?"

"Yeah?"

"Look, it's none of my business-"

"Then you probably shouldn't ask." I glance up at her to see if she's really upset with me. She doesn't seem upset. This is the kind of thing Landon would probably say, I think. They had kind of a banter relationship. Is she trying to use me to replace Landon? Most likely. Then again, I'm probably doing the same with her if I'm being honest.

"Probably. Yet, here I go. Are you and Trent..." I feel my cheeks get red. I let it hang, hoping she'll fill it in for me.

"Are we what? Together? Have you asked him? What'd he say?"

My eyes widen at all the questions she's firing at me. "No. I haven't asked him."

"He's your brother. Go to him first. Then, come to me and tell me exactly what he says."

I frown. "That's awkward. More awkward than asking you."

"Why?"

"He's a boy."

"He's your brother. You can ask your brother about who he's dating…and then you can tell your friend about what your brother said. That's how this works."

"You still didn't answer my question. Did y'all…"

"Sex and being together are different things. Believe me, I've learned the hard way."

The bell rings. She plasters a fake smile and beams, "Gotta go. Text me."

⌒

After school I meet with Rita. She finally tires of my silence and speaks. "I understand you're grieving. Let's try to work through this. Landon was a very important part of your life and to your growth. Don't shut everyone out."

Too late.

Forty-Five

THE WHOLE SCHOOL BEGINS TO BUZZ OVER THE excitement of prom. It's difficult for me to get excited over prom, even if it is my senior year. I can still feel Landon's absence everywhere, especially with an event like this. I'd planned to double date with him and Rachel. Landon had been working on planning an after party. I told Rachel that we're still going—together. Landon would've had a stroke at the thought of us missing prom.

That night, I call Trent. He hasn't been back to visit in weeks, true to his word.

"Sarah? Are you okay?"

"Yeah, I'm fine…"

"Sorry. Just, you never called before. Usually, you just text."

That's what I should've done tonight. I take a deep breath. "Well, I wanted to ask you something that would be too awkward to text. Now, I'm thinking it might be too awkward to ask over the phone."

"You can ask me anything."

"Sure about that?"

"Positive."

"Remember when you were telling me and Landon about Rachel? You know I saw her leave your room after the funeral. Did anything…happen? I mean, I haven't seen Maggie around. I wanted to ask before because I noticed she wasn't at the funeral and then I saw Rachel…and I'm being nosy. I'm sorry. I just wondered if maybe you wanted someone to talk to about…"

"My love life?"

"I guess."

"And you are being nosy."

"Are you mad?"

He groans. "Nah. I'm not mad. Maggie and I broke up. I had a really hard time dealing with Landon's death, and I was upset she didn't make it to the funeral. She couldn't leave. I might have overacted, but I needed her."

"Trent, that's understandable."

"She wasn't being supportive. I didn't feel like she was, anyways. We've been talking a little since then."

"Think you're going to get back together?"

"Maybe. Most likely. I don't know. I don't think she's the one for me. Even though she's almost like a female replica of me, but with less muscles."

I laugh at his attempt of a joke. "She's probably not the one then. Sorry. I did like her. Was… Rachel being supportive?"

I hear a heavy, deep sigh through the phone. "Rachel understood my loss because it was her loss, too. She felt it. Rachel is… special. She's special because her and Landon have been attached at the hip since elementary school. She's like a kid sister, but then she's not. It's confusing. I'll be honest with you, I'm confused. If you're asking if I feel things for her, yes. Of course. How could I not?"

"Then why not be with her?"

"I can't pursue a relationship with a high schooler. It wouldn't be fair to either one of us. I could never hurt Rachel.

I try not to, but I know I have. Landon would kill me if I ever hurt her. He'd kill me now if he could. Might still do it. Knowing him, he would haunt me and love the theatrics of it."

I laugh and so does he. Trent asks me how things are going with Noah. I keep it vague. He asks if I've been thinking about colleges. I tell him that I'm seriously considering attending in Lexington. He said he'd love it if we went to the same school. Before I know it, we've been on the phone for over an hour. I hang up happy about the progress we just made in our bonding but sad too. I want happiness for Trent and Rachel and the answer seems so simple. But life's never as simple as it seems.

⁂

On the night of prom, Rachel comes to get ready at my house. I turn on some music to try and get us in the mood. Denise comes to my room to help with make-up and hair. For a moment, the three of us lose ourselves in fun and behave like normal teenagers getting ready for prom. We dance and laugh around my bedroom and bathroom. Melissa calls for us to get downstairs for photos. My dress is princess style, baby blue, with scattered stones on the bottom. It has a heart neckline that has various stones and beads forming an elegant design around the bodice. The dress reminds me of Cinderella's, and right now, I feel like her in this mansion with my prince charming arriving any minute. Rachel is wearing a slim fitted, A-Line, black dress with sparkling rhinestones arranged around the neck and snaking around the sides. The dress has thin, see through, nude material on the back with stones scattered along in an intricate design. Her brown hair is piled on top of her head with big curls. Only two small loose curls hang on either side of her face. She looks stunning.

We take a few photos of the two of us and a few with Denise, as well. We try serious poses, silly, and natural poses.

Rachel takes the camera and takes a few of me with Melissa, Richard, and Denise. The doorbell rings, and Denise hurries off to answer it. My eyes grow wide, and my mouth waters when I see who walks in.

Noah.

Noah has always been extremely handsome. There's always been something special about him. Noah in a tux is breathtaking. He wears all black except for his vest and tie. They're silver. Rachel reaches over with a tissue to dab the corner of my mouth. "I think you have a little drool there."

I swat her hand away, embarrassed, because that's probably true.

His eyes are wide and his mouth is slightly open. I can see his hand shaking as he comes over holding up a beautiful, white orchid corsage.

"Wow. You look-" He clears his throat. "You're stunning."

"Thank you. You too." I want to face palm myself for how lame I probably sound. Noah shifts from one foot to the other. I can hear the plastic popping from his fingers squeezing the corsage case. "Is that for me?"

"Will you wear it? I'm sorry I showed up unannounced. I've been trying to give you your space, but-" I watch his eyebrows furrow and hear a slight break in his voice. "But I really wanted to be the one to escort you to prom. If you'll let me." He quickly looks over to my parents. "If your folks will let me also?"

The room is thick with tension. How could anyone possibly tell him no when he looks so vulnerable and sincere. The back of my eyes burn and Denise quickly waves her hands in front of my eyes. "No, no, no. Do not mess up this masterpiece."

A giggle escapes me and it seems to lighten the mood. Noah bites his bottom lip. I hold my wrist out to him. He opens the plastic container and places the corsage on my wrist as Melissa takes several photos. We take a few photos of just the two of us and one with my parents.

I give Noah a hug and look up into his eyes. "There's a slight catch. I'm kind of a package deal. Rachel's with me tonight, so… think you can handle being both our escorts?"

He chuckles as Rachel rolls her eyes. I ask Rachel to come over for a photo, but she shoos me off.

"He's your date, too," I insist.

She gives an awkward laugh. "Stop. He's not my date."

Then, we hear a low voice from the top of the stairs speak, "That's right, he's not."

We all turn to see Trent slowly descending the stairs, dressed in a sleek, fitted tux. He looks like a Hollywood actor, polished and handsome. I didn't even know he'd come back home. *How long has he been sneaking around the house?*

He walks up to Rachel, who looks like a deer in headlights. He takes her hand. "Will you allow me to take you to prom in Landon's place? I can't promise I'll be as good of a dancer."

Her eyes glisten with unshed tears as she swallows hard and nods. He gives her a dazzling smile and leads her over to stand by us. We pose for a few more photos. Trent and Rachel take a couple of pictures of just the two of them.

We're all surprised when Trent says, "Landon always liked to take silly photos." Trent sticks his tongue out and tries his best to appear silly, but it comes over awkward and stiff for him. No one can control their laughter.

Trent further surprises us with a rented limo. We all hop in with Trent sitting next to Rachel, and Noah and me across from them.

"You look gorgeous." He smiles at her. She blushes and then he adds, "Both of you. Both of you girls look beautiful."

Noah takes my hand and holds it. Trent looks like he wants to hold Rachel's hand, but he doesn't. I can't help but wonder how Maggie feels about this, or if she knows.

We don't dance immediately upon arrival. I admire the decorations. The twinkling lights strung from the ceiling. The blue and white balloons floating about as the strobe lights change colors. A disco ball hung in the center of the dance floor.

We mingle with a few of our friends. Landon had always been the dancer of our group. Noah wanders off, but I can't see where he goes because he's lost amongst the crowd. A familiar ballad comes on as he reappears. Noah wastes no time leading me out to the dance floor as the theme song to the Breakfast Club fills the room. I laugh as I close my eyes and rest my head on his shoulder as we sway to the music. I open my eyes to find Trent dancing with Rachel. She looks as though she's on cloud nine. She always has a look of utter adoration when she's around him.

When the song is over, Noah gives me a twirl. "Thanks for the dance, princess."

I laugh, and we make our way to the rest of the group. Keaton, Emily, Jeff, Tara, Rachel, Trent and a few others are all in a circle. We stay on the dance floor and dance a few songs together.

I whisper to Noah that I'm ready to go. I remember that we rode with Trent and Rachel, though. We tell them we're thinking about leaving early. Trent whispers something to Rachel, making her blush. She nods and gives him a shy smile. He tells us to go ahead and take the limo. We all walk out, and Trent goes over to talk to the driver. I ask Rachel what their plans are.

"Trent suggested that after the limo dropped y'all off, we ride around in it. Maybe go through a drive thru and get some food to snack on." She tries to sound casual, but I can tell she's beyond excited.

Once again, I can't help but wonder where this is going. Has Trent decided to go ahead and pursue a relationship with Rachel, or is he planning to still get back together with Maggie? I'm happy for Rachel; I just hope she doesn't get hurt. Trent comes back and tells me he'll see me at home.

Instead of the limo pulling up to my house, we're in front of Noah's. Noah tells me to stay in the car as he hops out. He jogs around the limo to come open the door for me. He takes my hand to help me out and bows. I laugh as I pull my hand away to cover my face. "You're being so cheesy!"

He pulls me into a hug and kisses my forehead. "But you love it."

I nod and look up into his kind eyes. "You're right. I can't believe it, but I do. I love it."

He nods his head toward his truck. "Come on."

We hop in the truck and somehow, I already know where we're going. The truck bounces along the bumpy gravel as we pull up to the clearing. I hold my prom dress up as I step over twigs and moss. "Oh my gosh." I giggle. "I'm going to fall in heels. They keep sinking into the ground!" I yelp as I almost twist my ankle.

Noah swoops me up into his arms. He carries me over to our spot. "Oh shit."

"What?"

"Your dress. You can't sit in the moss. Hold on." He places me down on my feet. I wobble and he laughs. "Are you good?" He holds his hands out ready to catch me. When I nod, he shrugs out of his tux jacket and places it on the ground.

"There. Sit."

"What about your jacket?"

"It's easier to get my jacket cleaned than your dress with all the beading and—whatever. I'm trying here, c'mon."

Noah helps me ease down on the ground while in my constricting prom dress. The night is perfect. The stars twinkle in the clear sky. The moon shines brightly over the water. There's no mosquitos or bugs flying around. Just a light breeze.

"This is so much better than the lights and noise."

"It is," he agrees.

I blush and whisper, "I loved tonight. I didn't think I would, so thank you."

He nods in understanding. The loss of Landon is still weighing heavy on me, but Noah made the night so wonderful. *And Trent.* He too, helped make tonight special. Noah cups my face in his hand and whispers, "The night's not over."

His thumb caresses my lower lip as he stares into my eyes. I sigh and try to fight back tears. The look on his face and the way he spoke to me is filled with so much devotion.

"I love you," My voice trembles.

I'm falling hard for Noah, and it scares me. I'm unsure if I love him because of the comfort and connection to my past, or if it's simply Noah himself. I do know in my heart that I do love him. We stare into each other's eyes as he leans in and places a soft kiss on my lips.

He barely pulls back, but I reach up and cup his neck pulling him back to me. I open my mouth and he doesn't hesitate. I lean back and bring Noah with me. Slowly, he eases his body on top of mine. I feel him in all the right places. My body craves his touch. My heart is beating so hard he must feel it against his chest. He deepens the kiss as his hands explore my body. I need more. I don't know exactly what I want more of, I just know I need more.

But Noah doesn't give me more.

He pulls back and searches my eyes. He gulps and his voice comes out hoarse, "I'm not going any farther with you. Not tonight. God, I hope someday soon, but tonight has been perfect. I want it to always be perfect for you. You're too raw from everything that's happened. I'd feel like I was taking advantage of your emotions."

My chest rises and falls. I feel like he just popped my bubble. He raises an eyebrow as his hand eases under my prom dress and creeps up my leg. "But—we can do *other* stuff."

I bite my lip and nod my head. He smiles and asks, "Yeah?"

"Yes."

I hope and pray nobody is watching at the window when Noah pulls up in his truck. He leans over and gives me a kiss full of promise of future things to come. He pulls back only enough to whisper against my lips, "Good night."

I walk into the house expecting to find Melissa waiting for me like she did after Homecoming. She was so excited for me. Instead, it's dark and quiet. I see a faint light coming from the den. I'm nervous as to what I'll find. She's hasn't been in a good place since Landon's death, although she is trying and I do understand.

The television is on with the volume turned low. Melissa is wrapped in a blanket on the couch sitting upright asleep. There's an open book on her lap, and there's a giant mug of coffee on the table next to her.

"She tried to stay awake, but she's been exhausted."

I jump at the sound of Richard's voice.

"Sorry. I didn't mean to scare ya."

"No, it's fine. She looks peaceful. I don't want to wake her."

"She'd love to see you and hear all about the dance. But you're probably right. She's finally sleeping peacefully. There's always tomorrow morning."

She'd been waiting up for me. I feel a tightness in my chest and a burning in my eyes. I tip toe over to her. I grab the remote and turn off the television. I slide the book from her hands. I stick a piece of mail off the table into the book as a bookmark. I ease her down to where she's lying on her side. She barely stirs but remains asleep. I adjust her blanket, but before backing away, I lean in for a hug. I lightly kiss her temple and whisper, "I love you, Mom."

Forty-Six

TRENT DOESN'T SHARE ANY DETAILS ABOUT HIS night with Rachel. He eats breakfast with all of us and then tells me goodbye and leaves to go back to school. I think about his school. I also think about how he said he'd never return to town, but he did. Throughout the day, my mind continues to wonder about Trent and his decisions.

When the bell rings ending first hour, Noah walks me to my next class. As we walk, he says, "Why don't we go grab a bite to eat after school?"

It's to discuss our relationship. He doesn't specify it, but we both know that's what we're going to do. Graduation is approaching and we're both about to have life changing decisions. I feel uneasy because if there wasn't any question about our relationship, he could ease my mind now by saying that. He's always been big on telling me to have faith in us. I tell him that sounds 'great,' and the rest of the day drags on.

Rachel asks me about my plans for graduation during lunch. I tell her I'm still up in the air. Plans usually don't work out and my life has been so unpredictable. I might just go wherever the wind blows me.

"I'm going to try and graduate early."

I drop my fork. "*What?* Like this year?"

"Maybe not May but this summer it might be possible. I know I don't act it but I'm advanced. I'm already ahead. I'm short like two classes."

"Oh. Wow. That's impressive."

"I can't go another year here…without…"

"Him."

"Yeah." She licks her lips and then perks up at me. "We could be roommates! Think about it? There are so many horror stories about freshman roommates." She bats her eye lashes and makes a sad puppy dog face at me.

I squirm in my seat. "Can I think about it?" She appears stunned by my response so I quickly add, "It's not that I wouldn't love to room with you. It's just… I'm kind of wanting to start fresh somewhere. You wouldn't understand…"

She nods enthusiastically. "Yes, I do. I totally get it. I want to start fresh, too. I'll give you plenty of space. I get freaked out by the idea of rooming with a stranger. Plus…" She sighs, "I know all about plans not working out…"

She doesn't finish. I already know her answer, but I don't voice it. She had plans with Landon. I chew on the inside of my cheek. I fear Rachel is about to break down into tears. I gently touch her arm and squeeze my lips together. I nod my head and her face lights up.

Her eyes are bright with unshed tears, and she throws her arms around me. "Yay." She wipes her eyes and gives a weak chuckle. "Roomie."

We never discuss a backup plan in case we don't get into the same schools. I tell her the ones I already applied to, and she suggests two more for me to apply to. After lunch, I go to the counselor for the paperwork for those schools. It's late but I haven't missed the deadlines.

Noah is waiting for me after school by my locker. We

discuss how our last classes went as I get what I need from my locker. Our conversation is light, even on the way to his truck, but there is tension in the air. As we get in the vehicle, he asks if cheeseburgers sound good, and I reply with a simple "yeah." We become silent as he pulls out of the school parking lot.

I'm surprised when he takes the drive-thru instead of us going in to eat. When I recognize the road he takes toward the end of town, I can't help the smile that spreads across my face. We're heading in the direction toward our spot. I turn the radio up and stare out of the window as he drives.

We're still quiet as we get out of the truck and follow the dirt path. Noah sits our bag of food down and lays a blanket down on the grass. He sits down first and pats his lap. I smile as he grabs my hand and pulls me down onto him. He reaches over for the bag of burgers and pulls one out for me. We eat with me sitting on him and watching the stream flow.

After we finish eating, Noah wraps me in a tight embrace. He nuzzles my neck and whispers, "I love you, princess."

I lay my head back against his chest and grab ahold of his arms, squeezing them tighter against me. "I love you."

He turns me around to where I'm straddling him. He takes a deep breath and releases it. "I have to join the army. There's no way around this. I've thought long and hard about it. I dread it for several reasons. The idea of leaving my family, my friends, the only place I've ever known, and most of all, the idea of leaving you scares me. It. Scares. Me. But what scares me more, is not becoming who I need to be. I want to make something of myself. I want to be somebody." I try to interrupt him, but he stops me. "I'm going to do this. Just like you're going to figure out who you are."

I stare into his eyes. "I know who I am, Noah. I may have had a confusing year, but I know who I am."

He gives me a sad smile and shakes his head. "You're eighteen. You don't know anything."

I punch him in the shoulder. "You're eighteen!"

He clears his throat and raises an eyebrow. "I'll be nineteen this summer."

I feel myself sinking into myself, but he pulls me closer to his chest. "Please listen to me. Hear what I'm trying to say. Your life has been…" He shakes his head and cups my face. "You've gone through more than any teenager should. And you're stronger than anyone else I know. While I'm away, trying to become a better version of myself, for *us*; I want you to take some time to focus on you. I want you to have an opportunity to discover *you*, before we move any further with *us*. Not Olivia. Not Sarah. You." He gently cups my face. "Discover who you are without others trying to say who you should be."

I know what he's thinking but won't say. I've had the same thoughts. *Who am I? Who do I want to be? Is this connection we have real?* Am I really in love with him for him or for the comfort and familiarity he offers from my former life?

I ask him when he'll leave and return. I guess he takes that as a good sign because his shoulders relax.

"I'll have to report for basic training two weeks after graduation, but I'll have a leave in December."

I lean in for a kiss. Noah hesitates but doesn't stop me. The kiss begins soft but turns more passionate. We kiss for a while before I pull away.

"Let's focus on just being with each other for now," I suggest.

Noah smiles, but his eyes are intense. "You've been my only focus since you stole my seat your first day of school. Yesterday, tomorrow, now, I'll always be focusing on you. Even if I can't be here with you, know that."

He rolls us over to where he's on top of me. He supports his weight with his arms as he kisses me. I feel his desperation. In the back of my mind, I feel like this is the beginning to our goodbye.

Forty-Seven

S THE DAYS GO BY, NOAH AND I SPEND AS much time as possible together. We double date a couple of times with Rachel when she has an occasional date here and there. We also double with Tara and Jeff, and Emily and Keaton. Tara still can't believe Noah and I haven't slept together yet. We go and visit Trent once, and Maggie joins us for dinner. Most of the time, however, we go to our spot. I know that we're quickly approaching the deadline for our time together, but I try not to dwell on it. But there are constant reminders of it at school and home with graduation preparations.

Rachel and I finally begin to receive our acceptance letters. At first, we're discouraged with the first couple of schools accepting one or the other but not both of us. However, we finally both receive acceptance letters from the same two universities. One is in Lexington where Trent attends and the other one is in Colorado. I almost feel like this is a cruel joke forcing me to choose between the two worlds I've been torn between. Really, I wanted some random school, completely separated from both, yet here are the two schools to choose from with Rachel. I try to leave the decision up to her, but she's scared either way. She has a fear of never getting over Trent if we go to the same school as him, but she's also uncomfortable attending school that far away from home. She says she'll blindly follow me with whatever decision I choose.

I call Rachel around ten at night to tell her which university I'm leaning toward. The one in Lexington offered me a full ride on a soccer scholarship. But Trent turned out to be my deciding factor. The loss of Landon was so hard on me, and though I don't want Trent to become a crutch, being so far away would be like losing him as well. I secretly think she was relieved, but she didn't let on. After I hang up with her, I call Noah. He's excited that I decided to stay close to the area, so when he comes to visit on leave, it'll be easier for him to visit me and his family. It'll still be a drive, but at least we're still in the same state. In the morning, I announce my decision to everyone else over breakfast. Everyone beams with pride that I was offered a soccer scholarship and they're elated that I'll be attending the same school as Trent. Even though Melissa wanted me to attend a closer university, like in the next town over, she's grateful I at least chose to attend one with another family member.

✐

There's a moment of silence during graduation in Landon's honor. Even though he wasn't in our class, he had made such an impact on the entire student body. When they call the name "Sarah Randall," I don't hesitate. I stand tall and walk across the stage with my head held high.

After the graduation ceremony, we have a celebratory family dinner in my honor at my favorite restaurant, Taste of Tuscany.

I decide that now's the time to tell them I've legally changed my name. Melissa is hurt, as was to be expected. She understands my choice but still hurt I wouldn't keep the name she'd given me. Richard and Trent both nod and smile at me in an understanding way. Denise wants to change her name, too, of course.

∽

The day before Noah is to depart, we go back to our spot. I'm not panicking. I guess it's because I don't feel I'll ever really lose him. Somehow, lying against his chest with his arms and legs wrapped around me, I feel confident for the first time in a long time that everything is going to work out.

Suddenly, Noah pushes me off him and strips himself of his shirt. He gives me a mischievous grin as he leans into me. My heart is racing as his arms wrap around me. I wet my lips and stare into his eyes. He has determination in his piercing eyes. I'm lifted off the ground. He begins carrying me and then breaks into a hard run. I latch onto him in confusion. Then, I realize he's running towards the waterfall and we're about to run out of ground. I scream as he jumps. We hold onto each other as we plummet down toward the water. It's not that far of a drop, but I still scream and squeeze his neck. Right before we hit the water, he captures my lips. The water covers our heads, and he still holds me as he pushes us up through the water to the surface. We gasp for air and then laugh, still holding each other.

"I love you," he kisses me again. "Just so you know, that's exactly what it's felt like since you came here."

I look at him with confusion. "What?"

He stares into my eyes, "Our relationship. Falling in love. It's happened fast but it's been pure adrenaline. It's been the most terrifying and exciting part of my life."

The sun is at the perfect angle to cascade over the water. It shines on his sun kissed skin, making his eyes and the water droplets sparkle. I want to sketch this moment. I have the sudden urge to tell him not to move while I run to grab my supplies. I'm in awe by how gorgeous he looks and how beautiful this moment is. No matter what the future brings, this moment will forever be sketched in my mind.

I watch as the smile on his face slowly fades away. His face become serious as he looks at me. He takes my face into his hands and brings his lips crashing to mine. We become frantic. We can't stop kissing as we push ourselves through the water to the shoreline. My clothes stick to my skin and it's a little awkward trying to remove them, especially since I'm trying to hurry. Noah and I bump heads as we both tug on my shirt. We begin laughing so hard we collapse against each other on the ground.

I smile as I stare into his hazel eyes. "Why can't anything ever be easy?"

"Because we're rushing. And we shouldn't be." I think he's going to back away from me, but instead, he slowly takes the bottom of my shirt and gently begins pulling it from my skin and over my head. The movement is so slow and deliberate, it makes it more intimate. Then he goes to the button on my shorts. Again, slowly and deliberately, he unfastens them and slides the wet material down my legs. Goosebumps prickle my skin from the water droplets and the light breeze. Or maybe, they're from Noah's eyes studying me.

"See? That wasn't so hard."

"No. It wasn't." His shirt is already thrown off somewhere in the grass, so I focus on his jeans. My fingers shake as I try to unfasten the button. He places his large hands over mine and helps steady my hand to unfasten it. He stands, and I slowly slide the wet, heavy material down his legs. His boxers are wet and stick to his legs, the thin material outlining *all* of him.

He looks down. "I can hold off on removing those if it makes you nervous."

"No." I bite my bottom lip. "I'm curious."

He doesn't say anything, merely raises his eyebrows. His eyes dance with mischief. I should be embarrassed and look away, but I don't. I feel my cheeks blush as I shamefully watch as he lowers his boxers. "Alright. Now—it's your turn."

He eases down and kisses me sweetly. Then he eases from my lips down to my jaw, and when he's at the crook of my neck, I feel his hands come around my back and unfasten my bra. With the hooks open, he gently presses my body against the ground where I'm lying on my back. He slides the straps down my arm as he trails kisses along my collar bone and shoulder. I place my hands in his short, wet hair as his warm tongue laps at droplets of water that have gathered between the dip in my breasts. His warm hands slide down my waist to the band of my panties. He hooks his thumbs under the band and then slides it down my legs until finally, I'm completely exposed to him.

Noah brings his lips to mine and I greedily welcome them. I can't get enough of him. He presses his body firmly against mine. I feel all the hard planes of his muscles and the sensation of the mixture of cold water droplets and his warm body heat. The pressure of his body pushes my back into the mossy ground. It's not exactly the most comfortable spot, but I don't want to end this moment. I hold him tighter to me. His hand comes behind my head to cradle it as he presses himself more firmly between my legs. The sensation causes me to release a gasp. He does it again.

"Sarah."

"Yes?"

"Let's go to my truck."

"Why?"

I watch as he seems to struggle to even swallow. "I need a condom. I have one in the glove compartment. Plus, this ground is hurting you. If we do this, it will already be a little uncomfortable for you. I don't want to make it worse."

As much as I hate to lose our physical connection, he's right. Standing up naked in front of him is ten times more awkward than being beneath him. I grab my shirt and throw it on and shimmy back into my wet, heavy shorts. I carry my undergarments in a wet, soggy ball. He slides back into his boxers.

Noah opens the tailgate. He reaches in the cab of his truck and pulls out some blankets we'd used for picnics. He arranges them in a nice pallet in the truck bed. He whispers, "Hop up."

As I climb into the truck bed, I wonder if I should undress myself again or wait and let him do the honors. He shuffles through his glove compartment and then comes back with a condom.

"Just in case you're wondering, I'm still a virgin. I have this because coach gave all the players a box. Safe sex and all that."

I blush. "I wasn't."

Noah raises a single brow and I blush. He crawls up the truck bed toward me. "Let's get you back out of these wet clothes."

Let's. I sigh as he begins kissing my neck again. My entire body feels more sensitive to every touch. The feel of his warm mouth. The touch of his strong hands. Even as strands of his wet hair tickle and leave tiny droplets in their wake.

We hold each other tightly as our bodies create a delicious friction. My legs squeeze him and hug him against me. I can't hold him tight enough. I want more. I want more of this friction, his hot kisses, his hands massaging my body, everything and more.

More. I need *more.*

Noah seems to read my mind or maybe he feels the same. He pulls away from me and slides his boxers down. Taking the condom packet, he rips it open and slides it on. I take a deep breath and I watch as Noah does the same, his chest rising and falling.

We're not frantic anymore. He positions himself on top of me, placing most of his weight on his elbows. I stare into those tender, beautiful hazel eyes as they stare back at me.

"I love you."

A soft smile spreads as he whispers back, "I love you. So much."

I say through a smile. "Then kiss me."

Noah bites his bottom lip and my heart melts. "I think I will." And he does. The sweetest and most tender of kisses. Slowly, he deepens the kiss. I tilt my head and open my mouth more giving him greater access. An ache begins to build. I can feel it building in Noah as his body tenses and he seems to be struggling with keeping his weight on his elbows. He begins to shift and I feel him between my legs. That delicious friction returning. A steady rhythm, but I need more.

I finally take the advice I'd been receiving in therapy and voice my concerns. "More. Noah, I need *more*."

It pays off because he listens. He presses himself against me more firmly as his hands begin to massage my breasts. He takes my earlobe and gently sucks on it. All these new sensations have my body singing.

"More?" He asks.

"More," I whisper. Even though I don't know how much more I can take, but I'm ready to receive whatever Noah Wallace can give me.

And what he gives me, is him. All of him. His body is stiff and tense as he eases himself in. I try to remain relaxed, but the stretching of my body makes it difficult. I won't lie and say it's comfortable, far from it. This is one sensation I could do without. Noah's eyes are dazed and he looks like he's seeing stars. He pushes himself further, until finally he's fully inside.

Slowly, he moves and slowly, I begin to relax. We're clumsy as we're trying to find a rhythm that we can both enjoy. Through it all, we kiss and hold each other. We find it and it's one of the most intense experiences of my life. We're so in tune with each other's bodies. His hands landing exactly where I need them to be. My hands rub along his side as I suck at his collar bone, feeling pure satisfaction when I hear his low moan of pleasure.

"I love you," Noah breathes into my hair. He kisses my forehead and then my temple. "I love you so much." He kisses my cheek and then my lips. He pulls away and stares into my eyes. "I could make love to you forever."

"Then do it. Make love to me forever."

"I think I will."

I hope you do, Noah.

His thrusts become stronger as we both hold on to each other tightly. Now it feels as though we're climbing. The pressure is so great that I don't know how I'll survive the fall. All I can do is hope Noah will hold me like he did when we fell earlier into the water. Hope that he'll hold me and I won't drown.

With each push, the building pressure increases. Sweat gathers at his temple and his arms hold me to almost a crushing point. "Oh God." He reaches down and hikes my leg up. The new friction and angle sends a new wave of sensation through my body. I gasp and dig my nails into Noah's skin. We both release a moan and hold onto each other as we finally leap off the edge. We dive down into each other in a kiss.

Noah holds me as we finally come back to the surface. Our chests rise and fall as we lay sideways facing each other. The skies above begin to darken. And like those dark, looming clouds, we know our time has officially run out.

⁓

On the drive home, we try to be normal, but there's a rising tension between us. When we're almost to the house, Noah connects to Blutooth. "Don't You Forget About Me" begins. We both burst out singing. I'm between laughing and crying by the time it's over, and we pull into my driveway. Raindrops fall on the windshield as we finish the song, even after he puts the truck in park. When it's over, we stare into each other's eyes, and reality slams into me that I won't see him for a long time. We reach for each other at the same time and pour all our emotions into the kiss.

He pulls away and bows his head. "I have to go."

I nod my head and sniffle. He looks into my eyes and rubs his thumb along my jaw. "I love you."

I give him another quick kiss, and whisper against his lips, "I love you."

Leaning in again, I kiss him with everything I have. Slowly, I pull away and get out of the truck. The light sprinkle wets my hair, but I don't care. I watch and listen as he starts the song again and lowers his truck windows. I can still hear it as he turns out of the driveway.

I go into the house and finish what little was left to pack. As I pack, a smile stretches across my face. I know most freshmen claim to be on a journey of self-discovery, but I'm on a new journey for the third time it seems.

"I knew who I was this morning, but I've changed a few times since then." I pack the painting I had brought from Colorado, along with my pencil sketch of my spot with Noah. I wrote another quote from Alice in Wonderland on this one as well.

"It's no use going back to yesterday because I was a different person then."

⁂

Before I leave, I go by to see Rita one last time. I walk into her office, and hand her my sketch pad. She smiles at the fully drawn portrait. I watch as her eyes move to the corner. A smile stretches across her face as she reads. *Alice Randall*

Olivia Stevens and Sarah Randall are the names of girls I used to know. Hello, my name is Alice Randall.

Find out what's next for the Randalls in…

THE NIGHT
That Changed Rachel

Other Books by
GAIL HARIS

Worth a Shot

One simple run-in got me more than I bargained for...and now I can't go back. It might be dangerous, but it might just be worth a shot.

Victoria Angel...

It was just a cup of coffee...that's all I was after. Some much-needed caffeine to get me through wedding dress shopping. That's it. But I guess the universe had other plans. How do I go from getting coffee to waking up in the hospital after being involved in a drive-by?

And how does my mysterious hero go from taking a bullet for me to getting arrested and put in prison?

His last name is Goodman, but according to the police, he's not at all a good man. However, it feels as though fate brought us together. The police don't agree...and my fiancé definitely doesn't either.

Tristan Goodman…

She thinks I'm her hero, which couldn't be further from the truth. Because of the business that I'm in and the people I surround myself with, there's always a target on my back, and anyone associated with me is in the line of fire, including the quirky yet gorgeous Victoria Angel.

I've brought nothing but danger to her life the minute she bumped into me in that coffee shop. I know she's not mine, but that certainly doesn't stop me from going after what I want. And what I want is an angel.

She'd be wise to end all contact with me, exactly like her fiancé wishes, but I can't leave her alone…especially after I have a taste of heaven.

Acknowledgements

THANK YOU!!! Thank you so much for reading WHO IS Sarah Randall! This book is very special to me and I appreciate it so much that you gave it a chance. There's an endless supply of books out there and precious little time, so I am honored that you chose this story to read. Thank you!! I seriously can't thank you enough!

I started writing this book **FIVE** years ago. So many times I started to give up on this dream, but Alice wouldn't let me. Her voice and this story just kept begging to be told. I'm so grateful for all the support I've received. I hope you all love the characters as much as I do. I can't wait for you to read what's next for them. *cue happy dance*

Gail Haris started out as my pen name, but this name has turned into something so much bigger. I feel that Gail Haris is all of us because, I know I couldn't have gotten this far without you. I thank God every day for the amazing support from my family, friends, and people that have come into my life recently offering nothing but positivity and encouragement.

Gail's Book Belles!!! My Facebook group! The encouragement from you all blows my mind. I love y'all!!!!

My book club—My tribe! You ladies are my monthly therapy session that keep me sane! You all encourage me to expand my reading library and help me grow in all aspects of life. I love you ladies!

The indie book community… It's basically the most amazing group of people. I appreciate every single person I've come in contact with and has offered any shred of advice! It may seem like something simple to you, but it's *gold* to me. Thank you for welcoming me into this world!

My Book Bitches! Georgia, Chelsi, and Jessica! Our

adventures and support for each other is something I'll always be grateful for! Love you bitches!

My mom! My love for stories and reading all genres was a direct influence from my mother. She not only encouraged me to read but set an example by always having a book in her hand. Thank you Mom for always encouraging me to read and write! Always you More!

My mother-in-law! Thank you to my mother in law who has become one of my best friends. Thank you for feeding me and my family when I didn't want to leave my computer! LOL. Your compassion and support played a huge role in me finishing this! I love you, Sweetest!

Holly, my brilliant editor! Thank you so much for helping me dig deeper with this story!! I appreciate our phone conversations so much! You're the best and I love you! I'm so thankful I met you at Book Lovers Con!

Kiki—I can't wait to see where we go with this series!!! I'm so excited to be working with you and your brilliant team! I appreciate all your encouragement and wonderful positive vibes!

The greatest set of friends and support team anyone could ask for!!! Thank you to Jill, Jessica, Jana, Jade, (lots of J names lol) Casey, and Mariann!! Thank you for being so supportive! And more than anything, always checking on me and keeping me sane! I value your honest feedback and input so much. You all definitely make up a huge part of Gail Haris. I love you ladies and appreciate our friendships!!

Author Jessy Lin. *squeals* Hey you remember that one time when we became published authors? WHAT?! This is crazy!! I can't believe we're doing this! I'm so proud of you and extremely lucky to have you by my side on this! I love you bestie!!!

This book literally would not have happened had it not been for my sister, Teresa. I didn't even know the indie book world existed until she brought me into it! She makes up a BIG part of Gail Haris. Teresa, I love you so much! There's no way any of this would've happened without you. You're the best sister and friend!!

Culley, my extremely sweet and gorgeous niece that is gracing the cover! I'm so proud of the young woman you're growing up to be. I appreciate you being so brave and letting me use you as my cover model. I'll never forget when I told you the idea for this story:

ME: a girl is kidnapped as a baby and raised by a woman she thinks is her mother and doesn't discover the truth until she's seventeen.

Culley: you mean like Rapunzel?

I really thought I was being original here. I really did. Turns out there's LOTS of stories like this LOL.

Stacey Blake for this GORGEOUS formatting! OMG! I'm beyond in love with this!

Rocio and Germán for the gorgeous photos and being the two greatest people ever!! So much love for you two!

To my girls. You both are the reason I strive to be a better person. You're the reason behind my decision to go after my dream. My dream now is that you both always chase your dreams.

To the man that doesn't get nearly enough credit for what he has to go through on the daily—my husband. The most amazing individual I know. You really are a saint babe! I love you. You're my Noah. Solid, patient, and so loving and kind. I love you so much! Thank you for always supporting me and just being there for me.

If I've failed to mention anyone, I'm truly sorry. I love you all and I'm so grateful for all the support. Thank you!

About the Author

Gail Haris believes in fairytales, love, and laughter as the best medicine.

She was born and raised in a small town in the Midwest. After graduating with a degree in Mass Communications, Gail went on adventures traveling in America and Europe.

Her favorite adventures still are the ones where she gets lost in a good book.

Her love for reading and traveling lead her to attend book conventions. Those conventions gave her the encouragement she needed to combine her passion for creativity and storytelling. Using coffee and her imagination she loves writing contemporary romances that blend laughter and true love out of everyday chaos.

When Gail isn't day dreaming in front of her computer, she's busy raising her two daughters with the man of her dreams. She loves traveling with her family and friends, binge watching television series with her husband, singing Disney songs with her daughters, and having huge family and friends get-togethers that involve lots of food and usually a cake.

She hopes by following her own dream of becoming an author, she can set an example to her daughters that dreams can become reality. Maybe she can encourage you too.

Never stop believing in love, dreams, and yourself. And coffee...don't give up on coffee.

Get in touch with Gail!

gailharis.com

gailharisauthor@gmail.com

Facebook Page: www.facebook.com/pg/authorgailharis

Facebook Group:
www.facebook.com/groups/2262583704056800/?ref=share

Instagram: www.instagram.com/authorgailharis

Book Bub:
www.bookbub.com/profile/gail-haris?list=author_books

Goodreads
www.goodreads.com/author/show/19815494.Gail_
Haris?from_search=true

Newsletter: mailchi.mp/c741d7956650/ghauthor

Made in USA - Kendallville, IN
1093691_9781734666816
04.28.2020 0859